I0724568

TORMENT

1
GODS & MONSTERS

LAUREN DAWES

Torment
(Gods & Monsters #1)

First Edition, 2014 by Momentum (Pan Macmillan Australia Pty Ltd)
Second Edition, 2017 by Lauren Dawes
Third Edition, 2021 by Lauren Dawes
Copyright © 2014 by Lauren Dawes

www.authorlaurendawes.com

E-book: 978-0-9876409-1-8
Print: 978-1-922353-68-9

Cover by Deranged Doctor Designs

For Phil and Evie

GLOSSARY

Aesir (n) – The sky gods. It is their belief they are superior to all other races in the Nine Worlds.

agarwaen (adj) – after a Shadow Walker has completed their training and survived the Final Test, this is the title they are awarded; literally translated as blood-stained.

Asgard (n) – The former home of the Aesir.

fade (v) – to dematerialize to another location with a thought.

Fall, the (n) – The time when the Norse gods were no longer worshiped and therefore lost their power. The Fall was the tipping point that destroyed the Nine Worlds, breaking down the highly organized and coveted hierarchy built by the Aesir. Factions split and different species within those Nine Worlds were strewn across the human world. Some prospered while some merely survived. The gods favored the cities created by humans while others, like the dwarves, preferred the furthest outposts of human civilization.

Final Test, the (n) – At the end of a Mare's training to become a Walker, a gladiator-style battle takes place where the last man (or woman) standing is awarded the title agarwaen.

Frigg – Odin's wife; the goddess of fertility, love and marriage.

Hel – The goddess of the underworld

Jotunn (n) – a giant.

Mare (n) – a dark elf. Pure-blooded Mares are believed to be extinct after a campaign by Odin over a thousand years ago to eradicate their species. To escape persecution, dark elves bred with light elves creating half-breed children whose features helped them to pass as light elves.

Midgard (n) – The home of the humans.

Morier(ea) (n) – a derogatory term for a Shadow Walker; literally translated as dark one.

Niflheim (n) – Home of the dead; ruled by Hel.

Norns (n) – Female beings who rule the destiny of men and gods. Compare: the Fates of Greek mythology.

Odin – The father of all gods and men. Sometimes referred to as the *All-Father*.

Shadow Walker (n) –Shadow Walker is the ancient name for any Mare trained to be an assassin because of their ability to 'wrap' shadows around them to conceal themselves. However, due to the extensive interbreeding with the light elves, the ability to shadow walk was lost but the name remains the same. Shadow Walkers were feared for their ability to enter a person's dreams and manipulate them.

Valhalla (n) – An enormous hall within Asgard that housed fallen battle heroes.

Valkyrie (n) – A beautiful female warrior created by Odin to take the bodies of men slain in battle to Valhalla. Their immortality is only possible while their swan feather cloak is in their possession. If this cloak is stolen, the thief is entitled to seven years of service from the Valkyrie. However, if the feathers are plucked from the cloak, the Valkyrie's immortality leaves them and they can be killed by a mortal wound.

Vanir (n) – The Vanir are the old gods who ruled before the Aesir. Sworn enemies of the sky gods, they are the masters of sorcery and elemental magic.

PROLOGUE

AT THE START OF TIME . . .

The hand around Loki's bicep squeezed harder to stop his struggle, the blood flow in his arm slowing, slowing, until finally coming to a stop. He was numb. He attempted to pull free from those strong fingers, but he got the handle of a hammer jabbed into his solar plexus instead, pushing all the air from his lungs and doubling him over. Loki's knees gave out, letting the hand feel his slack weight. They had finally caught up with him, but it didn't mean he had to make it easy for them.

"Walk properly or I'll break your legs and drag you," an all-too-familiar male voice thundered. Glancing over his shoulder, he could see the god's free hand gripping the hammer so tightly his knuckles had turned white. Loki sneered at him and let even more of his weight drop.

Without releasing him, Thor backhanded Loki, smiling as blood tumbled down Loki's chin from the freshly split lip. Loki stood up to spit on the other god's sandals and smiled back sardonically.

Thor glowered at him, raising his hammer as if to strike him, when a powerful voice jerked him to a stop.

"Enough!" The All-Father's voice crackled and carried from behind them, echoing resonantly.

Thor glared at Loki, hatred boiling behind his ice-blue eyes. The god's chest heaved with rage, his arm shaking with a fine tremor.

"Thor!" Odin boomed again, his tone not just a warning but a promise of punishment if Thor chose to ignore him. Loki blinked up at the other man, watching to see if he was going to listen to his father. Thor growled at Loki—baring his teeth—but lowered his weapon.

"Move!" Thor shoved Loki in the back, marching him forward once more. Loki stumbled—the ground becoming rockier, the air thicker. The breeze was hot on his face, the sun an oppressive beast beating against the skin of his bare body. The sting from the wound on his lip turned into a throb, pounding in time with his erratically racing heart.

A sharp rock bit into the heel of Loki's foot, hobbling him instantly. His blood trailed behind him, following him up to the entrance of the cave that would no doubt become his prison, its dark maw open and waiting for him. Fear turned his stomach to stone, a cold sweat breaking out on his brow despite the blistering heat. Loki slowed his pathetic march, coming to a stop on the sharp rocky ground just before the shadowy entrance. This time Thor wasn't so gentle with him.

Loki felt the full force of the war hammer in the small of his back. He chewed the inside of his cheek, not allowing the bastard at his back to know just how much that had hurt. Blood welled in his mouth until he either had to spit it out or swallow it. He swallowed, the metallic tang disgusting him.

"Keep him moving," Odin said, stopping at his son's side. Loki looked over his shoulder at the two men he had once considered his family.

Thor snapped his teeth, raising an arm, but Loki had no interest in being hit again. He put one foot in front of the other, shuffling along to his slow and drawn-out death.

The sudden change in temperature brought a rush of goose bumps to Loki's naked flesh. His eyes took a long time to adjust to the gloom. They marched him in near darkness until he was sure he would collapse. Hours could have passed, but there was no way of telling. He realized then he would never see the sun again. The further they moved into the cave, the darker and colder it became.

Water dripped steadily from somewhere deeper in the cavern, the sound bouncing around—echoing. The darkness seemed to be closing in on Loki, making his throat close up and suffocating him. Panic bloomed when the stench of raw meat and spilled bowels hit his nose.

There was a small curve in the passage up ahead. The fine hairs on Loki's neck suddenly stood on end. He slowed and the air behind him shifted as Thor no doubt readied to jam his hammer into Loki's back again. Loki picked up his pace, fighting the feeling of dread sinking its hooks into his skin.

As they passed through the curved passage, Loki sensed they had just entered a much larger section of the cave. The air seemed cooler, but it was still tainted with the smell of death. An orange flame jumped to life at his back, the glow casting shadows around the large underground chamber.

"Those rocks there," Odin commanded from behind him. Thor wrenched on Loki's arm, pulling him toward three massive limestone boulders next to a sheer rock face. Water was dribbling down the hard rock wall, trickling off, dripping into small pools at its base. Thor threw Loki down roughly, holding his arms down with one hand while catching a sinewy rope thrown by Odin in the other. Thor grinned down at him, satisfaction curling his lips smugly. He waved the rope in Loki's face, Loki following the motion with his eyes.

"We should be thanking you for these cords." Thor began binding his wrists together above his head. "We turned your son Vali into a wolf so he could tear them from his brother's body."

Loki's eyes widened. Craning his neck, he looked around the cave, his eyes coming to an abrupt halt at the body of his son, Narvi, left violated and discarded on the floor. His stomach was eviscerated, the contents of his abdomen congealing in puddles of blood on the cave floor. Loki could feel bile working its way up from his stomach. As he turned his head, vomit burned up his throat and exploded from his mouth. Despite his blackening vision and spotty hearing, Thor's satisfied laughter was clear and a rage began to build within Loki. Just as he tried to kick out of the other god's grip, Thor caught his ankle and tightened the rope around it.

"No!" a woman screamed. Straining his neck, Loki looked for the source of the sound, noting Odin was nowhere to be seen.

"Sigyn!" he yelled. "Sigyn!" He desperately called his wife's name over and over again until Thor cuffed him, breaking his nose. Cartilage snapped. Blood sprayed from his nostrils, covering his chest with warm droplets.

"Loki!" Sigyn's voice was high, keening—desperate.

"Sigyn!" he tried to call back, but his throat had filled with blood again. A cough racked his body, forcing him to swallow the blood back, then he tried again.

"She can't hear you," Thor said, looking down at him. "But you should know we made her watch." Thor was making a noose-like knot now. Roughly, he pulled it down over Loki's head and tightened it. Breathing became even more difficult. Loki forced air through his mouth; blood dripped from his lips and trickled down the back of his throat.

Satisfied with the strength of the knots and the bonds, Thor stood up. "He's ready," he called. Loki strained to see Odin coming back into the main section of the cave. Sigyn was at his side, her hands bound in front of her. Tears had dragged clean lines down her filthy cheeks, making her look pitiful. She hadn't even seen him yet. Her eyes were on Narvi's body, lying motionless on the ground.

Odin pulled an ornate dagger from the scabbard on his hip. The blade gleamed in the dimly lit cave, but Sigyn was yet to see it. With his eyes fixed on Loki, Odin ran the blade sharply across his wife's throat. Sigyn dropped from the All-Father's arms like a stone, her body slapping the ground like a piece of meat.

Desperate gasping filled Loki's ears, his wife's dying gurgles and breaths guaranteed to haunt him for the rest of his days. Loki screamed out wordlessly, the noose tightening around his neck until he was fighting for his next breath. Odin's sandals kicked loose stones as he walked over toward the platform Loki was bound to. His one clear, green eye seemed to pity Loki, while the obsidian orb in the empty socket of his right said you brought this on yourself. Loki tried to make his eyes say fuck you, but the delighted smirk on the All-Father's face said he'd failed. Loki struggled against his bonds, only to have Odin's hand land on his shoulder. "I would not bother to try to free yourself. I have warded these bonds to prevent you from fading away."

Odin smiled at the growl that broke free of Loki's lips.

"You do know why this has happened to you, don't you, Loki?" Odin asked. "You had my son killed, and then you refused to weep for his loss. You damned Baldr to the cold, vast wastelands of Niflheim. He is your daughter Hel's guest now, and will forever be. For the part you played, I have taken away your son Narvi so you may know the feeling of loss. I turned your other son against his own brother so you would know betrayal and guilt. I killed your wife for the simple reason that she would aid you."

Odin looked over his shoulder, his chin rising slightly. The shuffling of feet filled Loki's ears along with an ophidian hissing. The All-Father looked at him once more. "You remember Skadi, don't you?" His voice was smug. "She's brought someone to keep you company while you rot in this cave."

The snow goddess approached the platform slowly. Skadi's ice-blonde hair hung over her silver-frosted eyes. Everything about the goddess was white, except for her mouth. That was a bright scarlet red.

As more and more of Skadi filled his vision, Loki's eyes widened. Wrapped around her body was a huge white snake. As she stroked its horned head with a light fingertip, cooing softly to the reptile, it turned its red eyes to Loki.

The hiss that escaped its mouth sent shivers along Loki's skin. Its fangs were six inches long and growing. Its scales had an iridescent shine to them, its body an undulating rainbow in Skadi's pale hands.

"Let's give him a taste, shall we?" Odin purred, his green eye sparkling with amusement.

Nodding, Skadi brought the snake to Loki, holding its head over his foot. Poison pooled and dripped from its fangs, the sensitive skin on the top of his foot beginning to smolder where it landed. Loki cried out, gritting his teeth together.

"You'd better get used to that, Loki. You will be trapped here with this serpent until the end of time." Odin turned to Skadi, touching her gently on the shoulder. "Say your goodbyes."

Loki watched in horror as Skadi kissed the snake then placed it above his head. The snake's body coiled around a stalactite hanging overhead, its head and open mouth positioned over his neck and chest. Loki licked his suddenly dry lips, knowing he was staring into the eyes not just of death, but of torment and torture, too.

Odin touched him on the hip. "Enjoy your time together, blood-brother." The last word was a sneer. Despair rose up in Loki like a swollen river, the banks threatening to break. The sound of their retreating footsteps was what broke him. He yelled, he raged, he swore. He begged, he pleaded, he cried. But they did not return. Straining his eyes, he could see they'd left Sigyn's and Narvi's bodies to rot, to remind him of why he was being punished, why he must endure this torture.

A droplet of venom fell onto his throat and the scream that escaped his body left his throat raw. He could feel the poison sinking into his blood, burning, melting his flesh. Another struck him directly above his heart, his skin sizzling and smoking on contact with the poison. Loki screamed out wordlessly, writhing, pulling against his bonds until blood welled on his ankles and wrists and throat.

Another drip.

Another scream.

A part of him thought maybe this was what he deserved. He was despised by the gods. They treated him as a threat, as a rabid dog, not knowing when or if he was going to bite them. He was the trickster god, but it had been Odin who had welcomed him into the fold.

Drip.

A burning started through his body, an all-consuming wildfire that could never be extinguished.

Drip.

Odin. He was the one who deserved to be tied to the rocks. He was the one who deserved to smell the fetid breath of death as the corpses of his beloved withered and rotted at his feet.

Odin.

Drip.

Odin.

Must.

Die.

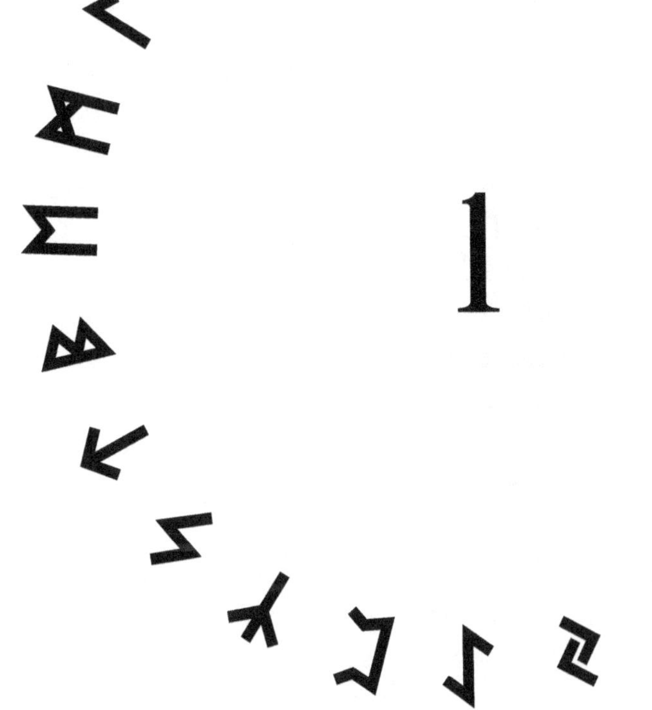

1

Darrion faded to the walk-up in South Boston, the weight of the twin Berettas under his arms a comfort. This was one of his warded safe houses and the gods knew he needed them. Although he realized he was a walking, talking target for any one of the rival guilds, he simply didn't give a fuck. Not tonight. Not any night. After sweeping his eyes around to see if he'd been followed, he glanced up at the rune carved above the front door.

The small symbol had been scratched out, which meant the protective spell designed to prevent gods and any other beings in the Nine Worlds from fading in and out had been tampered with. Darrion opened up the front door and silently slid inside.

The building's ancient heating system suddenly lurched to life, a dying beast that grunted and groaned as he bypassed the five flights of stairs to his apartment, and chose to fade there instead. He paused in front of the door, the hairs on the back of his neck prickling. He drew one of the twins silently. Approaching one side of the jamb, he reached out and tried the handle.

Locked.

With a growl in his throat, he faded just onto the other side of the door, ready. A delicate fragrance hung in the air. Honeysuckle, he thought. With narrowed eyes, he moved through the apartment, looking for signs of the intruder he knew was still there.

After a long silence, he was met with a hesitant female voice. "I mean you no harm, Walker."

He cursed. "Show yourself, female."

A woman emerged slowly from the bathroom on Darrion's left. She was wearing a white cloak that covered her head and shoulders, hiding her features in shadow. On her diminutive body, she wore a dress made of the sheerest fabric. A moment later, she drew the hood back from her blonde hair and got busy looking at the floor. Gods, she couldn't have been any older than sixteen.

He cursed her again, bringing the muzzle of the gun up to her forehead, teenager or not. "Who are you, and how did you find this place?" he snarled, baring his fangs.

The thick scent of her fear started to permeate the room, warring with the scent of honeysuckle. "Please," she begged, her fearful eyes fixed on his finger on the trigger. "My mistress sent me here to speak with you."

"Who is your mistress? How did you find me?" He could feel the air thicken as the fear consumed her. He breathed in that weighted air, feeling his stomach clench tight with need.

"M-my mistress is the queen," the girl stammered, the color draining from her cheeks.

Darrion sneered at the title. "What do you want?"

The female licked her lips. "She wishes me to tell you she has a request—a contract, if you prefer."

"I don't work for the Aesir," he spat back bitterly, lowering his arm but not holstering the weapon.

"Please." The girl started trembling visibly. "She said she would kill me if I did not come back with the right answer."

He leveled her with a cold, dead stare. "Your queen couldn't afford me."

"She has given me gold." The servant spoke in a rush, reaching into her cloak. Darrion raised his weapon again, training it on her head, so when she looked up again the muzzle was right between her eyes. She gasped in surprise, the coin purse falling from her hand.

She dropped to the ground, her shaking fingers reaching for the gold that had spilled out onto the floor. She started to cry, her sobs delicate—restrained—as if she was afraid to make any more noise. Darrion watched her pale head bob around as she worked, wondering why in the hell this girl was sent to him in the first place.

She seemed to have pulled herself together when she faced him once more. "Please . . . is there no way you would say yes?"

Darrion snorted. There was one way, but it would never happen. "Yeah, get that bitch down here to ask me herself, instead of sending me little girls."

The servant curtsied nervously and faded.

Darrion rubbed the back of his skull with his palm and holstered the Beretta. He fucking hated the Aesir—not because they had their heads so far up their asses they thought they'd invented the sun when they yawned, but because those pretentious fucks had persecuted his people for centuries. Odin had deemed the dark elves "too dangerous" to remain breathing and ordered that any Mare found within the civilian population should be captured or killed.

Gods, he needed a drink.

Finding his bottle of Maker's Mark, he tore the wax cap off and took a deep pull. The amber liquid burned on the way down. The bottle began to shake in his hand, his angry body finally signaling its intent. Wiping the back of his hand over his mouth, he put the bottle down and let out a deep lungful of air.

"Did my little handmaiden shake you up so badly, *morier*?"

With a guttural snarl, Darrion spun around, pulling a throwing knife from the holster on his thigh and launching it in the direction of the voice. The blade stuck into the wall, vibrating with the force still surging through the metal. The woman who had been his target had simply sidestepped the steel, unruffled by his aggression.

If she'd been going for inconspicuousness, she'd failed. Her blood-red gown was cinched in at the waist, pushing her breasts up until her warm flesh threatened to spill over the top. Darrion glared at the woman and reached for his gun.

"Leave the weapon where it lies, *morier*."

Darrion ground his teeth together, but stayed his hand. "I could have killed her, you know." He watched her with suspicious eyes. She didn't smell of fear yet, but there was still time.

"But you didn't," she replied smoothly, running a hand through hair the color of spun gold. Her shrewd blue eyes watched him move, watched him shift on his feet, positioning himself. "And do you want to know why?"

"Go on. Dazzle me."

"I still haunt your dreams," she replied, smiling insidiously.

Darrion bared his fangs at her, a rumble vibrating through his chest. "Don't flatter yourself."

The female laughed—a high, tinkling sound that grated on his eardrums.

"You think I couldn't finish you in the time it would take you to inhale your next breath?" he snarled back.

She waved away his threat with a casual hand. "Don't you want to know what the job is?"

"I couldn't give a—"

"Odin," she murmured. Darrion's mouth hung open for a second before he pulled his shit together. He couldn't be falling apart. He was a goddamn Walker—the best there ever was. He searched her face for any signs of dishonesty.

He didn't see any, but that didn't mean a goddamn thing.

"Kill Odin," she repeated.

A pause hung between them.

"You're asking the impossible."

"Nothing is impossible," she purred back.

Staring into her face, his next words came out as a low growl. "I should just kill you now."

"I'd be gone before you reached for your weapon."

He smiled widely, showing her his fangs. "Who needs a weapon?"

Her pupils dilated, but he smelled only lust, not fear. Darrion inhaled deeply, taking in the fragrance. His body stirred at the memories that came along with that particular bouquet.

She cleared her throat and jerked her royal chin forward. "You think I came here unprotected?"

"No, I don't think you're that stupid. A whore, sure, but not stupid."

Her delicate expression darkened. "How dare you!" she hissed.

He chuckled sardonically. "Slit your wrists, sweetheart," he said dismissively. "It'll lower your blood pressure." He stalked away, pleased with this reaction. The great unflappable queen had just proved otherwise—though when he looked back at her, she was in control of her emotions once more. This was the woman he knew. This was the woman he remembered.

He took out one of his daggers and sank into an armchair in the corner of the room, picking at the dried blood beneath his fingernails. "So tell me, O great queen, how am I supposed to take out Odin? The last I checked, he was truly immortal." Odin was not like the other Aesir. You could kill any god if you did enough damage to their body. But Odin . . . Odin was different.

She stared, drawing out the silence. Darrion picked at the blood. Finally, she said, "There is a way for him to die."

Darrion raised a brow. "Even if that were true, you think I'll believe you?" he snorted. "You want your husband dead? Why?"

Her blue eyes clouded over with rage. "I cannot stand his infidelity any longer."

His infidelity? Darrion thought wildly. She was the one who ushered people in between her legs like it was a movie theater about to close its doors for the screening. He focused on the tip of his blade for a second. Without lifting his eyes, he murmured, "I'm all ears."

"Kill Brynhildr and you can kill him."

His eyes cut to hers, skeptical. "How does that work?"

She came two paces closer to him, dropping to her knees. Although he was disgusted by her, disgusted with himself for burying his body into the well of hers so many times before, he still found her curiously arousing. His cock stirred slightly at the sight of her on her knees before him.

She shuffled forward, parting his knees with her hands and sliding in between his thighs. "Bryn has a feather cloak that holds her immortality. Destroy the cloak, you destroy her, and Odin can be killed."

Darrion stilled the knife in his fingers. He didn't trust her. She could be feeding him false information just to fuck around with his head. It wouldn't be the first time. "Why have you sought me out, Frigg?"

She smiled at him innocently, but it was like having a viper smiling at him: cold with death not just a threat, but a promise.

"You are the best," she said. Her hands ran up the inside of his thighs toward his hips. Fingertips brushed over his partial erection. Her head dipped and her tongue moistened her lips. There was no way in hell he was going to let her get her mouth anywhere near him.

He placed the tip of the blade under her chin and tipped her head back, trying to read her face, trying to decide whether he could trust her and her information. Frigg's eyes suddenly darted to the side, drawing Darrion's attention there too. He turned to glare at the two males who had faded in, daring them to get involved, but Frigg waved them back with a casual flick of her wrist.

"I've seen decomposing bodies more appealing than what you are about to offer me. Get up, my queen."

Her eyes flared with anger, but she managed to get herself back onto her feet. Crossing her arms over her chest, she looked at him impatiently.

"So, will you take the contract? I can pay you whatever you want."

He stood up and slid the blade into the holster on his thigh. Odin was his ultimate hit. He had dreamed of a time when he would be able to put a blade through the All-Father's heart, to hear his final breaths shuddering from his lips, to know that the god could no longer hunt his people down and take parents from their children.

Darrion refused to let his memories take over, but like a roiling ocean during a storm, there was no way to stop them. He heard the echoes of the screams—smelled the blood. He heard his father's final words to him. He remembered the way he had abandoned them all. With a shudder, he refocused on the room.

"Don't insult me with your money, *my queen*." Darrion's voice was sharp like a shard of glass and as dark and menacing as a gun muzzle pressed to someone's temple.

"Will you do it?" she asked somewhat impatiently.

"I'll think about it," he snarled back.

The woman smiled slyly—knowingly—her lips tilting up at the corners. "Good." She stepped back and looked at the two men who had faded in to protect her.

He turned around. "Now get out."

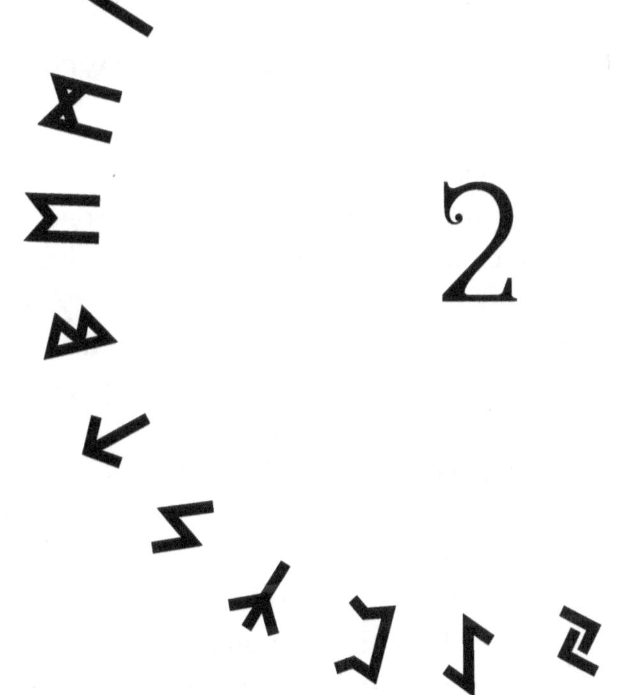

2

Korvain wiped the blood from his favorite curved blade against the pants leg of the guy who'd just had a real intimate introduction to the weapon. The fuck had apparently pissed off the wrong people.

He looked around the apartment. It was nice, if you liked the idea of wanting to slit your wrists just for something to do.

Everything was white, or at least it had been. Now it was spattered in the mark's blood, painted in the stuff. The shag rug where the piece of shit was laying had gone from pink to red. Soon it would be brown as the blood dried to a hard crust.

Message sent.

Korvain's pocket began to vibrate. Palming his phone, he answered it and held it to his ear. "Speak."

"Sit rep?" Darrion's cold voice asked on the other end of the phone. Korvain glanced around the room, nudging his mark with the toe of his boot. "End game."

"Good. Report to me."

Korvain hung up and slid the phone back into one of the pockets of his black cargoes. He faded from downtown Boston back to Dorchester, stepping out of a dark alleyway beside a cheap brothel. Under the haze of red-tinged lighting, there was a set of dingy stairs leading to the upper level, syringes and bent spoons littering the treads.

Korvain opened Darrion's office door and froze. His boss had the tip of a throwing knife in his right hand, the concentration on his face unmistakable.

"Don't move," Darrion said icily, his blue eyes fixed on a point just over Korvain's left shoulder. Korvain did as he was told, standing stock-still, hardly breathing. Darrion had trained him, had taught him almost everything he knew about killing. Korvain knew what the man was capable of, how good he was with a blade in his hand.

Darrion drew his arm back above his head and released the blade in a downward chopping motion. The blade sliced the air perfectly, flying just a hair's-breadth from Korvain's ear. The blade landed in the wooden board behind him with a sharp *thunk*.

Korvain released the breath he'd been holding and straightened up. Darrion stalked past him to retrieve the blades he must have been throwing at the wall since he'd called Korvain back in.

"What took you so long?"

"I didn't realize you were timing me," Korvain replied in a cold voice. He entered and stood with his back to the wall.

Darrion took up the same position as before and took aim once more. *Thunk. Thunk. Thunk.* "I have another assignment for you." His voice was calm, level, matter-of-fact. It was a little too calm—unnerving Korvain and sending a chill down his spine.

"Why didn't you just text me the details?"

Darrion looked at him with a hard edge in his pale eyes. "Delicacy is required."

Korvain's suspicions were instantly raised. When was Darrion ever delicate? When his boss wanted secrecy, it meant it was someone important, not like the piece of shit lesser god he'd killed earlier.

Thunk. Thunk. Thunk. "This is a once-in-a-lifetime hit. If you can make the mark disappear, you'll get paid triple what you usually get, plus I'll take five years off your contract."

The muscle in Korvain's jaw jumped. "I'm listening."

Thunk. "You can't fuck this up if you take it." *Thunk.* "If you do," *thunk,* "you know what happens."

That sound was *really* beginning to irritate Korvain. "Okay. Want to tell me?" he asked, his molars clenched together, grinding.

"A Valkyrie," Darrion replied calmly, throwing a blade.

Korvain barked a harsh laugh. "A Valkyrie?" he asked incredulously. "Why not ask me to kill Odin himself?"

Darrion turned, throwing the new blade in his hand. It hit the wall behind Korvain, but not before slicing open his cheek as he reflexively dodged to the side. He hadn't been fast enough. And that pissed him off. The rage that simmered within Korvain whenever he was around Darrion began to boil over, making him see black spots when he blinked.

He felt the first warm rivulets of his blood tracking down his cheek, dripping off his chin. Korvain swiped the blood away with the back of his hand.

"Laugh again and I won't miss," Darrion warned, his voice low, his nostrils flaring with rage. He turned back to his original target and threw the last blade.

Thunk.

"All right, so you want a Valkyrie dead. There's just one little problem." That was a fucking understatement. The Valkyries were just like Odin: truly immortal. Korvain's statement was greeted by silence, the fucking cricket-chirping kind of silence. He pushed on. "They're untouchable. Unless you've figured out a way to strip them of their immortality, you'll never even get close to hurting them."

Darrion's cold blue eyes turned back to him, and the strangest expression came onto his face. As the two Mares stood there, eyes locked, Korvain could have sworn his boss was actually smiling.

"You've found a way?"

The Mare's head inclined slightly.

"Why don't you kill her yourself, then?" Korvain asked.

"I'm asking you to do the job."

Korvain started to pace. You didn't say no to Darrion. You negotiated until you found a figure worth risking your life for. "Fifteen," he said. Darrion's eyebrow arched. "Take fifteen off my contract and I'll do it."

Korvain had another seventeen years left of a seventy-year term as Darrion's attack dog.

He could see the animosity and resentment growing in his boss's eyes. "Seven."

Korvain squeezed his sweat-slicked hands into fists. "Twelve."

"Ten."

A pause. Korvain released a deep breath. "Ten."

Darrion nodded, the deal done. "Your mark is Brynhildr."

Bryn was Odin's first creation, his oldest Valkyrie, his strongest. Korvain's mind started turning over all the possibilities, the opportunities, the options. "How?"

"Have you heard about the Valkyries' feather cloaks?" Korvain shook his head. "This information has just come to my attention—it's from a source I don't trust entirely, but I don't trust anyone entirely," Darrion said mildly. "Apparently Valkyries have a feather cloak they must keep in their possession." He took another dagger from the holster on his thigh and slumped down into a chair. Picking under his fingernails, he said, "Strip the feathers off the cloak and they become mortal again. Strip the feathers and you can kill them."

"Who told you this?"

Darrion pinned Korvain with an icy stare. "I told you, a source."

"An untrustworthy source," Korvain reiterated, holding that stare.

Darrion inclined his head slightly, his neck muscles twitching infinitesimally. Korvain blew out a frustrated breath. Darrion probably didn't even trust himself, he was so paranoid.

Korvain said, "This is what I've understood: Get the cloak. Strip the cloak. Kill the Valkyrie. Are we about on the same page here?"

"Yes. Kill her, Korvain, and I will take ten years off your contract. Fail and I'll own you for the rest of your unnatural life."

Korvain sighed. Well, how could he say no to that?

3

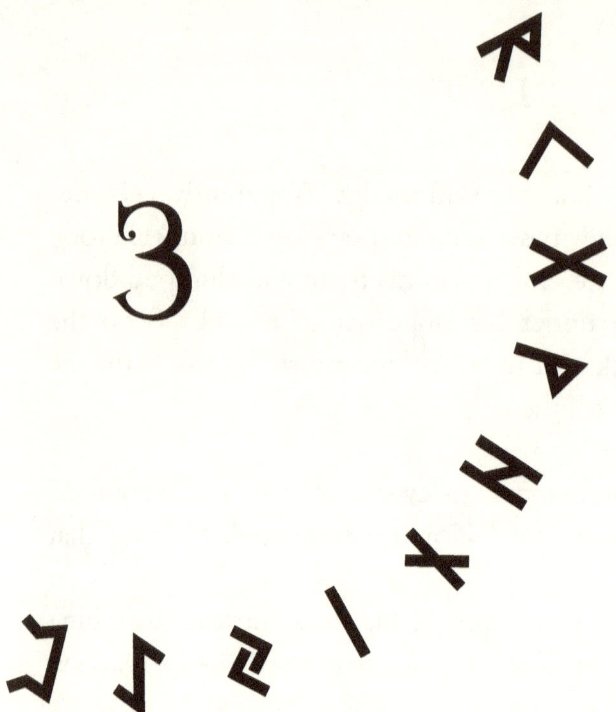

Frigg faded to her house in the affluent Boston suburb of Charleston, the house her darling husband had bought for her as a peace offering. At her back were her two most trusted Aesirean guards, Skoll and Hati. Seeing Darrion again had left Frigg shaken, uneasy. He was still the best lover she had ever had, even with his mean streak.

She turned to her men. "Leave me." The goddess waved them away as she swept upstairs to take a bath. Her handmaiden, Fulla, was waiting in her room. The poor thing was still shaking from her encounter with the Mare.

The young woman turned her wide eyes to Frigg when she entered. Dropping to the floor in supplication, she addressed Frigg as she'd been instructed. "My queen?"

"I wish to take a bath. Draw one for me."

"Yes, my queen."

Fulla scurried off, the white gown she wore trailing after her into the bathroom. Frigg walked around her room, touching all the things she found precious: her perfume bottles, her cosmetics, her priceless pieces of art. She had been called shallow before, but she saw it as appreciating the finer things in life. Besides, it was Odin's money that had paid for them all. And that was half the fun.

The scent of lavender filled the room suddenly, the steam from the hot water spilling into the bath drifting lazily through the air. Fulla reappeared, her cheeks pink from the heat.

"Do you wish me to help you undress?"

"Of course," Frigg replied, moving toward the three-sided dressing mirror in the corner of the room. Fulla followed her, her eyes respectfully fixed on the ground. Frigg stared at the young woman in the mirror's reflection.

"You are quiet tonight," she murmured thoughtfully.

Fulla cleared her throat delicately. "Yes, my queen." Her nimble fingers started in on the silk buttons on the back of Frigg's couture red gown.

"Why?"

Fulla looked up, her guileless blue eyes wide. They were the exact color of cornflowers at the height of spring, and Frigg hated her for it. "It matters not," she mumbled, continuing down the line of buttons.

Frigg frowned a little, shrugged and looked back at her glorious reflection. Although the fabric was loose now around her body, she could not breathe easily yet. Her corset was still firmly in place.

With her hand on Fulla's slender shoulder, Frigg stepped out of the dress. Beneath the yards of scarlet taffeta was matching silk lingerie.

Her handmaiden returned from hanging up her dress, coming

to stand at her back to unlace the blood-red corset. Inch by inch, Frigg could breathe once more. Fulla removed the shell of silk and whalebone and swept it away into the closet to join countless others.

Walking into the bathroom, Frigg's nipples puckered as her feet hit the cold tiles, the cool hardness rippling through her body. The bath was nearly ready. Removing her undergarment, she slid one foot into the water to test the temperature before stepping in fully. When she was submerged, Fulla entered the room.

"Will you be needing anything else, my queen?"

Frigg waved the girl away, asking her to shut the door behind her. Silence engulfed the room. She closed her eyes with a deep sigh, relaxing into the smooth granite tub. Water lapped at her chest, tickling her skin.

Darrion's eternal hatred of Odin had worked in her favor as she knew it would. Of course there were other things to set in motion, and they would be, as soon as her little birds came back with the information she sought.

Her whole body flushed at the memory of when she had last seen Darrion. Although she knew he despised the Aesir, she'd had to have him. She'd had to know what it was like to lie with a Mare. And he hadn't disappointed her.

His lovemaking was more about dominance than tenderness. He had tied her up, stripped her down, made her come. He was the most magnificent lover she had ever had the pleasure of fucking. She shivered, her body remembering the number of orgasms he'd managed to wring from her obedient flesh.

Frigg stayed in the tub until the water cooled. Calling Fulla back in, she got out and had her handmaiden rub fragrant oil into her skin before sliding into a silk robe.

"Finn has returned," Fulla said in a low voice, not meeting

Frigg's gaze.

"He has? Where is he?"

"In your bedchamber, my queen, as you requested."

"Good," Frigg purred, brushing past the young woman and stepping into her mood-lit bedroom. Finn was sitting on the chaise longue at the foot of her bed, his arm slung casually over the back of one of the most expensive pieces of furniture in her collection. His hair was longer in the front than at the back, covering most of his violet eyes. His skin was bone-white, his musculature that of an athlete.

"Finn," Frigg said, her voice low, tempting. The demigod lifted his eyes to her, the violet appearing through his fall of black hair.

"My queen."

"Have you found the location?"

He nodded, his smile revealing perfectly straight white teeth. "I have."

"Tell me where he is. Tell me where I can find him." Frigg had been searching for this place for nearly one hundred years—ever since Odin had discarded her love like it was nothing more than cheap rags.

"New Mexico."

She could feel the smile curl her upper lip. "Fulla! I need a map. Now!" The handmaiden returned with an atlas, bowing submissively after giving it to Frigg. Frigg spread the book wide in front of Finn.

"Where in New Mexico?" she demanded.

His eyes danced over the country, finally landing near the Texan border. "There." His finger pointed at a set of mountain ranges hemmed in by arid ground and sparse woods. Frigg leaned in closer.

"Carlsbad Caverns," she muttered, reading the name beside

the dot. Her eyes traced a path from there back to Boston. She smiled to herself.

Close.

So close now.

"Fulla, some clothes! Now!"

The girl rushed to her closet and pulled out a gown in a deep blue that brought out Frigg's eyes.

"The gown will get ruined. Get me something easier, simpler!" Frigg snapped, irritated by the stupidity of the girl.

Fulla paled and darted off, reappearing with a basic T-shirt, a pair of dark blue jeans and hiking boots. "Will this be sufficient, my queen?" she asked breathlessly, her arms trembling as she offered the items to the goddess.

"Yes, yes, fine. Give them to me."

Frigg slipped the robe from her slender shoulders, not caring whether Finn saw her flesh. She got dressed quickly, finally placing her feet into the ugly brown leather hiking boots, and faded from her house.

By the time she reached the caverns, the temperature was near freezing. She wrapped her arms around herself and headed toward the dark mouth that would lead her underground.

"My queen?"

Frigg turned suddenly. Skoll and Hati were waiting a few feet behind her. "Did you follow me?" she snapped.

"Yes," Hati replied.

"We cannot leave you unprotected." This came from Skoll. His cool gray eyes were unapologetic.

"Fine." She spun around once more, stepping over a shallow railing and onto the cold limestone floor.

Both men clicked on flashlights, illuminating the way. As she walked, her two bodyguards remained silent except for the shuffle of their feet on stone. Frigg's breath puffed out in front of her face, a reminder of just how cold it really was. Walking deeper into the cavern, she felt the hairs on the back of her neck begin to prickle.

But she could not turn back. She was so close. Darrion was in her pocket now, but she needed someone else. She needed to know that if Darrion somehow failed, Odin would still die. And there was only one person in all of the Nine Worlds who hated Odin more than Darrion and herself combined.

They walked until her back ached and her calves burned. They walked into the blackness of that cave until she was sure they would find themselves in another part of the country when they finally made it back out again. They walked until they reached a blind corner where the struggles of a god possessed could be heard.

She had found him.

She had found Loki.

Korvain had faded to an address in Southie, keeping to the shadows of the house on the opposite side of the street. It was a piece-of-shit neighborhood, no stranger to the red and blue lights of the police and the sound of gunshots in the dead of night.

The houses looked stretched out and stuck together; sometimes there was a little laneway separating them. They were like conjoined twins in a way, identical but wanting their independence all the same.

The lights of the house he'd been watching finally flicked off, the mark opening the front door and taking the porch steps two at a time. Korvain inhaled deeply, the male's scent hitting his nostrils. This was the demigod he was chasing.

Korvain pulled the shadows closer to his body, wrapping them around himself to muffle his footsteps. Skirting around the light, he approached the car quickly. Korvain withdrew the garrotte wire from a small pouch, his fingers wrapping around the metal handles. He stepped onto the sidewalk just as the demigod paused and looked over his shoulder.

The guy's blue eyes searched the darkness. He leaned forward, trying to peer through Korvain's shadow-swathed body. Korvain stopped breathing, holding his position. When the demigod turned back around shaking his head, Korvain struck.

Using his height advantage, he looped the wire over his mark's neck and yanked back. With nothing but a thought, Korvain sent the shadows wrapped around his body rushing forward, infesting the other man's skin and swallowing him from the view of the humans in the houses surrounding them.

Dragging the demigod further into the shadows, Korvain drew the inky blackness in closer to ensure the sounds of his death would be muffled, too.

Desperately scrambling to get the air back in his lungs, the demigod's fingers snatched at the wire. Korvain knocked the back of his knees, dropping him to the ground. He kneeled beside him, not taking away the strain on the wire, watching as the last of the guy's life drained from his body. Korvain's face remained perfectly impassive—bored even—until the fighting finally stopped.

The familiar smell of death trickled into his nostrils. A final gurgle escaped the male's throat as Korvain released his grip. His blue eyes were now ringed by red, the burst blood vessels like fireworks against the whites of his eyes.

Dying was not pretty. Dying was being stripped bare. Dying was being humiliated as your bowels released. There was no honor in it.

Korvain lay the body down on the small patch of lawn and went through its pockets, finally finding the guy's keys. He picked up the body and stashed it in the trunk before getting into the driver's seat and backing out of the driveway. Gods, it had been so long since he'd felt the need to dispose of a body, but this wasn't an ordered hit. This was just something he had to do to get the bigger job done.

Korvain started driving west, getting onto the freeway and heading toward some marshlands, where the body wouldn't be found for a little while. He pulled in at Millennium Park. Gravel crunched under his boots, and he was comforted by the fact he was the only thing moving for miles.

Popping open the trunk, Korvain cleared the mark of ID, pocketing his phone and wallet. When he was clean, Korvain wrapped the shadows around them both and started off towards one of the boardwalks leading to the wetlands.

4

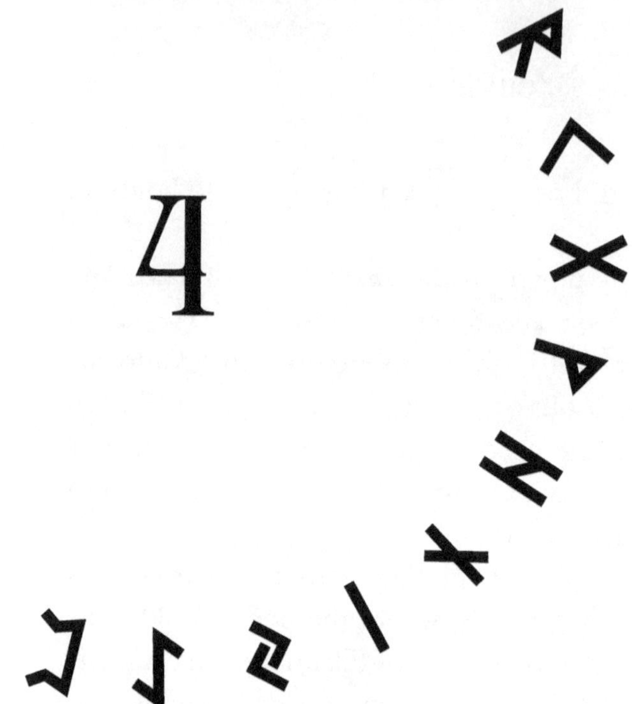

Bryn sat at the bar, her eyes drifting from face to face, as humans and gods alike milled around the bar on the first floor of Odin's Eye. On the floors above her head, she would have seen the same thing: humans rubbing shoulders with gods—not that the humans would have known that.

On the second floor was a nightclub; the floor above that, a gentlemen's club. At the base of each set of stairs leading up to the floors above stood two bouncers regulating who came through the doors of each section. The different services the Eye provided meant it was one of the busiest establishments in all of Boston.

At the front door tonight was one of her Valkyries, Maverick. Normally Bryn would have two bouncers working together, but Mav didn't like working with anyone, especially not the humans Bryn mainly employed as muscle.

Bryn took a sip from her glass of 42 Below and stood up to her full six foot two height. A few men close by turned their heads, looking her over from head to toe with an appreciative eye. Her slim body, blue eyes and plaited blonde hair made her the subject of many males' wet dreams. She hated that she looked like she did; she simply drew too much attention.

But that had been the point, once upon a time.

Ignoring their lust-filled eyes, she strode purposefully through the crowd, clearly uninterested in conversation. As the crowds parted, she made her way over to the front door. Mav had stepped aside to let a group of men in, her shrewd eyes looking over each of them in turn. The men were making a beeline for the stairs, no doubt heading straight to the third floor.

Mav's arm shot out just as the last man trickled through the door. Her palm landed on his chest, bringing him to an abrupt stop.

"Not you," she rumbled. Bryn was used to Mav's voice, but the male seemed to cringe back from it. Mav was supermodel stunning, but her voice box had been damaged before she became a Valkyrie, marring her throat with thick scars. The result? Her girl didn't like talking so much.

Mav's real name—the name that had been bestowed upon her when Odin had given her immortality—was Gunner. Like all Valkyries, she had pale skin and golden hair, but Mav's hair was shaved close to her scalp. Bryn didn't know the real reason she'd done it, but if it was meant to scare people away from her, it sure as shit worked.

Everyone gave Mav a wide berth.

Everyone.

Except for Bryn.

The sword tattoo on the undamaged side of Mav's neck sat starkly against her skin. Like the real blade she could summon, the black steel inked onto her skin seemed to gleam under the lights. It moved with her body, the steel catching images and mirroring them. Bryn's own tattoo was much the same and the humans stared at it openly.

Bryn's gaze skimmed down the human's body, checking him for any visible weapons. "You carrying?" she asked him.

The guy's eyes jerked to Bryn and he shook his head mechanically. "Where are you and your boys heading?"

"Level Three."

Bryn looked over her shoulder, seeing that his friends were already being swallowed up by the dim stairway. Catching the eye of her head of security, she cocked a brow at him. Mason touched the button clipped to the front of his shirt and his gravel voice filled her ear.

"Bucks' night."

"They clean?" she replied, holding his gaze across the room. They were speaking on a channel reserved just for them.

"Yeah."

"How's capacity?"

"Not even half."

Bryn looked back at the guy Mav had stopped. Her girl had a sixth sense when it came to human's thoughts and feelings. She'd obviously picked up on something in his head. "Sorry, Level Three is full. You'll have to wait down here for your buddies."

"Bullshit," he replied, spitting the word at her.

Bryn arched a brow at him and Mav took a step closer to her, shielding Bryn's body with hers. That was Mav, though: the perfect soldier.

Bryn looked pointedly at Mav, then back at the male. "You want to try that again?" Bryn asked, one hand perching on her hip. Her feminine voice was a stark contrast to the chill of menace rolling off her body. This looming threat was often enough to stop men like this in their tracks.

The human's eyes shifted from Bryn to Mav, taking in the firm muscles of Mav's arms and the breadth of her shoulders. His own shoulders slumped in defeat.

"Yeah, all right."

Bryn and Maverick watched him shuffle into the bar and sit down on a stool. Turning back to the other Valkyrie, Bryn asked, "You all right?"

Mav nodded.

"Need a break?"

She shook her head.

Bryn sighed. "All right." Turning around, she walked toward the bar and took up her post once more.

Mist, Bryn's lieutenant, was behind the bar restocking the shelves with Skyy and Johnnie Walker Blue. Mist's sleek blonde bob rode her jawline, swaying ever so slightly as she moved from the shelves to the bar top.

Bryn picked up her glass, the ice cubes knocking together as she took a sip. The vodka slid down her throat, burning slightly. Feeling the stab of a new headache assaulting the front of her skull, Bryn cradled her head in her hands and massaged her temples.

She hadn't been sleeping. She couldn't even remember the last time she'd gotten a full night's sleep. She tried to remember what time she'd made it to bed the previous night. Two am? Three? Who the fuck knew. All she knew was that running a human business was harder than the whole Choosers of the Slain gig they'd all had to endure before the Fall.

Now, she had to deal with employees, taxes, employee taxes, suppliers, distributors, maintenance, living costs . . . it made her want to go back into Odin's service for half a second, but then she remembered why she'd left in the first place.

"I'm going to go upstairs," Bryn announced, picking up her glass and heading toward the stairs.

"How're things, Boss?" Mason asked as she walked past. Mason was shorter than her by a good few inches. His hair was cut short—a no-nonsense type cut. His hazel eyes were slightly too small for his face, but they were always watchful. He'd saved her ass on a number of occasions.

"Good, Mason. How's Sophie?" Sophie was his German shepherd. Mason was too focused on his career for anything more in his life. Except for that dog.

He loved that dog.

His face lit up at the mention of her. "She's good. Real good."

Bryn smiled and made her way up to the next level. The deep, thrumming beats of the nightclub reverberated down to the marrow in Bryn's bones, her headache taking on a life of its own. Acknowledging the bouncers at the door, she continued on until she hit the gentlemen's club.

Level Three was every man's fantasy come to life. All tastes were catered for, with only one rule in place: Don't touch the girls. Bryn scanned the crowds, spotting the six bouncers she had littered around the room in addition to the two at the door.

The walls were painted blood red, the floors carpeted in the same color. The bar was shiny and black, manned by one barman and a stack of girls wearing next to nothing, carrying trays balanced on their palms. The stage jutted out from the wall opposite the bar, a "T" shape that thrust out into a crowd of dark wooden tables and black leather booths.

The group of men who had come through before was loitering near the bar—waiting for the entertainment to start for the evening. Bryn deposited her empty glass on a nearby table on her way to the end of the stage.

She climbed the few stairs and pushed past the crushed velvet curtain. The absence of the bouncer assigned to keep an eye on the backstage area struck Bryn first.

"Cherry, where's Winta?" she asked. Winta was a demigod. Nobody knew who his father was. His mother was human—a schoolteacher who'd had a one-night stand twenty years ago resulting in Winta. It happened with increasing frequency, especially since the Fall.

Cherry turned to Bryn. "He's not here." She was softly spoken and one of the only females working there who wasn't a goddess.

Bryn cursed and pulled the small phone from her pocket. Scrolling through her contacts, she found Winta's number, punched the call button and got ready to rip the bastard a new asshole for not turning up for work.

The damn thing rang out. Bryn tried the number again, but got the same ring-out-to-voicemail routine. Spinning around, she caught the eye of one of her other guys.

Adrian was a light elf, his pale green eyes and blond hair highlighting his heritage. Elves were slight of build, but still had preternatural strength on their side. There were only light elves left now. The dark elves—the Mares—had been wiped out under Odin's command.

"What's up?"

"Winta hasn't shown up for his shift. You got any friends who can fill in tonight?"

Adrian retrieved his phone from his pocket. "Yeah, I know someone." "You trust him?"

"With my life."

"Good. Get him here, but tell him he'll have to ask for me at the back door. He can't fade into the building."

Adrian began dialing, Bryn waiting to get the guy's details. After a few yeps and yeahs, Adrian hung up.

"He's coming."

"What's his name?"

"Korvain," he replied. Adrian glanced up as the Nine Inch Nails song "Closer" went stereo. "Looks like Kara's up." Bryn watched as Adrian took up his position, mirroring the stance of the other bouncers around him, arms locked across broad chests, legs shoulder-width apart. Men flocked to the stage area, planting their asses into the booths surrounding it.

Kara stepped out onto the stage. She was dressed in a red corset reminiscent of their uniform in Odin's army of Blonde and Buxom. The men were already foaming at the mouth, and she'd only just started to grind and gyrate along with the heavy beat.

Kara's large breasts swayed gently to the slow, dirty rhythm of her dancing. Before long, all the men were standing, waving folds of bills in her direction.

Satisfied everything was running smoothly, Bryn went down to the nightclub on the level below, pausing to talk to her bouncers for a moment before stepping into the darkened room. Where Level Three was red, Raven was as black as the feathers of the bird it was named after.

The crowds of beautiful people parted before her, throwing furtive glances over their shoulders. She ignored them, just like she always did, but she did notice one male approaching her. No doubt he was being egged on by his buddies, who were sitting at one of the banquet tables that lined the walls looking on, slapping each other on the back in congratulations.

She stopped and turned toward him. The male was shorter than her, but then again most men were. His hair looked black, and he had a swagger that said he knew how good-looking he was. He was good-looking, but she wasn't interested. When he was within arm's reach of her, he ran the back of his fingers down her bare arm.

Bryn's teeth snapped shut, and she growled. The human smiled a million-dollar smile and stepped close enough that she could practically taste the sweat beading off his body. Tilting his head up to her ear, he said, "How are you doing, beautiful?"

"I was good until some asshole invaded my personal space and touched me without permission," she replied, making sure to keep her voice sugary sweet.

He stepped back with a puzzled expression on his face.

"That means you, asshole," she snarled. "Back the fuck up."

His eyes widened, but he did as he was ordered, scurrying back to his buddies with his tail between his legs. With a shake of her head, Bryn proceeded in the direction of the bar. She was breaking in a new bartender tonight.

"Dex, how are you doing?"

The human looked up from pouring a drink and smiled. He had more piercings than she'd ever seen before, but he came with good references, and from what she'd seen so far he worked hard.

"S'all good, Boss," he grinned.

She didn't return the gesture. "Good. Give me a yell if you need anything." She turned toward the door when Mason's voice crackled to life in her ear.

"There's someone down here asking for you."

"Who is it?"

There was silence before he said, "Korvain."

"I'm coming down. Show him into my office."

Bryn walked back down the stairs until she hit the first level again. Turning left, she pushed open a door that opened up into a long hallway stretching out in both directions. At the end of the hallway on the right was the door leading out into the back alley and staff car park, but Bryn turned left and made her way down the hall. On her left was the unisex change room; on her right was her office. Mason was standing guard outside her office, his massive arms crisscrossing his chest.

"Says he was asked to come by."

"He was." She put a hand on his arm to move him out of the way, but he didn't budge. She looked at him, her hand squeezing his arm gently. "I'll be fine."

"He looks like an ax murderer," he muttered. "A Calvin-Klein-looking motherfucker, but still an ax murderer." Mason's chest heaved up and down, but when she patted his arm he moved.

Stepping past one of the only humans she actually liked, Bryn opened up her office door and stopped dead.

Korvain was sitting on the edge of her desk, his black eyes glittering in the overhead lights. Although he was sitting down, she could tell he was taller than her by more than just a few inches. His short hair was black, matching his eyes and the dark slashes of his eyebrows.

He was bigger than any other mixed-breed light elf she had ever seen, if that was what he was. With the dilution of dark elf blood and the extensive inbreeding of gods and humans, he really could have been anything. His arms were as big as her thighs, crossed tightly across a stomach so well defined that his abdominal muscles threw their own shadows from under the material of his shirt.

Her eyes took in the breadth of his shoulders, the size of his chest. Bryn swayed suddenly, her hand shooting out to catch the doorjamb to keep her balance. Gods, his scent was intoxicating.

She had a sudden vision of his body on hers, pressing into her. Bryn watched as his eyes seemed to grow darker, his luscious mouth parting in the most seductive way. She shook her head.

"Korvain?"

After a long, hot, lingering look, he dipped his chin slightly.

Her eyes slid shut as another flash of them touching intimately assaulted her. Letting out a breath, she pinned him with a look that usually sent men into hiding. "Mind getting your ass off my desk?" she snapped, stalking past him to sit in her huge leather chair.

With a cocky grin, he pushed himself off the edge of her desk and lowered his muscular body into the chair opposite her. His eyes raked over her upper body like he was thinking about her naked.

"Adrian says I can trust you with my girls up on Level Three."

"How can you know for sure?" he replied, his voice washing through her, tightening the muscles in her lower body. The cadence was mesmerizing, and she got another flash of him whispering erotic things into her ear while his chiseled, naked chest pressed against hers.

She let out an exasperated breath. "I trust Adrian. He trusts you. That's enough for me. Besides," she leaned in closer, "if you fuck around with them, I'll fuck around with you. You know who I am, what I'm capable of."

She sat back and watched in frustration as his lips curled into an amused smile.

Fucker.

Korvain drank in the sight of Bryn. She hadn't been afraid of him when she'd walked into the room. She'd been aroused by his presence. Now she was threatening him with death. The Valkyrie was braver than he thought she'd be. And he had to admit it was such a fucking turn-on.

Her blonde hair was pulled back behind her, a braid trailing over one shoulder. His fingers curled, wanting to know the softness of it, the silkiness, as he ran it through his fingers. The darker part of him wanted to know whether he could use all that hair during sex, to control her, to dominate her.

Her eyes were enthralling, with two separate rings of color that somehow swirled together, unique to Valkyries. The first ring was denim. It hugged her pupil, until the outer ring of sky blue started to take over.

His eyes drifted languidly down to her neck, studying the distinctive golden tattoo beneath her ear. Next they swept down to the hollow of her collarbones and then to her chest. She had nice breasts, but hid them behind a crew-neck tee, as if she was trying to take away some of her femininity by covering herself up.

His body had responded to the wave of gardenia her body had given off. The scent was still lingering in the air, and stuck to the back of Korvain's tongue. He wondered idly how she would respond to him taking her right here, right now, on the desk.

Bryn sucked in a sharp breath.

Korvain smiled.

She wanted him. There was no doubt about that.

"Have you ever done work like this before?" she asked, clearing her throat again. When he didn't answer, she went on. "My usual guy didn't show up. I can't afford to leave my girls unprotected." Her cheeks flushed with color, and he realized she rambled when she was nervous. He found that . . . endearing.

"I can do the job. Don't worry about that," he replied. Her eyes remained a little longer than necessary on his mouth.

Bryn seemed to study him for a long minute before she nodded, her braid bouncing on her shoulders. "I'll show you upstairs then."

Korvain followed her up the stairs, passing by two bouncers at each set of doors. The males tensed when they saw him, their hands reaching for the weapons under their arms. He smiled at them innocuously before walking on.

When they finally reached their destination, Bryn lead the way into the room. Korvain's eyes made a sweep of the huge space, landing on each bouncer for a second, assessing him. When he spotted Adrian, he lifted his chin in acknowledgment.

"I'm going to put you out on the floor so you get a feel for the place," Bryn said, pressing a button attached to the collar of her tee. "Fallon, I need you out the back with the girls."

A guy fell out of formation at the back of the room and came toward them. Korvain could smell he wasn't human as he passed them by.

"Take Fallon's position by the emergency exit," Bryn said. "Keep the men from touching my girls and from getting too trashed. I don't allow drugs here. You see any, confiscate them, then report it to me." She pulled an earpiece, a mic and receiver from her back pocket and handed them to him. "Don't be afraid to throw any of the men out if they're getting out of hand. I run a high-class establishment here. I won't stand for any shit."

Korvain accepted her words, clipping the mic to the front of his shirt. "You're on frequency three up here," she told him. "Questions? No? Good. See me at the end of the night for the money I owe you."

Bryn stalked away, straightening her T-shirt and tossing the silken length of her braid over one shoulder. Korvain inhaled, tasting her scent, trapping it in his nose.

Putting his back to the wall, he scanned the crowd. Humans mingled with the gods, rubbing shoulders with them, sharing drinks with them. The dancer on the stage was wrapped in a PVC piece—Korvain assumed it was a nurse's outfit. It hugged and exaggerated every one of her curves, flattering or not. She tottered on her heels, eye-fucking the crowd as she bore down on the pole at the end of the T-shaped stage.

He watched the males with their money flapping in front of their faces, watched the other bouncers position themselves more advantageously around the room. Topless waitresses walked backward and forwards from a shiny black bar on the opposite wall to the stage, their hands filled with loaded trays, their garters stuffed with green.

"Hey, my brother." Adrian's voice came over the earpiece in his ear. Korvain glanced over at his boy.

"Hey."

"If you do good tonight, she might ask you back."

Korvain snorted. "I don't need the work. I'm just doing you a favor."

His eyes made another sweep, landing on a woman who was walking toward him. Her hips looked like they were well oiled and moving independently of the rest of her body.

She stood before him, smiling and batting her fake lashes. Now that she was closer, Korvain could see she had the dual-ringed eyes of a Valkyrie.

"Hi," she purred, draping herself across his shoulders. He bit back the threatening growl when her fingertips walked up his chest and his throat until the backs of her fingers caressed his chin and jaw. He caught her hand, pressing his thumb into the nerve on the inside of her wrist until she winced.

"I don't like being touched," he warned. The blonde drew her arm away, cradling it to her chest protectively. When he looked back into her turquoise and navy eyes, she'd put her seductress smile back on.

"Are you new here?" she asked in a honeyed drawl.

He smiled, showing her his teeth. Her pupils dilated in response. "What's your name?" he asked.

"Kara," she breathed, her cheeks flushing, her pink tongue darting out to moisten her bottom lip.

"Well, Kara," he lowered his voice, dipping his head until it was next to her ear, "Get back to work so I can get back to mine."

Kara gave him a suggestive smile and turned to walk away. Her fluid, feline gait drew many eyes as she passed, and her being out on the floor seemed to be encouragement enough for one of the guys at a banquet table to grab her arm and pull her down onto his lap. She laughed throatily and brushed off his advance, but began to struggle when the man's hands locked around her waist, stopping her from standing up and leaving. Korvain was the first to react, his long gait closing the distance quickly.

"Get off me!" Kara shrieked, her hands pushing at the human as his fingers climbed up under her skirt. As she strained to pull away, her delicate neck muscles corded and Korvain saw a patch of scar tissue, about an inch wide and two inches long, just under her ear. He had half a second to wonder what it could mean before Adrian arrived to back him up.

"Get the girl out of here," Korvain growled, already reaching for the man and hauling him out from behind the banquet table. His legs flailed and kicked, thrashing against Korvain's hold. Korvain dragged him through the crowd and pushed his face against the wall, scattering a group of men in his wake.

With his knee, Korvain separated the male's legs, pinning his arms out to the side and keeping pressure on the back of his neck with his forearm. Korvain's free hand skimmed down one side of his body then the other, searching for any concealed weapons. There was a small bulge in his jacket pocket. Dipping his index and middle finger inside, Korvain pulled out a couple of packets of small white pills.

"What have we here?" he asked the human. The male was sweating now, trickles running down the side of his face. Korvain glanced up, looking directly into the camera above them. Jerking his chin toward the exit, he looked back at the human and twisted his arm until he screamed. Then, keeping a tight grip on the arm, Korvain sunk his fingers into the back of the male's neck and frog-marched him out of Level Three.

Bryn was waiting for them on the landing. She gave the club patron a cursory once-over before saying, "This way." She pushed open a concealed door directly opposite the stairs.

Inside, the room was shadowy and cold. The walls were black-painted bricks. A metal slab of a table was in the middle of the floor, a matching metal chair behind it. A single bare bulb hung from the ceiling. Korvain forced the man down into the chair, holding him in position with his heavy palms on his shoulders.

Bryn stood on the other side of the table, just outside the reach of the dim light, her face and shoulders masked by shadow. Even though the human couldn't see her eyes, her stare was hard. The piece of shit fidgeted, more sweat breaking out on his brow, down his back and under his arms.

"I hope you have an explanation," she said in a cold voice. The male shivered under Korvain's palms but remained silent.

"She asked you a question," Korvain said softly, the edge of violence in his voice unmistakable. The man jumped, whimpering pathetically. Korvain's fingers dug in, warning him not to move an inch.

Bryn stepped away from the shadows and approached the table. Reaching inside the human's jacket breast pocket, she pulled out his wallet. Flipping it open, she studied his ID, her blue eyes flicking to him and then back to his photo.

"Alex Jones," she said in a quiet voice, "What are doing in my establishment? And with a quantity of drugs that I can only assume you intend to sell?"

"I want my lawyer," he stammered. "I'm not saying anything until I've spoken to my lawyer."

Bryn laughed. The sound was as cold as the look in her eyes. "We're not the cops, so I can tell you right now that's not going to fly. I'll give you one more chance, though. Tell me why you're selling drugs in my establishment."

Alex glared at her, saying nothing.

"Fine. I'll get the cops involved. Is that what you want?"

The silent act continued.

Bryn shrugged and slid a phone from her pocket. "Have it your way."

Korvain stood there, restraining the man, watching the Valkyrie. A few minutes later, she hung up, pegging Alex with a hard stare. "Cops will be here in a few." She glanced at Korvain. "I can take it from here. I need you back in Level Three."

Korvain slid out of the room, but he wasn't going anywhere while that piece of shit was in the room with her. Setting his back against the wall, he waited until the cops arrived ten minutes later before returning to work.

5

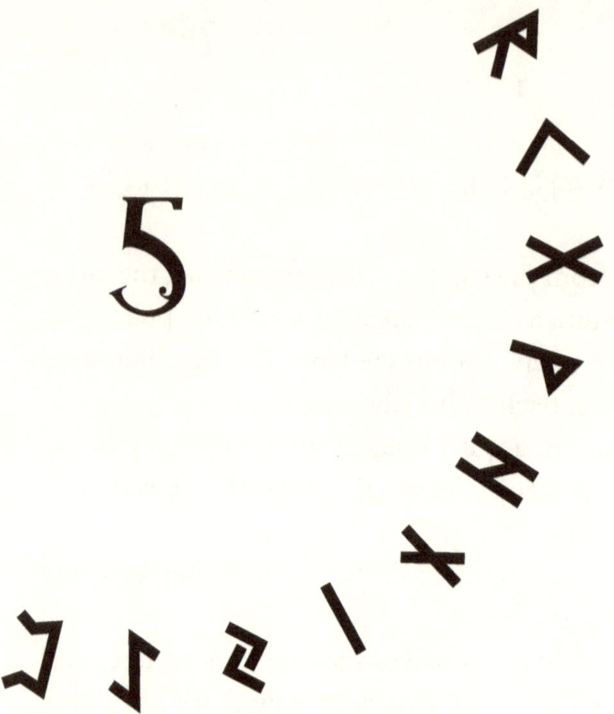

He could feel his body wasting away, but was powerless to stop it. He was immortal, not invincible. Flesh burned and healed. Blood ebbed and flowed. Breath rose and fell. And still he was bound to the boulders.

Pain.

Hunger.

Thirst.

He felt it in the tiny pinpricks on his skin, in the spasms of his decaying organs.

His lids cracked, opening slowly to look upon the only other living thing sharing his torment and misery. Ruby-red eyes stared down at him. As always, the serpent's maw gaped, its fangs bared. He knew every single detail of its body.

Venom welled slowly, dripping down one of its fangs. It hung there—trembling—before finally dropping.

He didn't scream, merely winced as the drop of poison rolled from his chest, tracking down his ribs and sliding onto the stone at his back. A moan escaped his lips, a moan that signaled his defeat, his surrender. Squeezing his eyes shut tight, he didn't even have the strength to buck against the bonds anymore. He was wallowing in his pain when he heard it.

Straining his ears, he listened. He could have sworn he'd heard a voice. It wasn't the first time it had happened, but he reacted all the same. He managed to lift his head, eyes rolling around sloppily in their sockets before exhaustion crashed over his body.

Are you a penitent man? a voice asked. It was smooth—silky like a well-polished piece of silver.

He tried to swallow moisture down into his dry throat, his tongue rasping against the roof of his mouth. Such thirst he felt. Such hunger, too, but he tried not to think about that.

Well, are you?

"Who are you?" he managed to croak. Was that actually what his voice sounded like?

Salvation, the voice whispered, the word echoing a hundred times over until his ears rang.

His tongue made another pass over his lips. "Where are you?" He waited for the response, clinging to the idea that he wasn't alone like it was a life raft and he was drowning at sea. This was the first contact he'd had in . . . he paused. Squeezed his eyes shut once more.

He remembered speaking to the bodies of his wife and son for a while, but they never spoke back. He remembered cursing them for having been killed, begging them for forgiveness, screaming at them to help him. Eventually he stopped when the fetid flesh fell from their bones, filling the cave's belly with a stench that made his eyes water.

They'd never answered him before. But this voice had.

Maybe this was real . . . Maybe . . .

"Hello?" he called. Desperation stabbed at him as he was met with silence. "Hello? Hello?"

He waited. He heard breathing. Rapid breathing. They were close, whoever they were. He strained his eyes, searching the darkness. "Whoever you are, help me!" he yelled, his voice cut up and bleeding like he'd swallowed glass shards.

He waited for their response, peering past the shadows. The breathing sounded closer. Yes! It *was* closer. He held his breath to hear them more clearly, to pinpoint where they were.

What he heard was . . .

Silence.

Infinite silence crashed over him.

He wailed at the ceiling. The breathing had been his own. Horror seeped into his bones. He was losing his grip on reality, losing his sanity. Immortality was the cage keeping his body alive and functioning, but his mind was up for grabs.

His eyes rose to the ceiling above him. The serpent—his jailer in this prison of torture—had not moved an inch since it had been placed there. Venom dropped from one fang, and the cycle started all over again.

I have watched you wither. I have watched you writhe. I have watched you beg for your release. Yet you have not asked the All-Father for forgiveness, the voice whispered once more. The silky quality to the voice made him think it could be a woman. His skin was smoking, slowly being eaten away. Soon the poison would be in his blood, his heart betraying his body by pumping it all around under his skin.

"Why should I ask for forgiveness?" he wailed, staring at the stalactite-covered ceiling. "What do I have to be sorry for?"

Do you forget the reason you are here? the voice asked, growing impatient.

"No," he ground out. "I have not forgotten. Nor will I forget who put me here."

And what would you do if you were free?

He smiled for the first time since his imprisonment. He'd thought of nothing else. "I would kill him."

A satisfied purr traveled through his head. *Would you now?* A rumbling chuckle reverberated around the room. *And how would you do it?*

He moistened his lips with another swipe of his tongue. "I know a way."

And would you use that knowledge? the voice purred.

"Yes," he croaked.

Yes? Do you swear to it?

A harsh laugh grazed his throat. "This is fruitless. I am not free."

If you were free?

It was only a dream. "Yes," he whispered, closing his eyes.

His answer echoed around him, slowly disappearing, until the cavern was plunged into silence once more. He soaked in the silence, the conversation he'd just had playing through his mind. This wasn't real. This conversation. This deal. None of it was real. He slumped back, sinking into the dark oblivion of his misery.

Then you are free, the voice replied.

Confusion and doubt crept through his rotting mind. What game was being played here? What trick? The silence continued on around him, the doubt spreading. He was not free. He was—

The bonds that held him in place suddenly slackened against his skin. They were . . . gone. He could breathe again, move his arms and his legs again. He wanted to get up, but feared what would happen. His body was nothing more than bones kept hostage inside his fragile skin.

Be sure to keep your end of the deal, Trickster.

He started by rotating his wrists and ankles, letting the feeling come back to them. Next his knees and elbows, then he sat up and the world swam in front of his eyes.

Hunger burned his stomach. Food. He needed food.

Perhaps it is time to punish the serpent for the role it played in your captivity. Consume its flesh and learn how the world has changed around you, that seductive voice said, nudging him in the direction he'd already been heading in.

When he felt he could, he swung his legs off the platform and placed his feet on the cold, rocky ground. Slowly and unsteadily, he staggered to his feet, clinging to the rock walls for support until he made it to the bones and rags that had been his son.

Lifting the rags, he took the blade attached to the leather belt his son had once worn. He was shaking from hunger, from insanity, from disbelief. He eyed the serpent hanging from the ceiling, hearing the hiss of warning—ignoring it.

Climbing clumsily onto the platform, he licked his lips. His body shook violently as he raised the blade and struck, severing the serpent's spine in one movement. Blood flowed down his hand, his arm, dripping off his elbow from where his knife had plunged into the snake's flesh. It was cold and it was liquid. He thrust his mouth under the flow, drinking his fill of that cool blood, then pulled the body free from the rock.

Taking it to the cave's floor, he peeled the skin off with weak fingers and feasted on the flesh, dead now but still twitching. As he bit into it, it writhed between his teeth. He ate until he passed out, his eyes closing, his stomach full, his mouth moist with blood, his head almost bursting with knowledge about this new world he was a part of, buzzing with names of people, of places, of strange new objects, with unfamiliar ideas, strange concepts. The rush of knowledge was dizzying, almost sickening—yet he had only one thought as he let sleep drag him under.

He was free.

6

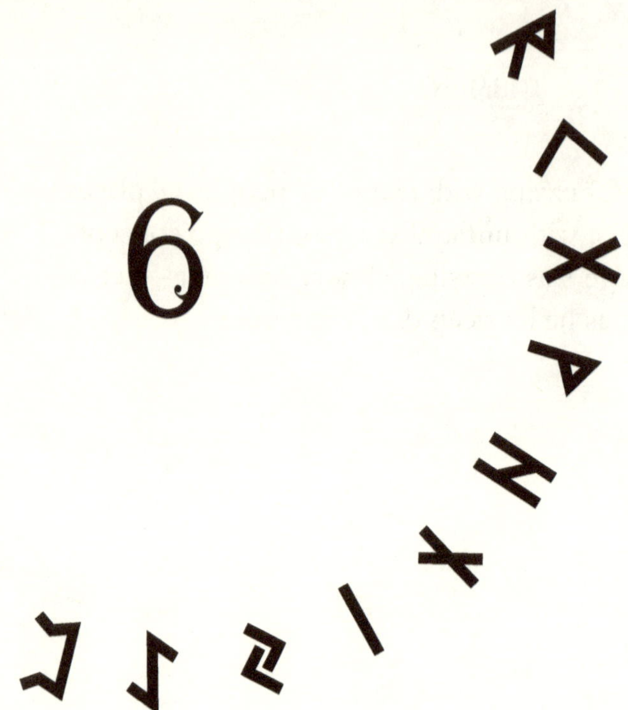

Bryn sat back in her chair and let out a deep breath. The cops had just discreetly left through the back door, the human trying to sell drugs in her club cuffed. Outside the interrogation room, Korvain had been waiting, watching the door like a loyal guard dog.

His presence had shaken her up more than she wanted to admit. There was an animalistic rawness to him that made him both seductive and dangerous to her. The images that had flashed through her mind when they'd first met had left her with a need she had never experienced before. She didn't understand what they meant, only that she knew she wanted him.

A quick glance up at the clock above the door told her it was only just after midnight. There were at least another three hours of night left for the humans to throw their money away on booze and women.

Rubbing the itch from her eyes, Bryn looked over at one of

the dual screens she had set up on her desk. The CCTV cameras streamed through to it, flickering from wide-angle shots to close-ups on each level every few seconds.

Every floor was packed, the people crammed in until the only way they could move was to rub themselves up against one another. Her eyes scanned the screen, looking for her bouncers. Each of them was exactly where she needed them to be.

Bryn's eyes finally settled on the image of Korvain up on Level Three. He was bigger than Adrian—wider, too. The room was heaving with people, but there was a large perimeter surrounding Korvain like people were afraid to get any closer than a few feet. She wasn't surprised. She could practically see the menace billowing from his body in large, thick waves.

His dark eyes flickered upwards, looking directly at the camera above his head. A blast of heat hit Bryn's body, her skin tightening, her muscles trembling. A gasp escaped her lips and she forced her eyes away.

"Get a fucking grip, Bryn," she chastised herself softly. She looked back at the screen, finding Korvain had gone back to watching the crowd with hooded eyes. She was losing her mind, the sleep deprivation finally catching up with her. She looked at the mountain of paperwork she needed to attend to and heaved a heavy sigh. Picking up the first invoice, Bryn got to work.

When she finally lifted her tired eyes again, it was three in the morning. The music had stopped and a quick glance at the surveillance cameras confirmed Raven and Level Three had been cleared of patrons.

She was stretching out her back, yawning, when there was a knock on the office door.

"Yeah."

Mist opened the door holding a fabric bag in her hand.

"We're done."

"How'd we do?"

"The bar took about ten large. I don't know about the other two levels. Someone's going to bring the take down soon." Mist slid the reproduction copy of William. T. Maud's *The Ride of the Valkyries* off the wall and opened the safe with a few expert flicks of her wrist. After placing the money in alongside another three bags, she replaced the picture and leaned on the wall, her arms loose at her sides. "Are you going to be much longer?"

Bryn looked down at the pile of paperwork. She'd hardly made a dent in it. "I'll get as much done as I can before the others come down with the take."

Mist gave her a sympathetic look and slipped from the room silently. Ten minutes later there was another knock, breaking off her concentration. Glancing at the camera placed outside her office door, Bryn saw it was Korvain.

"Come in," she called, hating how her heart was already beating like a snare against her ribs. The handle turned and Korvain filled the doorway. His shoulders barely fit in between the jambs, his head almost touching the top. He looked down at her, his black eyes glinting.

Bryn could taste her pulse on the back of her tongue, and she pressed herself into her chair. She let go a shaky breath, hiding her discomfort by going on the defensive.

"I'm busy."

"I can see that," he murmured in response. Her eyes flickered up, and she saw that his were raking over her body. He licked his lips, drawing her eyes down to his mouth, and she couldn't stop them there.

She took in all of him: his shoulders, his chest, his stomach. Her eyes became transfixed on his waist, his hips. His legs were thick with muscle. She could see that clearly even through the fabric of his pants.

Korvain cleared his throat. "You told me to come and see you after my shift."

Fuck. "Yeah. I did. I owe you for helping out tonight." Pulling open a desk drawer, she found a small locked tin and placed it on the desk. Reaching into another drawer, she took the key and slid it into the lock. Bryn started counting out the green, placing three hundreds on the desk.

She slid the money toward him, pulling back when Korvain's fingers touched hers, pausing there for a second longer than what was socially acceptable.

"Thanks," he murmured, holding her gaze hungrily.

Bryn couldn't stop the shiver tracking down her spine. "You did a good job tonight. If I ever need help again, I'll give you a call."

When he didn't respond, Bryn turned back to her work with a frown. "I've got a mountain of paperwork to do," she said tersely, gesturing at the offending pile of paper in case he needed visual aids.

His dark eyes fell to the desk, the corners of his mouth curling slightly. "I'll leave you to it then."

Korvain stepped out of the office, pocketing the three hundred he'd earned, and turned toward the exit. Even though Adrian had told him he couldn't fade into the building, Korvain had still tried. If the protection was anything like what he had on their place, he could have breached it. It wasn't until he'd made it inside that he'd understood what had stopped him. There were runes painted on the walls, passing as part of the decor. The pattern seemed random, but it was a very powerful ancient verse meant to protect the building from unwelcome visitors fading in and out.

As he reached the door, one of the other bouncers, the one who had seen him into the office when he'd first arrived, stepped in front of him.

The male was human—as most of the bouncers were in this place. He had his muscular arms folded over his barrel chest, his doubting hazel eyes on Korvain's face. "Is she allowing you back?" he asked, his deep voice rumbling with an unspoken threat.

Korvain stared down at him, forcing the other guy to crane his neck back to maintain eye contact. "Who wants to know?"

"I'm her head of security. I want to know if I can trust you, trust you to have my back if shit went south."

Korvain's dark eyes looked him over. Not even a hint of fear. Silence filled the space between them. "Yeah, I got your back," Korvain replied.

The guy relaxed visibly, his shoulders drooping. "Good." He offered Korvain his palm. "I'm Mason."

"Korvain."

Mason frowned.

"Yeah, I know it sounds weird," Korvain said. "I had parents with a strange fucking sense of humor." He laughed to put the other man at ease. Mason laughed, too.

"Does it mean something?"

"Korvain? No." Korvain told the lie with a tight-lipped smile.

"Look, I've got to get home. I hope you can make it back here. I heard you handled yourself real well up there." Mason turned and left him in the dimly lit hallway.

Korvain didn't mix with humans, but when he did it never went well, so this response from Mason was unexpected. Ducking left, Korvain pushed down on the metal bar across the door and stepped into the cool night. The door slammed shut behind him and he faded back to the house he shared with Adrian and his sister.

The front door was unlocked when he arrived on the front step. With the door shut behind him, he heard Adrian's voice carry down the hallway.

"My brother. You hungry?"

"Yeah. I could eat," Korvain called back, locking the door at his back. Fading into the house would have been so much easier, but it was a safety issue they didn't want to handle.

Above the door, they had a rune carved into the wood to prevent any unwanted visitors. It was the same as the runes used in the club, just more rudimentary—less powerful. It prevented most people from fading in, but it wouldn't stop everyone.

When Korvain rounded the corner, he saw that Adrian had somehow crammed his body into an apron that was straining across his chest, the slogan "Kiss the Cook" distorted over his wide pectorals.

"That's a good look for you, Ad. I'm sure you'll make someone a very nice wife someday."

His best friend laughed and threw a dish towel at him. "Did you remember to pick up some milk, sweetie?" he asked in a falsetto, laughing again.

"What are you making?" Korvain asked, still chuckling, pulling out one of the stools under the breakfast bar.

"Just reheating what Taer made for us earlier."

Korvain smiled. "She's a good kid."

"Yeah, but don't let her hear you calling her that."

Adrian spooned some pasta onto a plate for Korvain and handed him a fork. "What happened to the dealer you caught?"

Korvain chewed slowly, swallowing before answering. "Cops hauled his ass away."

Ad whistled through his teeth. "No shit, eh? I thought he would have squealed after Bryn put the pressure on him."

Korvain shrugged.

"So did Bryn ask you to come back in again?"

Korvain shook his head, loading another mouthful of pasta onto his fork. "She said she'd call me in if she needed help again, but didn't say when."

"Well, if Winta is a no-show again, I'll make sure she calls you in to cover. I've never seen the men behave so well before, with the exception of that cocksucker with the wandering hands and the drugs. You scared the shit out of them."

"I have a habit of doing that," Korvain replied.

Adrian laughed out loud, but somehow managed to keep on shoveling in food at the same time.

When his plate was scraped clean, Korvain took it to the sink to rinse and placed it in the dishwasher. "I'm beat. I'll see you tomorrow sometime."

The two clapped palms and Korvain dragged his ass upstairs to disarm and clean up.

He stripped his body of weapons, the twin Sig Sauers under his arms going straight into the safe in his closet. His karambit and the garrotte he always carried went into another locked chest.

He never worried about concealing the weapons he was carrying with clothing. He could cover them all with the shadows he called to himself, hiding the telltale bulges and outlines.

He stripped off his clothes then padded barefoot into the bathroom, twisting on the taps in the shower. The hot water quickly filled the room with steam. Korvain dragged deep lungfuls of the stuff in through his nose, shaking off the tension in his shoulders and back.

Tonight had been good. He'd gotten into the club and managed to make Bryn trust him by pulling the sniffer dog routine. Tipping his head back, he let the spray soak through his hair, the water's scalding fingers running down his face and along his neck. Alone with his thoughts, he ran through the plan once more.

He'd already known the layout of the club from Adrian before he got the invite, so no other recon was necessary now he'd seen it. Plus he'd made contact with Bryn and managed to gain her trust. That hadn't been part of the plan—just a bonus. If things continued on the way they were, he would have her blood on his hands and ten years off his contract sooner than he'd anticipated. He grinned, knowing how sweet that was going to be.

Korvain turned off the water and stepped out onto the white tile, wrapping a towel around his waist, then wandered out into his bedroom, letting his skin dry in the air.

Pulling on a pair of sweats, he left his chest bare and stretched out on top of the sheets. He relaxed his body, closing his eyes, and thought about Bryn. In his mind, he saw her dual-toned eyes, her alabaster skin. He smelled the shampoo she used, the scent of her skin.

He thought she'd be in her office still, having fallen asleep while doing that oh-so-important paperwork, but when he entered her dream, her body was tangled up in the sheets of her bed as if she'd been unsettled before finally drifting off.

Bryn's lean legs were splayed—the only exposed flesh—the sheets pooling in the depression between her thighs and along the length of her torso. The long expanse of her naked legs held his attention for longer than it should have. His body stirred at the thought of what was being hidden from him beneath the sheer cotton.

He forced his eyes to keep moving, trailing up her body to her face. Her braid had been taken out, and her honey-blonde hair—kinked from being restrained all day—was fanned out on her pillow, a halo of gold.

Korvain approached her slowly, his bare feet soundless on the thick-piled carpet. He was still a few feet from her bed, but he could smell that fresh, sweet smell of gardenia on her skin.

Her deep, even breaths filled the air. He paced his with hers, drawing in her fragrance, filling his lungs with that sweet temptation.

Bryn's eyes began to flutter open. She inhaled deeply, her eyes opening wider as she no doubt caught his scent. He knew the exact moment when she realized she wasn't alone. Her whole body became rigid, and her hand rose to her neck, her fingers near her tattoo but not quite touching it.

"Who's there?" she asked, sitting up. She clutched the sheet against her body, her gaze darting around the darkness. He stayed silent. Her hauntingly beautiful eyes pierced something inside him, some long forgotten part of himself. "Korvain?" she asked, her voice soft and unsure.

He remained where he was. Frowning, she ran a hand through her long hair and lay back down again, forcing her body to relax.

Sleep. His command was whispered directly into her subconscious. Bryn obeyed, her eyelids drooping slowly, her breathing leveling out. He had done enough. She would wake up wondering whether his visit to her had been real, whether he had actually been in her room.

The answer was both yes and no. The dream realm was real when he was the one manipulating it. She would remember the encounter, but still try to pass it off as a side effect of an overactive imagination.

Korvain left her to sleep's drugging influence and opened his eyes in his room once more. Rolling his head to one side, he looked at the little neon numbers staring back at him patiently from the bedside table. It was almost five in the morning. With a groan, he flipped over onto his other side and went to sleep.

7

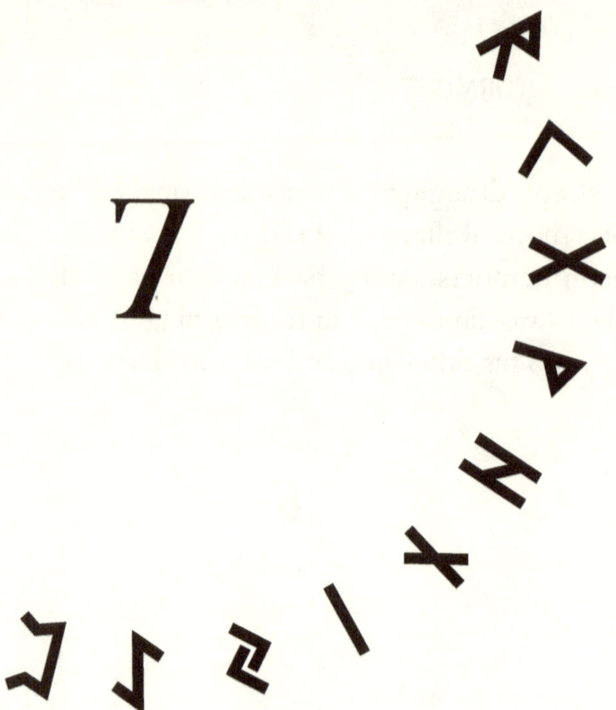

Odin paced his house in Beacon Hill, the slap of his Tom Ford loafers hitting the dark marble like a hammer against his skull. The news he'd just received had left him in a cold sweat.

Only two of the three Norns had answered his summons. Odin had been taking their counsel since the beginning of time. They knew all that has been, all that is and all that will be.

"You're sure?" He directed his question to Skuld.

"Be in no doubt about what we saw, All-Father," she replied meekly. "Loki has broken free of his bonds." Skuld fingered the ash tree pendant at her throat as she spoke, the nervous gesture not going unnoticed. Her hair shone like burnished copper, falling down her back in glossy sheets while her green eyes glowed softly from beneath her heavy fringe.

"That's impossible," he snarled back, dragging a hand through his hair and then loosening his tie when that wasn't enough to still his nerves. Unbuttoning the top button of his jacket, he added, "The only way he could have broken free was if someone set him free. Those bonds were unbreakable, and that snake . . ." He had breathed his own immortality into that snake. "That snake . . ." he faltered again. He hadn't been able to see through the snake's eyes—to know its thoughts—in about a week. He hadn't wanted to consider what it had meant at the time, but now . . . now there was no doubt in his mind.

Skuld's sister Verdandi touched her arm and sat forward, poised to add her two cents to the conversation. "It would be advisable—" Odin shot her a dark look. Her choice of words was no accident. She sighed. "You may need to take some measures to protect yourself, Odin." Where her sister had bronze hair, Verdandi's was pale, tightly bound at the back of her head.

"You think I don't know that?" he replied. "If you're going to advise me, at least give me something more helpful than that." The savagery in his voice was beginning to surface, to morph into all-out rage. The woman's eyes darted nervously between his real green eye and the obsidian glass in his right socket. Odin paced a tight line, cutting backward and forwards along his oriental rug. He might have the advantage, given it would take Loki a while to find him, but presumptions were dangerous things.

At the height of his power, Odin wouldn't have cowered at anyone's threat, but times had changed. Since the Fall, the gods and goddesses of the Nine Worlds had spread far and wide. The gods didn't wield the same powers anymore—the Aesir weren't as feared as they had once been, and since losing his Valkyries, Odin knew he had become somewhat of a joke. Nobody respected him anymore. He didn't even have any loyal guards left.

He had to find Loki before Loki could find him. Yes, Loki would be lost in this new world—friendless, ignorant, powerless.

It shouldn't be too difficult to locate him.

"That would take time, Odin. Time you don't have," Verdandi said, startling Odin. Had his thoughts really been so clear on his face?

He ignored the woman's warning. "I could send out my spies," he announced, thinking out loud.

Verdandi's eyes darted to her sister's. "There is no one who would stand by you now."

The truth of her words stung, wounding him. "Don't presume anything," he replied, letting her see his real rage for the first time.

"Perhaps there is a better way?" Skuld said softly, drawing Odin's attention away from her sister. Odin looked over at her and cocked an arrogant brow.

"Pray, tell, what is that better way?"

Skuld examined her hands in her lap. "Might I be so bold as to suggest you reconcile with Brynhildr?" After taking a deep breath, she bravely looked up at him once more. "That is who Loki will ultimately look for."

Odin squeezed his eyes shut tightly. Of course Loki would be coming for her. She was his only weakness—even before she became his Valkyrie . . .

Odin had been walking among the humans in Midgard when he happened upon a small village by the seaside. He was watching the humans as they toiled in the sun, sweat beading off their brows. They were cleaning the nets they had used to catch fish that morning, removing tufts of seagrass and other debris. Their knives cut through the weeds, often catching a man's fingers as he worked. Odin wondered idly what it would be like to work like that, to sweat and bleed so you could feed your family.

He was watching one man in particular. His great broad shoulders were wider than any other man's, his arms and chest dotted with scars. His face was stern, his blue eyes cold. Odin recognized what he really was. He was a warrior unable to die an honorable death, too old to live and die by the sword.

"Fadir!" a young girl called. The man looked up, the harsh lines of his face melting away as he looked at the young girl running toward him. She couldn't have been any older than twelve. Her blonde hair was the color of the noon sun, her eyes the exact same shade as her father's.

The man scooped her up in his arms, hugging her tightly. The girl's slim arms wound around his huge neck, squeezing.

"Brynhildr, what are you doing here?" he asked. "Your mother would be furious to know you have left the house."

The girl's wide smile turned into a frown. "She's making me sew hides for the winter. I hate sewing," she replied, pulling a face.

The young girl's father laughed at her, tapping the end of her nose playfully. "You may hate it, but you'll be thankful for those hides come winter."

"Odin?"

The All-Father shook his head slowly, shrugging off the memories. "Brynhildr will not speak to me."

Loki blinked rapidly. It was so bright, and he hadn't even reached the mouth of the cavern yet. He had slowly been picking his way over the stony ground, his bare feet bleeding profusely, a wake of crimson smears behind him.

Loki shielded his eyes with a bloodstained hand and grunted as another sharp shard of limestone bit into his heel. He propped himself up against the cold wall for a moment, collecting his breath and his thoughts.

"The caves will be closing in five minutes, folks. Five minutes," a disembodied voice announced.

Loki jerked upright, sliding into a cool shadow along the cave wall before he could be seen. When he thought it was safe, he peered around the corner and saw a man standing no more than thirty feet away at the bottom of a long trail. He was wearing a long-sleeved gray shirt with dark green pants. On his head was a large wide-brimmed hat.

The man began walking back up the steep track he'd obviously come down, herding the other dozen humans who had been standing at the railing with him. Loki forced his body to move, to give him just a little more. He covered the small distance to the railing at a hobble. Clambering over smooth boulders at the foot of the walkway, he rolled onto the path that had been filled with people no more than five minutes before.

He lay there for a minute, letting the cold seep into his skin. The world as he had known it was now gone—he understood that now. He'd been so focused on escaping the cavern and the bones of his wife and son that he'd barely thought of the future— where he would go, what he would do, how he would survive— but he had eaten the flesh of the serpent of knowledge, and the new world did not frighten him. It would not be the world he had known, but he knew it nonetheless. It would be strange and new, but not unfamiliar. He knew all he would need to know.

Climbing to his feet, he ascended the snaking walkway out of the cave, clinging to the railings to support himself. The muscles in his legs had wasted and barely held his weight. Loki finally emerged, staggering around in the dying light, drawing in deep breaths of fresh, clean air.

His watering eyes surveyed the landscape around him. The cave opened into a shallow valley, surrounded on all sides by hills that threw their dark shadows over him, digging their fingers into the back of his neck. Above him, all he could see was a great expanse of pale blue sky and many steps still to be climbed before he would finally be free of the earth.

After testing the steps, he found them to be built strong. It took him a long time to climb them, exhausting his already weakened body. With shaking legs, he finally made it to the top and had slumped down to rest for a moment when heavy footsteps approached.

Too tired to care, Loki stayed where he was—head bowed, breathing labored, the weight of the new world upon his shoulders.

"I'm sorry, sir, but the caves are closed up for the night. I'm going to have to ask you to leave."

Loki squinted at the man, but said nothing.

The man put his hands on his hips, looking exasperated. "Sir, did you hear what I said? I'm going to have to ask you to move along."

Loki licked his lips, recognizing the words the man had spoken as English. "I don't know where I am," he said, the strange new language feeling wooden on his tongue.

The man's eyes drifted down to Loki's chest. Loki had put his dead son's clothes on. They were torn and stained, but at least they covered his nakedness. Loki put his arms across his chest protectively.

"Well, sir, you're at the Carlsbad Caverns in New Mexico."

"New . . . Mexi—" he began saying slowly, trying the words out.

"New Mexico. The United States," the human repeated. He squatted down next to Loki, frowning under the large brim of his hat. "Are you all right, sir? You don't look so good."

"I don't know how I got here," Loki replied softly.

The man took off his hat, wiping the sweat that beaded there away with the back of his hand. He glanced around as if looking for someone.

"You got a car here, sir?"

"Car?" Loki asked. He frowned, wondering if he had the right word. "An automobile?" he clarified.

"Yeah, an automobile," the man repeated with a strange expression on his face. "You got one of those here?"

Loki shook his head.

The guy blew out a frustrated breath. "Well, how'd you get here then? With a group? The last group left a few hours ago."

"I didn't come with a group." Loki's stomach grumbled angrily.

"You're hungry," the man said. Loki blinked up at him, not denying it. The man looked around again, searching. "Look, I have to shut the front gates in ten minutes. The phones don't work so good out here, so how about I take you back to my place, and you can call whoever it is you need to call so they can pick you up and take you home?"

"Home," Loki said wistfully. He didn't have a home anymore. The glory days of the Aesir were over.

"Yeah, home," the human repeated. "I'm going to help you stand up now, okay?"

"Okay."

The man hooked an arm under Loki's armpit and lifted him up easily. "Dang it, you hardly weigh a thing. Where'd you say you were from again?"

"I didn't."

The man tipped his hat back, giving Loki the once-over. He must have decided he seemed harmless enough, because he began ushering him toward a large flat space with many lines painted on its surface. It was called a . . .

"Parking lot," Loki murmured, surprised at his ability to recall the information.

"Yeah, a parking lot," the human muttered. "That's my truck over there, you see it? The red one? We'll just take it nice and easy and get you in the cab, okay?" Loki allowed him to lead him, leaning on the man heavily. It was slow going, but eventually they made it. Loki sat in the front of the truck while the human walked around the hood and got into the other seat beside him.

"My name's Mike, by the way." Mike stuck his hand out in a peculiar way. Loki mirrored him and Mike took Loki's hand in his, shaking it firmly.

This new world was a strange one, indeed.

"Well, let's get home." Mike turned the key, the engine coming to life with a loud roar.

Loki tried to relax into his seat as they drove away from the cave. He passed the time by watching the small clock on the dashboard change. The hand had moved almost the whole way around when Mike slowed the truck and pulled into a driveway.

Up ahead, there was a small house with a wraparound porch. A woman appeared in the doorway, smiling at Mike through the windshield.

"That's my wife, Nancy," Mike told him, unclipping the strap crossing his body and getting out. Loki followed, shivering at the drop in temperature when he slipped out of the cab.

"Nancy, this is . . . ah, say, what is your name?" Mike asked. Loki approached the porch cautiously, unsure whether to give his real name or a false one. Did humans still know of the gods? Even if they did, would they know who he was?

"I am Loki," he answered, watching them both for any reaction.

"It's nice to meet you, Loki," Nancy said without hesitation and a friendly smile. "Won't you come in?"

Loki glanced at Mike, who encouraged him with a bob of his head. "Go on. You can make your phone call and have dinner while you wait for whoever is going to come and pick you up."

The house was warm inside. Loki looked around, able to name all the things contained within it. He still didn't understand how it was possible, but that snake had known everything there was to know about this new world.

"Would you like some coffee, Loki?" Nancy asked.

Loki looked at her, knowing his eyes must have been wide. "Please," he managed to croak out.

Nancy smiled warmly and disappeared around a corner. Mike took his elbow then, turning him around. "The phone is right over there." He indicated a small table near the door. "Call whoever you need to call."

Loki's gaze remained on the phone, but he took no steps toward it. "I do not have anyone to call, Mike," he finally admitted.

Mike gave him an uneasy smile. "And you don't remember how you got to the caves today either?" His voice had dropped in volume.

Loki shook his head.

Mike went to remove his hat, remembered he wasn't wearing one anymore and dropped his hand. "The police station won't be open right now, but if you don't have anywhere to go, I won't turn you out. You can stay here tonight with us, then tomorrow I can drop you off at the police station in Carlsbad. The folks there will be able to help you out."

Loki tried on a smile. "Thank you."

"Mike?" Nancy called from the other room. Mike looked over his shoulder and excused himself. Loki was left alone and his stomach twisted into a tight knot of anxiety. He had been alone for far too long already. To take his mind off the gnawing sensation, he wandered around the room looking at the photographs and trinkets lining the shelves of a bookcase.

When Mike reappeared, Loki was sitting in one of the armchairs facing the television. He had been watching the news, learning about the current government and the war it was fighting. He guessed not everything had changed then.

"Here's your coffee, Loki." Mike handed him a white mug. Loki peered over the rim, seeing his haggard reflection in the dark liquid. He knew about coffee. He just had no idea what it tasted like. Bringing the mug to his lips, he took a shallow sip and forced himself to swallow it down.

Mike laughed, taking the mug from Loki's hand. "If you don't like it, don't drink it," he said. "Nancy isn't well known for her ability to make a decent cup."

"I heard that!" Nancy yelled from the kitchen. She sounded upset, but Mike was still grinning at him.

Loki and Mike watched the rest of the news in silence, although the human made some strange noises while watching a story about a football team.

"That's my team," Mike announced proudly. "Cardinals, all the way. You got a favorite team?"

Loki shook his head, but before Mike could say anything more, Nancy walked into the room, a dish towel in her hand. "Stop trying to convert him, Mike," she said, exasperated. "Anyway, dinner's ready."

Loki followed Mike and Nancy out of the room and into another where a small square table was set up.

"Take that seat right there," Mike said, pointing to the one directly ahead. Loki sat down and stared at the plate of food in front of him: a piece of fish, peas and beans. At least that looked familiar. He was so hungry he could feel his mouth moisten as his eyes took in the feast he'd been presented with.

Putting a piece of thin paper in his lap, Mike asked, "Loki, would you like to say grace?"

Loki idly fingered his own piece of paper folded neatly beside his plate. "Grace?"

"You know—a prayer to God to thank him for this food."

Loki cocked his head to the side. "To which god?" he asked, confused. Nancy and Mike looked at each other. "You know what?" Mike said with an unsteady smile. "Don't worry about it. I'll say grace for us."

Loki watched as Mike bowed his head, mumbling some words under his breath before both he and Nancy finished with "Amen."

"Is that all?" Loki inquired, looking between Mike and Nancy. "No sacrifice is needed?"

Mike gave him a puzzled look. "Ah, nope, that's it." Picking up his knife and fork he added, "You'd better get eating before it gets cold."

Loki stared at the cutlery. He knew of these tools, but watched how Mike used them before trying it himself. He found it much simpler than he thought it was going to be. How strange it was, though, that they now prayed to only one god. Had they forgotten already?

After dinner, Loki was shown into a bathroom where he could wash and change into some of Mike's old clothes. He paused on the stairs coming back down when he heard Mike and Nancy talking together in hushed tones.

"You just found him there?" Nancy asked.

"Yeah. In those rags he was wearing. It looked like he'd been abandoned there, but for a lot longer than just a few hours."

Nancy sighed. "Are you sure he's safe?"

There was a long pause before Mike spoke again. "He seems harmless to me, but I'll stay awake tonight just to make sure. Would that make you feel better?"

"Yes, darling, that would make me feel much better. Thank you."

Loki coughed loudly, giving them a warning before continuing down the stairs. When he appeared in the living room, Nancy was lying on the couch with her head in Mike's lap. His fingers were brushing away her hair carefully, tucking it behind her ear in slow, languid movements.

Loki found a place on the other small sofa. Breathing in a deep breath, Loki felt a faint vibration in his body. He had felt it while he was bathing also but hadn't given it another thought. It seemed stronger this time, though.

"Mike, where is New Mexico in the United States?"

Mike's hand paused in stroking his wife's hair for a moment. "New Mexico? Well, it's in the southwest of the country, right between Arizona, Texas and Colorado."

Loki inclined his head to show he understood what he'd been told. "And what is that way?" He pointed over his shoulder. He wanted to get his bearings.

Mike frowned before he answered. "Ah, lots of states, Loki. There's Oklahoma, Missouri, West Virginia, New York."

"Oh."

"I have an atlas here somewhere. I can show you if you like?"

Loki nodded. "Yes. I would like that. Thank you."

Nancy sat up so her husband could go and get the atlas, smiling kindly at Loki.

"You really don't remember anything?" she asked gently.

Loki shook his head. "It is as if I've just been born into this world."

"All right, here we go." Mike placed the open book on the coffee table in between them. Loki slid from his chair and looked at the map.

"So, we're here," Mike said, his finger coming down to stab New Mexico in the belly, "and here's Oklahoma, that's Tennessee, West Virginia, Pennsylvania. . ." His fingers kept skimming over the different states, but Loki could hear only the vibration in his body, feel the pull in his blood.

Odin was in the north-east of this country.

He was there.

Loki could feel it.

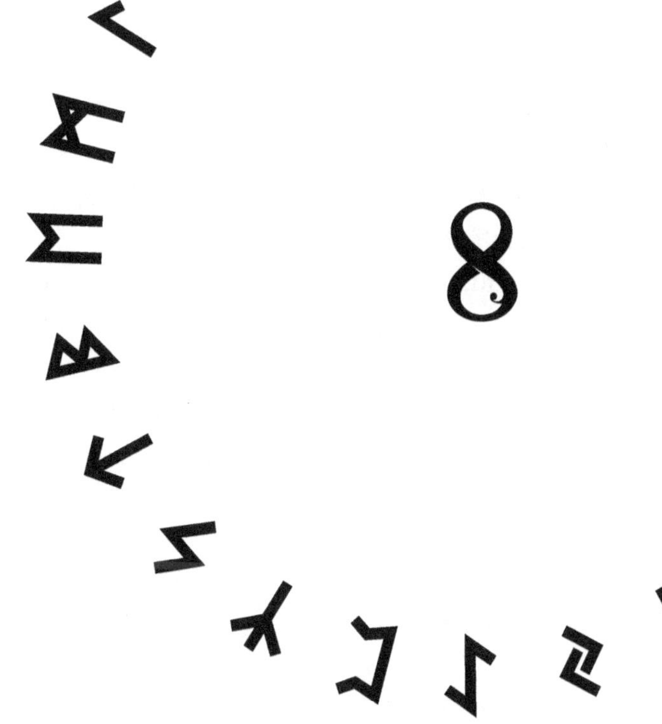

8

Taer's kick came in low, slamming into Adrian's kneecap. A hiss escaped his lips, a throb climbing his leg where she'd struck. Adrian's teeth snapped together as he tried to breathe through the pain. He went down on one knee, grabbing Taer's leg and slamming a full-knuckled punch into her shinbone. She winced and, after retreating a few steps, paused, breathing heavily through her nose. Her guard dropped, and Adrian took the opening with a satisfied smile.

Pushing off with his rear leg, he landed a flat-footed kick to her abdomen. The force of contact threw her off balance, swiveling her body around. She let out a string of obscenities as she fell in a heap on the floor, pain riding her body.

It was over and she was the loser.

His sister was good, but she had to be better.

"Don't let your guard down—you drop your hand when you kick. And keep your balance even on both feet," he said, offering her his hand and pulling her up off the padded floor. Taer dusted herself off, glaring indignantly at him.

"Again," she demanded, still breathing heavily.

Adrian smiled, flashing his fangs and stretching out the leg she had struck. Even though he had beaten her more times than he could count, he had to respect her tenacity.

"Enough for today." His stomach raged suddenly, reminding him of how long they had been sparring together, and how much he needed to refuel his body. "But you do need more practice."

Taer shrugged on a leather dagger holster that crisscrossed her small chest. "I know I do, but you're working at the club all the time."

Adrian wiped the sweat from his brow using the hem of his tee. "Yeah, well, that's a necessity. I try to give you as much time as I can afford." Picking up an identical dagger holster, he slid it over his shoulder before pushing his Beretta into the waistband at the small of his back.

Taer pushed open the side door to the garage, stepping out into the cool breeze.

"You know you could ask Korvain to teach me. I'm sure he'd make a great teacher," Taer said, going for nonchalance, but not pulling it off.

"I don't want you bothering him, Taer," Adrian warned. She'd had that walking death wish in her head ever since he'd moved in with them. "He's no good for you."

She huffed. "You don't think anyone is good for me." Taer opened the back door, her eyes scanning for threats just like he'd taught her.

"That's because it's true." Sliding the holster off his shoulder, he placed it on the counter then took out his gun.

Taer grabbed a bottle of water from the fridge, tossing one to him. "You know, I'm not a little girl anymore." He caught the bottle and took a deep drink. Adrian glanced at his sister, only able to see that small, fragile child who had hidden in his shadow as they grew up.

She was his apprentice now. She wanted to become a Walker—she wanted to become agarwaen—but the reality was she probably wasn't going to make it until he made her harder to kill than the other apprentices out there.

All the guilds subjected their apprentices to a Final Test in some form, but Darrion's was by far the most brutal. It was his sick idea of sport to pit all the apprentices from the current quinary against each other at the conclusion of their training to see who would walk away unaided and who would be put back together and sent home in a pine box. There could only be one winner. If an apprentice was badly maimed in an attack, and unable to compete further, the winner would kill them at the conclusion of the fight just to prove his loyalty to Darrion.

They had all done it.

And they all had the words inked onto their back to demonstrate their continued loyalty.

Odin had hunted Mares almost to the brink of extinction, so Darrion's methods made no sense—it was madness to pit the best warriors of their race against one another, eliminating the strongest—but no one dared question him.

The locks on the front door slid open then, shaking Adrian from his grim thoughts.

"My brother."

Adrian glanced toward the hallway. Korvain was covered in sweat, his shirt sticking to his skin and highlighting the muscular planes of his abdomen. His broad shoulders filled the doorframe, dwarfing the rest of the room. His biceps were like tree trunks, his thighs much the same, all twitching with brute power.

Korvain was the last of the pure-blooded Mares. He truly was the best example of what their race had been. He was two hundred and fifty pounds of rippling muscle and impending death. He was a living, breathing dagger through the heart.

"Hey," Adrian said.

Korvain pulled his tee over his head and threw it on the table beside the door. There was a choking sound, and when Adrian glanced over at Taer, she was having trouble swallowing the water she had in her mouth. She coughed, turning bright red.

Korvain's dark eyes slid to her, a small smile that looked wrong on his harsh face turning his lips up at the corners. "You all right there, Little Fox?"

She coughed again and made a strangled sound before running up the stairs. Korvain threw his head back and laughed—a deep, throaty noise. He took up the recently vacated stool, snagging the bottle of water in front of him. He swallowed the rest of the contents and crushed the bottle in his giant palm.

"How's her training going?" he asked.

Adrian shrugged. "Not bad, but not great either. She's getting to know the movements well, but her timing is still off. Reaction time is good, but she doesn't think much beyond that." He took another sip from his water bottle, letting the cool liquid swirl around his mouth. "It makes her vulnerable, because she's not thinking ahead and planning the counters."

Korvain watched him carefully as he spoke, but didn't offer any advice. "I'm glad I don't have an apprentice," he said under his breath. The truth was Adrian would have preferred not to have one either, but it was a case of taking Taer on or letting her become another one of Darrion's concubines. And there was no way in hell he would have let that happen.

"All right, well, I'm going to crash," Korvain announced, stretching out his nearly seven-foot frame. The vertebrae in his back popped and he rolled his neck to loosen everything up.

As he stalked away, Adrian got an eyeful of the tattoo that spanned the width of his best friend's shoulders. There in the old language were the words *Death before dishonor*. If Adrian had looked in the mirror, he would have seen exactly the same thing etched into his own skin.

The words were their contract with their guild master. Darrion's blood had been bound with the ink, and if they failed in their objective he could take their lives. It was like having a gun perpetually trained at their hearts.

The microwave chimed, drawing him out of his thoughts about Darrion.

"Tay! Food!" Adrian called up the stairs, pulling the hot bowl from the plate.

"I'm not hungry!" she shouted back a minute later. "I'm too busy dying of embarrassment."

Adrian shrugged and began shoveling the food into his mouth.

Odin didn't know where he was going. He was just wandering around the streets of Boston, restless, the conversation with Verdandi and Skuld lapping at his head. Gods, he needed a drink to calm him down. He kept on walking, though, and when he lifted his head, he realized where he had inadvertently walked to.

Odin's Eye.

One of his former Valkyries, Gunner, was at the door . . . but she didn't go by that name anymore. She used Maverick now instead. She eyeballed him uncertainly as he walked by, hands shoved in his coat pockets, his shoulders rolled forward. He glanced at her quickly then looked away. From the corner of his eye, he could see her mouth moving while her hand rested near the collar of her shirt. A few words were spoken quickly before she stood at ease again.

Odin walked the block, ignoring all the other bars and nightclubs, cutting back and walking past the Eye once more. Bryn was standing beside Gunner this time, her hard eyes fixed on him from across the street.

Dammit, he didn't know what he was doing. He was one step away from being a stalker. How ironic that was, he thought . . .

Every day, Odin would go down to the docks and watch Brynhildr's father toil. And each day, Brynhildr would run down to see him, telling him of what her mother had made her do that day. The man would wrap his arms around his daughter and hold her tight, and there was an ache in Odin's chest each time he saw it.

That was what he wanted. He had sons, but he longed for a daughter. For hundreds of years, he watched the humans with their sons—teaching them the family trade or business—but the girls were always left behind doing menial jobs by the hearth. He wanted more for them. He wanted a daughter of his own to teach, to make her feel more important than she would just being somebody's wife.

"Are you here to see me?" Bryn asked. Odin jerked back from the sound, not having seen or heard her approach. She looked at him warily, measuring him visually, before stepping off the road and onto the sidewalk in front of him.

"I . . ." he faltered, his mind lost to the memory of something he still regretted to this day.

Bryn was dressed in a T-shirt emblazoned with the name of

her club. "What are you doing here, Odin?" The tone of her voice was venomous, her hands held tightly at her sides.

He met her hostile eyes and took a deep breath. "I need to speak with you."

Giving him a reproachful glare, she asked, "About what?"

He glanced up and down the street suspiciously. "Something that doesn't need to be discussed in public. Can we go somewhere more private?"

Silence seemed to suspend time between them. She would say no. He knew it. Why would now be any different from the dozens of other times he had tried to come and speak with her over the last few decades?

She turned around without answering, making her way across the road—effectively dismissing him. And all he could do was watch on. What was he thinking? She hadn't changed her mind about him. She still hated him.

"You'd better come to my office," she called over her shoulder.

Odin stared at her, dumbfounded. She had never given him the time of day before this.

Bryn was across the street now, walking down the alleyway beside the club. Odin followed, the scent of garbage drifting into his nostrils. Up ahead, a door opened, golden light pouring out onto the asphalt. Bryn ushered him through, closing the door behind them both.

Leading the way, Bryn opened the door to an office. She waved him toward the chair facing her desk as she sank into her own, facing him, her expression frustratingly unreadable.

Odin undid the button on his single-breasted suit jacket and sat down, his legs crossed at the ankle. Cynically, her eyes traveled over his attire.

"Nothing's changed, has it?" she murmured.

He looked down at his designer suit, brushing a few pieces of non-existent lint away from the lapel. "I'm afraid I don't understand."

She smiled, but there was no humor to it. "The suit, the French cuffs, the diamond tiepin . . ." She waved in the general direction of the items mentioned. "Nothing changes."

Bryn pulled open a desk drawer and took out a bottle of clear liquid. Screwing the top off, she took a mouthful from the bottle. "You want a drink?" she asked after swallowing. He knew she didn't expect a positive answer, but he gave her one all the same.

"A cognac wouldn't go astray."

Her lips puckered distastefully. "It's vodka or nothing."

He sighed. "Vodka will have to do then."

Bryn handed over the bottle and sank back into her chair, watching Odin take a measured sip.

"So you said you wanted to talk. I'm busy. I don't have all night."

He placed the bottle back on the desk, inclining his head slightly.

"I have come to ask you to return to my side."

"Why?" she asked stiffly.

"I miss you."

"Bullshit. Tell me the real reason."

"That is the real reason, Brynhildr. Isn't that enough?" He truly wasn't lying. He did miss her. She was his first Valkyrie, his first daughter.

Odin could hear her teeth grinding furiously at the use of her full name. "I told you there would only be one way for me to return to your side."

He stared at her blankly, masking his rising rage. Bryn had granted him this audience. He couldn't fuck it up. "You could ask me for anything else and I would give it to you, but I will not allow that boon." His words were soft, his tone even softer, but inside his blood ran like fire through his veins.

"I think Kara has suffered enough."

"She broke the rules, and she was punished for that."

"I know she did, but after she served you honorably, dutifully, for a millennium, you couldn't have spared her that humiliation?"

Odin blew out a breath. It was true Kara's honor had been lost, but it was her own doing. She had made the decision to break his rules.

"Kara has always been . . . flighty."

"So expelling her from your service was the way to fix that?" There was a sharpness to Bryn's voice she hadn't been able to fully disguise.

Odin's chest rose and fell. "I left her her immortality."

Bryn's brow rose. "Yes, but you banished her. How well did you think she was going to take that rejection?"

Odin was tired of talking about Kara. He focused his one clear eye on her. "Bryn. Please."

He wouldn't beg her, so that was as close as he was going to get to it.

The Valkyrie shook her head, her braid swinging behind her. "You have my answer, Odin. Unless yours changes, don't bother coming back here."

He looked down at the hands folded in his lap, mulling over his options. "Final answer?" he asked, glancing back up, trying to ignore the animosity barely veiled in her eyes.

"Yes," she hissed. He stood up and left the office, trailing down the hallway and out into the cool air. As soon as he was free of the protective runes, he vanished—fading out of Bryn's life once more.

Loki stayed awake all night, stretched out on the couch while Mike dozed in the nearby armchair, thinking about the new world he lived in, working through everything he'd learned about it, piecing it all together.

He left Mike and Nancy's place early the next morning before either of them had woken up. Even though he hadn't deserved it, their kindness wouldn't soon be forgotten.

He had something more urgent on his mind now, though.

Revenge.

His hatred of Odin had not waned with time. If anything, it had grown stronger, until it was all-consuming.

In his pocket were the pages he'd torn from the atlas showing the United States. He had faded to a city called St Louis, wandering the streets, seeking out other gods, seeking out answers to the questions burning on his tongue. Had the humans forgotten? Were there any that remembered, or knew their stories, the Eddas?

The sun was dipping low on the Mississippi, shedding its golden light, rippling off the surface of the water. Loki knew he had to find a place to bed down for the night. God or not, he still had no money, forcing him to sleep on the streets with the filth and debris of human society, people addicted to substances they injected into their arms, fingers and toes. Of course he knew of these drugs, but now he saw firsthand what they did to the frailty of the human body.

Turning his back on the Gateway Arch, he headed into downtown St Louis, scanning the alleyways as he passed. Down one of them, he saw two men huddling over a small flame, a spoon in one of their hands. He approached discreetly, watching them melt a brown powder in the metal bowl of the spoon. When the liquid began to bubble, one man filled a needle while the other man held out his arm.

Loki watched in morbid fascination as the man receiving the injection went limp, his mouth hanging open, his eyes rolling back in his head. The man with the needle then did the same thing to himself, his teeth holding a tourniquet tight against his arm.

Puzzled, Loki backed away from the two men quietly, turning and walking away as quickly as he could from what he had just seen.

Loki walked on, the night thickly draping around him. Streetlights went on, but the stretch of street he was on was dark, the lights broken or flickering. The urgency to find shelter pressed on his mind.

He was so caught up in his search that at first he didn't see the man up ahead leaning casually against the side of the building until he coughed loudly and spat on the ground. Loki's eyes swept over him. He was not as tall as Loki, but he had more bulk on his frame despite being an obvious street person—Loki could smell his stench from where he stood.

He kept his course, walking past the man, who fell into step beside him.

"You got a light, buddy?" the man asked, producing a crudely constructed white stick from a pocket in his pants and placing it between his lips.

"No. I do not," Loki replied, slowing his steps.

The man grunted. "That's too bad." He slowed to a stop. "Hey, are you looking for somewhere to sleep? Maybe need something to eat? I know a place that'll have space for us if we leave now."

Loki stopped, turning toward the man. "You know where I can find food?" Mike had made the same offer to him. Perhaps these humans were okay.

The man shrugged one shoulder. "Well, yeah. You hungry?"

"I am," Loki replied.

The man turned back in the direction they'd just been walking. "Come on then. The soup kitchen's back this way. I'm Butch, by the way."

Loki let the man—Butch—lead him. He thought it strange that he kept glancing over his shoulder, but when Loki looked, there were only stray cats prowling from darkened alley to darkened alley. Loki turned back and saw Butch watching him.

"You got nice threads, my man. You haven't been on the street very long, have you?" He chuckled. "I bet you haven't even seen a real winter."

Loki shook his head. "I am new to this country."

Butch chuckled again, but it was derisive this time. "That explains the accent then."

Loki peered anxiously at the dark streets around them, asking, "Where is it that you're taking me?"

Butch glanced back at him. "Not far. Just another block."

As they walked, Loki's thighs began to burn, proof that his strength had not yet fully returned. They rounded one final corner, and Loki ran into Butch's chest. He felt all the bones of his ribs, smelled the stench of sweat-drenched clothing, musty with age. Loki looked around, taking a step back.

"Have we arrived?"

Loki dropped to his knees suddenly, an immense pain radiating out from the back of his skull. A strike to his stomach pushed all the air from his body, leaving him gasping to draw air back into his lungs. Another strike to his kidneys sent him sprawling forward onto the sidewalk.

Then he blacked out.

When he woke, only a few seconds had passed. He was on

his back, staring up at Butch, who was talking to someone else standing near Loki's feet. Loki tried, but couldn't get his body to move.

"He's fresh. Check his pockets. He's got to have some green on him."

There were hands suddenly all over Loki, pushing and prodding, fingers dipping into his pockets. "He doesn't have a thing," a male voice announced.

"Fuck, I need to score, man." Butch's voice and face were strained.

"Look, take his shoes. We can sell them."

Loki lay there as the boots Mike had given him were wrenched clear off his feet. He may have cried out. He may not have. Before the men left, Butch loomed above him.

"Welcome to St Louis," he sneered, kicking Loki in the side of the head. The last thought Loki had before the darkness swallowed him was that he was lost in this new world of his.

9

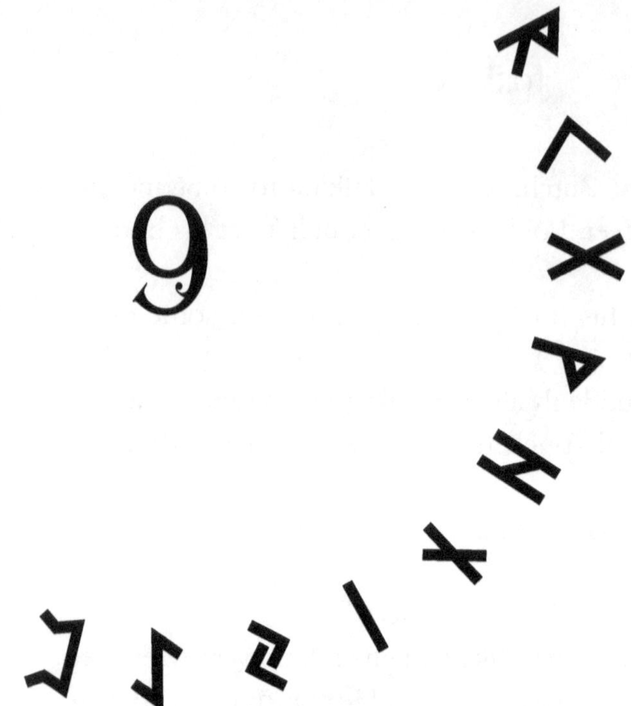

The whole situation was getting fucking ridiculous. Darrion had relegated this job to Korvain, but his patience was beginning to grow thin. Korvain hadn't hit his mark yet, which meant Darrion couldn't hit his own mark. He needed Odin dead, but he was barely holding on to his self-control. He could feel it fraying, could sense the snap ready to come.

He knocked on the door, his massive fist hammering the wood—letting it feel all his anger and frustration. Adrian's sister appeared through the glass panel, the color draining from her face when she caught sight of him. She opened the door, but kept the chain on.

"Taer," he purred. She was a temptation—there was no mistaking that. She was all sleek lines, pale green eyes wide with fear and a mouth he wanted wrapped around his cock. "You think a chain is going to stop me, little girl?"

"What do you want?" she replied cautiously, trying to hide the shake in her voice.

He smiled, baring his fangs. "Your brother's best friend."

"What do you want with him?" she returned, obviously feeling a little braver with the door as a shield in front of her.

Darrion let some of the malice leak from his pores. Taer stiffened.

"Where's Korvain?" he asked again, lowering his voice, letting her see the malignancy in his cold blue eyes.

"Out back in the garage," she squeaked.

Giving Taer another fang-filled grin, Darrion walked back down the stairs and continued up the cracked driveway. The chain link fence that ran alongside it was bent out of shape like a car had decided to get all up close and cozy without taking it out to dinner first. Glancing to his left, he noticed the curtain in the bay window closing suddenly, as Taer retreated quickly from the glass.

Up ahead, the pull-up garage door was opened halfway, light spilling out on the driveway like golden blood. There was a grunt, and then another, as Darrion pulled the door up the rest of the way. His two best assassins were grappling, each trying to overpower the other. Korvain had the bulk, but Adrian had the speed.

Korvain tackled Adrian to the ground, his knees close to Adrian's body. One arm tangled under Adrian's neck, the other under his opposite arm to control Adrian's head.

"What are you going to do now, my brother?" Korvain asked. His tone was cocky, but the strain was evident in his voice.

Adrian smiled, showing the full length of his fangs. With quick, sure movements, he positioned his left arm against Korvain's thickly corded neck, pressing into it. His right arm burrowed under Korvain's armpit so he could clasp his hands together.

Adrian used the leverage of his caged arms to open up a space between their chests so he could maneuver him easily with a series of grappling movements. He managed to slide his body out from underneath Korvain's and, finally grabbing Korvain's leg, slid the bigger man toward him, repositioning his arms around his waist. Korvain grunted in surprise, then laughed.

"All right, Ad, you got me."

Adrian smiled again, releasing his hold. Getting to his feet, he offered Korvain his hand.

"Well, that was sweet," Darrion drawled, enjoying the flash of surprise and anger in their eyes when they both looked up. He let the door slide shut, closing them all in together.

Korvain grabbed his shirt from the floor with an angry swipe of his arm, the tattoo across his shoulders glistening with sweat.

"What's doing, boys?" Darrion asked, watching them both predatorily. Adrian's startled eyes flashed to Darrion's face. He was almost as tall as Korvain, but the light elf blood flowing through his half-breed veins would never allow him to achieve the same bulk.

Gesturing at the training pads and weapons littering the blue mats around them, Korvain replied, "Training." His voice was dark, threatening.

Darrion cocked a brow at the man. "You want to lose the attitude?" Korvain simply stared, his dark, bottomless eyes boring into him. Darrion returned the favor. "We need to talk."

Korvain screwed the top off a water bottle, glancing over at Adrian. "Give us a minute, my brother?"

Adrian's hesitant eyes bounced between the two of them, but in the end, he nodded and left. Once they were alone, Korvain said, "So talk," putting his lips to the bottle.

Darrion began, walking around the sparring mat. "I need an update." Korvain had sat down onto the mat and started stretching out his twitching muscles. When he looked up, a bead of sweat dripped down the side of his face. "I'm working on it."

"You're not working hard enough on it." Darrion's reply was cool, calm—at complete odds with what raged on the inside.

"Look, I'll get it done."

"When?" he snarled back.

Korvain stood up. "What's the fucking rush?" he asked, towering over Darrion—crowding him. But size wasn't everything.

Darrion bared his fangs. "You don't want to do that, morier."

Korvain's much larger and longer fangs flashed in reply. "You may be my boss, but watch your fucking mouth."

Darrion laughed in his face.

"Fuck you, Darrion." Korvain's voice boomed in the insulated room. "You came here for an update. You got one. Now leave me the fuck alone so I can get on with it."

Darrion's skeptical gaze bored into him. Korvain never flew off the handle. Ever. He was just like Darrion in that way. Cold. Heartless. But as Darrion probed, he found Korvain's emotions were all over the place.

The muscles in Korvain's jaw jumped violently. "Stay out of my fucking head, too."

Darrion pulled back. He wanted his kill. He had waited too long already. "I want this done in forty-eight hours, morier, so I suggest you stop fucking around in here with Adrian and get the job done."

"And if I take longer than that?"

Darrion approached the huge male, tilting his head back so he could still look him in the eye. "You know what happens," he replied in a cold drawl.

"I'll get it done."

Korvain's whole body was vibrating with anger. His hands had bunched into tight fists and he wanted to drive his fingers into Darrion's throat, but he held on to that anger, that raw energy. He knew better than to goad Darrion into anything more than a war of words.

The tattoo on his back made sure he couldn't cause any physical or mental harm to Darrion. He'd tried it once. It felt like ten thousand volts were traveling through his body while he was hit by a freight train. So, yeah, he hadn't done it since then.

His whole existence as a Walker was one brutal lesson after another, but lesson number one had always been the same: Don't get attached to the mark. If he saw them as a real person, things got complicated. They were not his friend. All he had to do was figure out a way to fulfill the contract and cover his exit. Kill them as quickly and discreetly as possible and walk away, forgetting the gurgling last words, the desperate begging, the rage, the hate, the fear.

Darrion stared at him with his empty, cold, blue eyes. Eventually, his boss nodded curtly and faded from the garage. Korvain snarled at the empty space where Darrion had been and started striding the length of the floor.

"Fucking cocksucker," he grunted under his breath. Korvain didn't know what was stopping him from completing the job. Normally he would have done the necessary recon, figured out a plan and executed it within a few days. That was why he was the best: He had the least emotional attachment to the mark. They were the object standing in the way of another sliver of time off his contract.

"She's nothing," he spat. "She's dead already. She just doesn't know it," he added, still pacing the blue mats, curling his hands into tight fists over and over again.

"Korvain?" a small voice asked from the side door. He glanced up, finding Taer standing there, her small body trembling. He couldn't blame her. Darrion was a scary motherfucker: cold, calculating, manipulative. It was also no secret that the bastard had had his eye on Tay ever since he'd found out she was Adrian's sister.

He slid his anger back into its box. "What's up, Little Fox?" He watched as her whole body sagged against the frame of the door. She was training to be a Walker, but he knew the Final Test would break her. She just didn't have the will to survive like her brother did.

There could only be one winner in that contest, and the fucker had to have nerves of steel and the ability to block all emotions out. By simply being female, Taer was already at a disadvantage.

"I thought he was going to kill you."

He'd had exactly the same thought. "I'm still here," he said, rubbing a hand through his short hair. His answer somehow gave her the courage to come a little further into the room.

"I thought you were in trouble in here . . ." she stammered, playing with the edge of her tee nervously, eyes downcast.

"Nah," he replied steadily. When it was obvious she wasn't going to speak again, Korvain began picking up the equipment he and Adrian had been using to spar with: daggers of varying sizes, short swords, sticks.

He was so preoccupied with cleaning up, and his standing order to kill Bryn, that he was completely oblivious to the other person in the garage with him. He had no idea anything was different until the whisper of clothes against skin made Korvain spin around.

Taer stood before him completely naked from the waist up. She had the body of a woman, but instead of being all curves and grace, her stomach was flat and toned—training with Adrian had honed her body into a carefully crafted weapon.

He took a step back, frowning, too shocked to form a coherent thought.

"Taer, what are you—?" Squeezing his eyes shut, Korvain was sure when he opened them he would find it all a dream. He cracked his lids.

Nope.

Still Taer.

Still very naked.

She glanced down, her cheeks flushing. One arm came across to cover her breasts. Her body trembled, her skin covered in goosebumps. "I don't know what I'd do if you were killed, Korvain. I—" She blinked up at him with doe eyes.

Korvain approached her in two large strides, picking up her shirt and holding it up against her naked upper body. "Taer, please cover yourself up." Gods, he couldn't even look her directly in the eye.

"I want—" she began, but Korvain silenced her, his fingers gently touching her mouth.

"You don't know what you want, Tay."

Her pale eyes filled with tears. "But, I . . . I want you to know I care about you. A lot. And . . ." she trailed off.

"Tay," he said soothingly. "You don't know what you ask."

She shook her head, dark hair like satin ribbons falling over her shoulders. "Please."

"Little Fox," he murmured, rubbing her arms gently.

Her eyes snapped back to his, anger filling them with a black flame. She pulled away from him roughly. "Stop calling me that! I'm not a little girl anymore." She snatched her shirt from him, cradling it to her chest.

"Okay. I'm sorry, Taer." Korvain put his hands up defensively. He was one of the best assassins in the world, yet a little girl had him cowering away in a corner. What. The. Fuck.

"Taer, if Adrian saw you like this, he'd castrate me . . . for starters."

Their eyes met. She was trembling visibly, tears on her cheeks. She turned her back to him and abruptly faded out of the garage. He had known about her little crush on him. He'd just had no idea how far the infatuation went. And he certainly had no idea she'd act upon it.

"Fuck me," Korvain breathed, dragging his palm across the back of his head. He looked around aimlessly. "Just . . . yeah . . . fuck me."

10

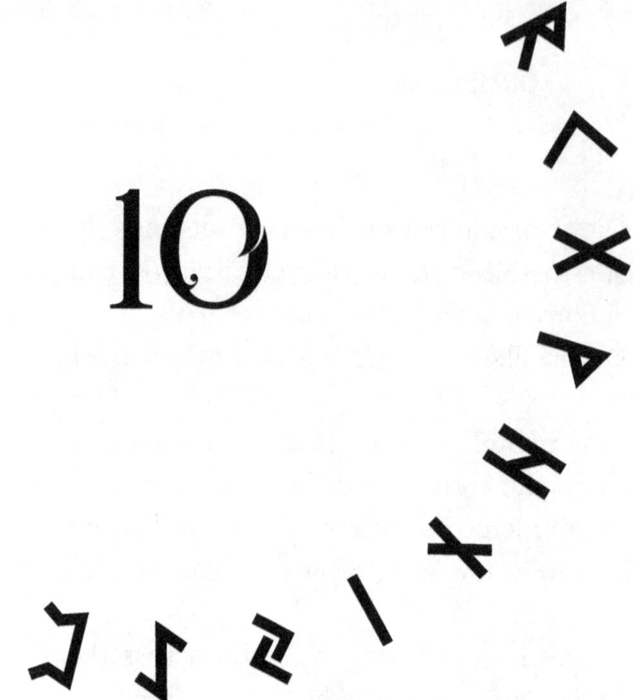

oki woke with the sun's hot rays on his face. Lifting his hand to brush the prickling sensation away, his bloody fingertips were greeted with puffy skin. He winced when his fingers landed on one sensitive eye socket. Sitting up slowly, he squinted at his surroundings, taking stock of the situation. He was where he had been the night before, lying on a slab of pavement splattered in his own blood.

Blood stained his mouth. He tasted it on the back of his tongue. He swallowed, trying to get rid of the metallic dryness, when something small shifted around in his mouth. Loki spat into his hand and found a tooth, his tongue probing the space where it had once been.

"Man, they got you good," someone said above his head. Loki looked up, shielding his face from the sun, temporarily blinded by the light.

"Who are you?" he demanded, instantly going on the defensive. He would not be tricked so easily again.

"Me?" the man asked, crouching down beside him. "I'm Andy." He eyed Loki's bruised and beaten body in a detached sort of way. "You got your ass handed to you last night."

Even though Loki didn't understand the words, he understood the meaning. "Yes, I suppose I did . . . *Andy*." He looked at the man, at his wiry blond beard and wide-set green eyes. He was not a human, but one of the Aesir—there was no doubt in Loki's mind—but who was he? Loki had never seen him before.

"Well, if the cops see you just hanging around on the street bleeding like you are, they'll lock you up. So let's get you out of here and cleaned up." Andy offered Loki his palm, but Loki hesitated.

"Look, you can trust me," Andy said, seeing how he paused. Loki didn't know whether he could or not. But what other choice did he have? He had been looking for other gods without results, and now a god had found him. With a slow inclination of his head, he took the proffered hand and was hauled to his feet.

As soon as he was vertical, Loki tried to put weight on his right leg, but winced. Andy crouched down and inspected his ankle.

"Could be broken. All you need is some time to recuperate. Think you can fade?"

Loki nodded gingerly, discovering a new ache in his neck. "I think so, yes."

"Well, all right. Take my arm and I'll show you where to go."

Loki put his hand on Andy's arm, closing his eyes as the vibration of a fade overtook his body. One second he was in a stinking alleyway and the next he was in a small, cramped apartment stinking of mildew. It wasn't much of an improvement.

"Are we still in St Louis?" Loki asked, clutching the wall when the room wouldn't stop spinning.

"Whoa, why don't you sit down for a second?" Andy said, grabbing his arm and directing him to an old green couch. Loki slouched into the worn cushions and stared up at the other god. He was vulnerable right now and he hated it. He needed to find out who Andy was and how much he knew before he could rest.

Loki licked his lips and looked Andy in the eye. "Do you know who I am?"

Andy's eyes skirted around the room before finally landing back on Loki. "Just some guy down on his luck?"

Was he lying or telling the truth? "But you knew I was a god. How?"

Andy shrugged his shoulders and sank down onto the coffee table opposite the couch. "How do humans recognize their own family members?" he asked in reply. "I just did. Can't you spot other gods?"

Loki thought about that for a moment. "Yes, I suppose I can."

"Well, there you have it," Andy said and stood up, clapping his hands together then rubbing his palms nervously. "Are you hungry? I can make you something, or would you prefer to take a shower first?"

Loki looked down at his bloodstained hands. "I would like to bathe, then I'll eat."

Andy bobbed his head, a jerky movement. "No problem. I'll show you where everything is."

He led Loki into a small, windowless bathroom and left him alone there for a minute.

"Here are a fresh towel and some clothes to put on," the god said a moment later. Loki took the things from Andy's outstretched arms and shut the door.

Resting against the lip of the basin, Loki disrobed. His ankle still hurt, and he couldn't put any real weight on it yet. Stripping the bloody shirt Mike had given him from his body, he dumped it on the floor beside him. He struggled to remove the pants, but managed. They, too, joined the shirt on the dark green tile.

He hobbled the few steps to the shower and turned on the taps until hot water beat against the grimy floor. Loki stepped inside the cubicle and shut himself in with the steam.

The blood that had been caked on his face and body dissolved with the water, running pink down the drain at the bottom of the trough. His face was still tender to touch, so he washed it clean as gently as possible.

When his aching body felt a little better, Loki dried himself, slid into the new clothes and left the bathroom. Andy was at the stove cooking something that smelled like the stew Loki's wife had once made. On the countertop, there was a fresh loaf of bread and a knife—and suddenly Loki knew who he was.

"Andhrimnir."

He had been the cook in the halls of Valhalla. They had never met, but he was sure it was him.

"Don't go by that name anymore," Andhrimnir said gruffly. The god pulled out two wooden bowls and filled them with the thick stew. "Hungry?"

"Yes."

He placed one bowl in front of Loki where he sat at the small counter and fetched him a spoon to eat with.

The rich food filled the gnawing hole in Loki's stomach, helping him heal the injuries he had sustained the night before. Loki was scraping at the bottom of the bowl when Andhrimnir took it from him and spooned another ladleful into it.

Sliding it back in front of Loki, he mumbled, "You need to eat more to heal yourself." Andhrimnir cut off the heel of bread and dunked it into his own bowl of stew.

With the spoon poised in front of him, Loki looked at the other god, softly asking, "Have you seen many others?"

Andhrimnir glanced up from his bowl. "Yeah, occasionally. Some of the Vanir live around here, but not many."

"Have you seen any other Aesir?"

Andhrimnir's eyebrows rose. "Around here? No, not so much. That's why I settled here."

The next question burned on the tip of Loki's tongue, but he had to be very careful about how he asked it. "And what of . . . Odin?"

"Odin?"

Loki hid his interest, looking back down at his bowl. Andhrimnir remained quiet for a time before Loki heard him inhale deeply.

"Odin is where he has always been since the Fall."

"Which is?" Loki nudged casually, spooning some more stew into his mouth, chewing, swallowing.

"Boston. He's in Boston, Massachusetts."

Loki let out a breath and sat back into the bar stool, his spoon abandoned in the bowl. "Is it far?"

Andhrimnir shrugged. "A bit over a thousand miles."

Loki's mind churned over the new information quickly. He was only one thousand miles from Odin, but he needed to get to his Valkyries first. He looked up at Andhrimnir. The other man was watching him with a fearful look that hadn't been there a few moments before.

He knows who I am. Loki had to move quickly now. "Do his Valkyries still reside with him?"

The other god dropped his spoon into his bowl of stew, splashing some of the contents out onto the countertop, and took a step back.

Loki's eyes darted to the breadknife sitting between them just as Andhrimnir's did. Loki looked back at the other man before throwing his still-healing body over the countertop, toward the knife. His bowl went flying, hitting the ground and spitting bits of meat and vegetables everywhere. Andhrimnir leaped for the knife too but was a fraction too slow, and Loki's fingers wrapped around the hilt.

Andhrimnir backed away from Loki, his hands up, his eyes wide. Loki stalked around the counter towards him.

"Tell me about the Valkyries," he hissed, thrusting the knife into Andhrimnir's fearful face.

Andhrimnir stared at the blade perilously close to his eyeball. "I swear, I don't know about them."

"I don't believe you." Loki pressed the tip into the skin just below Andhrimnir's right eye and applied the slightest amount of pressure without breaking the skin.

"Okay!" Andhrimnir screamed. "Okay," he repeated quietly, defeated.

"Start talking," Loki demanded.

Andhrimnir's face drained of color, but he managed to stammer out a few words. "The Valkyries split from him."

"When?"

"I'm not sure. I h-h-heard rumors it was right after the Fall, and others saying it was more recent than that—a hundred years or less."

"And where do they reside?"

"Boston, I think."

Loki could feel the satisfied smile pulling on his lips. Odin had done half his work already. He had been wondering how to approach the Valkyries without the All-Father knowing, but the arrogant asshole had already alienated them.

His pale eyes fixed on Andhrimnir's face once more and he smiled. "Thank you." He pulled the knife away from his eye and settled it near his hip instead.

The other god looked relieved for a second, right before Loki sank the blade into his belly. Andhrimnir cried out in pain, dropping to the floor with both hands pressed to the wound, the knife still protruding from his belly.

Getting down onto his knees, Loki took the hilt into his hand again and repositioned it under Andhrimnir's rib cage. The god cried out again, but didn't fight. With a push, Loki thrust and twisted the blade upwards through the god's heart, killing him.

Loki got off his knees unsteadily—Andhrimnir's blood staining his hand—and looked around the apartment. He had eaten his fill, but still required more suitable clothing than what Andhrimnir had provided for him. After dressing in a pair of jeans and a long-sleeved T-shirt, he took the god's wallet and coat from the rack near the door and faded from St Louis.

When Loki arrived in the city of Boston, the thrum he associated with Odin had lessened. Perhaps it was because so many others from the Nine Worlds seemed to reside in the city, but for whatever the reason, the vibration was weaker—diluted somehow.

Still disoriented by the new world he was now a part of, he found himself sitting in the shadows of a tree in a small cemetery in the center of the city. For some reason, he felt at peace there. The timeworn headstones jutted out of the ground like the broken teeth of giants.

He watched the humans walk by, going about their days, oblivious to him and everyone else around them. They held small phones to their ears, not speaking to the people who stood shoulder to shoulder with them. They were moving together as one, but disconnected from each other also. More than once he spotted a light elf towering above the crowd.

As the day wore on and the number of humans dropped off, the vibration started to get a little stronger and Loki realized why Odin had chosen to make this city his home. The humans' energy along with the others' seemed to distort his.

When the temperature started to drop and he began shivering in the light jacket he'd taken from Andhrimnir's apartment, Loki decided to move on. He stretched out his legs, his knees popping in protest after being in the same position all day. He left the confines of the cemetery behind him, following the pull of Odin's energy.

When he passed by a large glass-fronted shop, his steps slowed, his eyes clamping onto something taped to the other side of the glass. He leaned in closer for a second before entering the shop and tearing the piece of paper off the window.

"Hey! You can't—"

Loki glared at the woman behind the counter and left the shop, clutching the thin piece of parchment in his white-knuckled hands. It was a poster for a place called Odin's Eye, on Tremont Street. It could simply be a coincidence, but he doubted it. If someone had the gall to use the All-Father's name, perhaps that person could lead him to Odin's Valkyries.

Folding up the paper quickly, he stuffed it into his pocket and held the address in his mind, his body vibrating with his fade. When he got there, he looked up at the unassuming building. He couldn't be sure if it was the place. There was no sign on the outside, no street number on the building, nor the surrounding buildings. As his eyes looked over the facade, they paused just above the door.

On the lintel, carved into the stonework, was a small rune. Loki squinted at the symbol, realizing what it was, what it meant. This had to be the place.

He decided he would return later on in the evening and try to gain entry then. Turning around, he started walking, following the tug of Odin's energy.

Loki crossed a large park still filled with people despite the drop in temperature, despite the setting sun. Around its fringes were vast buildings made from red bricks and white stone. They rose to great heights above his head. Passing down one of the streets, he closed his eyes and drew on the link with his blood brother.

He was still going in the right direction.

Opening his eyes once more, Loki crossed Branch Street, but paused at a cross street. A new energy signature hummed, and it was too similar to Odin's to ignore. Glancing around, he took a few steps closer to a house on the adjacent corner. Looking above the doorway, he found the same symbol of protection that had been on the club. Loki was studying the building when the front door opened and a woman stepped out.

Loki pulled out the paper from his pocket, pretending to study it intently. He kept one eye on her, but the woman's bicolored blue eyes passed over his face without any recognition. Her pale hair was tied back from her face, exposing a tattoo on her neck that looked like a silver sword.

Valkyrie.

His whole body pulsed with a barely contained frenzied energy as he tried not to strike out there in the street. He would bide his time and come back for her. He only had one shot at it and he had to get it right.

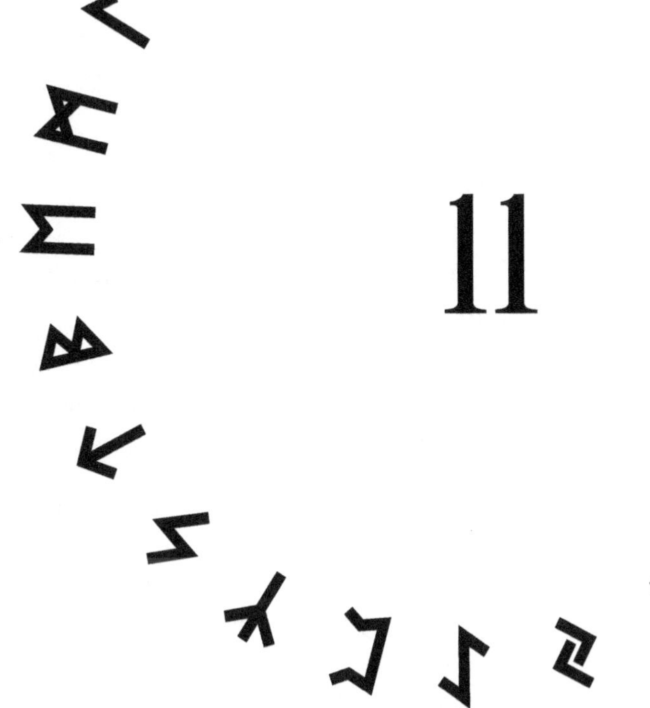

11

Odin heard the screech of a car alarm blaring into the night, jolting him from his sleep. He had been dreaming about that awful day, the day his grip had finally broken. Shaking his head, he sat up. With his elbows on his knees, his head sank into his hands.

Disturbing dreams about his past haunted his sleep—thoughts about Bryn, mostly. Thinking about the rift between them filled Odin's heart with a hollow ache. After Kara's banishment, he had assumed Bryn would help the Valkyrie out and then return to him. Kara had needed to be punished, not Bryn, but somehow—inadvertently—that was exactly what he'd done.

Nearly one hundred years later, she was still as determined as ever to prove him wrong, to live her life away from him.

The alarm was still going, making his head throb. Pushing himself off the bed, Odin peered out the window, frowning. As he looked, the lights flared and the horn stopped, the night returning to blissful silence.

Odin let the curtain slide from his fingers, blocking out the world once more. He needed to find a way to get Bryn back to him. He needed to protect her . . .

After watching Bryn's father for two human years, Odin had seen Bryn grow into a beautiful young woman. She was almost fourteen now, her long blonde hair glossy with health, her blue eyes intelligent, yet playful. She wasn't a little girl anymore.

Bryn came to see her father without fail whether it was raining, hailing or snowing. And her father was always happy to see her, still crushing her to his body when she flung herself at him.

One day, before Bryn had come to see her father, Odin let himself be seen by the humans. He walked the docks as he had always done, but this time, the humans noticed him—studying him with suspicion in their eyes.

"Brander Gunnarsson," Odin said, reaching the male.

Bryn's father looked up from his work, his blue eyes watchful. When he straightened up to his full height, he said, "Yes?"

"I have come to make a deal with you."

Brander's eyes studied him intently. "What kind of deal?" No doubt he was thinking this was about his work.

"Do you know who I am?"

Brander shook his head, his grip on the bone-handled knife he'd been using on the nets tightening.

Odin smirked at him, leaning in a little closer. "Take a guess."

"You only have one eye, like the All-Father does, but you cannot be him."

"Why not?"

Brander laughed suddenly. "Because the All-Father does not stroll among us mortals for sport." He turned back to his work, dismissing Odin. "Leave me now. I have work to do and not enough sunlight to do it in."

Odin paused momentarily before reaching out and taking the man's shoulder. He let him feel the strength in his body, the current of electricity burning through his fingers. "I am who you believe me to be. I am Odin."

The human stumbled back, looking at Odin with continued skepticism, then reached for the stone pendant at his throat, clutching it. The pad of his thumb ran over the protective rune inscribed there.

Odin watched him slowly unravel. So many emotions passed over his face: disbelief, contemplation, confusion, conflict. The humans believed in the gods, but never expected to meet them.

Shakily, Brander reached out to a sack of grain piled up behind him and sat down, the knife slipping from his fingers and clattering to the wooden dock.

"No . . . you can't . . ." Brander shook his head. His eyes were fixed on the ground. When his breathing had returned to normal, he looked up into Odin's face. "Are you really him?" he asked sincerely.

"I am. Now, about that deal."

"I don't know what a fisherman would have that you would desire, but you can have anything." He swallowed. "You are the All-Father."

Such reverence he spoke with. Odin kept the delight from his face. Slowly, he said her name. "Brynhildr."

Brander shook his head slowly, his eyebrows drawing together tightly. "I don't understand."

"Your daughter. Brynhildr. I want her."

In an instant, the veneration was gone. The human was suddenly shaking with anger. "You cannot have her. She is still a maiden." His rage spilled over, his veins bulging in his neck, his face turning scarlet. "Go and spread your seed elsewhere." He threw the words angrily, Odin's wrath long forgotten.

Brander's defiance angered Odin. Nobody said no to him. "I will have her, Brander, whether you agree or not. This was just a courtesy—a courtesy you do not deserve, but a courtesy all the same."

"She is not yet fifteen! What use do you have for her?" Brander cried, anguished.

"I will not take her yet. When she is eighteen I will return for her. She will not marry. You are to ensure she remains pure." Odin's tone left no room for argument.

"Wh-what are you going to do with her?" the man stammered, fear turning his sun-browned skin white.

Odin smiled. "I have special plans for her."

Odin shook the memory from behind his eyes. He remembered that day so clearly, but had not thought about it for so long. He also remembered what had happened when he returned for her on the day of her eighteenth birthday.

The god lay back down on his bed and closed his eyes. Sleep was elusive, but ultimately it came.

Loki pulled Andhrimnir's wallet from the back pocket of his jeans and flipped it open. Inside were lots of pieces of plastic: some with photos, some with numbers, some with strange little shiny pictures in the corner. He pulled out the one with *Visa* written on it, turned it over and studied it. This had to be the one that turned into money.

Sleep had been tugging at him for hours now. He needed to bathe and eat and rest. Walking along the streets of Boston, he found a suitable inn and entered, approaching a long bank of counters.

"Good evening, sir. How can I help you?" a woman asked him from behind one of the desks. Her hair was coiled up on top of her head, her kind, dark eyes smiling at him.

Loki stepped closer to her slowly, tentatively. "I wish to sleep," he said.

"Of course, sir." She started tapping on the keyboard in front of her screen. "Is it just you?" "Yes."

"We have an executive room available. It's one hundred and ninety-five dollars per night." She looked up at him and smiled. "Would you like to take it?"

"Yes."

"Great." She beamed, pressing a few more keys. "How long are you intending to stay with us, sir?"

Loki didn't know how long it would take to execute his plan. "A week," he muttered offhandedly.

The human smiled again, her fingers tapping the keyboard quickly and efficiently. "I'll just need some ID and a credit card."

Loki pulled Andhrimnir's wallet from his pocket and took out his license and credit card. He handed it to the woman, who frowned at the photo. Loki quickly changed his features enough to pass as Andhrimnir, but not enough to be unrecognizable as himself. It was a subtle shifting of features—changing the shape of his nose slightly, widening his eyes a little, making himself appear shorter, when in fact it was all an illusion.

When the human looked up, she frowned again, then looked down at the photo once more. "What brings you to Boston, Mr. Metzger?"

"Business."

She smiled, bobbing her head in understanding, before saying, "The card went through fine." She placed the license and credit card on the counter alongside another plastic card. "This is your room key. You are up on level six, room four."

Loki pocketed all the plastic and turned to leave.

"Mr. Metzger? Do you need any help with your luggage?" the human called out after him.

"No . . . thank you," he replied, walking over to the bank of elevators and pushing the "up" arrow. As the elevator took him up to his floor, his mind worked over the plan that had suddenly been put into play.

He knew the location of the first Valkyrie. He could find out where the rest were from her, and when the goddess wasn't of use to him anymore, he would kill her, cut out her heart and ensure Odin found her.

12

"My brother, you awake?" Adrian called through the door. Korvain rolled over, rubbing the sleep from his eyes. Afternoon sun trickled in past the blinds, casting a soft orange glow over the room. Fuck. He'd slept away most of the day.

Pulling himself up onto his elbows, Korvain said, "Yeah." The sheets dragged down his naked chest as he moved, pooling at his hips. Adrian pushed open the door and stuck his head inside.

"I just got a call from Bryn. She needs you tonight. Winta's still a no-show."

"Yeah, all right. What time?"

"An hour."

Korvain nodded and fell back onto the mattress, throwing a forearm across his face. The door snicked shut, leaving him alone with his thoughts.

Tonight could be the night he killed her.

Tonight could be the night he wiped ten years off his contract with Darrion. That thought alone spurred him into action. He showered and got dressed, arming up and hiding the small arsenal on his body with carefully positioned shadows. He went downstairs to find Adrian biting into a sandwich over the sink. The other man glanced up and grinned, his mouth trying to say a word that came out garbled. "What?"

Adrian swallowed. "Sandwich?"

Korvain shook his head. "Nah, I'm good." He stood there for a minute. "I'm going to go early. I need to talk to Bryn."

"About a permanent job?" Hope shone in his eyes. "I knew you fucking liked it there."

Korvain smiled. "Yeah. Something like that."

Taking the back door out of the kitchen, Korvain faded to the rear entrance of the club and pounded on the steel door. Half a minute later, it swung open, making Korvain take a few steps backward to avoid being hit.

Bryn stood there looking straight at him, one hand on each side of the doorframe. Today she was in a pair of tight jeans and another fitted tee. This time the logo of the bar was scrawled over her breasts. Korvain knew he was staring, but somehow he couldn't stop himself.

"I'm glad you came," she said, snapping him out of his stupor. His eyes climbed the rest of her body until they hit her face. He could have sworn her cheeks were bruised with color. Before he could call her on it, she threw something in his face.

Korvain pulled the fabric away and looked at the shirt. It was like Bryn's, just black instead of white and about ten times bigger. He brought his arms down and cocked a brow at her.

"If you're going to work here, you'll have to look the part." She stepped back from the doorway. "Change room is there." She pointed down the hall about fifteen feet away. "Questions?"

"Yeah, is anyone else here yet?"

She shook her head, her braid sliding against her back. "Not for another half an hour."

Korvain watched as Bryn disappeared into her office. He could attempt to find her cloak now and kill her before the rest of security turned up, but half an hour wasn't a lot of time to play with. Besides, he had no idea where her cloak was, nor did he have any idea where to start.

He wasn't about to rush this. He had to be patient. Making his way down the hall, he pushed into the staff change room and dropped the shirt on a long bench that sat in the middle of the room surrounded by lockers. Keeping his weapons shrouded in shadow, he stripped off the holster that held his Sig Sauers, the thigh holster for his blade and the garrotte wire.

He was dragging his shirt over his head when the door to the change room opened and closed with a soft click. With his back to whoever had just walked in, he quickly peeled his shirt off the rest of the way, dumped it on top of his weapons and turned around.

"Nice tat. Does it mean anything?" Kara stood in the doorway, her eyes at half-mast. She was in a silk robe the same shade as the turquoise ring of color in her eyes and wore a pair of clear heels.

Her eyes were fixed on his chest, absorbing every inch of his muscular body. Korvain felt violated, but could do nothing to stop it.

"No," he replied, hearing the hostile tone of his voice. "What are you doing here? I thought you girls got dressed upstairs."

"We do, but I heard you were here early, so I thought I'd come and talk to you." The sound of her voice had desperation written all over it.

"Talk about what?" Korvain shoved his arms into the new shirt, irritated with Kara showing up like this. Surely she'd already received the message that he wasn't fucking interested loud and clear.

"Don't feel like you have to cover up for my sake," she said in a slinky drawl, her hand clutching at her throat, her pupils dilated. Korvain narrowed his eyes at her as she slithered her way toward him. Shaking his head, he slipped into the top of the shirt and pulled it down his torso.

The hungry look on her face dimmed slightly at the brush-off, but she wasn't ready to give up on her prize just yet. Her long fingernails were painted in a color complementing her eyes, her fingers fluttering impatiently as she reached for him.

Korvain bit the inside of his cheek to stop a vicious snarl from escaping. "What are you doing?"

Tilting her head back, she looked him in the eye. "I wanted to thank you for saving me from that man the other night."

Korvain pulled her hands free from his body and put the bench between them. "You're welcome."

The Valkyrie pouted and sashayed in his direction again.

"Kara—" Before he could finish his sentence, the Valkyrie's mouth was on his, her tongue pushing against his lips. He growled and pulled away from her, ignoring the dark, hungry look in her eyes.

From the corner of his eye, Korvain saw that the changing room door was now open. He could see Bryn standing there, her mouth hanging open, her hand still on the handle as she took in the scene in front of her.

Fuck.

Korvain took a step back from Kara, his hands up in front of him.

"I was wondering where you were," Bryn said softly. "Now I see what held you up. I'll, ah, leave you two to it." She retreated from the room; the look on her face—annoyingly—made his chest hurt.

He rounded on Kara, trying his best to keep his anger in check. "What the *fuck* do you think you're doing?" he snarled, his hands bunching into fists at his side.

Kara stared at him, a look of satisfaction in her eyes. "I was thanking you."

Korvain glared back at her, then at the door where Bryn had been. How much had she seen? Did she know that it was Kara who had come on to him, or did she only see her mouth plastered onto his?

"You're wasting your time," Kara said, drawing his attention back to her. Her seductress face was gone, a scorned, angry look in its place.

"Excuse me?"

She signed tersely. "Bryn. You're wasting your time with her. She's uptight. What you need is a sure thing."

Unbelievably, she pressed her body against him again. Korvain didn't bother muffling the sound of his irritation this time. Kara had the good sense to pull away from his tightly wound body, to step back. Self-preservation had finally kicked in.

Thank the fucking gods.

"Stay away from me, Kara," he hissed, scooping up his weapons from the bench. He shouldered his way out of the room, the sound of Bryn's office door slamming shut bringing his head around.

Bryn had heard everything Kara said, and the words stung.

Pressing her back against the closed door, she angrily wiped away the tears threatening to spill down her cheeks. Why was she upset by this? Korvain didn't belong to her. He could kiss or fuck whoever he wanted. But seeing Kara with him made her feel like she'd just been stabbed in the back.

Her eyes landed on the bottle of 42 on the top of her desk. Lurching forward, she grabbed the thing with both hands and took a deep pull. When there was only an inch of clear liquid left at the bottom of the bottle, Bryn collapsed into her desk chair and buried her head in her hands.

She didn't understand this feeling of jealousy. It didn't make any sense. Was she upset that Kara had gotten her claws into Korvain, or was it something else? Seeing their lips fused together had brought the memories of the dreams back to her. In one of them, Korvain's lips had been pressed to her mouth like that. Her lips tingled even now with the sensation.

She had woken up from another bout of disturbed sleep. She'd only been able to get a few hours at a time, and each time she'd woken she'd gotten up to walk a lap of her apartment. Her feet had pressed into the soft carpet when she swung them off the bed, her toes curling into the pile as a need to feel grounded became overwhelming.

Not bothering with a robe, Bryn had padded out of her room in a tank and boxers, making a beeline for the freezer. Pulling one of the squat glasses from the drying rack, she'd poured a few fingers of vodka into it and brought the rim to her lips. She was swallowing the first mouthful when she'd seen a figure looming in the living room. Putting the glass down, she'd squinted into the darkness.

She knew there was no way anybody could get up there and

laughed at her own stupidity. She had the best charms and modern technology in place. She was seeing things. The insomnia was making her hallucinate.

Draining the glass, she'd placed it in the sink and wandered back through to her bedroom. But as soon as the door was shut firmly behind her, the hairs at the base of her skull had stood at attention. She felt eyes on her.

The same huge shape she'd seen in the living room was now in the corner of her bedroom. Flipping on the light switch, she'd squinted at the glare until her eyes adjusted. She'd looked over at the corner and slammed her back into the door as she stepped away from what she'd just seen.

Korvain was standing casually against the wall. His arms were pressed across his chest, a dark, sensual look in his eyes.

"Korvain?" she'd croaked.

Pushing himself off the wall, he'd approached her with a rolling, predatory gait. His hips seemed to move independently of the rest of his body. Her eyes had been fixed on his waist, her tongue swiping moisture onto her lips involuntarily. He reached for her, but instead of touching her, he'd flipped the light off again. Darkness descended, yet she could see him so clearly in front of her.

"Bryn," he'd murmured, and his hand slid over her cheek and cradled her face against his palm. A shuddered breath of contentment had left her lips. She had wanted to feel his touch like this since the first time she'd met. She'd longed to know the warmth of his skin. He moved in closer, bringing his mouth to her ear. "I can't stay away."

She'd moaned and felt her body go slack. He pressed himself into her, letting her feel all the strength he had in his muscles, letting her feel what was straining against her belly.

Korvain had dipped his head until their mouths were mere inches apart. His warm breath had brushed over her face, his spicy masculine scent getting trapped in her nostrils.

She'd arched her back, her hips jerking into his, craving him, and causing him to suck in a seductive hiss. "Kiss me," she breathed, pushing her chest out. A raw, needy sound burst from down low in his throat and he meshed their mouths together.

There had been nothing tender or sweet about the kiss. It hadn't been the tentative meeting of two mouths, but a rushed push toward something they'd both wanted—what they'd both needed. His tongue expertly coerced her to open for him. She'd allowed him entry, and he'd explored her mouth, tasting her completely.

She'd melted in his strong arms, her hands gripping his biceps trying to hold herself upright. Heat bruised her body, pushing more satiated moans from her throat. She was already lost in him when he'd pulled back, sucking on her bottom lip as he did.

She was panting, looking deeply into his eyes. He'd smiled and scooped her up effortlessly into his arms. He'd walked her to the side of the bed and laid her down gently, pulling the blankets up to her chin.

"Sleep now." It was a command she had no way of disobeying. Her eyes had slid shut, and when they opened again, it was late afternoon. She had slept for around six hours straight—something she hadn't done in years.

Sitting up in bed, she had touched her lips and smiled.

Loki faded directly from his hotel room back to the red-brick house he'd seen the day before, the house where he knew a Valkyrie lived. He looked at the building, feeling the life force of the woman inside. The plan he had come up with was simple, but he believed it would yield the results he needed.

He walked up the steps to the stoop, altering his appearance slightly to make his hair black instead of blond, and his eyes brown instead of green. He injected just the right amount of panic into his expression as he began knocking frantically on the front door.

The Valkyrie opened the door cautiously, her eyes taking him in quickly. When she saw the dread clearly etched onto his face, the door swung open all the way.

"Sir? What's wrong?"

Loki faked a shudder. "Please help me. Someone just ran over my dog."

The goddess's eyes widened as she peered out onto the street. "Where?"

"Just across the road! Please! You have to help me."

The Valkyrie looked back into his face, compassion coming to her eyes. "Of course. Just let me get my coat."

As soon as her back was turned, Loki followed her into the house, treading softly. He closed the door quietly behind himself, stalking her toward a closet at the end of the long entrance hall. He was only a few feet away when he tackled her from behind.

Pulling her to the floor, Loki shifted his weight directly on top of her shoulder blades. She instantly struggled against him, trying to throw him off, a hand reaching, straining, for the tattoo on her neck. Knowing he had to subdue her, Loki twisted one arm behind her back, holding her still while his eyes searched for something heavy.

On the nearby sideboard, he spotted a large crystal paperweight. Loki reached for the weapon and brutally brought it down onto the top of her head. The Valkyrie's wild struggles stopped instantly, her body going limp beneath him.

Loki rolled off her and stood up, brushing himself off. He knew he didn't have a lot of time. He started up the stairs, making for her bedroom. That was where her cloak should be. He looked through her closet without finding it, but as soon as he opened up a drawer full of her undergarments, Loki saw the ash box taking up more than half of the space inside.

He pulled the box free and inspected the contents. The pure white feathers shimmered in the light, and as Loki slid his hand inside, he felt the softness of them against his palm. A satisfied grin pulled up his mouth. He was so close now.

With cloak in hand, Loki started back down the stairs, but paused when he heard whispering.

"Mist?" the Valkyrie said desperately, unable to conceal the whimper in her voice. "Please. You have to help me. Someone just forced their way into my house . . ."

Loki recognized the name. It was another one of Odin's Valkyries. A rush of adrenaline flooded his bloodstream as he realized he could kill at least one more Valkyrie that night. But was that what he wanted? Did he want to exact his revenge so quickly? No. Loki wanted Odin to suffer as he had suffered all those centuries trapped beneath the ground.

Focusing only on his current task, Loki crept down the stairs silently until he reached the bottom. The Valkyrie was propped up against the wall, blood gushing from the wound to her head. Her hand shook where it pressed the phone to her ear, her eyes widening when she saw that Loki had returned.

"Help me!" she screamed into the phone just as Loki reached for it. She threw it across the room out of his reach. A feral roar left Loki's throat as he backhanded the woman.

Her eyes rolled back in her skull and she listed over to one side. Dumping the cloak on the ground, Loki yanked the wires hanging from a phone sitting on a low table from the socket. He bound her hands and feet with the wires, leaving her propped against the wall. Loki slapped her to bring her back around. She came to with a loud gasp, her eyes cracking open widely when she realized he was still there.

"Where are the other Valkyries?" he demanded.

The goddess shook her head. "I'll never tell."

Loki bared his teeth at her in a humorless smile and picked up the cloak. He fingered the feathers gently, enjoying the look of pain on the woman's face as he did so. "Tell me where the others are," he repeated, more softly this time.

"I'd rather die than tell you," she spat back venomously.

Loki shrugged. "Have it your way then." He tugged the first feather free, enjoying the way she shrieked out in pain. Blood welled from the cloak where the feather had been plucked, the color slowly staining the surrounding plumes.

When the ground was littered with half a dozen feathers and pools of blood, he paused. "Tell me where the others are."

The Valkyrie's teeth were clenched against the pain, the muscles in her neck cording. Wordlessly, she grimaced and defiantly shook her head. Loki snapped his teeth at the woman. "All you need to tell me is the location of one other Valkyrie and I will stop all this. I will stop your misery."

Loki could pinpoint the exact moment his words had pushed through the haze of her suffering.

"Do you swear it?" she asked, her voice hoarse from screaming. "Do you swear you'll let me live?" Her chin shook as she spoke, tears trembling in the corners of her eyes. Loki inclined his head slightly.

The waiting tears suddenly ran down her face, mixing with

the blood already staining her skin. "Svava lives on Myrtle." Her brow puckered as she spoke, the betrayal she felt as she told him exactly what he wanted to know pleasing Loki.

"And the others?" he pushed.

She sobbed, a ragged sound from deep within her chest. "Lime, River, Tremont and Revere."

Loki stroked the woman's hair out of her eyes and smiled at her gently. "There. That wasn't so hard, was it?"

The Valkyrie dropped her head into her hands, her whole body wracked with sobs. Loki tilted her chin up and forced her to look in his eyes. "Thank you," he said gently, with conviction. The woman closed her eyes and slammed the back of her head against the wall behind her, squeezing more tears out as she did.

Loki rocked back onto his heels and stepped away, the cloak still in his hand. He stroked it absently, waiting for a sense of ease to overtake the woman. For so long he had dreamed of doing this, of hurting Odin as badly as Odin had hurt him. He had plotted and planned and this night was the first of many to come.

He took in the broken Valkyrie, and grabbed huge fistfuls of feathers, ripping them free and tearing fresh screams from her throat. She twisted and bucked against the bonds, writhing while blood dripped from the cloak onto the floor at her feet.

When there was only one feather remaining, Loki took the Valkyrie's chin in his hand again and forced her to look at him. With his teeth, he plucked the feather free. The cry that left her mouth rebounded around the room, his mouth pulling up into a satisfied grin. The torrent of blood flowing from the plucked cloak meant only one thing: The Valkyrie was mortal.

Reaching around to the small of his back, Loki pulled the knife he had taken from Andhrimnir's apartment free and dragged the Valkyrie onto her back. Her eyes widened when he climbed on top of her body. Straddling her waist, he lifted the dagger above her.

The blade flashed, arcing toward its target. The steel plunged through flesh, through bone, until the hilt rested against her breast. Deep red heart's blood erupted from around the blade. The god watched as her eyes started to dull, her mouth working over words that would never be spoken. She coughed, spraying blood all over his face and neck. It trickled like a river from the corner of her mouth, pooling behind her neck. And when her body went slack beneath him, maniacal laughter bubbled up from his throat.

She was dead.

And he had done it.

With an overwhelming sense of joy, Loki rolled from her body and got to his feet. The Valkyrie's death would be discovered a lot sooner than he had anticipated since she had been able to make that pitiful phone call for help, but before leaving, Loki walked around the former Valkyrie's home, touching all of her belongings, leaving smears of her blood everywhere he went. He wanted whoever discovered the scene to know how much she had suffered before she was finally killed. He wanted them to know that eventually their blood would be spilled like this. He left something special as well, to throw them off the scent—to turn the remaining Valkyries against Odin.

13

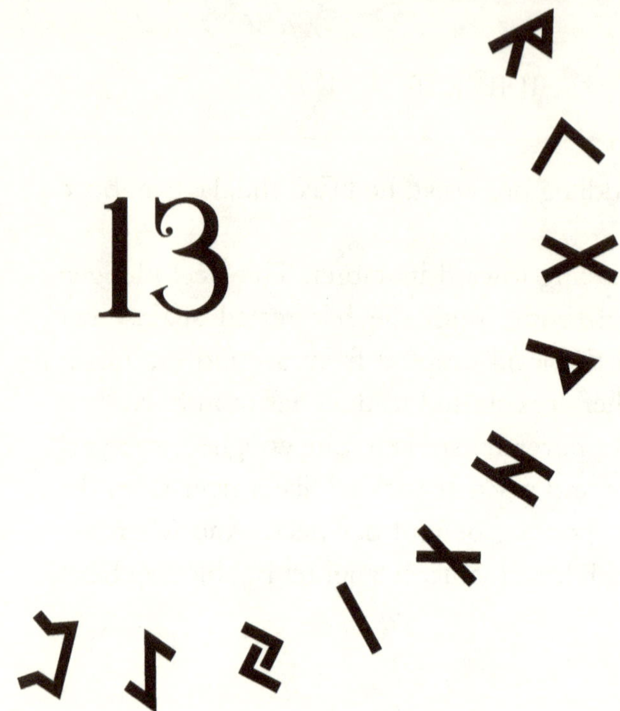

Bryn rolled over restlessly, kicking the sheets off her body with her feet. She'd been awake since she'd gone to bed a few hours before, her mind a writhing mess of thoughts with Odin front and center—among other things she had no intention of contemplating.

She knew he wasn't giving her the whole story. But that was Odin—only letting her know just enough. He wanted her back, but that wasn't a newsflash. What she wanted to know was why now? Why was he so desperate to have her agree to return now? He thought he'd hidden his desperation from her, but she'd seen right through him. She knew. Something had scared him, but what?

Closing her eyes to force her body into sleep, she saw Korvain's face as if his image had been burned into the back of her lids. She turned over onto her stomach, pulling the pillow over her head and groaning into the mattress. He was the other thought she had promised herself not to think about.

"Forget about him," she whispered into the dark room. "Bryn, forget him." She tried to repeat the mantra, but her body refused to see the logic, responding to the memories instead by dragging every illicit detail back to the forefront of her mind.

"Forget who?" a masculine voice asked softly.

Bryn sat up quickly, her eyes scanning the familiar silhouettes of her bedroom furniture. Everything was as it should have been. With her pulse racing, she lay back down, but couldn't shake the feeling she wasn't alone. It was just like when she'd dreamed of Korvain before.

Her hand plowed through her long hair. "I must be fucking hallucinating again." Rolling onto her side, she closed her eyes and tried to sleep until she felt the heat of another body beside her. She reached for the tattoo on her neck, attempting to summon her sword, when strong fingers wrapped around her wrist, stopping her.

She was flipped over, coming face to face with Korvain. Her body reacted without permission, without sense. It remembered the last time he'd touched her and craved more—so much more. Heat bloomed between her legs, and her breasts tightened at the dark, sensuous look in his eyes. She nervously licked her lips as his eyes burned with a hunger she wanted to physically feel.

Painfully slow, he lowered his head, his lips like the softest suede against hers. She opened for him, surrendering herself, and relished the feel of his insistent, persuasive tongue exploring her mouth.

Gradually, he loosened his grip on her wrist, stretching her arm above her head. He did the same with her other arm, easily holding both of her wrists with one hand, his hot, strong fingers branding her. His free hand skimmed over the tee and boxer shorts she'd worn to bed, touching her, further heating her hypersensitive skin. His fingertips inched up the fabric, caressing her softly, and making Bryn's mouth go dry.

Her hips rolled forward when he reached the edge of her shorts, desperately urging him to keep going when he pulled away. He smiled, flashing a monstrous set of fangs at her as he did, and grazed a light finger just above the elastic waist. She groaned in frustration, eliciting a small, satisfied chuckle from Korvain's chest.

"Patience," he chastised gently, running his nose along the length of her neck, starting just beneath her ear. "We have all night." Bryn shivered involuntarily, hearing the raw and erotic promise in his voice.

Releasing her wrists, he positioned himself beside her, propping himself up on one elbow. In a possessive move, he kept one large hand splayed across her stomach while forcing a knee between her thighs, opening up her body. She knew that if he wanted to, he could easily have his hips there instead, and she would let him. She would welcome his weight and relish the touch of his body.

Lowering one arm, she curled her hand around the back of his neck, the other arm coming to rest above her head. Still staring deeply into her eyes, his fingers toyed with the hem of her shirt, skating over her skin beneath the fabric and veering closer and closer to her heavy, aching breasts.

"Gods, you feel good," he purred down into her ear, the vibration going all the way through her. Another, stronger shiver consumed her body, causing her breathing to accelerate. His broad shoulders moved with his own deep, hungry breaths as he looked down at her with such . . . longing . . . such craving.

She reached out to touch his face, running her fingers along his slightly stubbled jaw, along his full bottom lip.

He was breathing hard, the words, "Fuck, I need you," barely audible. She gave him his answer with one look, her eyes sliding shut when his mouth passionately crashed into hers . . .

She was suddenly jerked awake. "Bryn!" Disoriented, and slightly embarrassed, she looked around. Light was flooding in from the hallway, her bedroom door thrown wide open. She blinked and rubbed the back of her hand over her eyes.

"Bryn!" She felt like she was coming out of drug-induced sleep. Focusing on the sound of Mist's voice, she fixed her eyes on the other Valkyrie and was instantly awake. Mist was shaking, her face pale, her mouth drawn into a tight line. In her trembling hand, she clutched a phone.

Sitting up, she asked, "Mist? What is it?"

Mist extended a quaking limb toward her. She was clenching the phone so tightly her fingers were mottled white. Frowning, Bryn pried the phone free of her fingers and put it to her ear.

At first, she couldn't hear anything. Then the screaming started. The sound of it chilled her blood. Looking at caller ID, she recognized the number as that of one of her Valkyries, Rota. There was a strange ripping sound, another scream of agony. Then the connection cut out. Bryn dropped the phone, the blood draining from her face.

Bryn stood up. "Mist. Wake the others." Mist was sobbing now, her eyes red raw. "Mist!"

Mist's sapphire and indigo eyes finally focused on Bryn's face. Bryn touched her shoulder, pulling her face closer. "Go wake the others." She said the words slowly, carefully.

Mist stood motionless for a moment before running from the room. Bryn stared down at the phone, her fear and shock draining from her. A new sensation began fighting for dominance. She let it come, knowing that it would be the best she could hope for:

rage. It burned white-hot in her veins, threatening to swamp all rational thought.

Marching over to her closet, she pulled on a pair of tight jeans and a tee. She swiped the tattoo on her neck, and her sword filled her palm. The balanced weight, the smell of the steel, filled her with a sense of calm, with a desire for retribution. The gold blade seemed to hum in her hand, begging for the taste of blood.

When she turned around, the others were assembled in front of her.

Mav was wearing leather pants with a black leather vest. Her sword hung at her side, her fingers idly stroking the pommel, the black steel glinting dangerously in the light.

Kara was wearing a short skirt and red velvet bustier. Her long hair had been tied back, a short sword resting against her shoulder like a baseball bat. Bryn saw the sadness in Kara's eyes as she looked at Bryn's sword. Kara would never again hold the red sword she had once possessed, the sword that had been made for her hand to hold.

Bryn forced herself to look away. Kara didn't need Bryn's pity—not now. Instead, she looked at Mist. Her girl looked more collected. She had wiped the tears clear of her eyes. Now they were filled with a fire to hurt whoever had gone after Rota. The blue blade she carried had yet to be drawn.

Bryn moved towards the door. "All right. Let's go."

Once outside in the alleyway beside the club, Bryn said, "I'll go with Kara. We'll meet you there." Kara's ability to fade had been taken away from her when Odin had taken her sword as one final fuck you for her indiscretion. Now, the Valkyrie had to rely on a car they kept parked behind the club to get around. Bryn was already moving towards the BMW X6 when Mist stopped her.

"We go together, Bryn," she said. "Always." Bryn looked at her second-in-command for a moment. She was right. Splitting up wasn't going to help anything. If Rota was in trouble, they were stronger together.

"Okay."

Mist sped through the early-morning traffic without stopping. Bryn's stomach knotted as she ran through all the possible scenarios. She had wanted all her Valkyries to live together, but many of them had decided to strike out on their own—to live their lives in a way they had never had been able to under Odin's rule. Unwilling to be as controlling as the All-Father had been, she respected their wishes, but asked them to stay within a ten-mile radius of the club for the sake of safety and to ensure they warded their houses well.

Even with all those precautions . . .

Perhaps she had been foolish to let them go.

Bryn was shaken from her confused thoughts when the car came to an abrupt halt against the curb. They all remained where they were for a moment, everyone scanning their surroundings for threats as their instincts demanded.

Bryn was the first one out of the car, the others following closely behind her. As they approached Rota's open front door, Bryn knew they were too late. The stench of death was in the air, the sickly scent of freshly spilled blood in her nose and on the back of her tongue.

Mav went in first, sword drawn. Bryn followed her soldier in, eyes constantly moving. They stopped at the large congealed puddle of blood on the floorboards in the entrance hall. Bryn swallowed bile.

"Gods," Mist said in a whimper, dropping to her knees. Her sword clattered to the ground beside her. Kara dropped to Mist's side, her head bowed. Bryn didn't feel like she was in her body, that what she was looking at was even real. She dragged her eyes from the bloody scene, fixing them on Maverick.

"Mav, find her cloak," she ordered.

Mav disappeared up the stairs without a word, her black sword drawn. Bryn forced herself to look at everything around her, to see the evidence of what were, perhaps, Rota's last minutes of life. Bryn moved through the living room, taking stock of all the blood smears on every piece of furniture. She had stepped into the adjoining dining room when something dark caught her attention. Closing in on the long dining table, she reached out and found a black feather placed in the middle. Bryn picked up the plume and stared at it, unable to suppress her increasing rage. It was a raven feather, which meant only one thing.

Bryn felt Mav return, a tall shadow standing in her periphery. Stuffing the evidence of Odin's involvement into the pocket of her jeans and covering it with the bottom of her shirt, Bryn glanced towards the doorway. "Did you find it?" Mav shook her head, the anguish she couldn't voice plain on her face.

And that was when everything became real . . . Rota was dead by Odin's own hand.

Bryn felt her legs give out, betrayal slamming into her like a sledgehammer. Throwing out an arm, she steadied herself against the sideboard. How could the All-Father have done this to her, to them? Why had he done it? White noise buzzed in her ears, drowning out all other sounds.

It was only the tentative touch on her shoulder that drew Bryn out of her shock.

"Bryn, we have to get out of here," Mist said, her face slowly swimming into focus. "Did you hear me? We can't stay here. Whoever did this could come back."

Bryn's jaw flexed at the thought of Odin showing his face.

Pushing herself upright, Bryn led the way from Rota's apartment, shutting herself inside the car while the others piled in.

Bryn couldn't even recall their drive home. All she knew was that when she snapped out of the maelstrom of anger and grief, they were back in the safety of Bryn's apartment. They sat together in the lounge room, each silently contemplating what had happened.

Kara hugged her body tightly; Mist's arm was over her shoulders, a blanket covering them both. The others had no idea of Odin's involvement, but Bryn did, and she'd be damned if she let him take any more of her Valkyries away.

"I'll take first watch," Bryn announced, breaking the heavy silence. "Nobody can fade into the building, so we're safe here—we just need to keep a lookout and check anyone who turns up at the door down on the street. All of you get some sleep. Mav, I'll wake you up in a few hours to take over."

Mist and Kara shuffled off to Mist's apartment, just down the hall, leaving Bryn with Maverick. The haunted look in her girl's eyes made Bryn's chest tight. Placing her hand on Mav's shoulder, she said, "We'll find out what happened. Don't worry." With a despondent shrug, Mav walked off down the hallway and shut her apartment door firmly behind her, cutting off any more words of encouragement Bryn could offer.

Unable to stand being in the apartment, Bryn made her way down to her office, where she sat in the dark, intently watching the security camera feed and letting all her anger rage and roil.

Pulling the feather out of her pocket, she stared at it in the dim light, as if it would suddenly provide all the answers to the questions running through her head. It had to be more than a coincidence. Odin was the only god who knew the Valkyries' one weakness, and he was known as the raven god. He had kept two ravens, Huginn and Muninn, while the Valkyries had been in his service. Odin had killed Rota, and he was coming for the other Valkyries. What other explanation was there? He knew Bryn would never willingly leave her sisters. Had his desire to have her back in his life become so singular that he would do anything in his power to remove the other Valkyries from the equation altogether?

Bryn scrubbed a hand down her face, exhausted. "Fuck."

Loki needed a weapon.

He had gone into Roxbury despite being discouraged from going there at night. Ignoring the clerk at the inn and his warnings, Loki faded to the poverty-stricken Boston suburb, searching for what he required. Every street he had been down so far had been deserted, and Loki was about to concede defeat when he caught sight of a man standing alone up ahead.

As the distance closed between them, Loki could see how the human's dark skin helped him to blend into the surrounding shadows, his clothing only adding to the disguise. He was unaccustomed to seeing such dark skin on a human, and Loki found himself fascinated. The man looked up, hearing the scuff of Loki's shoes, and stood up to his full height when he was a few feet away. Loki looked at the man from the corner of his eye, and as he passed, the human muttered something quietly.

Loki stopped and turned. "What did you say?"

The guy looked up the street, left and right, then did it again. When he was satisfied nobody else was around to hear him, he said, "What are you after?"

This expression puzzled Loki, but the man proceeded. "You

looking to score?"

"Score what?" Loki asked. The man who stole his shoes in St Louis had spoken of scoring.

The man's eyes made a sweep of the surrounds again before they met Loki's gaze. "You want smack? I've got smack."

"What is this smack you are talking about?"

The man's eye twitched before his face clouded over with irritation. "Heroin, man," he replied. "Fuck it. Get outta here, man!" He turned away from Loki and started walking up a small laneway between the houses.

Loki called after him, "Are you an apothecary?"

The man turned around, glowering at Loki. "What are you talking about, man?" The human started inching his way closer to him, his interest obviously piqued.

"Apothecary. Alchemist. Herbalist."

The man's expression changed from confusion to comprehension with the last word.

"I ain't got no weed, only the hard stuff. So you want it or not?" A bitter acrid smell that clung to his clothes got stronger as the distance between them closed. "Yes. I wish to . . . score." The vernacular the human had used felt strange coming out of Loki's mouth.

The man's lips tilted up in a smile, showing more than one golden tooth in his mouth. Jerking his head around, he said, "This way then."

Loki followed him to a large black car parked on another street close by. The human opened up the back and leaned in. There was a popping noise and a side compartment opened.

"How much do you want?"

"I do not know."

The guy looked over his shoulder and shook his head. "For

real? Look, how about a gram?" He produced a small plastic bag with whitish-brown powder in it. "It'll cost you two hundred."

Loki eyed the bag held up in front of his face. "I don't have two hundred."

"Then get the fuck outta here."

Loki straightened his back. He had seen the effect of the drug on humans in St Louis. He could use it to subdue the next Valkyrie. Perhaps it was a better option than the gun he was seeking. It would certainly be quieter.

"I don't have two hundred. But I want the heroin." He took the plastic bag from the man's fingers and disappeared it into his pocket. When Loki looked up again, the dealer had a weapon pointed at his chest.

Moving faster than the man, Loki stepped aside, grabbing the body of the pistol and twisting it free of the human's grip. Loki's free hand slammed into the man's unguarded midsection, doubling him over. Ramming his elbow into his nose, Loki felt cartilage pop and the first warm droplets of blood as it sprayed in a small arc, covering the man's face.

The dealer dropped to his knees, clutching his nose; a wet coughing filling the night air. Loki picked up the weapon from where it had landed and looked it over. It seemed like a simple enough design.

Pointing it at the man's head, he pulled the trigger. A mass of bone and brain matter burst over the back of the car and pavement, the sound too loud in Loki's ears. He leaned down and studied what was left behind, and he was once again reminded of the fragility of man. Loki really did wonder why Odin liked them so much. They were so weak, so easily misled and taken advantage of. He laughed. Perhaps that was it. With a thought, he faded back into his room at the hotel, the gun still smoking in his hand.

Walking calmly into the bathroom, he turned on the shower. Placing the gun and the drugs on the countertop, he got under the spray in his clothes. The sinkhole gurgled softly, swallowing every trace of blood from Loki's clothes. When they were finally clean, he stripped them off and left them to dry.

14

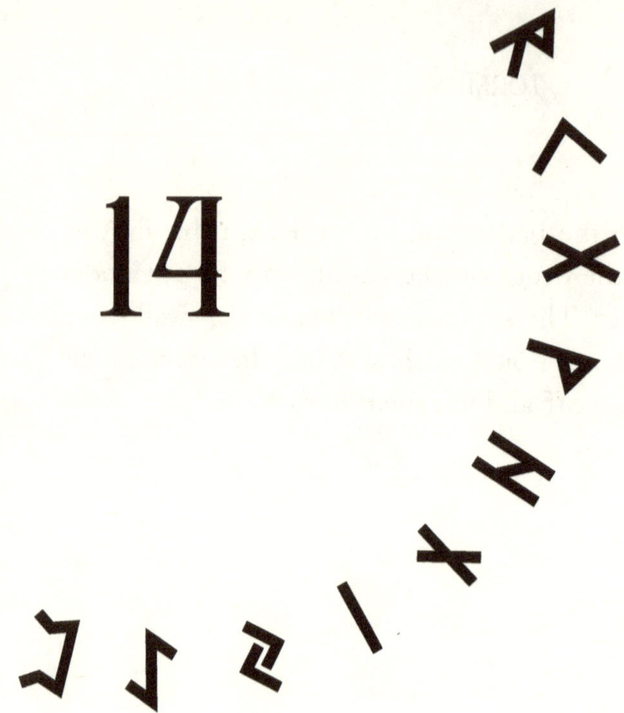

Korvain woke to the sound of his phone vibrating on the nightstand. Reaching out, he felt around for the device and answered the call.

"Korvain?"

Korvain sat up in bed, wiping his face with the back of his hand. "Bryn?" His chest tightened a little at the sad tone of her voice. "What's wrong?"

A long pause.

"Nothing's wrong . . . I just need to see you down at the club."

"Okay. I'll be there soon."

He ended the call and dropped his phone into the tangle of sheets. Looking over at the clock, he saw it was nearly six o'clock in the evening.

He dressed and armed himself before fading to just outside the rear door of the club in the darkened alleyway, the anticipation of seeing Bryn again putting him slightly on edge.

He raised his fist to the door, but before he could knock, the door snicked open automatically. Puzzled, Korvain looked up, spotting a small, carefully concealed camera positioned on the door. Bryn must have seen he'd arrived and let him in remotely. He pulled open the external door and stopped.

He listened and heard . . . absolutely nothing.

The club was quiet—no-lights-no-music-no-people quiet. He went through the door that led into the Eye, his gaze sweeping the room. There was absolutely no movement, the lights off, the hum from the small refrigerators behind the bar the only sound. Turning around, he headed in the direction of Bryn's office. A sliver of light pushed out from beneath the door, a soft sound like sobbing flowing through the wood.

Korvain turned the knob and eased the door open with his foot, the light spilling out onto his lower body. Bryn looked up briefly. She was curled up in her office chair, her eyes red, wet streaks trailing down her face.

An unfamiliar feeling floored Korvain—a foreign, wrong feeling that threatened to pierce the armor he had worn since entering Darrion's service. It left him desperately trying to catch his breath, to force air into his lungs. But when he looked at Bryn so close to breaking, he pushed the cloying feeling aside and focused only on her.

"Where is everyone?" he asked gently, easing the door closed behind him. Her scent engulfed him instantly, stirring his body.

"Club's closed for the night."

He let his surprise roll over him before replying. "Why?"

Bryn shrugged and dragged herself out of the chair, only to reach for a desk drawer. She pulled out a bottle of vodka and cracked the lid, dropping it into the trash can beside her.

Uncomfortable didn't even begin to explain how he was feeling

. . . but that wasn't the only emotion surging through his body. "Look, I'll come back later."

He turned to leave, but Bryn's whispered words stopped him. "Don't go." Sucking in a deep breath, he turned to her again. She had the bottle at her lips now, tipping it back, her throat working down the liquor as if she was dying of thirst. Korvain winced. There was that feeling again. He rubbed absently at a spot in the middle of his chest. "You want to tell me about it?"

"No." Bryn tilted her head back and took another mouthful. Her eyes slid shut, her face contorting before straightening out again. When she opened her eyes, there was pain sitting behind them.

Korvain approached the desk. Bryn's wary eyes watched him, her fingers cranking down harder around the glass in her hand.

"Are you sure you don't want to talk about it?" he asked gently, perching himself on the edge of the desk, facing her. Bryn moved the chair back a little, hugging the bottle to her chest.

"No."

He was getting tired of hearing that word. "I've been told I'm a good listener."

She sighed, defeated. "Just forget about it, Korvain." Bryn ran a hand through her hair. "I don't even know why I called you," she muttered under her breath.

He frowned at her. She had asked him to come. She had asked him to stay. Why was she pushing him away now? Leaning forward, he took the bottle from her fingers.

Bryn tried to snatch the bottle back, but Korvain drew away from her, taking the bottle and placing it on the desktop beside him.

"Give me the fucking bottle . . . Now!" she said.

When Korvain denied her with a shake of his head, she lurched forward. She lost her balance, the move sending her sprawling into his arms. He caught her easily, taking her weight and holding her close. She struggled in his arms, pushing and swearing to break his hold. Locking his thighs around her hips, he drew her in closer to his chest.

"Just let go, Bryn," he murmured softly.

"No," she cried. "No, no, no!" Her delicate fist landed on his chest, slamming into his body over and over again. "No." The last word was barely a whisper. Bryn had collapsed into his arms, shuddering, her face pressed into the hollow of his neck. He felt something wet slide down his skin, slipping in under the collar of his shirt.

He knew as soon as he'd drawn her in that he shouldn't have. He was getting too close. Lifting his free hand, he went to push her away, but found he couldn't do it. She just fit too perfectly against his body. Pumping his hand into a fist a few times, he finally flattened his palm on her back and began rubbing slow circles. Bryn's body calmed almost instantly, her sobs slowing. She relaxed even further into his arms until he was wearing her like a second skin. Dipping his head, he stuck his nose behind her ear and drew in the scent of her hair.

He didn't know how long they stayed like that—him holding onto her, her hanging onto him like he was the only solid thing in her life, but it was her rasping voice that finally broke the silence.

"One of my girls was killed last night." Bryn stumbled, the last word coming out broken. "She . . . her body was gone, but there was enough blood on the ground to tell us that she was—" she coughed, "dead." Korvain let the words sink in.

"Are you sure? I thought Valkyries were immortal. Could she have just been taken somewhere else?"

She made a noise in the back of her throat, pulling away to look at his face. "Immortality is a lie," she replied. "Cut us and we'll bleed, do enough damage to our bodies and we'll take our last breath just like everybody else."

"But what about . . ." He paused, stopping himself from revealing too much.

"About what?"

He stroked her long hair down her back, enjoying the softness of it more than he should have. "Nothing."

Bryn exhaled sharply. "Korvain, can I ask you a favor?"

"Name it," he replied, running strands of her thick blonde hair through his fingertips like he'd wanted to do the first time he'd met her.

"Can you please keep a close eye on the other Valkyries out there?"

"Kind of like security?"

She bit her lip and looked away for a moment. "I'd pay you, of course."

"Of course," he muttered to himself. "How many are we talking here?"

Bryn pulled away from his arms, scrubbing her face with a hand. She inhaled deeply. "I have," she grimaced, "*had* ten, but now that Rota is gone, there are nine altogether—the four of us who live here and another five, who all live in and around Beacon Hill. I've spoken to them all, the others who don't live here, but they don't believe they're in any danger where they are."

He studied her solemn face. "But you think they are."

"Yes."

"You know something more, don't you?"

She met his intense stare. "Yes."

"But you're not going to tell me, are you?"

She shook her head slowly. "No."

She was holding something back. He didn't blame her—everyone had their secrets. It was just that some were bigger than others. Blowing out a frustrated breath, he said, "I'm going to need to know who I'm looking out for if I'm going to be able to protect them."

Bryn's eyes darted to the bottle of vodka. "I'm going to need that if I tell you." Korvain passed her the bottle, watching as her throat worked down the liquor.

She wiped the back of her shaking hand across her mouth. "Odin. I think Odin is the one after them."

Korvain whistled through his teeth. "You're sure?"

"No, but there are too many coincidences," she said.

He shrugged—deciding against pushing for more information—and crooked his finger at the bottle. Bryn handed it over, their fingers brushing. She seemed to shake herself before sitting down in the office chair, grabbing a spiral notebook and a pen as she did. With her head bent over the paper, she scribbled down something then handed it to him.

"These are the names and addresses of the five Valkyries not living here. If you could just check on them, I'd really appreciate it." He looked at the list. "Can you go and check on the girls now?" she asked, her fingers tapping nervously on the cover of the notebook.

"Sure."

When Korvain was outside in the hallway, the tightness in his chest emerged once more, stronger this time. He looked at the closed door and cursed. He wanted to be back in there with her. He wanted to be close to her again.

But then he remembered with terrifying clarity; he was supposed to kill her. "This is no time to be getting fucking attached." Dragging a hand down his face, he left the building and faded away. He would get a grip on this. He had a job to do, but he didn't have to enjoy doing it.

The scent of the Valkyrie's perfume hovered in the air behind her, setting up an easy trail for Loki to follow. The click, click, click of her heels echoed, bouncing off the walls of the surrounding buildings. On a street corner, she paused and peered over her shoulder.

Then she disappeared.

With a soft curse, Loki faded too, having no doubt she would be going straight to her home. He was right. He rematerialized at the walk-up on Myrtle clearly protected by runes, just in time to see his prey throwing harried glances over her shoulder and fumbling with the keys in the lock.

The disjointed tangle of metal fell to the ground in her panic. Stooping down, she snatched at them, dropping them once more before finally securing them in her hand. As she stood up, Loki wrapped one hand around her shoulders and chest, bringing the syringe of heroin to her neck and depressing the plunger before she could scream out for help. The woman's body instantly went slack in his hands.

"The wonders of the modern world," Loki muttered to himself. Potato-sacking her over his shoulder, he picked up the keys and let himself in—away from the prying eyes of any humans who may have been watching.

Loki dropped the Valkyrie onto the living room floor, her head first hitting the edge of the granite coffee table before cracking against the floorboards. The scent of blood immediately flooded the room, hanging there like a heavy perfume. Loki sucked in a deep breath, savoring it, rolling the flavor around on his tongue. At the rate he was killing, he would have his revenge on Odin sooner than he had planned.

Leaving the unconscious Valkyrie behind, Loki left the living room and started up the stairs. Up on the landing, he followed the long hall runner down to the end, to the bedroom that stunk like the goddess downstairs.

The walls were painted a soft shade of pink, the bedspread and dust ruffle on the large bed a slightly darker shade. Running along the opposite wall to the bed were a series of doors. Opening the first, Loki discovered a bathroom, but behind the second was a walk-in closet.

Flicking on the light, he dropped his eyes to the ground, searching for the ash box her cloak would be in. There were shelves stuffed with clothes and shoes, but no box. His gaze drifted up. There. Putting his feet on a lower shelf, he boosted himself up and dragged the small wooden crate toward him.

Inside, the white swan feathers gleamed.

With a smile curling his lips, Loki took his prize back to the Valkyrie in the living room. He kicked her awake and her glassy eyes blinked, trying to focus. The drug was running through her blood, holding her hostage in her own body, but she flinched at his approach, making soft mewling sounds of protest at the back of her throat.

Crouching down, balancing on the balls of his feet, Loki stroked some of the blonde hair from her face and placed a finger over her mouth. "Shh. You'll wake the neighbors." Loki laughed, dragging his fingertips over her brow, pressing them inside the wound, watching the blood stain his skin. The Valkyrie—Svava, Loki thought her name was . . . not that it really mattered—sucked in a pained breath. Loki saw tears well, heard her breathing become rapid and irregular.

Her blood had run into her hair from the gash, painting the pale strands red. He could tell by the wild look in her eyes that she wanted to move away, but the drug held her still, imprisoning her for Loki's pleasure.

Dragging the box closer, he opened it and reached inside. His bloody fingers smudged the feathers as he took the cloak out and looked it over. The Valkyrie's pitiful protests were the perfect soundtrack as Loki fingered one of the feathers, running it through his hands softly. If he listened closely, he could hear the soft rasp against his skin.

Cutting his eyes back to her face, Loki toyed with one of the plumes, watching the pulse at her throat bang violently against her skin. Enjoying her reaction, he tugged at the feather, pulling it free, watching with morbid delight as the Valkyrie's skin turned gray. Her body convulsed uncontrollably, doubling her over. In his hands, the cloak wept crimson tears. A well of blood formed where the feather had been plucked. It quickly became a steady stream, dropping to the floor with a soft tap, tap, tap.

Still in the fetal position, her chin tucked into her chest, the Valkyrie finally stopped shuddering. Loki took another feather, polluted and pink, in between his thumb and index finger and plucked it with relish.

The drug must have been wearing off, because she screamed that time. It was wordless, but no less satisfying. More blood welled and joined the steady stream already dripping from the cloak. A grin pulled up one corner of his mouth, and as he watched the blood travel down his hand, his wrist, his forearm, the scent of her pain flooded the room.

Loki would draw this death out. The first Valkyrie hadn't felt true pain. He was still euphoric over finding her and getting what he wanted so easily. But this female . . . he would make her feel it all. One by one, he stripped her cloak of every single feather until it looked as if she was lying in a cloud.

Ignoring her pathetic attempts to beg him to stop, Loki plunged his dagger into her chest, carving out her heart.

Two down.

Eight to go.

15

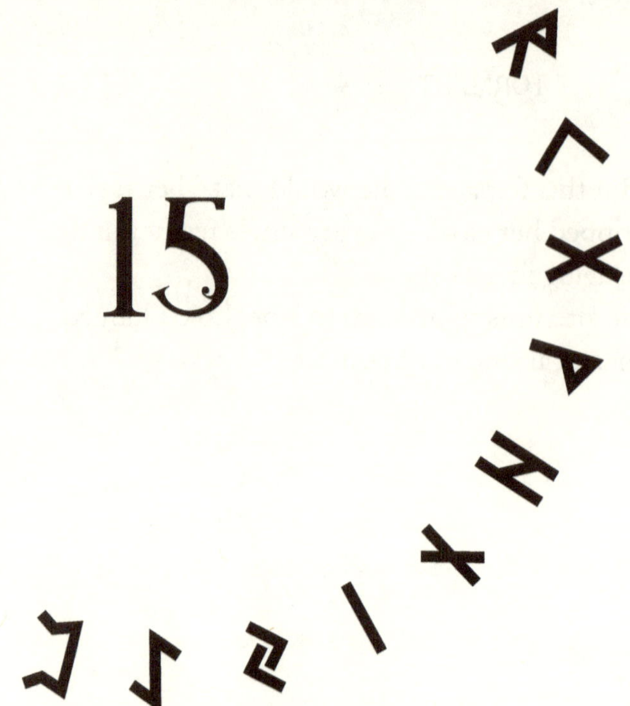

Eir stepped out into the still dark early morning, having finished her shift at Massachusetts General Hospital aching and stiff. Working for nearly twenty-eight hours straight in emergency took it out of her, but she wouldn't have traded it for anything in the world. Besides, she wasn't really doing that much—the doctors did more, worked harder. And she was used to it.

Her natural ability to heal had helped her through the years of study. Before modern medicine, a cold could kill someone. Now, there were drugs to help with everything—even the fight against cancer. She had to train and retrain just to keep up.

Eir flexed her hands, feeling them still tingling from overuse. Her palms would be sensitive for the next twelve hours or so until she'd healed herself. It was funny how that worked—she could help people to regulate their breathing or improve their circulation just by laying her hands on them, and they would improve almost instantly, but it would always take her longer to heal herself.

"See you tomorrow, Eir!" Stacy the receptionist called as Eir waved her goodbyes. The double glass doors slid open, a rush of cold air greeting her. She could have faded straight home, but she found the fresh air helped her heal a little faster. Turning left, she started walking back toward her house in Beacon Hill.

Inside the small pocket of her bag, her phone started to ring. She fished it out and held it to her ear with her shoulder. "Bryn?"

"Hi, Eir. How are you?"

She checked for traffic before stepping out into the road—even as sparse as it was at this time, there were still idiots driving around. "I'm good. How are you?"

"Good."

Silence.

"Is something wrong? Has somebody been hurt?" She glanced at her watch. "I'm just leaving work now—I can be at the club in a minute."

"No, it's not that. I just wanted to check in on you, see how you're going."

"I'm busy with work, but everything else is fine."

More silence.

Bryn never called without good reason. Eir was on Grove walking toward Myrtle, the hush of her soft-soled shoes barely making a sound on the pavement. She drew her purse strap closer up her shoulder. She didn't have to worry about people mugging her in this neighborhood, but when she glanced up and noticed a tall man propped up against the side of a house, she decided to cross to the other side of the road just in case.

She glanced back over her shoulder nervously, horrified to see the man had disappeared. The hairs on the back of her neck prickled. She picked up the pace, still holding the phone to her ear. "Look, Bryn, I'm sorry, but I have to go. I'm walking home."

"You're what?" Bryn demanded. "Gods, fade home now. Call me when you get in so I know you made it back safely."

A chill went down Eir's spine at the urgency of Bryn's tone. "Is something going on?"

"It's nothing. Call me when you get in." The line died. Eir slipped her phone back into its pocket, momentarily taking her eyes off what was going on in front of her.

As she looked back up, she yelped, slapping her hand against her neck. It felt like she'd just been stung by something, but that was impossible. It was too cold for mosquitoes. Eir's skin suddenly felt warm all over.

She walked a few more steps until she lost control of her limbs, staggering, tilting to one side, and catching herself against a wall. Her breath faltered like she was dragging mud into her lungs. Her head began to swim, her vision coming in and out of focus. Panicked, Eir tried to fade back to her house, but nothing happened.

She slumped down onto the ground, her eyelids feeling heavy. A shadow obscured her vision. She sensed it was a man, and he wasn't human. He crouched down in front of her, two fingers sliding along the side of her neck, feeling for her pulse.

The world slipped out of focus then and she was violently dumped into a black abyss.

Korvain had seen it all, but was too far away to intervene in time.

The Valkyrie had struggled on for a few steps before collapsing against a red-brick house with black shutters. Her attacker crouched down to take her pulse, an empty syringe in his hand. She barely moved as he slid his arms under her legs. Korvain kicked into motion, his long stride eating up the distance.

"Hey," he yelled, much louder than normal. The man's head jerked up and around. "Get away from her." The man stood up, his eyes meeting Korvain's before skimming his body, assessing his size and strength.

"Stay out of this, *morier*," the man spat. Korvain fucking hated that name, but it told him two things. First, the fucker knew he was a Walker; second, and more importantly, he was also a god.

Korvain pulled his karambit from his shoulder harness and twirled it in his hand before positioning the blade down against his palm, ready. "I said leave her alone.'

The guy smiled and immediately pulled a gun on him, training it at his chest. "I'd like to see you make me."

Korvain closed the distance immediately, smoothly sidestepping to the left. The other male tried to track his movements with the muzzle of the gun, but Korvain was faster, locking his arm under the god's raised arm and drawing the extended limb flush against his chest. Korvain hooked the double-edged, talon-shaped blade behind the male's forearm and made sure his slash was deep enough to cut the tangle of tendons beneath his skin. Running the length of the blade down towards his wrist, Korvain flayed muscle from bone, drawing a pained grunt from the man's throat. The god tried to pull away, but it was pointless. Korvain was like a pit bull; his jaws were latched on and he was intent on drawing more blood.

With a satisfied smirk on his face, Korvain raised his free elbow and slammed it repeatedly into the side of the other male's temple, stunning him momentarily. Fluidly, Korvain twisted the gun from the grasp of the god and shoved him away roughly.

He stumbled back a few unsteady steps. Glaring vehemently at Korvain, the man wrapped a hand over his injured forearm, an angry, wild sound vibrating out from between his tightly pressed lips. Driven by anger and desperation, he lunged toward Korvain's hand, towards his gun. Korvain circumvented the movement, repositioning himself to drive a sharp knee into the man's thigh. Howling in pain, the man bent over, giving Korvain the opportunity to strike the god's chin with his karambit.

Blood instantly welled, looking black in the night. Hooking the blade into the crook of the male's elbow, Korvain forced the limb to bend inwards and up. The god snarled at him, his eyes glowing fiercely.

Realizing his disadvantage, the god faded from Korvain's grip and immediately reappeared behind him. As Korvain spun around to face him, the god wrenched the gun from his grip, smashing the butt against his head, breaking open the skin above his eye. Korvain grunted, trying to wipe the blood away from his eyes with the back of his hand. When he could see again, he swiped at the god aiming to cut open his belly.

There was a pop as he lunged, and the coward faded from the scene, but not before slamming his foot into Korvain's kneecap. Korvain roared out loud, the blood pounding in his ears, but kept his weapon ready in front of him.

Silence reigned in the quiet street. Korvain's chest was heaving. Blood flowed freely from the cut above his eye, and his knee screamed each time he put any pressure on it, but at least the girl was safe. Korvain crouched down and watched her chest rise and fall steadily with her breathing.

When it was clear the god wasn't going to be coming back, Korvain picked her up carefully, ignoring the pain that shot up his leg. Blood seeped slowly from his hairline, trailing down his forehead, over his eye and along his cheek. It dripped on the Valkyrie in his arms, but there was nothing he could do about it.

He couldn't fade with the weight, which left him only one option. Korvain wrapped the shadows around him and the woman in his arms and started in the direction of the club.

The sun was beginning to lighten the sky when he finally made it there, the last of his shrouding shadows dripping away with the new day. Eir had started to come around while he'd been walking, mumbling through the drug haze, pushing weakly against his chest. He held her closer, softly murmuring into her ear to calm her down. It had worked for a while, but she was starting to throw off the effects of whatever had been forced into her body and was getting restless.

Arriving at the club, Korvain propped her up on her feet, wrapping his arm around her waist, and began pounding on the back door. He looked up into the camera installed there, and the door clicked open, leaving Korvain to usher the injured Valkyrie inside.

16

Bryn was in her office, working through some of the invoices that kept coming in even though the club had been closed for three days already. She couldn't afford to let it continue that way, but she wasn't ready to face reality yet.

Her head jerked up when she heard what sounded like a sledgehammer going to work on the back door of the club. Glancing at the monitor to her right, she saw Korvain standing there, looking up at the camera. There was a dark shape beside him, but she couldn't make out what it was.

Bryn buzzed him in and got up from behind her desk, instantly fearing the worst. When she made it out into the hallway, Korvain was holding the door open with his foot and carefully bringing in the shape she'd seen. There was a feminine moan and Bryn started to run down the hallway, blind panic threatening to take hold.

Eir was limp in his arms, just barely holding onto consciousness.

Bryn knew something was wrong when Eir had failed to call her ten minutes after she'd hung up, but she'd reasoned that she was just being paranoid, being overly cautious. Now she knew better.

"Korvain, what happened?" she demanded, feeling for Eir's pulse. It was weak and thready. "Gods, take her upstairs so we can look her over."

Korvain's muscular shoulders spanned the width of the hallway as he motioned for Bryn to open the door leading into the Eye and to the stairs of the upper levels. She shook her head. "Can't get to the apartments that way. Take the elevator at the end of the hall." She led the way past her office door and around a corner. The elevator was only designed to hold two people at a time, and Korvain took up that quota with his height and width alone. He still hadn't let go of Eir, who was tucked up closely to his chest.

When the doors slammed shut, all Bryn could smell was him; all masculine spices and the faintest hint of cologne. But the scent of blood was stronger. Her eyes drifted down to Eir, looking so small in his arms.

"What happened to her?" she asked, distracting herself from how close they were standing.

"I was following her home. A god came out of nowhere and injected her with something. I don't know what. He was going to take her somewhere. I fought him off."

Bryn's thoughts clouded. Was it Odin, or had he sent someone to do his dirty work for him this time? Snapping herself out of her dark thoughts, she looked at Korvain, noticing the blood oozing down his face. How had she missed that? "Did you get hurt?"

"Nothing I can't handle," he replied in a rumbling voice that only further stoked the fires of her attraction to him. The elevator lurched to a stop, the doors opening with a soft ping.

"Follow me." Bryn stepped out of the elevator and led him to her apartment, feeling a little leery about having Korvain in there. She never brought anyone into her inner sanctum.

Bryn opened the door wide and ushered them in. "Put Eir on the couch." As he did, she set about collecting supplies to clean up Korvain while whatever was in Eir's system wore off.

"Do you know what she was stuck with?"

Korvain shook his head, not meeting her eyes. "I should probably go." He moved toward the door, but Bryn jumped in front of him. Like hell she was just going to let him walk out of there looking like he did.

"No, you're not. Sit down." He sidestepped her, but she matched it, blocking his way again. "Sit. Down."

He finally looked at her. His dark eyes were bottomless. Bryn felt like she could trip and fall into them and never touch the bottom.

"I'm fine," he ground out.

She saw his fangs for a second. It was unusual to see a half-breed with such large incisors. "Well, that's great. But you got hurt protecting one of my Valkyries because I asked you to. I'm not letting you leave without cleaning you up first. It's the least I can do."

His eyes narrowed to slits and she suddenly felt cold. Then the moment passed, as Korvain turned his huge body around and stalked toward one of the chairs at her small dining room table.

He slumped down into the thing like he was completely and utterly exhausted and looked over at Eir. Bryn pulled up a chair and sat in front of him. She couldn't get close enough with his legs in the way. Forced to stand up, she loaded a sterile pad with saline and leaned into his body, her legs within the confines of his huge thighs.

She heard his breath catch in his throat, but she ignored the sound. The cut above his eye was deep, but thankfully it had stopped bleeding. He wouldn't need to have stitches if his body kept on healing him. His eyes slid shut as she worked.

His hair was both rough and soft against her palm as she cleaned the wound right on his hairline. "What made the cut?"

"The butt of a gun."

Ouch. "Did you repay the favor?"

His eyes opened slowly. "Yeah."

She focused again, soaking the wound with saline. He hissed.

"Sorry."

"Don't worry about it," he rumbled. She had to lean in a little closer to see if she'd gotten all the blood, but as she did, his huge chest lifted beneath her body and then shuddered as he let the breath go.

His hands landed on her hips. They were only resting there gently; there was nothing possessive about it. He looked at her, liquid onyx eyes asking for permission. As much as she wanted to, she stepped back and his hands fell away from her body, hanging at his sides.

"It's clean enough," she managed to say, keeping the shake from her voice. Her focus fell to the ground because she just couldn't look at him right then. That was when she noticed the small pool of blood on the tile beside the chair leg. It was dripping from the inside of Korvain's sleeve.

"Take your jacket off," she demanded, rifling through the first-aid kit again for more gauze. "And your shirt."

"What?"

"Your clothes. Take them off."

Korvain stood up to his full height, dwarfing Bryn for a moment, and slid the leather from his upper body. His black tee was stuck to his shoulder, a small hole through the fabric. While he stripped, she checked on Eir's breathing and pulse rate, and when she turned back around again, Korvain had shed the shirt from his body before planting his ass back down. His weapons harness was slung over the back of the chair. She frowned. She hadn't even seen that he'd had one on.

She looked more closely at the wound. "Gods, you've been shot." Bryn looked over at Eir again, wishing she would wake up. She was the one qualified to look after the sick and injured, not Bryn. The Valkyries had once been dubbed the demigods of death for good reason.

Bryn looked through the kit again, pulling tweezers and more gauze out, lining it up on the table. Leaning in closer to Korvain, she probed the entry site with her fingers. He hissed again, but didn't flinch.

"I'm sorry. I'll try and be quick."

"It's fine," he ground out. "Is there an exit wound?"

Bryn pulled him forward, highly aware that his face was trapped somewhere in her cleavage. She inspected his shoulder, then loaded up some gauze with saline, pressing one pad to the front of his shoulder and another to the exit wound at the back. She stood there putting pressure on the wound, their breaths matched in pace and depth.

She suddenly felt very self-conscious, painfully aware of how she felt about this male, about the way her heart fluttered restlessly against her ribs.

"Thank you," he murmured. The words were barely a whisper, but they drew her attention back to him. She stared at him, transfixed by his harsh face and large body, his bare chest. There were scars there, a lot of scars. Her mind skittered back to how he had comforted her in her office, how he had stroked her hair.

He was such a contradiction.

With his uninjured arm, he reached up and brushed some stray strands of hair from her face, tucking them behind her ear. His fingers remained there, warm against her already heated skin.

He traced the planes of her jaw, rubbing his thumb across her bottom lip when he reached her chin. Bryn's heart pounded in response, her mouth going dry. Memories of her dream bombarded her, and she wanted to press her mouth to his. Her tongue darted out to moisten her lips, Korvain's feral eyes watching—waiting.

Keeping the pressure on his shoulder, she leaned in closer until their faces were less than an inch away.

She felt his warm breath on her cheeks. She could smell only him and she wanted to taste only him. Their mouths had barely brushed when Eir suddenly started coughing; great hacking coughs that shook her entire body.

"I'm going to be sick," Eir moaned. Bryn pulled back, dropping the gauze and running for a trash can to park under her Valkyrie's head. Eir threw up quietly into the container while Bryn stroked her back gently. When Bryn looked over at Korvain, he was shrugging his jacket on.

"I should go."

Bryn knew it was for the best, but . . . "I still want to—" She stopped, pausing at the hungry look in his eyes. Oh, fuck.

"Yes?" he asked in a dark, sensuous tone.

She willed her blush away. "I want to bandage your shoulder up before you go. Can you wait ten minutes?

17

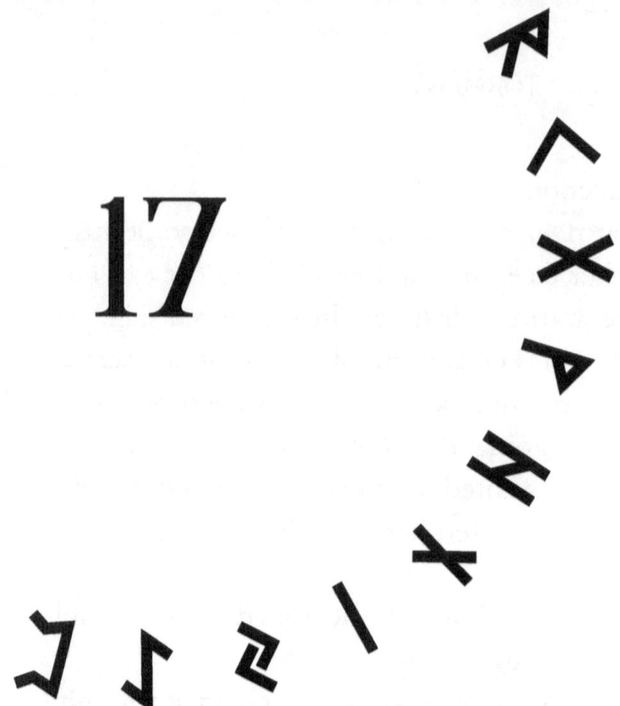

Odin woke up feeling like hell. He sat up, throwing his legs off the side of the bed and rubbing his eyes with the heel of his hand. Staggering up to a stand, he pulled the blinds up and looked down at Boston Common from his bedroom window.

The humans were swarming around like they always did, phones pressed to their ears, coffee cups clutched in their hands. It was no wonder they had stopped worshiping him—even the gods who had replaced him weren't being worshiped as much anymore. Humans now spent all their time worshiping easy communication and a caffeine rush.

Odin stepped back from the window and set about getting dressed for the day. After showering, he padded over to his closet filled with designer suits, all perfectly tailored, all perfectly appropriate for the god he was. He put on a dove gray single-breasted with matching vest and a blood-red tie.

When he was dressed, he stepped out of his building and breathed in deeply. He had come into the habit of going for a walk in the mornings. He found it cleared his head of the dreams that were coming with increasing frequency. Scanning left and right, he stepped off the curb in between the cars parked outside his house. A strange smell suddenly assaulted his nose. It smelled faintly of rot with the metallic edge of blood. He squinted, trying to see past the dark tint of the car beside him.

His eyes widened. "Gods," he whispered, stumbling back a step.

It was Rota. Rota was behind the wheel of the car, her head tilted back at a strange angle that exposed her throat. Her skin was gray and her eyes were still open, staring unfocused at the inside roof of the car.

He had to get her out of there before the owner of the vehicle found her and called the human authorities. Being the All-Father, it was in his power to fade multiple people at once with no need for physical contact. Glancing around to ensure he was unobserved, Odin focused on Rota and faded her bloated body back into his house, calmly walking back inside afterward.

In a detached way, Odin studied her body. The Valkyrie must have been dead for a couple of days at least. A large dark brown stain bloomed on the front of her chest, and when Odin pulled the side of her shirt away from her body, there was one bloody feather laid over the hole where her heart used to be.

Odin sat back on his heels, his mind reeling. It had started. It had started and he was powerless to stop it. Climbing to his feet unsteadily, Odin had only one thought and that was to get to Bryn. He faded to the club on Tremont, slipping down the alleyway. Standing before the giant metal door, he knocked loudly.

Nothing happened.

With a quiet snarl, he tried again, hammering his fists against the steel until the skin split over his knuckles.

"Yeah?" Bryn's crackling voice asked. Odin looked at the small box the sound had come from.

Pushing the button, he said, "I need to see you."

There was an immeasurable silence before the intercom buzzed back to life. "I've said all I need to say to you."

Odin got in close to the box, shielding his words with his body. "It's about Rota."

Silence dropped between them. Bryn's voice was angry when she spoke. "You better not be fucking around with me here."

"I'm not."

A few seconds later there was a click and Odin stepped inside the club that bore his name. Bryn was standing in front of her office door, her expression a mixture of wariness and irritation.

"I didn't expect to see you so soon," she said.

"Believe me, I wouldn't have come if it wasn't important."

She moved out of the doorway so he could slide inside the room. "I didn't invite you back here to catch up on old times, Odin."

"Of course not," he replied dryly. Odin unbuttoned his suit jacket and sat down, legs crossed at the ankle, his black angora socks covering the distance from his shoe to the end of his trousers.

Bryn had walked around to her side of the desk as he got settled in. Planting both palms on the top, she leaned in. "What do you know about Rota?"

He looked up from his socks, holding her blue gaze. "I found her body." Disbelief flashed in her eyes. "I don't believe you," she spat, standing up and putting her back to the wall, creating more distance between them.

"It's true. I found her body this morning in a car parked in front of my house."

"How convenient." Derision dripped from her words.

"Bryn, I swear to you that's the truth."

She laughed darkly. "You really are the father of lies, aren't you?"

"I apologized for that."

"No amount of apologizing will make up for what you did to me, to all of us."

He bit back the growl sitting at the back of his throat. "Bryn, I need you to come with me." He continued despite her disgusted look. "I need you. I don't think you're safe here. Not anymore. Come home with me. I can protect you there." He reached out his hand, hoping to placate her, willing her to accept what he was saying as truth. "Please."

"I don't need your protection, Odin. I need protection from you." Yanking open a drawer, she pulled out a raven feather and dropped it on the desktop. "Care to explain?" she asked caustically.

A frown formed between his eyes as he stared at the black feather. "I'm afraid I don't understand."

"You don't understand?" she snapped savagely, jumping up from her chair. "Understand this then: Take your lies and your deceit, and get out of my life." Planting her hands on the desk, Bryn leaned forward aggressively, her words coming out softly, dangerously. "I knew you were cruel, Odin, but not so cruel as to kill your own creations to serve your agenda."

Kill his own creations? Odin tried once more to reach for her, to let her see reason, but Bryn lashed out.

Her whole body shook as she summoned her golden sword— the sword he had crafted just for her hand. Her blade was silky like molten gold and one of the only things that could mortally wound him. That was the price he had paid to have it created.

Odin stood up quickly, buttoning up his suit jacket.

"Didn't I teach you not to draw your weapon unless you planned on using it?" he asked callously.

Bryn's arm was by her side, but her knuckles were white around the hilt. Anger burned in her blue eyes. "Yes." Her voice was low, threatening. "So I suggest you leave before I use it."

Odin retreated from the room, closing the door behind him. He knew she wouldn't have come with him, but he couldn't tell her the real reason why he needed her under his protection yet. He had lied to her once about her parents. If he also told her how completely they were bound to each other's fates, she would kill herself just to spite him.

Bryn ran a finger over the tattoo on her neck, her sword fading from her hand. She hadn't wanted to threaten Odin, but if he'd stayed in her office a minute longer, she'd have been in very real danger of gutting him. Her whole body was still shaking with anger. How dare he come in and tell her that he had found Rota's body.

Her legs gave out from under her, slamming her back down into her old office chair. Odin truly was the father of lies, yet deep down she still wanted to be by his side. She was like a stray dog kicked and abused but still craving a master.

She was being ridiculous. She had been the one to leave him, and she would have done it ten times over again.

The day he had come for her was so clear in her mind. It was the day of her eighteenth birthday . . .

The man who had come to claim Bryn was handsome, as handsome as

Davin—the boy who lived in the next village. Her mother had let him into the house and sat down, shaking her head, saying "no, no, no" over and over again. Bryn stared at him openly, looking at the shiny black orb next to his remaining luminescent green eye.

"Do you know who I am, Brynhildr?" She shook my head. "No, I do not."

"I'm here to take you away from this life. I want you to come and live with me."

"Live?" she laughed. "I live here with my father and mother."

He sat beside her, turning his body turned toward her. She didn't feel frightened even though Mother was trembling terribly in front of them. "Your father said you can come with me, and your mother…" He paused and looked over at her mother. Their eyes met, and she wailed, burying her head in her hands. "Your mother also agreed to let you live with me."

Bryn shook her head. "I cannot be your wife. My parents will not allow me to wed."

"I don't wish to wed you, Brynhildr." He took her hand gently. His fingers were soft. She had never met a man with soft hands before. Her father's had been calloused from working hard since she could remember. "I wish to give you a job."

"A job?" She had always wanted a job—to feel useful. "What kind of job?"

"I want to have a special group of women who I can send out with my very important messages. They must be very beautiful and very hard-working." He tucked a strand of hair behind her ear. "Clearly, you are very beautiful, but are you hard-working?"

She nodded vigorously. "Yes. I work very hard. Just ask Mother. She can tell you."

The man didn't look at Bryn's mother, but she did. Mother was still holding her head in her hands, her shoulders shaking violently. Why was she so upset that Bryn was being offered a job?

"If you want this job, you must come with me now, Brynhildr," the man said, standing up and offering her his hand.

Bryn glanced from him to her mother. "Mother, don't be upset. I want to work. I have always wanted to work as Father does. You'll see! I'll bring money home and buy you the best meats and skins and—"

Her mother stood up and drew her close, crushing her to her chest and suffocating the words on her tongue.

"It's time to go," the man said, taking her by the wrist and pulling her away from her mother. Tears trembled in her mother's eyes. Bryn kissed her on the cheek.

"I shall return, Mother," she vowed.

She followed the man out the door, stopping him suddenly. "I don't know your name."

He took her hand, a strange burning sensation passing between them. It felt as if her body was filling up with white-hot light, scorching through her veins. Bryn gasped, closing her eyes, fighting the wave of nausea, the acrid taste of bile twisting up her throat. Her eyes flew open once more as if forced. The world began to shift in front of her, shattering like glass and falling into a thousand pieces. She screamed out as softly spoken words trickled into her ears . . .

Her heart pounded frantically against her ribs, beating against the prison of bones. When she opened her eyes again, she feared the world would be awash with flame, feared it would be changed—shattered—but the world was just as it had been before. It had not fallen apart. The man stood before her, holding her up with strong hands.

"What happened?" Bryn asked. "Who are you?"

He smiled at her, a warmth filling her chest at the sight of it. "I am Odin and you, Brynhildr, are now my daughter. I have just given you your immortality."

Bryn hadn't known the true meaning of the words he had spoken.

But she knew them now: *Purest blood that flows through my veins; I share the gift of everlasting life with her; she shall not age; she shall not wither and die; she will be immortal; forever at my side.*

That had been the last time she had seen her mother alive. Bryn had been bound to Odin, and told there was no possible way for her to return to her parents or her former life. She had wanted to hate him for a long time afterward, but soon there were other women who had joined his group of messengers. Bryn had wondered whether Odin had tricked them, too.

Bitterness grew inside her, a resentment, but her bond to the All-Father made it impossible for her to truly hate him.

18

Darrion closed his eyes and tapped into Korvain's energy. His blood came through the bond loud and clear, telling Darrion he was somewhere near Chinatown. Following the tether binding them, Darrion faded to within a few blocks of Korvain's location and headed north-east toward the pull of his blood.

He slowed when he felt the strongest throb of Korvain's presence. Looking up, his whole field of vision was taken up by one building. It was at least four stories high, made from the signature red brick many of the buildings in Boston were made from. There was only one door at the front and no windows. Above the door, the rune for protection was carved in the stone.

Clearly, the building was warded against gods fading in and out, so he couldn't get in that way. Walking along the length of the facade, he found the cool shadows of an alleyway just wide enough for one car to fit through at a time.

Ignoring the smell of garbage and stale piss, he walked down silently until he reached another door. He kept his distance, placing his back against the wall of the neighboring building while he surveyed the entrance.

The door was the same as the one out front: smooth without a handle in sight. Next to the door was a small intercom. Darrion's eyes drifted up to the camera positioned to look down at the door. Closing his eyes, he focused on his assassin. Korvain was in there. He could feel it.

The sun was no more than an hour old, not yet strong enough to heat up the day and burn away the chill of the night. He scanned the surrounds for somewhere to wait where he wouldn't be seen. There was a BMW X6 parked around the back of the building. If he lay on the ground and looked under the car, he could still watch the door and stay out of sight.

No sooner had he gotten himself into position than he saw another man show up, looking over the door like it held all the answers to his questions. Darrion thought he was human, but the fucker was too tall to be straight human. He inhaled, the familiar scent of Aesirean god on the air. Darrion bit back a nasty snarl.

The god's pale eyes were calculating like he was constantly thinking about his next move. Without warning, the god faded away from the building with a curse, and Darrion realized that someone was coming.

The steel door groaned as it was pushed open from the inside. Korvain's broad frame filled the space. Darrion delighted in the fact that he looked like shit. There was dried blood caked to his face and a hole in his leathers. As he stepped from the doorway, Darrion could tell his knee was bothering him, too. He took a second to wonder whether those injuries had come from killing the Valkyrie.

The Mare glanced in both directions before fading from the alleyway. Darrion followed, trailing their bond back to Korvain's house. Darrion rematerialized directly behind the bastard, turning him around with a firm hand on his shoulder.

The Mare spun around, taking the karambit from the holster under his jacket and raising it. When he realized it was Darrion, his body didn't relax an inch, but at least he lowered the weapon.

"What are you doing here? Did you follow me?" he snarled, his dark eyes churning.

Darrion ignored the questions like he always did. Instead, he looked over the Mare's face and hands, seeing the blood—hoping.

"Have you made the hit?"

Korvain flinched. It was a subtle movement, and if Darrion didn't know his Mare so well, he wouldn't have seen the slight tightening of his neck muscles. But Darrion did know him that well, and he had seen it.

"You know the consequences of not completing the assignment." Darrion's voice was dark, a prowling growl. He was so fucking ready to take Odin out. And waiting was not building his anticipation. It was irritating the fuck out of him.

Korvain's spine straightened, his shoulders rolling backward. "You don't have to remind me."

Darrion smiled at the Mare, baring his teeth. "This is your last warning, morier. I want it done."

He faded before Korvain could retort. Darrion had seen his reaction. He had broken the first rule of a Shadow Walker: Don't get close to the target. Gods, he had drilled it into him enough.

He knew his best assassin had been compromised, and if that had happened there was no way in hell the mark would be wiped out when the time really came.

Korvain cursed as soon as Darrion faded from in front of him. He knew. Gods, he knew he had gotten too close to Bryn. He hadn't meant to flinch, but talking about her as if she was disposable made his blood boil.

Korvain snapped open the front door, nearly pulling it from its hinges in the process. Adrian's head appeared from around the corner. He had that ridiculous apron on again, a spatula in his hand.

"Breakfast?" he asked.

Korvain bared his fangs at him with a hiss.

Adrian frowned. "What the hell happened to you?"

"Fuck. Just leave me alone," Korvain snarled, pushing past the other male and climbing the stairs. He couldn't deal with Adrian's perpetual cheer right that minute. The repercussions of his actions were still banging around in his skull. He hadn't killed Bryn yet. Darrion was impatient—but Korvain couldn't physically harm the Valkyrie now even if he wanted to.

She had cared for him when he was at his most vulnerable. Gods, she'd been so close to him. His body had beaten back the pain and exploded to life when she had pressed herself against him to clean the cut on his head.

He had breathed her in and smelled that fresh gardenia scent and crumbled. He shouldn't have even been there. He should have left Eir with Bryn and hauled ass, but somehow he just couldn't ignore her command to stay.

Korvain punched the hallway wall, bones cracking in his hand and wrist. Ignoring the throb, he threw open his bedroom door, knowing what he had to do. He took a cold shower to calm down, to wash away the memories of Bryn's healing touch on his body, to purge his memories of her intoxicating scent and his fierce desire.

The blood from his face washed away in pink swirls. His shoulder still stung, his knee aching every time he put any pressure on it. He twisted off the taps angrily, almost breaking the things off the wall in his rage.

Snapping a towel from the railing, he stalked through his room, wincing with every movement. He needed to heal. He needed to sleep in order to do that, but there was only one place he was going to go when he shut his eyes and that was straight back to Bryn.

When he pushed through the door into her mind, she was on the floor beside the couch, her head resting on her folded arms. Her breathing was deep and even, matched to Eir's, who was sleeping peacefully stretched out on the cushions. It seemed that whatever drug had been pushed into her system had finally worn off.

Korvain approached the sleeping pair carefully, touching Bryn's shoulder. Her head jerked up suddenly. Blinking, she simply stared at him for a moment.

"Korvain, what are you—"

He placed his finger against her lips and helped her stand. Gods, she was beautiful. He stared deeply into her blue eyes, knowing unequivocally that he would not be able to harm her no matter the order from Darrion. He had to protect her; he felt it in his bones, down in the marrow—deep in his soul.

She bit her lip, her white teeth sinking into the pink flesh. A low, possessive sound trickled from his mouth, a fresh wave of gardenia hitting him, staggering him for just a moment.

"Can I tell you something?" she asked quietly. He raised his eyebrows in invitation, knowing she would think this was just a dream. She swallowed nervously before meeting his eyes again.

"I wanted you to kiss me before—when you were here and I was looking after you."

He closed his eyes, letting Bryn's sweet words trickle in his ears. With his lids still squeezed shut, he rasped, "I liked that you were looking after me."

"Look at me, Korvain." Her voice cracked over his name. He did as he was asked and stared into her beautiful face. "Kiss me now?"

The blood in his body heated and, surging forward, he claimed her mouth with his. Their tongues met in a fierce struggle for domination, which he won when she moaned his name. The sound of her whimpers lit another fire within him, feeding the already glowing inferno.

He started angling them down the hallway toward her bedroom. He wrapped one arm around her waist, pinning her body against him while cupping her neck—caging her in. She molded to the front of his body as if she was made for him.

Exquisite heat shot through him at the different points of contact. He was so keyed up he could have taken her right then against the wall, but he treated her with the respect she deserved. Korvain's fangs began to thrum, the call of her blood scorching his nerve endings.

Running his nose along the length of her neck, he smelled the bouquet of her skin. He licked the side of her throat, teasing the vein to come to the surface. Her heart was beating so fast he could feel it against her skin. He kissed the long column of her throat, drawing soft moans from her lips.

Her back had finally hit the door at the end of the hall. Korvain reached behind her, twisting the knob and pushing open the door. Leading her in, he kicked the door shut and took a step back.

Bryn looked up at him shyly. "I can't get the image of you sitting shirtless at my dining room table out of my head." Her admission colored her cheeks. Korvain laughed at her gently, sliding his hands along her neck and stroking the side of her face with his thumbs.

"Well, I wouldn't want to disappoint you then."

He took a step back and pulled the tee from his body. When he dropped it to the floor, Bryn's eyes had glazed over. There was a deep-seated sense of satisfaction at seeing her reaction to his body. He was rewarded with another hit of gardenia. She approached him, stopping an inch away and looking in his eyes for permission. He nodded and felt her warm fingers trailing over his skin.

"So many scars," she murmured, lowering her mouth to the one above his nipple on his left pectoral. His breath left his lungs in a long shudder. She kissed another one of his scars, this one on his collarbone. Her tongue swept along his skin leaving a trail of goosebumps in its wake.

Catching the end of her T-shirt, he began inching it up her torso slowly. She moaned his name—a raw, guttural sound—and bit his still-healing shoulder. He hissed, the sound bringing her head up in a jerking movement.

"Did I hurt you?" she asked.

He shook his head. "Do it again," he replied hoarsely. Gods, he had dreamed of taking her blood into him, her teeth in his flesh only concreting the idea more firmly into place.

With a shy smile, she lowered her head once more. Her teeth sank into his skin and his whole body responded. The erection he'd been sporting since he'd kissed her suddenly became a monstrous hard length he couldn't hide away anymore. Bryn brushed up against his hips and gasped.

With a low, throaty sigh, he kissed her on the mouth while still working her shirt up her body. They had to break away when he pulled it over her head, but like two magnets, their mouths were fused again.

He hadn't touched her bare skin yet. Slowly, carefully, he rested his hands on her waist, remembering how he had reached for her before. Warm, soft flesh met his fingertips and he knew this was his version of heaven.

"You feel so good," he mumbled, forcing the words out from between their tightly pressed mouths.

With the tips of his fingers, he climbed up her torso. They gently undulated over each of her fragile ribs, rising and falling with increasing intensity the further he traveled north. When he brushed past lace, he knew he had found the underside of her bra.

Bryn's head kicked back and she groaned, pressing her fingers into his biceps. He growled low in his throat, slipped a finger into the top of her bra and pulled. Her warm breast filled his hand, her nipple peaked, hard and ready for him. Using the pad of his thumb, he rubbed that tight knot of flesh, reveling in the way her back arched and her hips jackknifed into his erection.

Korvain drank in the sight of her: her quickening pulse, her dilating pupils, her flushed skin. She was so ready for him. He walked her toward the bed until the back of her knees hit the edge. Lowering her body down, he stood back to watch her chest heave up and down, knowing he was responsible for it.

"I want all of you, Bryn, and I won't stop until I kiss every inch of your skin. I will bury my head between your thighs and lick and suck and suckle until you come, screaming my name."

She bit down on her bottom lip to stop the groan. Her legs scissored on top of the sheets, pushing them away and forcing them into a bunch at her feet. Dropping to his knees, he captured her ankles, stilling her legs instantly. The rest of her body, however, still writhed like a trapped snake.

The rolling of her hips and stomach was hypnotic. He planted one hand in the span between her hipbones, forcing her to calm. He leaned down to unbutton her jeans. The zipper shuddered open, revealing the top of her black silk underwear.

Bryn threw her arms over her face and groaned. Korvain released his hold on her body, sliding his hands up her hips to her waist. Her skin felt like warmed velvet against his palms, and the delicate scent of her arousal hung in the air.

As he pulled at the sides of her jeans, she lifted her hips to help him remove them. Inch by inch, he dragged the fabric down, revealing the cleft between her thighs and the long expanse of her lean legs. Korvain then pulled her panties off slowly, drawing more moans from Bryn's throat. Bunching up the fabric, he stuffed it into his pants pocket.

Starting at her toes, he stayed true to his word. He kissed her feet, her legs and her thighs, hovering just away from the place he really wanted to be.

"Please," Bryn begged, her toes curling into the sheets. He smiled up the length of her sinuous body.

"I'm going to make you come," he whispered. She whimpered and he lowered his head.

He wanted to taste her so badly, but he had to take it slow. He placed kisses along the inside of her thighs, moving closer and closer toward her slick core. When she grabbed onto his shoulders, guiding him closer, he pulled back and just watched her shudder for him.

"Korvain," she begged in a breathy voice. He chuckled and lowered his head once more. She was glistening already. He could see it and he longed to taste it. He swept his tongue through her trembling flesh, sending a spasm coursing through her body.

Her hips flexed off the mattress; her fingers dug into his shoulder. A haze of blood tinted the air, only adding to the drugging effect Bryn had on him. He made another long sweep, latching onto the tight knot of nerves at the top.

"Gods!"

He looked up at her, knowing how his eyes must have been swallowing shadows. "This is fantasy number one," he said, licking his lips appreciatively, "and you haven't disappointed."

He sucked her into his mouth once more, her spine bowing in response, her hands scrambling for purchase. He could feel her body twitch, getting closer to release. Her inner thighs began to tremble. He wanted it to be magnificent for her, so he increased his attention, redoubling his efforts.

His tongue was on her, in her, and when the tip swirled her clit, she finally exploded around him. She rode the orgasm up, her chest heaving with the effort. She cried out, her internal muscles pulsing, drawing it out. She arched off the bed, her hips rocking under Korvain's mouth.

She may have come, but he wasn't done with her yet. Using the flat of his tongue, he swept the entire length of her heart, lapping up her arousal and groaning when the flavor hit the back of his throat. He swallowed her down, tasting her completely.

"Stop, please," she begged. He ignored her pleas, smiling as she shuddered once more. "Korvain." She was desperate for him to stop, but he was desperate for her to come undone one more time. He shook his head and her hips jacked up off the bed once more.

She came apart, repeating his name over and over again until he could barely take it anymore. She crested the wave of her orgasm and lay limply on the bed, her breathing sharp and jerky for a while until she calmed down.

He looked up her body, hungrily licking his lips. "I've wanted to do that for so long."

19

Bryn slumped against the mattress, her breathing labored. She looked down at Korvain. His huge body pulsed with a juxtaposition of dangerous energy and protectiveness. She squeezed her eyes shut. Gods, if only this was real. If only he would really come to her and make her feel this way. Was it too much to hope for?

Deep down, though, she knew why he couldn't. She was too afraid of what Odin would think of her. This was the reason Kara had been dismissed from his service. Only virgins could serve the All-Father, although Bryn had never known why. Perhaps it was just Odin's need to have complete and utter control over them and their lives. Perhaps it had something to do with the power binding them together.

Whatever the reason, one thing still remained true: This could never happen in real life—but in her dreams . . . in her dreams there was nothing to stop her from fulfilling her fantasies.

He was licking his lips, sitting back on his heels while half her body was on the bed and the other half was draped over the side of it. She sat up slowly, aware of how her breasts swayed and the way Korvain's eyes watched them. He still had his pants on, his erection straining to get free.

"Come up here," she said, surprised at just how husky her voice sounded. Korvain smiled, revealing the tips of his fangs. He stretched out beside her, his large hands playing across her collarbone, dipping between her breasts. She laughed nervously when he trailed his fingers down the middle of her stomach and gasped when he dipped between her still-sensitive thighs.

"I've never let anyone do that to me before," she murmured.

"What?"

She glanced down to where his fingers were now stroking. "That."

"Really?"

She flushed at what she was about to say next. "I'm technically still a virgin." Admitting it now in this dream would be the only time she would leave herself so exposed.

Korvain's expression sobered and his hand stilled. He withdrew from her body slowly. Bryn reached for the fastening on his jeans, hoping to see how far the dream would take her.

"Don't," he said softly. She looked into his bottomless black eyes and frowned. His free hand smoothed the wrinkle away gently. "Let's just lie together for a little while," he said.

Confused, Bryn rolled over onto her side to hide her body from him. She didn't know why, but his rejection felt like a whole lot more than just a simple rejection. He pulled her onto her back, his dark eyes serious.

"Don't ever hide yourself from me, Bryn."

Don't hide yourself? Even in her dreams, she couldn't allow herself to cross that self-imposed line. She blew out a frustrated breath. "I had no idea I could dream this up," she muttered. Korvain brought her in line with his body, curling around her spine. His clothes rubbed against her lower body, a heavy reminder of just how seriously fucked up she was where Odin and his wishes were concerned.

She couldn't even dream about losing her virginity.

"We have time." His words vibrated through her back. She let out a deep breath and closed her eyes. He was all she could smell, all she could hear. She drifted off . . .

"Bryn? . . . Bryn? . . . Wake up." Bryn woke with a gasp, jerking back from the hand that had touched her shoulder. She blinked Eir into focus then looked around. She was propped up beside the couch, her face feeling like it had been flattened. She shifted, feeling wetness between her thighs. For a dream, it had been pretty damn realistic.

"Bryn?" Eir asked softly.

She squeezed her eyes shut and opened them again. Turning her head so she was looking at Eir, she asked, "How are you feeling?"

The other Valkyrie was sitting with her legs tucked in close to her body, her arms wrapped around her knees. She gave Bryn an unsteady smile. "Still a little off."

Bryn grunted, staggering to her feet. Her legs were really stiff. How long had she been asleep for? "Do you remember who attacked you?" she asked.

Eir shook her head, her long blonde hair cascading over one shoulder. Her face was a lot paler than normal, making her blue eyes stand out. "I was talking to you, then I was stung by something."

"You weren't stung. Someone stuck you with a needle. We don't know what you were injected with, but whatever it was, it seems to be out of your system now."

Eir rubbed at her neck. "Why would someone want to do that?"

Bryn sank down beside her on the couch. "Beats me," she lied. "You're just lucky Korvain was there. He saved you."

"Korvain?" Eir asked, rubbing her eyes.

"Yeah, one of my bouncers."

"Did he recognize the man?"

Bryn shook her head. "Look, I want you to stay here with me until we get this figured out. If someone is attacking Valkyries, I need to know you're safe."

"Of course. I'll go and get some clothes now." Eir stood up, but Bryn stopped her by grabbing her wrist.

"I don't want you going alone. I'll call Korvain later and get him to go with you. He can check in on the others, too."

Odin faded to the address of one of his Valkyries. He was no longer able to feel the pulse of her life—not that it mattered now. As much as he hated to acknowledge it, his time was over. There was nothing he could do to protect Svava or any of the other Valkyries. He had lost everything and everyone since the Fall, had no guards or servants to help him, no one to do his bidding. He didn't care, not really—Svava was expendable, just as his other Valkyries were, with the exception of Bryn. Bryn had proved to be his weakness in more ways than one, but he would defend her and what she represented for as long as his body could keep fighting.

Walking briskly across the street, Odin walked up the few steps to the front door and knocked. The door swung open slowly when his fist hit the wood, the smell of blood like a wall hitting his nose. What little light came from the street lights outside barely penetrated the gloom of the hallway as he pushed the door all the way open.

Kicking the door shut behind him, he stopped at the adjoining doorway of the living room, reaching around and flipping the switch beside the door. A chandelier dripping from the ceiling above flooded the room with a yellow light, illuminating the struggle that had taken place there.

One edge of the stone coffee table was bloody, hair and skin still glued to the corner with blood. Odin's eyes traveled down, seeing the large bloodstain on the floorboards. Stepping further into the room, he dragged his fingers through it. It was dry and flaking around the edges, but still slightly tacky in the middle. His eyes lifted to the underside of the nearby couch, noticing something small underneath it—a feather. Plucking up the bloodstained plume, there was absolutely no doubt in his mind that Svava was now dead.

Loki must have found her cloak and killed her right there on her living room floor, but Odin just couldn't figure out why he had taken her body. What good was the corpse of a Valkyrie to Loki? Standing up from his crouch, the All-Father retreated from the room, killing the lights as he did. When the front door was firmly shut behind him, he faded back to his apartment, contemplating whether to tell Bryn of the news or not.

She would like to know, but he doubted that she would like to see him again. Discarding the feather he'd taken from Svava's house, Odin sat down and tried to come up with a way to stop Loki before he could kill his most treasured possession.

Loki paced the cold floor of the underground room he had discovered below Boston's streets, the gun still in his hand. Everything had been going according to plan. He had injected the heroin into the Valkyrie's neck. She had passed out and he was going to take her back to her apartment and search out her cloak, but that damn Mare had come along and fucked it all up.

And he *was* a Mare—Loki had been able to sense the power in the purity of his blood—but that made no sense. Before the Fall, Odin had hunted down all the Mares, eradicating them from the face of the earth. Somehow, the bastard must have slipped through the cracks.

Loki looked over at the body of the only Valkyrie he had. He would have had two, but one he had given away—a gift for Odin.

It was frigid down there in the tunnels, but not cold enough to stop the decomposition process. Even now, a hint of carrion was in the air, threatening to take him back to the time when he was forced to suffer his wife's and son's rot and putrefaction. Crouching down, he picked up one of the feathers from the Valkyrie's cloak, blotted with blood, and twirled it between his fingers—thinking.

If the Valkyries now had a guard—one of the most physically powerful, dangerous beings ever to roam the Nine Worlds—it would make his job difficult, but not impossible.

He paused, letting an idea take shape. Yes, that could work. If he was to triumph, he needed to move not only quickly, but carefully. He only had one chance at succeeding in this new plan. Stashing the gun at the small of his back, he faded from the tunnels and onto Lime Street.

Houses lined the pavement, each of them joined with the same red-brick facade. He had passed through the street earlier on the hunt for the Valkyries he knew resided there when he'd seen the protection rune carved into the lintel above a yellow door.

He made his way back to the house and looked it over from his position across the street. From behind the blinds, the soft glow of a television radiated out into the darkness.

There was a car parked out the front of the house. Approaching it cautiously, Loki peered inside the window. With a glance up the street to confirm his privacy, he shoved his elbow through the glass.

The alarm began blaring. He watched as the porch light on the Valkyrie's house switched on and the locks on the door slid open. Hiding in the shadows beside the entrance way, he waited for the goddess to come out and inspect the damage. While her back was turned, he slid unnoticed into the house to await his prey.

Inside, the house was decorated in different shades of yellow, all blending together. Loki moved silently down the hallway, ducking into the darkened kitchen on the left. He heard the door close a few minutes later.

The stairs creaked. "What's the damage?" a woman asked. Loki froze. This was even better than he could have hoped for. There were two of them.

"Broken window. I didn't see who did it, but I'm calling the cops to report it," the other said.

He heard footsteps coming closer. Glancing up, he saw a phone attached to the wall just inside the door. The Valkyrie was coming straight for him. With a smile, he reached for his knife.

He disappeared into the pantry, pulling the door closed behind him just in time. The light flicked on. From the crack in the door, Loki watched as she picked up the phone and punched in a few numbers.

"Yes, hello, I'd like to report some vandalism . . . yeah, I'll hold."

Loki pushed silently out of the pantry, his eyes glued to the woman. Her back was to him, her fingers flicking through a magazine on the benchtop. He was within striking distance, so when she paused on one page, he stopped breathing, remaining completely still.

The woman shut the magazine with a snap. "Yeah, I'm here. I want to report some vandalism . . . yeah, someone broke the driver's side window of my—" The Valkyrie stopped mid-sentence, her eyes widening as she turned around and saw him. He struck her quickly, driving the dagger into her stomach. She dropped to the floor, the phone popping free from her hand. Loki could hear the human on the other end.

"Ma'am? Ma'am, you there? Ma'am?"

He picked up the receiver, setting it quietly back into the cradle before turning his attention to the Valkyrie bleeding out onto her kitchen floor.

Her dual-toned blue eyes were wide, both hands covering the ugly smile he'd punched into her abdomen. She sucked in a breath to scream out the other woman's name, but changed her mind; her lips sealed shut and tears began to stream down her face.

"You're the one, aren't you?" she asked in a bare whisper.

Loki didn't bother to answer. Instead, he crouched down in front of her. She whimpered and shuffled her ass backward on the black and white checked tile, one hand still pressed to her stomach, the other smearing blood everywhere.

"I know that wound won't kill you," he told her, "but I do know what will kill you. Tell me where you keep your cloak."

The woman's eyes clouded over with rage. "Never," she spat back.

He pried her hand away from the slice to her belly and pressed his fingers into her flesh. "Tell me, or I will kill the other girl. It's your choice: save your friend, or condemn the both of you to a slow, painful death."

He could see her trying to work over her other options. The thing was, she didn't have any. Loki was going to kill the other Valkyrie no matter the bargain. When the woman's determined eyes returned to his face, he knew she wasn't going to do this the easy way.

"Astrid! Run!" she screamed. Loki could barely contain his rage, angrily cuffing the woman across the cheek. Her head snapped back, connecting with the cupboards behind her. With fluttering eyelids, the woman passed out. He whirled around just as the other Valkyrie—Astrid—called out.

"Sigrun? . . . Sigrun, what is it?"

Grasping the syringe of heroin in his pocket, he lunged for Astrid's neck as she appeared in the doorway, and the point sank home. She tried to fight him off, but he depressed the plunger and took a step back. The Valkyrie scrambled away from him, her hand over her neck. He watched with morbid fascination as the drug hit her bloodstream, weakening her in an instant.

"Who—" she asked, her back hitting the wall opposite the kitchen door. Her long legs bent uncomfortably beneath her and she slumped to the floor, consciousness slipping away.

Loki turned back to Sigrun. Her hand had fallen away from the wound and blood stained the tiles around her. He knew he didn't have much time. To give him a little more, he pulled the phone from the wall and used the cord to bind her wrists and ankles.

Leaving the kitchen, he began his search for the ash boxes that were guaranteed to be in the house. The only rule constraining the Valkyries was that the box had to be kept in the place where they resided.

After thoroughly searching the bottom half of the house, Loki made his way upstairs. He walked into the first bedroom, his bloody hands touching sacred items like photographs and things from their old world. He pulled open the closet and rifled through until he found the first ash box. When he peered inside, the feathers looked like soft floating clouds.

With the box under his arm, he walked into the next bedroom and started his search. He found the other box hidden under the bed and pulled it out.

Back in the kitchen, Sigrun's blood had begun inching its way toward the doorway—a slick, glossy ribbon of color. Taking the first cloak out of its box, he ran the feathers through his hand slowly, carefully, before finally picking one and plucking it free.

Sigrun's eyes opened, a cry escaping her mouth. Her legs scrambling, she tried to push her body away from him. She raised her arm to summon her sword but found she couldn't move. Loki grinned. She pressed herself against one the kitchen cabinets further from him, groaning with each shift of her body. More blood flowed from the wound in her belly, dripping off her side. Sigrun's eyes found Astrid's slumped body against the opposite wall and tears started to well.

Loki stripped the cloak quickly, watching Sigrun's body writhe with each and every feather removed. When there were feathers littering the floor, and a fresh wash of blood spattered the tiles, he took his dagger and drove it through the Valkyrie's heart.

20

Darrion faded back to the office he had set up in Dorchester and immediately picked up the phone. Korvain's defiance was a slap in the face, and even though it killed him to do it, he couldn't have that in his guild. Losing his best assassin had now become unavoidable.

Walkers followed the orders they were given. End of story. If he showed leniency now, other guild masters would see it as a weakness and attempt to kill him. He had worked too damn hard to see his guild slip through his fingers.

He clutched the phone to his ear, listening impatiently to the ringing at the other end. Finally, Adrian answered.

"Yeah?"

"We need to talk."

Adrian swallowed audibly. "I'll be right there."

While he waited, Darrion pulled out his throwing blades and started launching them at the target beside the door. Each knife was perfectly balanced for throwing, perfectly tuned to him. He released the first one. It sliced through the air, landing in the wooden board with a familiar thunk.

Losing Korvain was going to be hard. He was the best there was. Hell, he was even better than Darrion had been. But defiance wouldn't be tolerated.

Death before dishonor.

Adrian knocked before he came in. Darrion threw his last knife at the target and retrieved them all before barking the order for Adrian to get his ass in the room. The Mare came in slowly, staring at him as if he was a loaded gun just waiting to go off. The funny thing was, he was right.

He was wound so damn tight he could snap at any minute.

"Sit down," he commanded. Adrian walked forward and sat in the chair—his back stiff, his eyes darting around. Darrion sat in his office chair, a throwing blade in one hand. He tested the tip with his fingertip.

He let Adrian sweat for a minute before finally speaking. "I have a job for you." Darrion watched his face for a reaction, but got none. "A Walker on a hit right now has been compromised."

Adrian's green eyes were fixed on the tip of the blade sticking into Darrion's thumb. A small bead of blood had welled, growing like a fattening tick against his skin.

Darrion could see the Mare wanted to ask who had fucked up their assignment, but he wouldn't—no matter how much he wanted to.

"I will offer you the same terms as the other Walker had. Triple the pay and. . . five years off your term."

Adrian's eyes widened. "Who's the mark?"

He smiled slyly. "Will you take the job?"

Looking stricken, Adrian sat back in his chair, but didn't relax.

When he finally looked Darrion in the eye, there was a steely determination in his gaze. "Give me ten off and I'll consider it."

His smile faltered. The fucker wasn't supposed to negotiate. Darrion needed it to be him. He needed the fucking irony. "Five," he spat back.

Adrian shook his head. "I'll go as low as seven."

Darrion looked at him darkly. "You don't negotiate with me. I offered you five, but now I'm not feeling so generous. You will do this job for me, and you will do it for one year off your service."

"I refuse," Adrian replied coolly, almost haughtily.

Fucking Korvain. He swallowed back a curse, maintaining his business face. "You will do this, Adrian, or I will take Taer out of the assassin program and make her the guild whore after I have had my fill of her."

The threat worked just as he had hoped. Adrian's eyes bulged for a second. He was trying to keep his cool. He was trying, but failing. A trickle of sweat trailed down from his temple; his nostrils flared.

Darrion laughed and leaned forward in his chair. "If you think you're upset now, wait till you hear who your mark is."

Korvain picked up his phone before it had even had the chance to ring. Hitting the accept button, he held it to his ear.

"Yeah?"

"Korvain?" Bryn's trembling voice came through from the other end.

"Yeah," he replied, his voice softening. "Is everything all right?" This was becoming a habit of hers that he liked.

"Everything is fine. I need you here," she said, and Korvain felt his blood pressure surge.

"Whatever you want. I'll come now," he blurted, cursing his whipped ass with every word.

He ended the call, running a hand through his short hair. He left the house straight away, only realizing when he faded to the club that he was still in a muscle shirt and sweats.

With a shrug, he approached the door and knocked—looking up at the camera as he did. The giant metal door clicked and he pulled it open. He took the elevator up to the living quarters on the top floor of the building, knocking on Bryn's slightly ajar apartment door.

Pushing it open, he called out, "Hello?"

"We're in here," Bryn called from down the hall. Korvain slid into the apartment and made his way down the hallway toward Bryn's bedroom. Memories from the dream came flooding back to him, sending blood south. His erection made a tent of the front of his sweats and he quickly tucked the length into the waistband.

He was about to push into Bryn's bedroom when she called out to him again. "Korvain, we're in here." With one last lingering glance at Bryn's bedroom, he pushed open the other door in the hall.

The Valkyrie was pulling the sheets up on a twin bed while Eir sat on the floor with a cushion hugged to her chest. Korvain looked over the healer. Her pale blonde hair, only a few shades darker than Bryn's, was scraped back into a high ponytail and there were deep purple bruises under her eyes. He hadn't noticed it last night, but there were a series of grazes up and down one of her arms that hadn't yet healed.

"How are you feeling?" he asked her.

Her royal blue and teal eyes were on the carpet she was picking at absently. "Much better, thank you," she replied, voice barely audible. "And . . .thank you for rescuing me," she tacked on just as quietly.

He acknowledged her gratitude with a slight incline of his head and looked at Bryn. "You wanted to see me?"

Glancing up, her cheeks flushed with a little color. "Yeah. Eir's going to move in here with me for a little while until whatever this thing is passes over. I need you to take her home so she can grab a few things, but I also need you to go check on the others."

"Wouldn't it be safer if I go by myself?" he asked.

"Yeah, it would be, but you don't know what Eir wants from her place and the others will probably believe there's a real threat if Eir tells them herself she has already been attacked."

It made sense. "When do you want us to go?"

"Now."

"All right."

Eir slowly got to her feet and left Korvain and Bryn together. With the other Valkyrie gone, he felt the air thicken, his need to touch Bryn's body almost suffocating. The silence filled the void between them. When it was clear she had nothing else to say to him, he turned to leave, stopping when he felt Bryn's fingers curl around his arm. His head spun around, his nostrils flaring when the faintest hint of gardenia hit the air.

"Shut the door," she said. "I need to speak to you for a minute."

He kicked the thing shut. "What's up?"

She dropped her gaze to the carpet, her toes digging into the pile. Gods, he had a flashback of those same toes curling into the sheets while he buried his face between her legs and made her come—before she had told him about still being a virgin. That little newsflash hadn't dampened his need to fuck her. If anything, it had made it worse; it made him even hungrier for her.

He focused on her bare feet, on the toenails painted the same shade of denim as her eyes. When she finally looked up at him again, she was flushed.

"I . . . umm . . ." She nervously fidgeted with the end of her braid, and he could tell she was holding something back. "Look after my girl, all right?"

"Tell me what you were really going to say just then," he said gently, taking a step closer.

Her eyes widened, but she shook her head. "It's nothing."

He growled softly, closing the distance between them. He hadn't thought. He'd just acted. He had denied himself in the dream. He didn't want to take her at a time when she thought it wasn't real. He wanted her in this reality, in this plane, where there would be no doubt in her mind about who she belonged to afterward.

He took her face in between his hands, and she melted, whimpered.

"Tell me what you were going to say." It was a demand. He couldn't help it. Where she was concerned, he wanted to be that primal asshole who protected his woman.

She licked her lips, unknowingly tempting him to kiss her. "It's nothing."

"Bullshit."

She cursed him under her breath, causing him to smile. "I was just wondering whether . . ." she groaned. Her chest rose and fell with a large sigh. "It's stupid."

"I don't care."

She stared at him for a moment before tilting her chin up in stubbornness. "All right. I had a dream about you last night."

A smile curved up his lips. When Bryn saw it, she added, "Just forget I mentioned it, all right?" and pulled away from him.

He slipped his hands onto her shoulders, stopping her. "What was your dream about?" he asked gently.

She was flush against his chest so when her nipples hardened, he felt them. His arousal was undeniable, forcing him to angle his hips away from hers.

"I dreamed—"

"Korvain?" Eir knocked on the door. "Are you coming?"

He stepped away from Bryn reluctantly, his hand dragging down the length of her arm as he did. "We aren't done here," he warned softly. Bryn blinked up at him in surprise, her mouth parting ever so slightly. He stared into her eyes, showing her that he was serious. After a few brief but intense seconds, he turned away and led Eir from the apartment.

He and Eir stepped out the back door of the club, fading to the Valkyrie's house in Beacon Hill. He inspected the rune above the front door—feeling the potency of the spell—as they approached the building. That was when he noticed Eir glancing around nervously. In an effort to stifle her fears, he stood sentinel on the stoop, his eyes surveying their surroundings as Eir worked the lock. The Valkyrie fumbled with the keys before finally getting the right one into the lock and turning it.

When the door whined open, Korvain turned and followed Eir inside. She flicked on the lights in the entrance hall as she went, illuminating the whole room as if the shadows were going to suddenly grow fangs and attack her. With a shake of his head, he shut the door behind him.

Eir wandered away from him. Grabbing her wrist, he pulled her to an abrupt stop.

"Wait here while I check out the place."

"I'm coming with you." Her eyes were fierce, but her voice was brittle with fear, betraying her true emotions.

"Fine, but stay close behind me."

Taking out one of his Sig Sauers, he moved through the bottom floor of the house with an efficiency he could only credit to Darrion's training. Eir trailed behind him, never more than two feet from his heels.

When they made it back to the entrance hall, she murmured, "Do you really think someone could be in here?"

"I'd rather not take the risk." His eyes lifted to the second level. "I'll go up first to check it's clear. You stay down here. I won't be long."

Her head jerked unsteadily. Korvain legged it up the stairs and conducted the same sweep, but found nothing out of the ordinary. He leaned over the balustrade from the mezzanine and called down to the Valkyrie.

"Come on up, but don't take too long. I'd rather check on the others sooner than later."

While Eir started rummaging through her closet for gods knew what, Korvain went down to the first level again. He peered through the curtained front window before looking at the photos standing in frames around the living room.

Bryn showed up in a lot of them, and a lot of them were from the early days. If he had to guess, he would have said the 1920s. Bryn looked great in a flapper dress. Her legs went for days. In many of the images, the girls posed with bright smiles on their lips. They all looked so different—so carefree.

Bryn especially looked younger. She didn't have the dark circles under her eyes that were a testament to the strain and stress she was living under now.

"I'm ready," Eir announced. Korvain spun around at the sound of her voice, having become so caught up in the past—so caught up in Bryn. The Valkyrie had a sports bag over one shoulder and a wooden box under the other arm. He studied the thing.

"My cloak," Eir told him when he asked.

"What's with the box?"

She looked down at the box and shrugged. "It's just what Odin gave us to keep them in."

"All the Valkyries have one?"

"Yeah."

He stored that piece of information away. "Right. Let's go." Taking the bag from her hands, he led her from the house, waiting while she locked it up again.

"We'll go to Sigrun and Astrid's place first, then Kristy's on the way back to the club."

They both faded to the address on Lime, and Korvain froze. All the fine hairs on the back of his neck were instantly set on end. Eir must have sensed the danger, too, whimpering his name. Without another thought, he pulled her behind him, calling the shadows to them.

"Stay here," he hissed. He was scaring her, he knew that, but if she were to get killed on his watch Bryn would skin him alive. Korvain willed the shadows to swathe Eir's body before stepping away from his charge and up the two steps of the stoop.

The instant he pushed the door open, he smelled the blood. His fangs throbbed and hummed, punching out through the gums of his upper jaw. Following his nose, he cautiously moved through the house, his Sig drawn, keeping his eyes swiveling for any other movement.

The coppery tang became stronger as Korvain walked toward the back of the house. On his right, against the wall, was a pool of blood, with smears disappearing under a swinging door on the left.

Standing on the other side of the jamb, he pushed open the door with his foot and stepped inside. The stench of blood and bowels was an almost tangible thing he could see and touch and feel. The color red was everywhere; on the walls, the floor, the cupboards, the fridge, the sink and splashback. Everywhere.

The tiles on the floor had once been white and black but were now red and reddish-black. On those same tiles were red smears from bodies being dragged through the larger pools of blood. He scanned the rest of the space. As they passed over the fridge again, he saw something white beneath it.

Crouching down in front of it, he reached underneath and pulled out two feathers. Both had been white, but now they were spattered with blood.

What those two feathers represented was the beginning of the end. Two in one night. Two already killed and one attempted murder. There was only one more Valkyrie who didn't have the direct protection Bryn could offer at the club, and Korvain knew time was running out.

He snarled down low in his throat. "The fucker."

Standing up, he disappeared the feathers and hauled ass out of there. When he got outside, Eir was shivering, her arms wrapped around her torso. Her eyes widened when she saw the blood on his hands.

"They're dead. Their bodies weren't there, but these were." He pulled the two feathers from his pocket and gave them to Eir. "We need to get to the last Valkyrie."

Tears began to stream down her cheeks. "Kristy," she whispered. Her fingers curled around the feathers and she looked at him. "Please. We have to save her. She's my twin. Please."

He nodded. "Take the feathers and fade back to Bryn. I need you to let her know what's happened to Sigrun and Astrid."

Without a word, she disappeared, fading back to the safety of the club. Korvain touched the karambit hidden in plain sight on his chest and faded to the last address on the list.

21

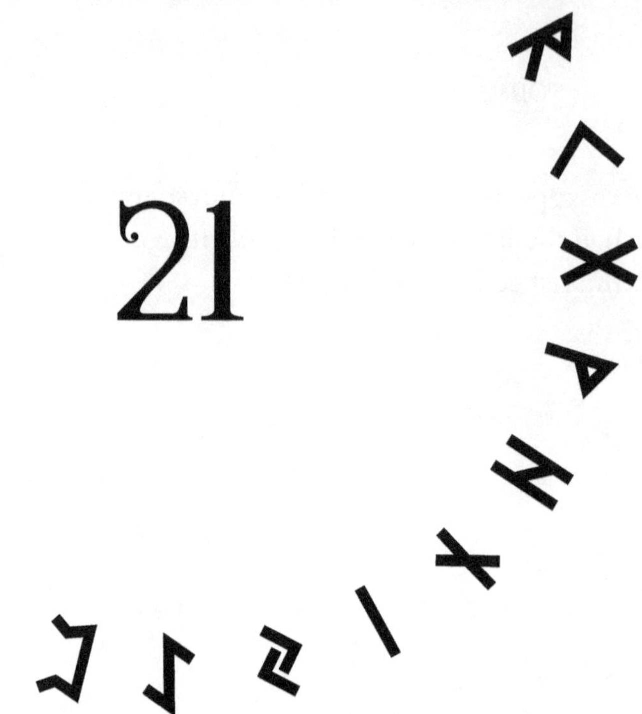

Adrian had bitten his tongue so hard he'd tasted blood in his mouth while he was talking to Darrion. Even now, he had no idea when he'd grown a pair of balls big enough to negotiate with the bastard. Nobody negotiated with Darrion.

And now he was bound to the contract. He had to kill his best friend, then kill Bryn at the club, otherwise Taer would be forced into sexual servitude like many of the other female Mares had been. Even their own mother had been one of their father's concubines.

Taer just happened to be turning all the rules upside down. But he wouldn't let that happen to her—couldn't let that happen to her. He'd worked too damn hard keeping her safe to fuck it up.

Fading back to the house, he unlocked the door and marched up to her room. He didn't want to kill Korvain, but if it was between him and his sister, Taer would win. He also knew Korvain would kill him before he managed to even get a scratch on the bastard.

He was just that good.

Adrian knew how it would play out: He would try to take out Korvain, who would, therefore, take him out. Taer would be left unprotected and Darrion would take her and force her into sexual servitude. It sounded like a hell of a lot of no-fucking-way to him.

Adrian knew he would be killed by Korvain. There was nothing he could do about that. But there was something he could do about Taer. If he made her stronger, she could survive Darrion's cruelty.

Her bedroom door was slightly ajar. Pausing, he listened to her deep, even breathing. Driven by the need to protect her, he pushed open her door and marched inside.

Taer was asleep with the blankets brushed to one side. The heat was cranked up in her room, causing beads of sweat to break out on Adrian's brow. Her dark hair was loose and splayed out around her head, a halo of inky blackness covering the pillow. She was wearing a tank top and a pair of satin boxer shorts on her narrow hips. Her ribs could clearly be seen through her tank, her hip bones poking out between the bottom of the fabric and the elastic top of her shorts.

"Tay, wake up," Adrian whispered.

She groaned and rolled over, putting her back to him, her shoulder blades and ribs pressing through her skin.

Adrian tried again. "Tay," he said in a much louder voice. "Taer, wake up!" He grabbed her by the shoulder, intending to pull her over onto her back when he was suddenly staring down the barrel of a Beretta 92 Steel.

His sister's green eyes were wide open. Adrian put his hands up in front of him in surrender. Taer blinked then lowered the weapon.

"Sorry, Ad," she said stifling a yawn. "Didn't mean to pull a gun on you."

"I never taught you to do that," he commented, watching her through narrowed eyes.

She yawned again. "Korvain taught me," she replied absently. "What did you wake me up for?"

He ignored her question. "Tay, I thought I told you not to bother him."

"I didn't!" she shot back, affronted. "He just offered up the info."

Adrian's hands balled into fists. He didn't have fucking time for this. "Whatever. Get up."

"Why?"

"Training."

She glanced at her clock. "It's like three in the morning."

"I'm aware of the time," he bit out, his irritation growing.

She lay back down again, curling over onto her side once more. "Then wake me up in three and haul me off to training then. It's too early," she mumbled.

Grabbing her arm, Adrian dragged her out of bed roughly. "Now, Taer. We train now!"

With a look of indignation on her face, she fumed, "All right! Fuck, Adrian! What's crawled up your ass?"

"Nothing," he spat back, picking up her sweatpants and throwing them at her. "Get dressed and meet me in the garage in five."

He turned and left her room, closing the door behind him. He glanced at the closed door at the end of the hallway. Was Korvain already home? Could he just go in and kill him now? It would put an end to a lot of Adrian's misery. He walked quietly along the carpet, then pressed his ear to the door and listened.

If Korvain was in there, he could simply slip inside and drive a dagger through his heart. Or maybe he could smother him in his sleep. Gods, what was he thinking? He didn't want to kill Korvain. He had to kill him, but wanting and needing to were two very different things. He would try to put it off for as long as possible. He turned quickly and walked back down the hallway. As he passed Taer's door, he could hear her grumbling to herself.

She turned up in the garage a few minutes later, dressed in loose-fitting pants and the same tank top she'd been sleeping in. Adrian dropped into a fighting position, attacking her before she was ready for him.

Blocking his attacks, she threw him off her. "Ad, what the fuck?" she snarled, shoving at the dark hair that had fallen over her face.

"Be prepared," he replied, ducking past her guard and slamming the heel of his palm against her breastbone, in between her breasts. Taer staggered backward, but righted herself by bracing her leg before she could fall.

"Watch it!" she hissed, falling into the same fighting stance Adrian had adopted, quickly putting her hair up into a ponytail. Before she was fully ready, he came at her again, and again—always finding the hole in her defenses, always taking advantage of her unpreparedness.

They sparred for hours. He ran drills fifty times until their bodies were slick with sweat. Taer called him something new each time his fist or foot connected with a part of her body. Her inventiveness with curse words really was impressive. They were both breathless, the air they dragged into their lungs tainted with Adrian's fear, Taer's anger, and their blood. She didn't question him once about why he was pushing her so hard.

And for that Adrian was thankful.

By the time sunlight was peeking through the dirt-encrusted windows along one side of the garage, Taer's torso, arms, neck and legs were beginning to bruise up. Adrian had hit her harder than he normally would have, fear driving him to toughen his sister up more quickly than he had previously been willing to do. All of his anger from the little chitchat with Darrion had thankfully drained away from his body.

Taer bent over, her hands on her knees, her breath rasping in and out of her throat. Adrian took a sip from the bottle of water in his hands and studied her. She was a good fighter, but she needed to be better. Looking up from underneath her dark lashes, she lifted a hand and motioned for the bottle.

Adrian pushed off from the workbench he was leaning on and passed it over. "You're a dick," she said after taking a long pull. Her breath was still wheezing in and out of her lungs.

"Is that all you got? You were calling me plenty of other things while we were training."

"Dick is only one syllable," she panted. "It's easier to say."

Adrian grinned despite himself and the clusterfuck he'd found himself in. "Come on. We're done. Food then rest. We'll start again at sundown."

Taer groaned, but shuffled out of the garage after him. "These bruises aren't going to be gone by tonight," she huffed.

"Suck it up, Princess. Life's hard. I'm just trying to make you harder."

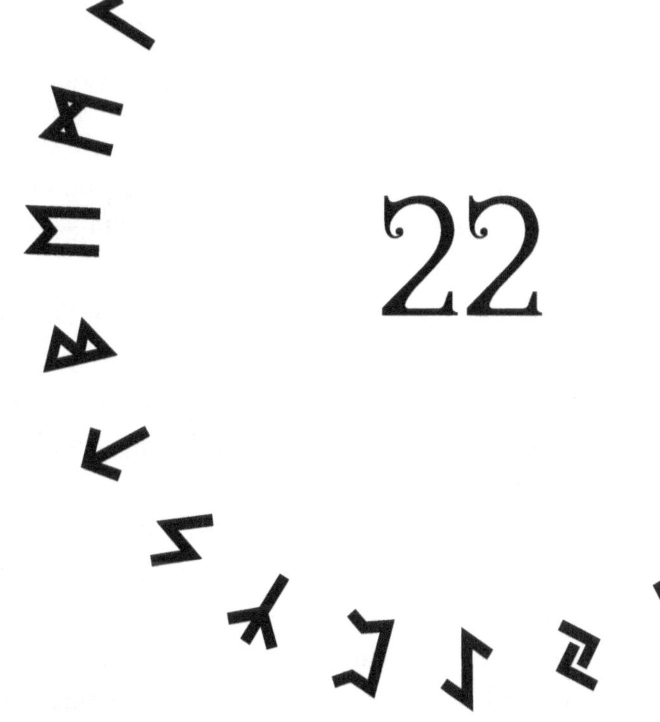

22

Frigg had been waiting for Fulla in La Perla for three-quarters of an hour, and she was incredibly close to screaming out loud. She had gone through the racks of bustiers, bras and panties, touching the silks, laces and satins. She had sampled all the perfumes and looked at all the robes, and yet Fulla hadn't returned.

Gods, she'd only sent the girl out to get her a latte while she browsed. How difficult could it actually be? She fussed with the waist of her emerald-green dress, then dropped her hand and stopped fidgeting.

Queens didn't fidget.

"My queen," Fulla said quietly from behind her. Frigg spun around to face the young woman, frowning as she did. In her hand, Fulla held up a white cup with a green logo on the side. Snatching it from her, Frigg took a sip and let the caffeine charge through her system.

"What took you so long?" she snapped impatiently.

Her handmaiden looked down. "There was a large line at the coffee house."

Frigg made a disgusted noise at the back of her throat and waved Fulla away. "Where is my money? I wish to buy something."

Frigg began to pull thousand-dollar silk kimonos and six-hundred-dollar corsets from the racks and threw them at Fulla to catch. Frigg breathed in a deep, satisfied breath. There really was nothing like spending her husband's money.

When Fulla couldn't see over the pile of lingerie in her arms, Frigg left her handmaiden to pay for her purchases and went to sit in the limo out front. Skoll stood sentry at the rear door. He opened it, allowing Frigg to slide inside the quiet, rich leather-smelling backseat. When she felt eyes on her, Frigg glanced up into the rearview mirror to see Hati staring intently back at her.

Hati's violet eyes smoldered at her. She smiled a seductive smile, biting down onto her pouty lower lip. She had had him many times before, the same way she had had Skoll many times before. Sometimes she even had them together. They were her personal guard and they would lay their lives down for hers, would do whatever she asked of them.

"You're staring, Hati," she purred, touching the part of her chest where her dress pushed her breasts up and over. His eyes darted down to her fingers and she could have sworn she heard him growl faintly.

Frigg caught movement from the corner of her eye. Fulla was coming toward the car, at least a dozen bags in her hands. Frigg glanced back at the male in the front seat.

"Later, lover," she said quickly just as Skoll opened the door for Fulla.

"What took you so long?" Frigg snapped, tossing her long hair over her shoulder.

"You had a large number of purchases, my queen. It takes time to ring them all up."

The passenger door opened and Skoll got into the car, all while Fulla rattled on.

Frigg waved her hand in the air dismissively. "Yes, yes. I don't really care." Turning her attention back to Hati, she said, "Back to the penthouse. I feel the need for a bath." She made sure to keep her eyes locked on Hati when she said the words. Turning his attention to one of the side mirrors, he smoothly pulled out into traffic.

They arrived at her Charlestown address, and Frigg waited for Skoll to open her door. She stepped out, running her hands down her dress, pushing out any wrinkles from the short drive home.

"Fulla, run upstairs and get the bath going." The girl practically jumped before hurrying off to do her bidding. Skoll pulled her purchases from the trunk of the car while Hati offered her his arm. She smiled slyly at him. He had never offered this courtesy before.

By the time they were upstairs, Skoll was placing the bags neatly on the chaise longue before backing out of the room. Fulla was still in the bathroom, monitoring the water temperature and level, while Frigg had Hati all to herself.

He was still staring at her with a desire she found so tempting. Usually it was the other way around—she would be the one to approach her guards to have her appetites sated. This was out of character for Hati, but she liked how his eyes raked over her body with such lust and longing.

He reached for her, and she smacked his hand away. Chiding him like a child, she said, "I am the one who does the touching." Frigg glanced over her shoulder. "Besides, we still have company."

Fulla chose that moment to turn the taps off. The hollow echo of the last few drops of water falling from the faucet followed her out. Her handmaiden excused herself from the room, her blue eyes never leaving Frigg's face. She knew Frigg would have no need of her to help her undress—not now Hati was with her.

Frigg sauntered away from her guard, making sure her hips swayed temptingly before demurely looking over her shoulder at him.

"I can't seem to take this dress off without some help, Hati."

She walked into the bathroom, hearing him follow. With her back still to him, she sat on the edge of the claw-foot bath and gently played with the still rippling surface of the water with her index finger. The diamonds frosting her fingers sparkled in the lights, the rainbow of colors ricocheting around the room.

When Hati's hand wrapped around the back of her neck, the pressure was just enough to make her moan with pleasure. He didn't say a word to her—he didn't have to. She slid from the lip of the tub and dropped to her knees, her fingers already reaching for the zipper of his pants.

Hati shook his head, giving her pause.

Frowning, she asked, "Are you denying me this?"

He remained silent before a smile formed on his lips. Frigg couldn't see what was so funny until he brought the blade of a knife in front of her eyes.

"What is this?" she demanded, attempting to get to her feet. Hati pressed on her neck, keeping her on her knees. She looked at her reflection in the blade, then her gaze drifted up.

Hati's face was melting away. His violet eyes gave way to pale green, his dark hair to blond. Somehow he gained another six inches and she was no longer staring at Hati. She was staring at Loki.

Loki bared his teeth at the queen of the Aesir. Her eyes were wide, her pupils dilated in fear. She knew what his appearance meant. It was death and pain and torture all wrapped up with a neat little bow.

"Loki," she gasped.

"Frigg. It's been a long time," he drawled back casually. His voice was rough from being quiet for so long. Passing as Hati had hinged on Loki remaining silent. He couldn't match the other god's voice well enough, and if his cover had been blown, his plan would have been compromised.

"What are you doing here?"

He studied her face. She wasn't stupid. Surely she'd already figured it out. "Guess."

A small line appeared between her eyes before smoothing out again. She cleared her throat in that imperious way that only she could. "You're here to kill me." She said the words without any inflection, without any emotion.

"Yes."

"I was the one to free you. I was the one who released you from your torture." Her tone rose with each word, desperation filling her slowly but surely.

He smiled benignly. "I know."

"But why?"

He laughed at her. Her ego would never let her see what she didn't want to believe. "Your husband took my wife away from me. So, I am taking his wife away from him."

It was her turn to laugh this time. "Odin is only my husband by title. He does not hold my heart."

He leered at her, sickened by her arrogance. "Nobody could

hold your heart." She recoiled as if he'd slapped her. Her eyes dropped, but when she looked up again, fire crackled and burned in her glare. "I freed you," she repeated. "You owe me."

Cocking his head to one side, Loki studied her face. "I owe you nothing."

With one swift slashing movement, the blade in his hand opened up the front of her throat. Frigg's hands flew to the wound, her fingers clutching at the place where the blade had cleaved through her flesh. Blood swelled and oozed down her hands, the trail quickening until it dripped from her forearms.

The goddess fell to the side, coughing blood, spraying it in a perfect arc around her head, a bloody halo. With his foot on her shoulder, he rolled her over onto her back and straddled her hips.

Frigg was dragging in deep, desperate breaths, gurgling noises escaping her ruined throat. With his blade tip aligned perfectly over her heart, Loki smiled at her one last time and plunged the steel through her ribs, puncturing the chest cavity. With an abrupt twist and thrust, it cut into the muscle that was responsible for so much.

When at last she lay still, Loki grabbed one of her arms and hefted her onto his shoulder. He dumped her into the nice hot bath, the water sloshing over the rim and spilling out all over the floor.

Sauntering over to the mirror, he looked at his reflection and began morphing his features into Hati's once more. When he was satisfied with his illusion, he stalked from the bathroom, walking out of the front door and into the early Boston afternoon with the queen's blood still drying on his skin.

23

Korvain faded a block away from the address on River. He didn't want to risk being seen by the god going after Kristy. Pulling the shadows around him, he legged it over to the address.

The little red-brick house was the last one on the street before it narrowed into a small walkway, opening up onto a square hemmed in by other red-brick houses that were so typical of Boston. He was closing in fast, seeing the silhouettes of people moving around behind the blinds as he passed.

The door of the last house swung open without warning and Korvain stopped. Light spilled out from the hallway, its fingers stopping just short of revealing him with his foot on the bottom step.

He recognized the god standing on the top step. It was the man who had tried to drug and kidnap Eir. Wearing a sneer on his lips, the god looked around, his eyes tracking everything before disappearing back into the house, only to reappear with a blonde-haired woman over his shoulder.

He was too late. Korvain shrugged the shadows from him just as the god faded from view. The guy had to be powerful to pull that kind of fade. Once any kind of weight was involved, fading was near impossible.

Korvain spat a nasty curse and entered the house. He'd been too late to save Kristy, but he had to know if her cloak was still there. Deep down in his gut, he knew the god had taken it with him, but that didn't stop him from checking. Climbing the stairs two at a time, he inspected every room before stalking around the bottom levels.

There was no box.

He hadn't even found any blood, or loose feathers, which he could only take as a good sign. Flicking off the last of the lights, he faded back to the club to deliver the news to Bryn.

Bryn sat back in her office chair and closed her eyes. She'd come downstairs to clear her head, to stop herself from thinking about everything that had happened to her in the last few days. Glancing at the clock, she figured Korvain and Eir wouldn't be too much longer either.

Sighing, she got started on the paperwork still begging for her attention. The buzzer being hit repeatedly finally drew Bryn's head up from the invoice she'd been looking over. Glancing sideways at the monitors, she saw Eir standing there. Bryn hit the buzzer to unlock the door and stepped into the hallway.

She felt rather than saw the other woman's distress. It hit her like an unstoppable wave crashing against her.

"Eir?" she asked, starting toward the rear door. Gods, she looked like hell. She sagged to one side suddenly, catching herself against the wall. Bryn took her by the shoulder, throwing her arm around her waist, steadying the woman. Eir's skin was white, her body trembling. In one hand she held an unzipped sports bag stuffed with clothes, and in the other, she clutched her ash box.

"Tell me what happened." Bryn led her toward her office, afraid she would pass out before they reached the elevator at the end of the hall. Taking the bag of clothes from her, Bryn pressed Eir's shoulders, forcing her into the chair. Bryn stepped back to face her, her ass resting on the lip of her desk.

Eir still clutched her cloak box firmly to her chest. The trembling hadn't gotten any better. If anything, it had gotten worse. Bryn pulled open her desk drawer and drew out a bottle of vodka.

"Here. Drink this," Bryn told the other woman, unscrewing the cap and holding the bottle out to her. She expected her to refuse, but when Eir's free hand wrapped around the glass, Bryn knew that whatever had happened was serious.

Eir placed the bottle to her lips and tipped. There was nothing graceful about what happened next. She choked, spitting the vodka back out all over herself. While she coughed, Bryn rubbed her back, murmuring softly to her.

When Eir had finally settled, Bryn crouched beside the chair. "Tell me what happened."

Eir's eyes met hers, wet and red. "Sigrun and Astrid . . . are . . ."

Fresh tears welled; Eir's body seemed to collapse under the weight of them. Her head dropped, her blonde hair raining down over her shoulders to hide her face. Bryn had a pretty good idea what the next word out of her mouth was going to be. Her spine stiffened and she stood up to pace. That was the only way she would be able to work off the angry energy battering her body.

"They're dead, aren't they?" Bryn's hands had balled into tight fists. "Eir? Tell me."

Eir's head bowed in defeat.

Bryn blinked, seeing red dots. Anger was not a strong enough word for how she was feeling. "Where's Korvain?"

"He—" Eir hiccupped. "He went to check on Kristy. He told—" Hiccup. "He told me to come back here. He told me to give you these," Eir added in a shaky voice. Bryn looked down at what Eir was offering and staggered back a step, her hand over her mouth.

Eir lowered her eyes and retracted her hand slowly, her fingers curling over the two bloody feathers lying against her palm. Bryn reached across her desk and picked up her phone, needing to hear the words from Korvain's mouth.

The thing rang for a second before Korvain's silky voice filled her ear. "Bryn."

Bryn squeezed her eyes shut, keeping the tears teetering there from falling. "Where are you?" she demanded.

"The back door."

Her eyes cut to the CCTV monitor. Korvain's imposing form seemed to step from the shadows themselves. She buzzed him in and hung up the phone. Looking at Eir, she said, "Go upstairs now. We'll figure out a safe place to put your cloak when I come up in a minute."

Eir seemed to shudder before she stood up unsteadily. Bryn followed her out of the room, watching her walk toward the elevator. With her bag on one shoulder, Eir leaned to one side looking like she would topple over at any minute.

When the elevator door had slid shut, Bryn turned and ran directly into something hard. Throwing her palms up, she dug her fingers into Korvain's hard, warm chest and felt herself beginning to fall apart. She looked into his onyx eyes, wondering—not for the first time—what it was with him that made her unravel so spectacularly.

His strong fingers cinched shut around her upper arms, his thumbs stroking softly. "Bryn, I'm—"

She pulled away from his body angrily, refusing to be seduced by his concern. "Don't say it! Don't you dare say you're sorry!" she hissed. She marched back into her office, snatching the bottle of 42 from where Eir had left it. She took a deep pull, feeling it burn down her throat and into her chest. Roughly, she wiped the back of her hand over her mouth, ignoring the shake.

Korvain kicked the door shut behind him, resting against it casually with his arms lightly folded over his muscular chest. Bryn had the strangest urge to be enveloped and held in those arms, but she shoved the feeling away.

"Eir told you then?" he asked quietly.

"Yeah, she told me. What happened? Couldn't you have saved them?" Bryn couldn't stop the sting in her voice. She was just so angry. With herself. With Odin.

He pushed off the door and stalked toward her. His huge body moved with a feline grace that seemed impossible for someone with his height and bulk. He was within touching distance now, but he kept his hands to himself.

Bastard.

"When we got there they were already dead—their bodies already taken."

She finally made herself look him in the face. His usual rough, I-don't-give-a-fuck attitude was gone. Instead, there was compassion. This only pissed her off further. She didn't need his pity. She needed him to protect her Valkyries.

In one long stride, she was in front of him, her palm raised. Korvain caught her wrist before the slap to his cheek could land.

Anger bubbled and she tried the other hand. He caught that too, stretching her arms above her head, holding her hostage.

Her pulse pounded in her ears. "Let me go," she seethed, struggling. Korvain pulled her into the heat of his body, trapping her against him. Pushing off, Bryn tried to land a kick somewhere on his body. She missed, being pushed up against the wall instead.

With her hands still held above her head, she had no choice but to breathe in his scent, to drink in the sight of him. Her body betrayed her first, heating up. Her heart rate increased and liquid heat pooled between her legs. What he had done to her in the dream was a sledgehammer to the front of her mind; she wanted his hands on her body so badly it stunned her.

Korvain's gaze intensified, zeroing in on her throat. She whimpered when he lowered his head to the base of her throat, his lips soft and warm and addictive. His fingers relaxed around her wrists, and her hands found their way to the back of his head, sliding through his short hair.

He seemed to purr at the contact, his hips possessively pressing up against hers before he pulled back slightly. She was instantly struck by how he'd felt against her; it was exactly how he'd felt in the dreams.

"I know you're angry," he murmured, his velvet-soft lips brushing against her collarbone as he spoke. She shuddered. "But there was nothing I could have done." He pulled back and looked into her eyes. "There is something else you need to know, though."

Bryn didn't like the seriousness in his eyes. She tried to push him away, needing to be apart from him to get her head together, but he kept her pinned against the wall with his hips. "I went to Kristy's house straight after I sent Eir away. I saw him."

"You saw him?" she asked, still acutely aware of her position, of how her breathing had accelerated. "You saw Odin?"

Korvain shook his head. "It wasn't Odin."

Bryn made a disgusted noise in the back of her throat. "He probably has some mindless goon doing his dirty work for him," she surmised.

Korvain pressed on. "This god, whoever he is, had Kristy over his shoulder. She looked unharmed—probably just drugged like Eir had been. He faded before I could react."

"I'm going to kill Odin for doing this, for targeting my Valkyries," she swore.

"What?" Korvain asked, finally stepping away from her body. "You don't even know it's him."

"Who else could it be?" she snapped back acidly. "He wants me back, and the only way the bastard knows how to do that is to take away everything I love, including the other Valkyries. And I won't let him get away with this again, Korvain. I just won't."

"So, you're just going to kill the All-Father?" he asked, incredulous. Korvain's disbelief needled Bryn, but when the words were spoken aloud, she could see how insane it made her seem. She knew of one way to kill Odin, but that information wasn't public knowledge. Biting the inside of her cheek, Bryn glared at Korvain.

"Bryn, we both know that's not possible."

Playing ignorant, she bit out, "And why not?"

"Because even though you say you hate him, I don't believe you truly do. Even though you say you'll kill him, the fact remains that you haven't yet." He brushed a strand of hair from her neck, revealing her tattoo. "I believe if you wanted revenge on him, we wouldn't even be discussing this right now. You'd already have your sword drawn and be on your way to Odin."

Bryn's anger went from a simmer to a rolling boil. Of course, he was right. Bryn couldn't cause harm to Odin any more than she could cause herself, or one of her Valkyries, harm. "If not Odin, then who?" she demanded, needing to blame someone.

Korvain's chest rose and fell with a heavy sigh. "I don't know. I promise you I'll do my best to find out, but that's going to take time." Bryn opened her mouth in protest, but he cut her off. "Kristy is still alive. Of that I'm sure. Let's focus on that. Think, Bryn. What's different with Kristy?"

"Nothing. Nothing is different. Whoever is behind this is going to pluck the feathers from her cloak and kill her." Odin, she thought. Odin is going to kill her.

Korvain pulled her back into his heat of his body. "No, Bryn." His voice vibrated through his chest, against her ear. Bryn had to get away from him, not sink further into the comfort he could bring, but somehow she just wasn't able to. Korvain added, "Every other kill has happened on site. This time Kristy was taken. Why?"

She leaned back to look at him, considering his question for a long moment. He was right. This was different. Why hadn't he just killed her in her home like the others? Her heart bounced into her throat when the answer came. "Gods, he's going to negotiate."

Korvain's lips thinned into a grimace, confirming her theory. "He knows he can't get the rest of you. This place is warded too well, so he has to draw you out."

The puzzle pieces were falling into place too quickly for Bryn to process. "How?" she asked softly, afraid of what he would say next.

"He'll establish contact with you somehow," Korvain said. "And the most logical way for that to happen would be by forcing Kristy to make a call to get you, or at least one of the other

Valkyries, to cooperate."

Bryn's stomach churned. She felt so helpless, hated not being able to do anything but wait for the bastard to call. She met Korvain's intense eyes. "I need to go check on Eir."

Without waiting for his response, Bryn left the office, riding the elevator up to the apartments in a daze. If Kristy was still alive, she had to get her back. There was no question about that. And if the god wanted Bryn in exchange, she would gladly give herself up. When Bryn pushed into the apartment, Eir was sitting on her love seat looking shell-shocked. Held loosely in her hands was her phone, and Bryn's hands flexed into fists at her side.

"Eir?" The Valkyrie looked up at her slowly. "Eir? What's wrong?"

Bryn's eyes fell to Eir's white-knuckle grip, fearing the worst.

"I just . . . listened to a voicemail I had. It was from Kristy."

Gods. Has he already called?

Bryn's heart was pounding hard against her ribs. Licking her suddenly dry lips, she asked, "What did it say?"

Eir's eyes began to water again, the first tear escaping down her cheek slowly. "She was excited we were going to catch a movie tomorrow night."

The knot in Bryn's stomach loosened slightly. The god hadn't made Eir's twin call yet, but she knew in her gut it would only be a matter of time, and when he did, Bryn would be ready to give him whatever he wanted.

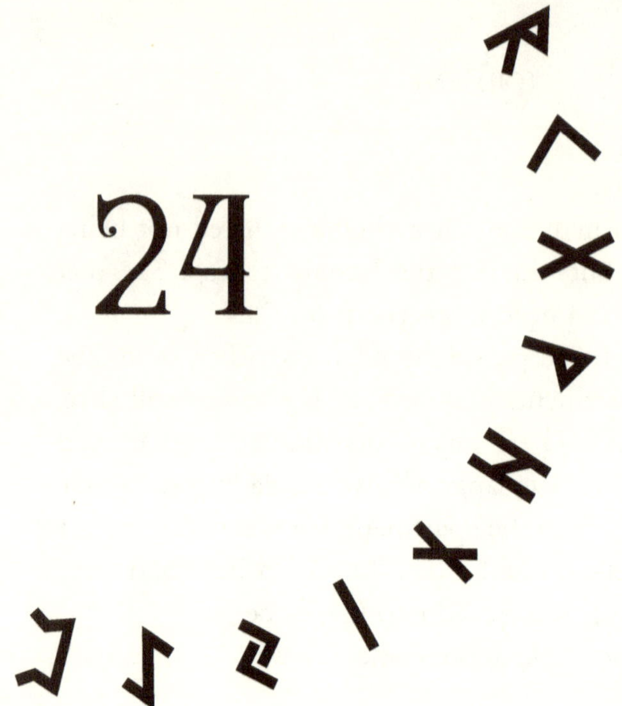

24

The doorbell to Odin's house rang, the sound booming and echoing around the marble he chose to surround himself with. Having done away with servants a century ago, he extricated himself from the powder blue Louis XV armchair in his formal living room and walked to the door.

Swinging the door wide, he took in the shaking mess of the young woman standing before him. She was a classic beauty with pale hair and Aesirean blue eyes. She was wearing a heavy looking overcoat more suited to a male than a female and her feet were bare despite the chill in the air.

"Fulla?"

Curtseying hurriedly, she gasped, "Odin—" Fulla swallowed convulsively, like whatever she wanted to say had suddenly become lodged in her throat. She shook her head and tried again. "Please, you must come."

His eyes scanned behind her. The street was quiet except for a few people ambling along in the park across the street. "Why? What's wrong?"

"Please," she cried, reaching for his hand. "You must come with me. It's the queen."

"Frigg? What's wrong with her?"

The tears that had sat in the young woman's eyes were suddenly streaming down her cheeks. With trembling hands, she pulled open the two sides of her coat and revealed what was underneath.

Odin felt cold.

Numb.

Empty.

He shifted his balance from one leg to the other, the only external sign of his uneasiness. Fulla still stood on his small stoop, her whole body shaking. Beneath the coat, her fine silk dress was drenched in fresh blood.

Even though he and Frigg were still married, they had not shared a kind word in nearly one hundred years. She had railed at him for his handling of the Valkyries, claiming he loved them more than he loved her. The whole idea was preposterous, of course. He loved his wife—he would until his dying breath, he suspected—but her jealousy knew no bounds.

The question Odin already knew the answer to stuck to the back of his tongue. He tried twice to ask what he intended to before giving up.

"Tell me," he finally said, his voice like cool steel.

"The queen . . . is . . . dead." Fulla's voice squeaked over the last word, washing away from her lips with a fresh wave of tears. She was shaking so badly now that her hand shot out and clutched at the side of his door.

He willed his legs to move. Taking Fulla by the wrist, he said, "I need to see this."

Odin faded them both to the house Frigg had demanded he buy her in the 1920s. Fulla opened the door for him, her eyes firmly fixed on the black and white tiled floor when he passed by her. Even at a time like this, the habit of subjugation was still deeply ingrained in her.

Not waiting for the handmaiden, Odin took the grand staircase to the upper floor and navigated his way to the master suite.

He had never been in there before. The room was opulent. A large French armoire took up most of the north wall, while an equally impressive canopy bed took up the east. It was drenched in rich burgundy silks, a canopy of twisted material overhead, crashing down the sides in a waterfall of color.

In the corner was a gilt three-way mirror, no doubt worshiped by his wife on a daily basis. It was true she was the goddess of love, but vanity and ego nipped eagerly at her heels.

Directly across from the bed was the door leading into the bathroom. He moved with purpose, determined to see for himself his wife's lifeless body.

Someone—Fulla he supposed—had laid Frigg out on the tile. The color had leached from her skin, but that wasn't what drew his attention. The huge unnatural smile carved into the front of her throat did. The flesh was smooth, but gaped like a mocking grin.

One hand was still caught on the lip of the tub, as if whoever had pulled her out of the water had done so hastily. He couldn't see the inside of the tub until he got a little closer. He forced himself to look at the bloodstained water. Carefully, he dipped his finger in to test the temperature.

"It's still warm," he announced, thinking aloud.

"Yes, All-Father." Fulla's answer came from behind him. Glancing over his left shoulder, he could see her pressed against the bathroom door, refusing to come in any further. Her body shook with a fine tremor, but he shouldn't have been surprised. The woman had never seen death before, and her devotion to Frigg was unwavering.

"Who found her?"

"I did," she whispered, her voice getting softer as she backed out of the room completely. "I came to tell her dinner was ready. When she didn't reply straight away, I entered the bathroom to find her submerged."

"And you pulled her free, too?"

"Yes."

"Did you leave her alone while she bathed, Fulla?" She was still fully dressed, which certainly indicated Fulla hadn't been with her.

"I . . . I . . ."

"She was not alone," a male voice replied from behind the handmaiden. Odin dragged his eyes off Fulla and turned his attention to one of Frigg's security guards. He couldn't remember if the man was Skoll or Hati.

"Which one are you again?" he demanded offhandedly. The other man's gray eyes clouded over with rage. "Skoll."

"Who was with her?"

"Hati."

Odin's skin began to itch. "Why?"

Skoll met his gaze full on, unflinchingly. "Do I really need to spell that out for you?"

Odin's chest rose and fell at the confirmation of his wife's infidelity. He hadn't wanted to believe the rumors, but perhaps burying his head in the sand hadn't been the best thing to do. He turned back around to the queen's body and crouched beside her head.

Frigg had always accused him of fucking his Valkyries, but he had never been unfaithful—not once. But she had. He wanted to resurrect her so he could kill her again, but that was beyond even his power.

He cranked his head back around to Skoll. "Where is the bastard?"

Odin's body felt like it was burning up from the inside. His fingers itched to tear Hati's skin from his bones, to boil the motherfucker's organs and feed them to his dogs. He wanted revenge. And there was nothing more dangerous than a god with revenge on his mind.

"I don't know. I can't find him." Skoll's voice was flat, irreverent.

"Well find him!" Odin roared, standing up to his full height, and brushing past Fulla and into the bedroom. Getting right up into the other guy's face, he shouted, "Find him and bring him to me!"

Skoll's lips pressed together, but he bowed slightly and left the room. Odin squeezed his hands into tight fists, his knuckles bulging. The desire to lash out was irresistible. With a roar, he punched out the glass in the framed mirror. The cacophony of shattering glass filled his ears—a tremendous reverberation echoing his outpouring of anger mingled with grief and disbelief. Sharp shards rained down on him, slicing his flesh. Gentle sobs finally broke through his anger.

Fulla was whimpering in the corner, as far away from him as she could get without physically leaving the room. She was too shaken to even remain standing. Odin was still vibrating with rage. Was it the news of her death, seeing Frigg's body, or learning of her infidelity that enraged him so? Perhaps it was a combination of all three that left him pissed off and ready to destroy the next person who spoke out of turn to him. Nobody did this to him.

Nobody.

Walking back into the bathroom, Odin collapsed onto the ground beside Frigg, his smoking jacket fanning out around his body, the knees of his silk pants drawing in the moisture almost instantly. He looked at his beautiful wife and the red slash across her throat, and began to weep for all he had lost.

He didn't know how long he stayed like that, but when he heard the whisper of footsteps on carpet, he lifted his head slowly and looked to the doorway leading into the bedroom, feeling the true weight of his grief.

Skoll was back—a grim look on his hard face. He looked at Odin. "I found him in his room, a hole blown in the back of his skull. It looks as if he killed her and then put the gun in his mouth and killed himself."

Odin's eyes traveled back to Frigg for a moment before fixing on the other male. "Why? Why would he kill her?"

"I don't know," Skoll replied, his voice rough. "Perhaps she had taken another lover and he was jealous."

Another lover? How many had his darling wife had? Whatever the reason, though, she was now dead and she had to be given the proper burial. Odin scooped her up in his arms, looking down at the woman he had shared so much of his life with.

Frowning, he gently repositioned Frigg's body on the tile and pulled a stack of wet, bloodied towels out from under the tub. Slowly, he pulled a feather free of the pile.

Odin's blood ran cold. It was one of his Valkyrie's feathers, which meant it hadn't been Hati who had killed Frigg.

It was Loki.

He stood up unsteadily, his calm demeanor melting away, his wife's body forgotten. She was already dead, and he would be, too, if he didn't warn Bryn.

25

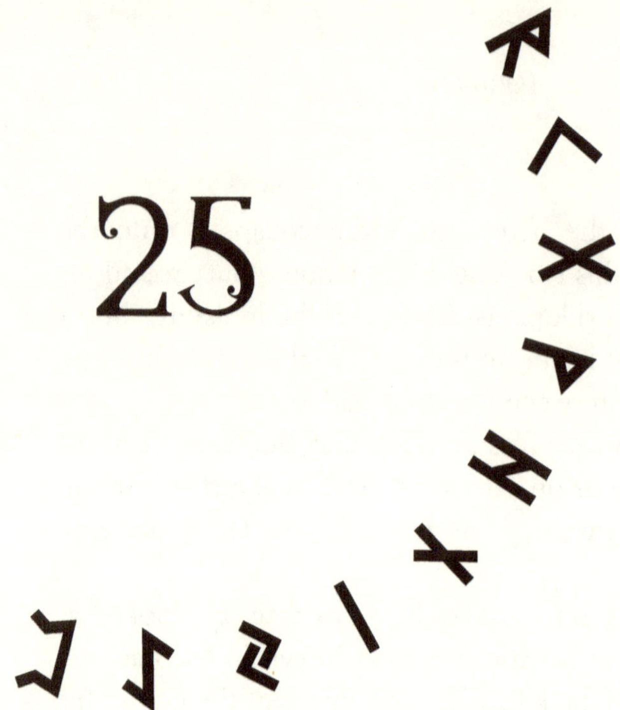

oki's blood was still pumping furiously through his veins, his euphoric high making his head swim. He had taken two, and now he had taken a third. He had to make a big enough statement to draw both Bryn and her Mare out into the open. He needed them to come to him. Looking at the Valkyrie laid out on his bed, he knew she would be the perfect bait.

Using a length of rope he'd bought from a hardware store, he bound her wrists and ankles then left her on the bed to come around. She would be unable to fade though. He made sure to top up the cocktail of drugs he was now using to keep the Valkyries sedated and pliant. Loki stepped into the bathroom, stripping off his bloodstained clothes and getting under the spray in the shower.

He grinned to himself. Two kills in one night plus a kidnapping. Odin wouldn't know what had hit him. After washing away the gore, he strode back into the room and over to the ash box containing the Valkyrie's feather cloak. He was tempted to kill her right then and there, but he stayed his hand. The bigger plan had been put into motion and he needed it to run smoothly.

Approaching the bed, he rifled through the woman's pockets until he found her phone. Thumbing through the recently dialed numbers, he found the one he was looking for. Hitting the green button, he held the device to his ear.

"Hello?" Brynhildr's voice was cautious.

"Brynhildr," he purred. "Remember me?"

There was silence on the other end for a heartbeat before her enraged response came. "Who is this?"

Loki laughed at her question, brushing it aside. "I'm hurt you don't remember me, Bryn. I have not been around for a while, but was recently . . . freed."

A few beats of silence were interrupted by her hissed response. "Loki?"

"Who else?"

There was silence on the other end of the phone, and Loki took delight in it. When Bryn finally spoke again, she sounded like she was ready to strangle someone.

"Where is she?"

Ignoring her question, he said, "I have killed four of your Valkyries, Brynhildr. I would have had five if your Mare hadn't stepped in." More silence. Loki glanced down at the blonde beauty trussed up on his bed like a suckling pig. She was still unconscious, her lush lips parted just a little. Where the needle had gone in, there was a crust of dried blood on the surface of her alabaster skin. "I do so wish to play with her," he teased, enjoying how Bryn's breathing increased in intensity. With a chuckle, he added, "She's safe as long as you cooperate."

"What. Do. You. Want?" She bit the words out.

So easy, he thought. "You, Brynhildr."

There was a low malevolent noise, but it was masculine, animalistic, and Loki knew who was listening in. He laughed. "Have I ruffled a few feathers?" he purred.

The Mare's voice resonated with menace through the phone—not the blinding rage Loki had anticipated. "I'm going to tear you apart with my bare hands. I'm going to—"

Loki did not wish to hear any more threats. "Bring him to heel, Brynhildr."

There was a tense but muffled conversation on the other end. "How can I get Kristy back, Loki," Bryn eventually said.

"Listen, and listen well. I have a question for you. How much do you value your life? Would you, oh, I don't know . . . give it up for one of your Valkyries?"

A trickled growl accompanied her answer. "Yes."

Loki smiled into the receiver. "Right answer. I propose a trade then. Your life for this Valkyrie's."

"No!" boomed the Mare as Bryn whispered, "Deal," into the phone. There was a loud crash in the background that faded quickly as if shut behind a door.

"When? How?" Bryn asked.

He laughed again. "I'll call again with the information you need. Bye-bye."

Loki hung up the phone and pocketed it. Throwing his head back, he laughed. He was going to get his revenge, and he would crush all of Odin's beloved in the process.

All the parts of his plan were coming together, but there was still one more blow to come for Odin.

Bryn hit the end call button and dropped the phone onto the couch. It had been Loki all along. She knew about what had happened between him and Odin, of course. She'd been warned to stay away from him, too. She could feel Korvain at her back and she spun around to face him, suddenly remembering what Loki had called him. Backing up a few steps, she put some distance between them. If what Loki had said was true, if he was a Mare, she hadn't just been fantasizing about fucking one of the most feared creatures in all of the Nine Worlds, but also a creature that shouldn't technically exist.

"You aren't going to him," Korvain snarled, his hands running through his short hair.

She gave him a dark look. "You don't get a say in this."

He was suddenly in front of her, his hands fisted tightly at his side. "You can't stop me from fighting for you," he hissed. She looked up into his dark eyes, seeing the shadows move there. The raw power beating off his body called to a deep part of her. She shook her head, fighting the feelings she was developing for him.

"Is what he said true?" She had to know. "Why didn't you tell me you were a Mare?"

His expression turned antagonistic. "Yeah, that would have gone down real well, wouldn't it? Or have you forgotten there's a kill-on-sight order on any Mare found in the general population?"

She was more than aware of it. She had an intimate knowledge of that fact. "That was a thousand years ago. There aren't any Mares left—not really. They're too inbred with the light elves."

He gave her a mocking look. "Thanks for the recap on the history of my species. The only reason we were hunted is because your All-Father decided he didn't like us."

"No! The reason he hunted you was because you were hunting us!"

He got up in her face, so close she could feel his roiling rage. "All we wanted was our independence." The words hissed out from between his clenched teeth, and Bryn took a step back from him. Running a hand through his hair, he began to pace, wearing holes in her carpet. "So, now you know. What are you going to do about it?" he snapped back acidly.

Bryn's hand moved instinctively to her neck tattoo.

She should have killed him right there and then, but when she thought about hurting him, her eyes inexplicably began to well with tears. Those tears joined an unimaginable throb in the center of her chest. The thought of hurting him . . . hurt her.

"If you're not going to kill me, you're going to let me help you. And I'm going to show you why."

Before she could protest, he hit the light switch behind him, plunging the immediate area into darkness. The only source of light was a soft golden strip shining through the kitchen from the hall.

"Korvain, what are you doing?" She could see him standing in front of her, his wide shoulders and muscular chest backlit.

"Proving something to you," he said fiercely. And then just like that, he was gone. Bryn blinked and looked around her living room.

"Korvain?" she asked, eyes still searching. She walked around the living room, checking behind the couches even though that was a stupid thing to do. "Where are you?"

Something hard and warm gripped her wrist and she was spun around so quickly that she lost her footing. The unseen force caught her other wrist and panic bloomed. She thrashed against the invisible bonds, kicking out her legs wildly, struggling to break free.

She looked over her shoulder toward the hallway. Eir had gone to bed hours ago, but she could still scream for her help. Bryn opened her mouth, her lungs filling with air when something was thrown over her mouth, too. A hand.

"Shh." Korvain's husky voice filled her ear. She could feel the heat of his body against her cheek. She blinked and he was standing in front of her again. Shadows seemed to be flowing off his shoulders like water, falling in sheets from his body.

Her heart went from simply pounding to jackhammering in her chest. He wasn't just a Mare. He was a Walker—a legendary Shadow Walker. They were believed to have been completely wiped out under Odin's orders and under Bryn's own golden blade.

She licked her lips, her mouth suddenly dry. He released her arms and she took a trembling step back. She'd thought he was dangerous before. Now she knew better. He was lethal.

He was looking at her with such intensity—like he could see deep down into her soul with those black as pitch eyes. "Still think I'm just a Mare?" His voice caused her to shiver. As it caressed her skin, she felt all of its sharp edges, like thousands of shards of glass.

She licked her lips again. "*Morier*," she whispered, fear making her breath hitch, adrenaline dumping into her bloodstream.

The snarl pushing past his bared teeth was frightening and Bryn's heart kicked under her ribs, upping the tempo. "Are you scared of me now?"

She thought about that for a second. She was experiencing a reaction that had been pummeled into her by Odin himself. During her time in his army, she had killed Shadow Walkers under his order, not once stopping to think about the reasons why. So was she afraid of Walkers? Yes. She had seen what they were capable of, how ruthless they were when they killed. They were the trained assassins who took out countless numbers of the Aesir in their fight for independence.

But was she afraid of Korvain?

She shook her head slowly. "No."

"I'm a Shadow Walker, Bryn. I'm also the last pure-blooded Mare in existence. I can disappear like that," he snapped his fingers in front of her face. "I can get inside your head, alter your perceptions, feed on your fears." He laughed, a short, sharp sound. "I can even make you feel things you don't want to feel." He stalked away from her, rolling his shoulders and neck as if working out a kink.

When he finally turned back around, he pinned her in place with his dark eyes. "I'm the guy you want on your team."

She shook her head. "No. Kristy is my responsibility, nobody else's."

"Dammit, Bryn!" he roared, crossing the room and gripping her by the upper arms. "Why won't you let me help you?"

This close, her nostrils were filled with his spicy scent. His chest was heaving up and down, his lungs working like a bellows under his ribs. She could see the points of his fangs from beneath his upper lip and her mind instantly turned to sex. Closing her eyes, she turned her head away from him, desperately trying to stop his scent permanently embedding in her memory.

"This is my own battle," she murmured. "And I can handle it on my own."

26

Eir rolled over onto her back. As the last vestiges of sleep slipped free of her mind, she tried to think what had woken her. She lay there for a moment, just listening to Bryn's apartment. It didn't make noises like her house in Beacon Hill did.

She remembered hating the noises it made when she'd first moved in back in the 1920s. Everything had changed for them so quickly that they were all left floundering, scrambling to find themselves, to establish new lives.

Kara had been banished and Bryn had learned the awful truth about her parents. Bryn had left Odin to care for Kara, and without Bryn there to hold them all together, eventually they had all left the All-Father.

Now they were starting to come back together. She sighed and moved over onto her side. She'd forgotten how good it felt to be with her sisters. She'd forgotten the peace she felt when she was with them.

Raised voices from the living room broke apart her silent thoughts. Sliding off the mattress, she padded to the door and opened it just a little. The hallway light was still on, blinding her for a moment before her eyes adjusted.

"You have to tell her," Korvain commanded. Eir could hear the anger in his voice, but she could also hear his compassion. She wouldn't have thought a man like that knew what compassion was, but she suspected that where Bryn was concerned he had all the compassion in the world.

"Don't tell me what to do. I swore I'd protect them all," Bryn hissed in reply. "She has a right to know. It's her sister."

Eir could hear Bryn pacing, could see her shadow tracking back and forth along the wall. Her shadow hand ran through her hair. "By blood, yeah, but by circumstance she's mine. Besides, Loki doesn't want Eir. He wants me."

Eir stumbled back from the doorway, the words bombarding her until she tripped and fell in a heap on the floor. Her sister. Her sister had been taken. By Loki. Her hands started to tremble and the nurse in her recognized the effects of shock.

"Fine. If you won't tell her, I will," Korvain warned. There was a dangerous edge in his voice, instantly making Eir's heart beat faster in her chest. It was her fight-or-flight reaction, and if she'd been face to face with him, she would have chosen flight in a heartbeat.

"No!" Bryn yelled, closer this time. "I don't even know what you're still doing here, morier," Bryn hissed. "I think you should leave."

"I'm not leaving, Cupcake, so get used to it."

"Cupcake? Who the fuck do you think you're calling Cupcake?" Eir felt the air quiver with magic when Bryn drew her sword. "I suggest you get out of here, Korvain."

There was a beat of silence. "Bryn, be reasonable," Korvain said in a deceptively soft voice. "Put your sword away so we can talk about this."

"I'm done talking. Get. Out."

"You need me." He bit the words out, barely restraining his anger and irritation.

She made a disgusted noise at the back of her throat. "Like a hole in the head. Now get out of my apartment, out of my club, out of my life, or so help me, I will strike you down where you stand."

"You don't mean that, Bryn," he said, attempting to pacify her.

"Leave, Korvain. Now."

Eir waited to see who would crumble first. The slamming front door gave her the answer. She sat there shivering, digesting what she'd heard. Korvain was a Walker. Bryn had called him *morier*. Now that she knew, she wondered how she'd not seen it before.

Hushed footsteps began down the hallway. Eir looked for a way to pull herself up when the door opened, spilling light into her darkened room.

Bryn was shaking, her confrontation with Korvain still affecting her, but her expression softened when she saw Eir on the floor. "Are you all right?"

Eir blinked up at the other woman, her teeth chattering. "Korvain i-i-is a W-walker?" she managed to spit out.

Bryn frowned as she helped Eir to her feet. "You're shivering. Why?"

Eir met the other Valkyrie's gaze, letting her see the truth.

"Gods, you overheard everything, didn't you?"

Eir's head bobbed unsteadily. "G-g-going into sh-shock. Wish I c-could heal m-m-myself," she replied, managing a shaky smile.

Bryn took her elbow and led her back to the bed. Gently, she folded Eir back under the sheets, motioning for her to move over a little.

To Eir's amazement, Bryn slid in beside her, curling her body around her own to share the warmth.

"I'm sorry you had to hear that," Bryn murmured after Eir's body stopped shaking.

"Were you going to tell me?"

"After I got Kristy back, yeah."

"But Korvain didn't agree with you?"

"Korvain," Bryn spat, stretching out onto her back. "Korvain lied to me." "How?"

Bryn picked at her nails, avoiding eye contact. "He just did. Just like every other male in this world."

Bryn had needed this. Eir was a healer—whether actively or a passively, she was still a healer—and just being close to her had soothed Bryn. Her soul just couldn't take it anymore. Korvain had lied about who he was, about what he was, about what he could do. And she had fallen for it all.

Hell, she'd almost fallen for him.

Almost? No, she had gone past the point of no return.

She had fallen for him.

She now wanted to know if the dreams were real, or whether he had simply engineered them. They had felt real to her, and that was what scared her. What if he had created those illusions? If he hadn't stopped them, she would have given herself to him completely.

She blew out a frustrated breath. "Lies are what brought us

here to the human realm."

Eir murmured her agreement against the pillow. "I remember."

"Yeah," Bryn replied bitterly. "So do I."

Bryn had been with Odin for nearly a year. Every day, she had begged him to be allowed to go see her parents. And every day, he had denied her.

"Do you remember the oath you took, Brynhildr?" he asked, looking stern—looking like her father would have.

Bryn let out a sigh. "Obey you in everything."

"I don't want you to go and see your parents."

"Why not? I want to see Mother and Father again. I miss them."

Odin cupped her chin and forced her to look into his eyes. The pale green one was compassionate. The black obsidian was not. It still made her uncomfortable to look upon it.

"Although only a year has passed for you here, ten have passed in the human realm. Your parents have passed away. They are with Hel now."

Angrily, she shook her head. "No! You lie. That cannot be true. It has only been a year!"

Odin looked affronted. "You don't believe me, your All-Father?"

"No!" she cried. "I won't believe it until I see it with my own eyes."

The air began to crackle and spark. Bryn rubbed her arms, her eyes still not leaving Odin's face.

"Willful girl," he boomed. "You won't rest until you see it for yourself, will you?"

Angrily, she shook her head.

"Fine!" he replied, throwing his hands up. "I will take you down to the humans for an hour and you will see for yourself I have not lied."

Odin had taken Bryn down to her old village, and she had hardly recognized it. The port was in the same place, but everything looked weathered and dull. The grass that had grown close to shore was dead and brown. Even the houses seemed to feel the weight of the years. According to Odin, ten years had passed, but it seemed as if more time had disappeared.

Odin followed at her heel, shadowing her every move. At first, it didn't bother her, but as they moved closer to her old house, she turned to him.

"Odin, can I have a minute alone, please?"

He studied her face for a long time before bowing and retreating a few steps to give her the space she so desperately craved. Bryn walked the rest of the way up her old street until she was face to face with the house she'd grown up in.

She couldn't believe her parents were gone until she saw it for herself. Raising her fist, she knocked on the door. When it opened, a young woman Bryn recognized from the village stood there. Her belly was swollen with child, her hand resting protectively against the new life.

She frowned at Bryn. "Can I help you?"

Bryn knew this woman . . . at least she thought she knew this woman. "Ingrid?"

The woman leaned forward to look at Bryn's face more closely. Recognition lit up her blue eyes. "Brynhildr?"

"Bryn," she corrected. "Did my parents rent out my old room to you?" she asked, looking over the other woman's shoulder and into the house.

"No, Bryn, they didn't."

Bryn looked at the other woman again and laughed. "Well, where are they then?"

Ingrid turned around when someone spoke behind her. She stepped out of the way and Davin, the boy Bryn used to have a crush on, filled the doorway. His broad shoulders filled the space, his forearms and biceps thick with muscle. No doubt he was a fisherman now, too.

"Davin, where are my parents?" she asked, getting a sinking feeling down low in her stomach. Davin stared at her with pity in his eyes.

"Brynhildr—" he began.

"Bryn," she replied out of habit.

"Bryn, your parents are dead."

Bryn heard the words, watched them fall from Davin's mouth, yet she couldn't believe them for herself. Her head began to shake furiously, tears escaping her eyes.

"No," she whispered.

"Bryn, they were killed after you were taken away. I saw it happen. A man with one black glass eye came to their house in the middle of the night with two wolves. He set the beasts on them both."

More tears. They burned as they rolled down her cheeks. But still she refused to believe the words. "No."

"I saw it myself. I was coming home from the tavern when I heard their screams. The wolves dragged their bodies out into the street for everyone to see in the morning. It was a message from the gods."

Bryn noticed Davin's hand went to the stone attached to a leather thong around his neck. The rune for protection was carved into it.

"We began to make more sacrifices to them, to appease them. We didn't want any other people in the village killed. I heard about a year afterward that some other families in the next few villages were also made examples of. Each time, a man and a woman were killed and their bodies were left out for the village to see. It only happened to the ones whose daughters had left the house unmarried.

"Everyone was scared—they still are. Now, daughters are not allowed to leave the house until they are married, and even then some parents don't let their daughters leave until they are with child. They know the gods would not strike down a woman carrying a new life."

Bryn stumbled away from the doorway, bile burning up her throat. It sickened her to know that Odin had killed her parents, and probably the parents of every other Valkyrie he had since brought into the fold.

She vomited up the contents of her stomach in front of her parents' house before running away down the street. Odin caught her—of course—and demanded to know what was wrong. She told him everything and he didn't deny it.

"Why?" she cried. "Why would you do that?"

"I am your father now and you are a goddess. You are immortal, and those people were only humans."

Bryn shook off the memories with a shudder. Even after all these years, she hadn't forgiven Odin for the part he had played in destroying her life. And she knew deep down in her heart that she would never be able to forgive him either.

Not ever.

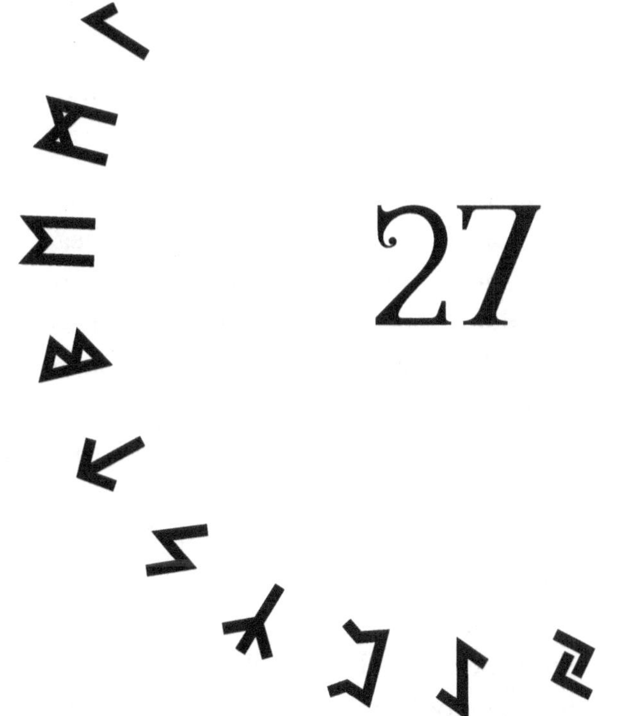

27

Korvain faded back to his house, rematerializing on the front steps when he heard a cry of pain coming from the garage behind the house. He peered around the corner, seeing the place lit up. Slipping off the porch, Korvain strolled up to the garage and pushed open the door.

Aggression, anger, determination and . . . fear tainted the air, stinging his nostrils. Adrian glanced up at his arrival and the air seemed to thicken. Korvain's best friend stared openly at him, a series of undecipherable emotions flashing in his eyes, making Korvain uneasy.

Adrian only dropped his defensive stance for a second, but that was all the time Taer needed. Taking advantage of his distraction, Taer knocked Adrian's practice blade from his grasp with a precise strike to the back of his hand. Adrian sucked in a hiss of pain, staggering back a step and clutching his injury.

Advancing on him, Taer swept his legs out from underneath

him, sending him crashing to the mats. A moment later, her weapon was positioned against his heart. Adrian blinked up at her, shock widening his eyes. Taer's tense body relaxed then, and she stepped back, lowering her weapon—tip pointing at the ground. Korvain couldn't see it, but knew she'd have a huge shit-eating grin on her face.

Korvain laughed out loud just picturing it. The noise startled Taer, who spun around and brought her weapon to the ready again. When she saw it was him, her face turned red and her gaze dropped to the floor.

"Excuse me," she muttered, placing her weapon back into the rack on the back wall and fading in front of his eyes. When Korvain looked back at Adrian, his friend was glaring.

"What was that about?" Adrian demanded harshly, stashing his practice blade next to Taer's. Adrian's clear hostility set the alarm bells ringing. Had Taer told him about what had happened between them?

"Beats me," he replied with a casual shrug.

Adrian's cool green eyes scrutinized him for a long minute before he turned away, scooping the rest of the sparring equipment up off the ground. That same uneasy feeling as before came over Korvain.

"Want to go out and play some pool or something tonight?" Korvain asked, clapping his best friend on the shoulder. He had to take his mind off Bryn's refusal to see things his way.

Adrian flinched away from the contact and Korvain noticed the lines branching out from around his eyes and mouth. He looked . . . strained, like an enormous pressure was weighing down on his shoulders.

That was when the thought hit him.

"He's done it, hasn't he?" Korvain asked, his voice flat and hollow sounding. If Korvain knew Darrion, the bastard had made it impossible for his best friend to refuse the contract.

Adrian dropped his gaze, unable to maintain eye contact. "I can feel his will working on me right now," he confessed.

"Fuck," Korvain said, lacing his fingers behind his neck and staring up at the ceiling, his mind working.

That was what happened when it came to an assignment. If Adrian had agreed to the terms put forth by Darrion, Darrion's blood would begin to work within him. His will would push against Ad's mind. It would start off as gentle whispers—a simple hushed breath that could be easily ignored—but as time wore on, the voice would get louder and louder until the only way to silence it would be by completing the assignment.

"I didn't want this, my brother," Adrian said. There was defeat in his voice—such defeat that it made Korvain's chest ache for him.

Korvain rested a hand on Adrian's shoulder, gripping it so he would finally look him in the eyes. "I know."

Adrian tilted his head in a jerking movement, his eyes closing for a moment then reopening. The compulsion.

"You all right, my brother?"

"Darrion's blood is strong. The compulsion is working quickly, but I think that's because I'm standing right beside you." He repeated the process; his head jerking, his eyes closing then reopening. When his pained eyes met Korvain's face again, he asked, "Is this what it's like for you? Do you feel his will so strongly?"

Korvain had never felt Darrion's will. The truth was his pure blood had burned through Darrion's compulsion almost as soon as the ink had dried on his tattoo. But Darrion didn't know that, and neither did Adrian.

"Yeah."

Adrian's head dropped, his chin touching his chest. "How can you stand it?" he whispered.

Korvain shrugged one shoulder. Up. Down. Slowly. "I don't wait to kill my mark. I just kill them." It sounded logical and easy, but for Adrian, it wasn't so simple. "What did he threaten you with? Adding years to your contract? Indefinite servitude?"

Adrian's eyes were suddenly blazing with rage and Korvain knew.

"Fuck," he cursed again, rubbing both of his palms over the top of his head while his fingers remained laced together. "Taer?" he asked, just to torture himself further.

Adrian's head jerked up and down. "He said he'd make her the guild whore."

"Motherfucker."

"*After* he'd had his fill of her." Adrian's words came out from between gritted teeth. Korvain wanted to punch something repeatedly—namely Darrion—for dragging Taer into this situation.

And he knew, he knew, he could have prevented it all by simply killing Bryn. Gods, he felt sick to his stomach even thinking about it.

"What am I supposed to do, Korvain? I don't want to kill you, but I can't let Darrion have my little sis either."

Korvain laughed at the other Mare. "What makes you think you could have succeeded in killing me anyway?"

This made Adrian grin, but the smile didn't reach his eyes. "Call it wishful thinking." He sighed and ran a hand through his shaggy hair. "Gods, there has to be a way out of this," he said.

When the idea struck Korvain, he let it sit there at the front of his mind for a moment—not touching it yet, just staring at it—contemplating it.

"Any ideas?" Adrian asked, doing his best to wear grooves into the sparring mats beneath his feet as he paced like a caged tiger.

"Maybe, but I don't know how we could do it." Killing Darrion seemed to be the most logical thing to do, but Korvain could see at least two potential problems already.

Problem One: When their tattoos were inked, they had sworn an oath not to take their master's life. Neither Korvain, nor Adrian, nor any other Walker in their guild could kill Darrion.

Problem Two: Whoever did kill him would become the new guild master. Whoever killed him would inherit all the assassins and all the territory Darrion had amassed—and Darrion had amassed a fuckload since taking over nearly five hundred years ago.

Having a guild master that powerful and well stocked was dangerous. Darrion might have sociopathic tendencies, but he knew his limitations. He was intelligent. He understood how guilds worked—probably because he had been in one since he was a child.

"What's going through that head of yours, my brother?"

Korvain looked at his best friend and smiled. "Trying to figure out how to do the impossible."

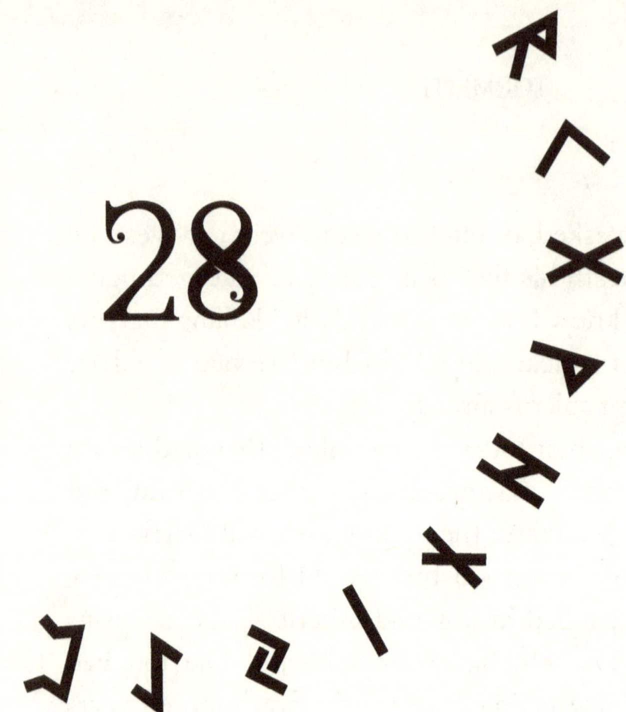

28

Eir was sitting on the couch in the living room, trying to figure out a way to get Kristy. Bryn had said she'd had a headache and would try to sleep it off before Loki called back with further instructions, leaving Eir to let the guilt eat at her.

Eir envied Bryn. She wished she could have forced her brain to stop so she could get some rest, but it didn't work that way. The knowledge that her twin had been taken by a psychopathic god did laps around her head, cutting deeper and deeper with each revolution.

She knew Bryn would take responsibility for getting her back, but Eir couldn't allow it. How could she when Kristy was her sister, her twin? She couldn't ask Bryn to risk her life.

She had given up enough already.

So, Eir did the only thing she could while they waited. She paced the living room floor because it was impossible to sleep knowing

Kristy was suffering. Anxiety stretched out inside her, settling in for the long haul even though her body cried out for rest.

In fact, the only way she could sleep now was if she had some anti-anxiety drugs to calm her down. Eir paused mid-step, a plan forming in her mind. She let out a breath and started toward Bryn's bedroom at the end of the hall, listening through the door for any movement.

Satisfied the other Valkyrie wouldn't be waking anytime soon, Eir retreated to her bedroom, closing the door behind her and began rifling through the hastily packed bag she had brought with her. After pulling nearly all of the contents out, she finally found what she was looking for.

She pulled the bottle of Valium with her name typed on the label all the way out, staring at it. She didn't use the drug often—just when she'd worked a particularly horrible shift and her palms were bothering her. It took a lot of energy to heal people and the knock-on effect it had on her was insomnia.

Convinced this was the best course of action, Eir walked back out into the kitchen to find a spoon when a shrill buzzing interrupted her thoughts. Near the door, there was a video screen next to a small numerical pad. Slipping the spoon into her cardigan pocket, she walked over to the screen. Looking the system over, she pressed a button with a green camera on it and the screen lit up.

Eir was startled to see Odin waiting at what appeared to be the back door of the club. With a galloping pulse, Eir tried to remember the last time she'd seen the All-Father. It must have been nearly a century ago. Biting her lip, she pressed another button that unlocked the door and went down to meet him. Riding down in the elevator, Eir's stomach flipped nervously. What was she going to say to him? What could he possibly have to say to her?

The car slid to a smooth stop. The doors opened lazily, letting Eir see that Odin was standing just inside the closed door. She was used to seeing him all powerful—perfect clothes, perfect face, perfect composure—but he was dressed in nothing more than striped pajamas, a smoking jacket cinched tightly at the waist and soft slippers.

"All-Father?" she asked softly, her arms wrapping around her stomach.

"Eir?" he asked, his eyes a little unfocused. "What are you doing here?"

She hugged herself a little tighter. "Bryn invited me to stay."

Did he know about the abduction attempt?

Did Bryn keep in regular contact with him?

"I need to see Bryn," he said.

"Okay." She turned back around to lead him down the hall, feeling his power wash over her. Even after all these years and after the Fall, he still had so much power over her body.

As soon as the doors of the elevator slid shut, a musty, metallic scent filled the space. She looked at Odin from the corner of her eye, noting the way his shoulders hung. Defeated. That was the word that came to mind.

The doors opened slowly onto the upper levels. Odin held out his arm to allow her to go first, and she quickly stepped out of the confining space. Odin followed at her back, but his movements seemed sluggish.

"I'll go wake Bryn," she murmured, closing the door of the apartment behind him.

"No," he said softly. "Please. I'll do it."

Eir didn't know whether that was such a good idea, but she shrugged and pointed out Bryn's door. Retreating back to her room, Eir sat down in the chair and popped the lid on the bottle of Valium. With shaking hands, she pulled out six tablets and placed them on the desk. With the back of the spoon she'd taken from the kitchen, she began crushing the circular blue tablets into a fine powder.

Admittedly, she didn't know how many it would take to render Bryn unconscious, so she was erring on the side of more rather than less. Eir felt the tears sitting in the corners of her eyes as she worked. She didn't want to do this to her friend, but she really had no other choice. In fact, every bone in her healing body was screaming at her to stop and think about her actions, but she shoved away all the doubts and focused on her twin.

She'd decided she would drug Bryn after Loki called back with the specifics of where to meet for the exchange. Eir would take her cloak and give herself up if her sister was freed. If that didn't work, well, she didn't want to think about what would happen.

Bryn sucked in a deep breath, waking suddenly. She blinked, scrubbing a hand down her face to wake herself up. When she was finally able to focus on the room, her eyes narrowed at the figure standing near the door.

"How did you get in here?" she snapped viciously.

Odin stepped forward, palms outstretched like he was pleading with her.

"Who let you in here?" she snarled again, throwing her legs over the side of the bed, her toes gripping the carpet. Still, Odin remained silent. Well, this was new. She peered at him, trying to understand what she was seeing. The usually impeccably dressed All-Father looked as if all he was wearing was an unbuttoned suit jacket covering a collared shirt, but the shirt was covered in black stains.

"Odin?" she asked, unable to hide the concern in her voice.

The god fell to his knees, a sob escaping his throat as he bowed his head. His shoulders had rolled forward, and he began to shake. Bryn's instincts kicked in as if they had never been separated, and she started toward him without conscious thought, before pausing less than a foot away from him. Studying him now that she was closer, she could see he wasn't in a suit but a smoking jacket over a pair of pajamas, and the black stains were actually red.

Blood.

Placing a hand on his shoulder gently, she shook her head. This was the first time she had allowed herself to touch him—to feel anything for him—in nearly one hundred years. And in all the time they'd shared, Bryn had never seen him unravel.

His body shuddered with her touch, the quiet sound of his sobs fading. "Tell me what's happened."

Raising his head, he said, "Frigg is dead." The words were spoken so calmly, she didn't know whether he was telling the truth, or lying to her in order to get his way. She looked down at him, seeing the blood, knowing he couldn't possibly lie about that. Odin was nothing if not unerringly devoted to his wife.

"What happened?" When he only blinked at her, Bryn blew out a frustrated breath. "I know you had nothing to do with the other Valkyries' deaths." The words tasted bitter on her tongue, but she admitted when she was wrong—even when she really didn't want to.

His focus sharpened, his shoulders and back becoming rigid. Bryn withdrew her hand.

"How do you know?" he demanded.

Sitting back on her heels, she looked into the All-Father's eyes, seeing the panic and concern he was unable to hide quickly enough. "I got a call from Loki. He admitted to killing Rota, Svava, Astrid and Sigrun."

"What did he say exactly?" Odin pressed.

She glanced away, wary of telling him too much. Would he help her get Kristy back? Did he even want to get her back, or was he still insisting that Bryn was the only Valkyrie he'd ever truly cared about?

Bryn inhaled deeply, letting the breath go slowly. "He has Kristy. He called to negotiate." She shut her eyes to hide her shame at being unable to protect Eir's twin. When she opened them once more, she said, "The only thing I don't understand is why. Why does he want me? And why is he targeting us?"

The All-Father shook his head. "He has reasons—reasons I refuse to get into with you." He was shutting down again, controlling the situation by withholding information until it was the most advantageous time for him to reveal it. It was, unfortunately, his MO.

She frowned. "You know why he's doing this then?"

Odin nodded—a short, sharp motion—but offered up no further explanation.

"And you're not going to tell me? Even though Kristy's life hangs in the balance?" she asked incredulously. "What the fuck is wrong with you? Why are you so desperate to get me back by your side? What's in it for you?"

"I only wish to keep you safe," he explained, looking unrepentant.

"The others be damned? Is that it?"

His expression hardened. "It is the way it has to be."

Bryn stood up and walked away from the man she had considered her father for nearly one thousand years. "I can't believe how callous you're being."

His eyes alighted on her face, the obsidian orb sitting in his right eye socket cold. "I'm being realistic. Their lives are inconsequential. I only wished to keep one of you safe, and that's you, Bryn."

Bryn wanted to throw her hands over her ears. She couldn't believe what she was hearing. She truly didn't know Odin.

"Get out."

"It's my prerogative to—" Odin began, launching into one of his usual holier-than-thou speeches, but Bryn cut him off.

"Get out of here, you sanctimonious sonofabitch, before I do something I'll regret." Her fingers were twitching for her sword, and so help her, if she drew the steel she would use it on Odin. She would strike him down right there where he kneeled.

29

The front door of Bryn's apartment slammed shut, shaking Eir's concentration. She had just gone back to crushing the pills when the shrill sound of a phone ringing down the hallway lifted her head from her clandestine work and made her heart pound. Quickly and carefully, she covered her desktop with a piece of paper and yanked open the door.

Bryn was already ahead of her, reaching for the phone sitting on the end of the kitchen counter. This was the phone call they'd been waiting for. Bryn picked it up and hit a button to put it on speaker phone.

"Yeah?"

"Brynhildr, so nice to hear from you," Loki purred on the other end of the line. Eir couldn't stop the shiver that rode her spine. Even before she'd joined the ranks of Odin's army, Loki had been the one god she had avoided at all costs.

"Where is Kristy? I want to speak to her," Bryn demanded.

There was a muffled sound like a hand over the receiver, then Kristy's voice came out on the other end, tinny and mechanical.

"Bryn?" she whispered hoarsely.

"I'm here, and so is your sister," Bryn replied, her fingers curling around the edge of the counter.

"Eir is there?"

"Kristy," Eir croaked. Pain blazed through her palm. When she looked down, she saw four half-moon gouges, blood welling slowly. "We're going to get you—"

Loki cut off her words by tutting into the phone. "Now, now, don't get her hopes up too high. I'm not even sure Bryn is going to do what I want her to."

Eir looked at Bryn, saw her face cloud with unimaginable anger.

"Just tell me where and when." Bryn bit the words off, spitting them out.

Loki laughed, the sound grating on Eir's nerves. She had already healed the damage to her palm, but had drawn more blood by doing it again. She whimpered and looked at Bryn.

"Six hours from now, the sun will begin to set. I want you to come to my hotel room with your feather cloak. I will set Kristy free if you are willing to replace her."

Eir clutched at Bryn's arm desperately. "Bryn, no. You can't. Let me go," she pleaded. Bryn's eyes locked on her and Eir knew she had already made up her mind.

"I don't want anyone else. I only want Bryn," Loki drawled. "If she comes tonight, I will stop going after the others. Bryn was the one I really wanted all along."

Tears leaked from Eir's eyes. "Please," she begged, shaking her head. "You don't have to do this."

Bryn turned her back on Eir. "Deal," she replied, her voice sounding hollow.

Eir wept as Loki gave them the name of his hotel.

"I'll meet you in the lobby at dusk," said Loki.

"Fine," Bryn replied through gritted teeth.

"And Bryn? Don't forget your cloak, otherwise we have no deal."

Bryn spat a nasty curse and hung up. Eir's head had dropped in defeat, her body feeling like lead. Bryn gently touched the top of her shoulder.

"You should get some sleep."

Eir looked up into the other woman's eyes. "What makes you think I'll be able to sleep now? You shouldn't be doing this, Bryn. Please. Let me go."

Bryn shook her head, her braid rasping against her back. "You heard Loki. He wants me." She let out a deep breath. "Odin got us into this mess, but I'm going to get us out of it. I'm going to take a shower and then I'm going to have a stiff drink."

This was Eir's only opportunity then. "I'll get the drink ready for you then. Go take a shower."

Bryn's gaze raked hers, but she sighed heavily and started down the hall. Eir returned to her room with the bottle of vodka Bryn kept in her freezer and closed the door behind her. Creating a funnel with a sheet of paper, she tipped the crushed Valium tablets into the vodka bottle and swirled it around a little.

She took it back into the kitchen and found a clean tumbler. She filled it up with the laced vodka and left it on the counter for Bryn to find.

Bryn let the scalding hot water spill over her head, soaking her hair completely. Her shoulders were tight, the muscles in her neck even tighter. Odin's words were going around and around in her head, the horrible truth she now knew gnawing at her.

She couldn't turn back time and bring her Valkyries back to life again, but she could prevent any more from being killed. She had to do this. Stopping the water, Bryn wrapped her wet hair in one towel and her body in another.

Stepping out of her private bathroom, the room felt cold around her. But then again, that might have had something to do with the fact that she was willingly walking to her own death by agreeing to the trade. Her spine stiffened. She would do it, though. She would do it for her girls. She would take a stand against Odin's self-serving agenda and sacrifice herself.

Bryn unwound the towel from her head and ran her fingers through her damp hair. She finger-combed it all together then quickly braided it down over her shoulder. She pulled on a pair of black jeans and a black tank.

Running her hand over the tattoo on the side of her neck, she felt her golden sword fill her hand, molding into the exact grip of her palm, warming under the heat of her skin. The sword had been given to her by Odin a few weeks after she'd entered his great hall in Asgard. He'd said it was specially calibrated to her touch. If someone else were to take the hilt, they would simply die.

She knew it wasn't a lie. She'd seen it happen with her own eyes. With a sigh, she willed the sword away and looked at her reflection in the mirror. Her features were drawn, probably because she wasn't getting enough sleep. She'd been too worried about Odin and Eir and Kristy and Korvain to be concerned about resting her body and mind.

Leaving her room, she made a beeline for the kitchen. A glass of 42 sat on the counter next to the sweating bottle. Eir must have known she wouldn't be stopping at just one. Grabbing the glass and the bottle, she slumped down into the sofa and brought the glass to her lips.

The icy liquid hit her tongue, the back of her throat. It slid down like a lover's caress, warming her chest and setting her frayed nerves at ease. Glancing at the clock above the TV in the corner, Bryn could see she still had another five and a half hours to wait until she could pull Kristy out of that hellhole.

Bryn took another mouthful of vodka, her head leaning back to rest on the back of the sofa. She drained the rest of her glass and poured herself another, filling the tumbler up to the two-thirds mark. She threw that back, too, reaching for the bottle to pour one more when it slipped from her hand and crashed to the floor.

Cursing, she bent down to pick it up, but ended up getting real close and personal with the carpet instead. The rest of her body tumbled after her, leaving her in a messy heap. The pile scratched the side of her face, but her limbs felt so heavy she couldn't move, no matter how hard she tried.

"Bryn?" Eir called from down the hall.

"Eir." Gods, was that her voice? Bryn sounded as if she'd drunk ten bottles of vodka instead of one. "Help . . . me." The words dribbled out of her mouth, spilling onto the floor with her.

Soft footsteps whispered across the floor. Eir's angelic face dropped into view. "I'm sorry I had to do that to you, Bryn, but you really left me with no choice. I can't let you exchange yourself for my twin."

And with that, she stood up and retreated from view. Bryn tried to scream at her to come back, but Eir was gone.

Bryn attempted to fight against whatever Eir had slipped into her drink, but her mind was thick, and thinking was like trying to wade through mud. She could feel the pull of sleep weighing down her body and mind. She tried to rebel, but the drug washed over her completely.

Bryn's eyes slid shut while her mind screamed out for help. Eir was going to die right alongside Kristy now, and Bryn was powerless to stop it.

Eir pulled Bryn's bedroom door closed and rested her forehead against the cool wood. Bryn had passed out a lot faster than she'd thought, leaving Eir to drag her limp body into her bedroom. Somehow she had managed to get her into her bed, too, although how she couldn't say.

Eir couldn't stop shaking. As a healer and nurse, she understood the why of it, yet couldn't stop it. The combination of adrenaline and fear shot through her body, hobbling her. She snuck out the back door of the club, propping a loose brick in the jamb to keep it ajar.

The hotel Loki had mentioned was only a block away from the hospital. She had even been to a conference or two there, so she knew the layout well enough to fade directly there.

She rematerialized in the underground parking garage attached to the hotel, her body still shaking. Taking a moment to collect herself, she pressed the side of her body up against the cold concrete garage wall.

Across her shoulder was a fabric tote bag holding the ash box containing her cloak. She shifted it around onto the other shoulder to avoid getting gouged in her ribs. She sucked in a few deep, cleansing breaths to steady her already shot nerves.

She could do this.

She had to do this.

Lifting her chin, she strode forward toward the entry, stepping directly into the lobby of the hotel from the garage. Her soft-soled shoes barely made a sound on the gray and white granite tiles covering the lobby's floor. The dark wood registration counters took up one length of wall, while an oriental-style blocked wall partitioned the other half into a lounge.

There were a few couples sitting together, wineglasses in their hands, quiet chatter filling the space with an unusually calming melody. She turned her body around in a tight circle, her eyes always scanning for the Aesirean god who held her sister captive.

A strong hand settled around the back of her neck, the fingers tightening. Eir stiffened and tried to step away. "Shh, don't make a scene," a male voice warned.

With a tremble in her lips, she looked over her shoulder at Loki. She had only seen him once or twice before, and always from a distance. Odin had never wanted any of them to associate with him.

Having him this close, she noted the feral look in his eyes. She had seen that look many times before when mentally unstable people were admitted to the hospital for a variety of reasons, from self-harm to harming others.

His smile skewed his face, cutting it in half with a sinister cast. "Remind me again of your name, *elskling.*"

She shivered at the familiar term. "I'm not your darling," she spat back at him, unsure where the fire had come from.

Something sharp bit into the small of her back causing pain to sear through her. "Your name, Valkyrie," Loki hissed, his fingernails digging into the delicate skin of her neck.

"Eir." Gods, she felt lightheaded. She weaved on her feet, but a strong hand around her waist stopped her from colliding with the nearby wall. She was vaguely aware that people were staring at her—not Loki—her.

Lifting her head was laborious, but she managed it. She blinked, seeing double. Loki's almost harmless sounding laugh rang in her ears.

"My wife," he announced, throwing one of her arms across his shoulders, or at least tried to. Loki was nearly six inches taller than her six feet two. One of his shoulders dropped to pull her up, the hand on her wrist squeezing tight.

"What . . . have . . . you . . ." she slurred.

"Shut your mouth," he hissed under his breath, then raised his voice so it would carry across the busy foyer. "She's simply had too much to drink. Let's get you to bed." His voice was happy, loud—too loud. His words seemed to bang around in her skull. She winced.

With his other arm securely wrapped around Eir's waist, Loki dragged her toward the bank of elevators. The tiles gave way to thick red carpets that hindered their movements even more. At least he couldn't fade with her. Their combined weights would have been too much.

They paused, and the next thing she knew, she felt the familiar vibrations—they were fading after all. Eir was shocked. Odin was the only god able to fade with another person, yet Loki had done just that with no effort. The room they appeared in looked well lived in. It smelled like it was well lived in, too.

Eir's head rolled on top of her shoulders like an unhinged gate, but she was just focused enough to take in the rumpled comforter, the trays of food with dull stainless steel covers on them.

"Where's . . . my . . ."

"Sister?" Loki asked, dropped her sideways onto the bed. Her tote was on the side of her body that hit the bed. It should have hurt when she landed on it, but strangely her body felt numb. She had felt this before.

"What . . . drug . . ." The words formed in her head, but her mouth, tongue and lips didn't want to make the leap from there. Whatever he had injected into her body was working quickly.

Loki's face was suddenly all she could see. "Your sister is in the bathroom, and I've injected you with a cocktail of heroin along with some other barbiturates."

Eir gasped, causing a smile to form on Loki's lips. He disappeared again, but Eir watched his shadows move around the room.

"Now," he said, rolling her over onto her back. He snatched the tote from her shoulder and flung it onto the floor. "Where's Bryn? Did she think sending you in instead would be enough?" As he talked, he took a rope and bound her hands and ankles.

When Eir kept her mouth shut, more out of necessity than will, he frowned. "It doesn't matter. I was going to kill your sister anyway. Now, I get two Valkyries to kill in front of Bryn."

Eir's chest squeezed tight. Not only had she damned her sister's life, but her own as well, and if Bryn did come—which of course she would—her life, too. Tears stung the corners of her eyes, gliding down her temples and soaking the messy sheets beneath her.

She had condemned them all.

Eir blinked up at the ceiling fixture, her lids getting heavier. She blinked more rapidly, hoping to fight off the feeling, but that only made it worse. She was lying out on a beach with the tide coming in.

Waves of darkness lapped at her feet, her calves, her hips.

Soon the waves would drag over her body and drown her. She blinked again, her eyelids slow and heavy. She tried to remain lucid, in control, but she could not win this battle.

The darkness finally swamped her and dragged her into the undertow.

30

Korvain had a plan. Granted, it was not a very good one, but it was a plan all the same. He'd come to the conclusion that no matter how much Bryn pushed him away, he would push back. Thinking she could take on Loki alone was insane. He'd seen firsthand how powerful the god was. If she thought she could defeat him without getting help from anyone else, she was delusional.

So here he was at the club, a crazy look in his eye that had everything to do with wanting to protect his woman. He wouldn't let her walk into the trap with her eyes closed so tightly. He just hoped he wasn't too late, that she hadn't received the phone call telling her exactly where the exchange was going to happen.

He approached the rear door carefully, his eyes always swiveling around for danger. He was well cloaked with shadows, but he never let his guard down.

Ever.

He was prepared to threaten his way inside, but when he arrived, there was a chunk of brick holding the door ajar. Kicking it away, he slid inside and shut the door firmly behind himself. The hallway was a tight squeeze for him, but he made his way down to the elevator and hit the dimly lit button on the side.

As he rode it up, he went through all the arguments he'd prepared. He was going to appeal to her intense loyalty to her Valkyries, tell her that if she somehow got herself killed, there would be no one to look after the club and the other women.

He rubbed at his chest, aching with the thought of Bryn getting killed. He didn't like it. Not one bit. He would fight for his woman into the deepest bowels of Niflheim if he had to.

The doors opened slowly onto the hallway that held half a dozen doors. Korvain moved to Bryn's apartment door and tried the handle. It was also unlocked.

Slipping inside, he scanned the immediate area for anything unusual. Bryn's delicate scent was everywhere in the room, and he took just a second to breathe her in, to hold her in his lungs before getting down to work.

He stalked toward her room knowing that that was where her cloak would be. He let out a breath and cracked open the door. He could see Bryn on the bed, her back to him. Her breathing was deep and steady.

Even though she seemed deeply asleep, Korvain wrapped more shadows around his body, padding his steel-toed boots so he made absolutely no sound whatsoever.

Walking over to her closet, he pulled open the door and began looking over the shelves and racks. His plan was to steal Bryn's cloak away from her so she wouldn't be able to go to the exchange. A mature approach? Probably not, but there was no way in hell he was going to let her go without him there to protect her.

So. Yeah. He'd turned into a caveman.

Whatever.

Korvain started pushing the clothes around on the racks, first wrapping them with the shadows swamping the small space. He couldn't chance Bryn waking up while he was stealing her most treasured possession.

He searched her closet for near on a quarter of an hour and found absolutely nothing. Frustrated, he turned back to the room and scanned the furniture. Bryn seemed to take the idea of Spartan living to the extreme. The only furniture she had in the room was a bed, a dresser and an oval cheval mirror.

He looked over the top of her dresser expecting to find trinkets and jewelry like other women kept. But the only things to adorn the top of hers were the two bloody feathers Eir must have given her.

Quickly and quietly, he looked through the drawers, but the ash box wasn't in there either. He even got onto his hands and knees and looked under her bed. Pressing gently against the boards, Korvain heard a soft creak.

Prying the loose board off, he found a small compartment. It was filled with dust, having probably being unopened for decades. Reaching inside, he felt around until his fingers brushed against something cool and hard.

He pulled the box free and opened it. There was no light to speak of, yet the feathers of her cloak gleamed brightly as if backlit from within. Reverently, he stroked one of the feathers, and Bryn moaned. He withdrew his hand quickly and shut the box.

With Bryn's ash box firmly in his hand, he turned to leave.

Bryn groaned and rolled over. When her face mashed up against something soft rather than coarse, she knew she wasn't still passed out on the living room floor. Her mouth felt dry as if all the moisture had been siphoned out of it.

She rubbed at her head, which was already throbbing, focusing her eyes on the clock on her bedside table and rolling into a sitting position. The movement was too fast; another volley of what felt like daggers through her skull piercing her brain all over, pulling a whimper from her dry lips.

She'd been unconscious for just over five hours. She had to go. She had to stop Eir from doing something stupid and crazy. Bryn looked toward the door and willed her body to move on her command.

She managed to stand, but once she was upright a roll of nausea swelled, threatening to spill over.

"Fuck," she hissed, her hand going to her stomach as if that was going to hold anything in. Sweat broke out on her brow, small beads clinging to her clammy skin. Whatever Eir had spiked her drink with, it had been strong.

Eir.

Bryn groaned in frustration. She was going to kill that woman when she got her hands on her. Didn't she realize just how dangerous it was? Didn't she know she could get killed? The only way to get her and her sister back now was to trade herself for them both. She just hoped she wasn't too late.

She staggered around to the other side of her bed, her eyes fixed on the false section of floor, about one foot wide and one foot long. Grunting, she dropped to her knees.

Bryn lifted the fake floorboards and reached beneath them. The forward movement made her head swim unexpectedly, forcing her to sit back on her heels.

With her equilibrium back, Bryn tried again. Coldness kissed her fingers as they searched for her ash box—the box that contained her feather cloak. She was up to her elbow now, half her arm buried under the floorboards. Back and forth, she swept the area, touching only dust. Desperately, she lowered herself to the ground and tried to look inside the cavity.

Empty.

It was empty.

Her cloak was gone.

She staggered to her feet, pitching to one side and catching herself on the edge of the bed. How could someone have taken her cloak? Nobody knew where she kept it. Not even the other Valkyries.

Black roses began blooming in front of her eyes. She whirled around and made for the door. She had to get to Eir, cloak or no cloak. She could worry about where it had gone later.

She staggered from her apartment, using the wall as support, swaying and fighting the combined waves of nausea and head spins as she went. Bile twisted up her throat. Bryn doubled over and vomited in the hall, no more than a few feet from her destination—the elevator.

Wiping the back of her hand across her mouth, she smeared vomit along her cheek, but was too focused on getting to Eir to care.

Once inside, she leaned heavily on the side panel of the elevator as she rode down to the lower level of her club. It opened with a ding and she stepped out, throwing her hands out to break her fall as her legs gave out under her.

Sprawled on the cold ground, reality seeped in. Eir was going to die because of her—just like every other Valkyrie who had died in the past week. It was all because of her.

Lifting her head, Bryn looked down the length of the dim hallway. A flicker of anger ignited into something more when she thought about giving up. Just because the situation was hopeless didn't mean there was nothing she could do about it. Even though it hurt, she pushed herself up until she was leaning against the wall, her eyes still fixed on the exit.

All she had to do was get there.

All she had to do after that was fade to the hotel.

She couldn't worry about what happened after that. She already knew what was going to happen. Loki was going to set the other two women free and she was going to surrender herself. She was going to sacrifice herself for her girls like Odin should have done for all of them.

Pitching forward, Bryn lifted herself off the ground and started down the hallway again. Staggering, she managed to reach the door without falling over.

A blast of cool air hit her in the face and chased down her neck, clearing her head just a little. It was enough for her to focus her thoughts on fading. There was a familiar vibration, and then she was there.

Bryn had faded into the parking garage next to a Honda Civic. Walking to the cool cement wall, she pressed her palms against it, resting her forehead there while breathing in slowly. Ready to face her fate, she made her way to the door leading through to the lobby, her breath misting a little in front of her mouth with each deep exhalation.

She twisted the handle and pulled open the door. A rush of warm air, low chatter and glasses clinking together greeted her. Moving among the humans, Bryn wondered how she was supposed to find Loki.

But in the end, it was Loki who found her.

His hand landed on her shoulder, his fingers gripping tight, crippling her. If they hadn't been surrounded by humans, Bryn would have drawn her sword.

She heard Loki's languid voice in her ear. "I wouldn't do that if I were you."

She turned her head just a little to see his profile. "I'm here," she managed to say, swallowing back more bile. "Now let the others go."

Loki started walking her out of the lobby, out of the hotel. Where were they going?

"Others?" he asked innocently.

If it wasn't for Loki's arm now tucked securely around her waist, she would have gone sprawling. "I know . . . Eir came to save her . . ." She swallowed again. "Her sister."

"That she did, that she did," Loki replied, nodding. They had come to a stop beside the boarded up fence of a construction site across the road. He smiled at her again almost benignly. She would have believed his innocence if it wasn't for the feral glaze in his eyes.

"Where . . . is she?"

"I'm taking you to her. Hold on tight," he replied in that same saccharine tone. Bryn felt the vibration as Loki faded them both to a new location. She hadn't thought it was possible for him to do that—only Odin had that kind of power.

Bryn set aside the whys of it for a minute to take in her new surroundings. Loki had faded them to what looked like an underground room. Water dripped somewhere, echoing around what must have been a huge space.

She turned her head slightly to look behind her. A giant wall of debris was at her back, which meant the only way to go now was forward.

"I feel I must warn you, Brynhildr. If you reach for your sword, I will have to sedate you." Loki's voice was calm, uninflected.

Honestly, it was just plain creepy.

But she knew she couldn't risk pissing him off. If her girls were somewhere down here, he was the only one who knew where.

Loki shoved her gently in the back, forcing her to walk ahead of him. The ground beneath her feet was concrete, but was littered with small chunks of rubble. Her head was still fuzzy from the drug yet to leave her system, so on more than one occasion she tripped and fell.

Before long her palms were cut, her jeans ripped and knees bleeding. Loki hooked his hand under her arm and hauled her to her feet once more. He stared at her, cocking his head to one side as he did. She could feel the beads of sweat beginning to form. She didn't want him to know just how fucked she was from whatever cocktail Eir had brewed.

To distract him, she asked, "So where are we?"

Loki was quiet for a long minute. "Take a look around. You tell me."

Bryn did look, but all she could see were huge pylons rising from the ground and smooth concrete walls. She knew they were underground; she could feel the dampness seeping into her bones. Looking up, she saw insulated pipes running along the walls, held up with large metal brackets.

"I don't know."

Loki smiled and prodded her again, keeping her moving at a pace just this side of too fast for her still scrambled brain. Bryn didn't know how long they had been walking. Honestly, she was having a hard enough time just walking in a straight line. So when Loki took her arm and hauled her to a stop, at first she didn't see why.

Turning to his left, he pulled on a handle in the middle of the wall. The wall wasn't a wall after all. It was a door that swung open on rusty hinges. The fetid smell of death and decay that poured out had Bryn holding the back of her hand against her nose.

Loki, however, seemed unaffected, moving behind her and giving her a little shove. Bryn stepped over the raised lip and into the corridor beyond it. Her head throbbed painfully. She wanted to cradle her head in her hands, to massage away some of the pain, but as she lifted her arms, she felt something sharp pierce her skin.

"Sweet dreams, Brynhildr."

31

Adrian had been cooped up far too long with nothing to do but fight the urges to kill his best friend. They were getting worse—bad enough that he had to physically remove himself from the house just so he could get some peace.

In the middle of a practice session with Taer, his phone had started ringing. Motioning for his sister to stop, he dropped his training mitts and scooped his phone up from the edge of the weapons rack.

"Adrian? Mason," the gravel voice on the other end said.

"Mason, what's up?"

"Club's opening tonight. I need you in for your usual shift."

He scrubbed a hand down his face. Thank fuck for that.

"Tell me about it," Mason replied. Adrian frowned. He must have said that last part out loud.

"Why was it closed?"

"I couldn't tell you. Bryn's not even going to be in tonight. Mist just told me to open it up and get everyone in. That includes your buddy. We could use him up on Level Three again."

"You got it."

He ended the call after the requisite goodbyes and finished the training session. Taer looked exhausted anyway. He had been pushing her to the point of breaking nearly every day since Darrion had forced the contract on him.

"Get some sleep. I have to work tonight," he told her, bumping her shoulder playfully as he walked through the kitchen, heading for the stairs. At the door at the end of the hall, he knocked.

"Yeah?" Korvain's voice rumbled through the wood.

Adrian stuck his head in the room, his brain already sparking out from being this close to his friend without a weapon in his hand. He squeezed his eyes shut and waited for the feeling to pass.

"You good, my brother?" Korvain asked, his dark eyes seeming to suck in the shadows in his dimly lit room. Adrian noticed he had palmed his karambit already. Gods, he was like a goddamn time bomb ticking away.

"Yeah, I'm good. Fighting the good fight." He shrugged and Korvain's fingers relaxed on the blade in his hand.

"What can I do for you then?"

He held up his phone and waved it back and forth. "Just got a call to go to work. The Eye has reopened and Mason wants you there."

But when he looked over at the other Mare, he didn't look pumped at all.

"Got something more pressing to attend to?" Adrian asked.

"Think that's a good idea?" Korvain asked with a raised brow. "You have orders to kill Bryn, and me."

Adrian grinned. "That's not going to be an issue. She's not

going to be there tonight, and I'll ask to swap with someone else so we won't be on the same floor."

Korvain sat forward on the bed, his eyes looking slightly wild. "Bryn's not there? Well, where is she?"

Adrian shrugged casually. "I don't know. Mason said she just isn't there. So are you coming or what?"

Korvain stared at the sheets for a moment "Yeah, I'm coming."

Korvain had tried to keep the fear from his eyes, but the news that Bryn was gone felt like a noose around his neck. If she was gone, it meant the phone call had come and she was quite possibly Loki's captive.

Adrian still stood in the doorway to his room, the look of pain as he fought the compulsion plain to see. By threatening Adrian into taking the hit on him, Darrion was getting exactly what he wanted. He wanted them both to suffer, and they both were.

Korvain fixed his attention on his friend. He knew his eyes would have been swimming in shadows, and his hand was on his weapon in case Adrian's control snapped and he had to kill him there and then.

"Get out of here, my brother. There's no need to torture yourself. I'll meet you there."

Adrian nodded woodenly and disappeared from the doorway. When the door snicked closed behind his best friend, Korvain let the all-out panic surface. Leaping from his bed, he dressed in black jeans and a black tee. Shrugging into the black leather holster that sat over his shoulders, he armed up—his karambit sitting over his heart. He pulled the shadows to it, covering it, making it blend into all the black he wore. Lastly, he pulled on his steel-toed boots, lacing them up tight.

He would go to the club and see what he could find out, but he wanted to see if he could get into her dreams first. Stretching himself out on his bed, he let his mind relax as he probed for Bryn.

He found the door into her mind, but no matter how hard he pushed, that door just did not open. It seemed to be stuck. With one last great shove, it inched open. He took a quick glance before the door slammed shut. Everything in her mind looked foggy, disoriented.

He tried to push in again, but it wouldn't budge. With an agitated huff, he pulled out of her head and returned to his bedroom. That little episode had done absolutely nothing for his already jacked up nerves. If she was unresponsive, she could be drugged.

Sliding off his bed, he beat feet downstairs and slid out the back door to fade to the club's back entrance. He wondered who was manning the office as he pushed the buzzer and looked up into the camera above the door.

To his surprise, it was Kara.

She looked at him like he was a lollipop she wanted to suck on long and hard. She leaned onto one leg, shifting her hips in an almost unnatural way. She was wearing a red bustier and micro mini that barely covered her southern assets. The heels she was sporting pushed her closer to six foot six rather than her usual six-two.

"Hi," she purred, her eyes looking him over from top to toe. Korvain didn't appreciate the eye-fuck from her, biting his tongue to stop himself from verbally tearing shreds off her. Hadn't she taken the fucking hint? He started to push past her, but she maneuvered that killer body of hers directly into his path again so that as he passed, he had no choice but to brush against her.

She moaned at the connection, reaching out to grasp his bicep. He grabbed her wrist and squeezed.

"Didn't learn your lesson last time?" he asked.

A slow, sensual smile spread across her lips. "Oh, yeah. Of course I did. I think I need to be punished for breaking your rules, though."

He cursed under his breath and moved away.

"I don't know why you're still bothering with her," Kara called out angrily, feeling the sting of his rejection.

Korvain was raging so badly on the inside that when he turned around to face the Valkyrie, he almost reached for his weapon. Instead, he flexed his hands into fists at his side.

"Who?"

Kara rolled her eyes—the perfect imitation of a teenage girl. "Bryn. Who else?"

"I don't know what you mean."

She made a strange noise at the back of her throat that, at a guess, meant something like *bullshit*. "I've seen the way you fawn all over her." She walked up the hallway, her body moving in a way that could be described as hypnotic . . . but not by Korvain. She was near his eye level with the four-inch heels on, so when she came to stand in front of him, he could see how glassy her eyes were. The Valkyrie was on something.

A low, feral sound vibrated through the air when her hand cupped what was oh-so-soft in the front of his pants. It remained that way, too, much to her displeasure. She looked up into his dark eyes, no doubt seeing how pissed off he was.

"You mind removing your hand?" he asked coolly.

"Don't like what you see?" she asked with a practiced pout.

His top lip peeled off his sharpened incisors. "No."

Kara released her prize, tossing her hair over one shoulder like it was no big deal. The truth was she was going to fall onto the next dick that came along to stroke her ego, to tell herself she was desirable.

Low self-esteem could be a bitch.

"She'll never give it up for you," she snapped scornfully.

He arched a brow at her, crossing his still fisted hands across his chest.

"Bryn. She'll never give it up. If you're after a Valkyrie, I'm the girl for you. I like it rough and bloody." Her blue eyes fixed on his mouth before she shook herself like a bird settling its feathers.

"Sorry. Not interested."

There was that pout again.

"Whatever. I have money to make."

She turned on her high heels and sashayed down the hallway and out into the main body of the bar.

Korvain let out a breath and rubbed his head a couple of times. When he was sure the coast was clear, he followed Kara's path and pushed into the Eye. The music assaulted his eardrums as if it was a physical force working against his body. The place was already packed, heaving with people chatting, drinking and grinding against one another to the heavy bass of the music.

Korvain's eyes scanned the bar, finding Mason staring back at him. He approached the other male, offering him his palm.

Mason took it before resuming his position, hands clasped in front of his hips, a stern look on his face. "It's good to see you again, Korvain."

"You, too."

"I need you up on Level Three tonight. You good with that?"

Korvain said, "Wherever you need me." Mason looked at his face like he was trying to see something that wasn't really there. "You're staring," Korvain added.

Mason guiltily dropped his eyes. "Yeah, sorry, my man. It's just," he paused, looked around. When he looked back at Korvain, he asked in a lowered voice, "Can we talk in the office?"

Korvain's interest was piqued. Mason led the way, Korvain following at his back. When the office door was shut, Mason turned around and looked like he wanted to be sick.

"You feeling all right?" Korvain asked.

Mason's hand went through his hair again. "Yeah, it's just . . ." He looked Korvain square in the eyes. "Look, I know about Bryn and the other girls. I know what they are."

"And what are they?" Korvain asked calmly.

The human pinned Korvain with a hard don't-fuck-around-with-me look. "Valkyries. They're Valkyries from the Viking times."

Korvain kept his expression neutral. He didn't want to confirm the human's suspicions.

"They're not suspicions," Mason snapped bitterly.

Korvain's stared hard at the human. *Did he just read my thoughts?* He snarled, unable to hold it back.

Mason blanched. "And . . . and I know what you are, and what Adrian is."

"And what's that?" Korvain could feel the temperature drop in the room, causing Mason to shiver.

"You're both Walkers," he said.

Korvain made a derisive sound at the back of his throat. "There's no such thing as Walkers anymore. Whoever told you they exist was yanking your fucking chain."

"The only one yanking my chain is you." Mason looked him square in the eye as the last word slipped off his tongue. "*Morier.*"

Mason only had time to blink before Korvain had him pinned to the back of the door, the toes of his steel-capped boots scraping the floor. Korvain bared his teeth, letting the human see his incisors, letting him know he knew what to do with them. He gave his baser instinct free reign. He recognized he was letting his beast out, but his woman was being held captive and there was not a damn thing he could do about it. He was working hard to keep all that aggression in check, but he wasn't able to stop some of it escaping.

"How do you know about us?" Fuck. His emotions were all over the place. Mason was gasping for air, gulping it down from around Korvain's slowly closing fingers. The human raised his hand slowly and tapped his temple three times.

Korvain spat a nasty curse and let the male go. Mason slumped to the ground, folding in on himself, sucking in the O_2.

Korvain was pacing the floor when Mason spoke again, his voice scratchy. "I don't know how to explain it. I can't do it with everyone—only certain people. I can read their thoughts. I only realized after listening in for a while that the people I could hear were gods—like the gods from our mythology. Bryn and the rest of the girls, I can hear their thoughts. I have to block them out most of the time."

"Can you hear mine?" Korvain demanded savagely.

Mason shook his head. "No. Your shields are too strong, but Adrian's are weaker. Sometimes his thoughts slip through."

All those hours of practice had paid off then. Darrion had made him strengthen and reinforce his mental shields for hours on end—until sweat had soaked his shirt and he'd been dehydrated. He'd designed it so his shields looked like an endless ocean at night—black and still.

"You and Adrian have the same . . . I don't know how to explain it . . . the same *feel*, I guess," Mason explained.

"Why are you telling me this?"

"Because I'm worried about Bryn. She never misses a shift. If she's not in her office, she's somewhere in the club, or upstairs. But I haven't seen her, and the other Valkyries don't know where she is either. They figured she was out talking to a supplier or something. I'm worried something has happened to her. I kept getting snippets of thoughts from the other gods about someone killing Valkyries. I need to know whether this is true or not."

Korvain blinked, seeing red. Mason knew too fucking much.

"If you're thinking of killing me, please don't. I won't say anything to anyone."

Korvain snapped his jaws shut, furious. If the gods were chattering, there had to be some kernel of truth to what they were saying. "How can I know for sure I can trust you?"

And then Mason laughed. "Do you really think I can tell people I hear the thoughts of gods and they won't think I'm crazy?" He shook his head. "I've learned to keep my trap shut about this shit."

Korvain stared at the man—a man who could be an ally. If he could read thoughts, he might be of use to Korvain.

"I'd like to help in any way I can," Mason said, somehow picking the thought from his brain. Korvain tightened up his shields. He had become lax around humans, but he would have to be careful around Mason.

"It's because you're upset. This is the first time I've been able to get anything other than a sea of black from you."

"Fuck you!" Korvain snarled, getting up into Mason's face. The human's eyes softened, though.

"You're upset because you love Bryn. I get that. I love her, too, which is why we need to get her back."

Love? Why was that word being thrown around?

"There is no *we*. It's just me."

"Please. I want to help. Tell me how I can help."

Korvain whirled away, thinking, thinking. Could he trust Mason? He seemed like a good enough guy for a human. He had the ability to search a god's mind. That would be useful somewhere down the line. Decided, Korvain turned back to Mason.

"Yeah, you can help. But I want a blood oath from you that you will not breathe a word about this—about Bryn and the Valkyries, about Adrian and I, about your ability. You got me? You break the oath, I'll kill you and you should know I take great pleasure in my work."

Mason looked stunned for a moment, no doubt getting a nice mental image of just how much Korvain enjoyed his work. "I'll make the oath."

Korvain freed his karambit and scored the palm of his hand. Roughly taking Mason's, he did the same. Wiping the bloody blade on his black pants, he slid his weapon back into place.

"What now?" Mason asked, looking at the shallow cut on his palm.

"Give me your hand." Mason did it willingly. The oath they were about to make would tie Mason to Korvain. It wouldn't be anything like the tie Darrion had with his assassins, but it would be strong enough that Korvain could feel where the human was.

Making sure there was enough blood pooled on Mason's palm, Korvain took some of that blood into himself. He could taste the man's loyalty like a fine wine rolling around on his palate. He truly was an honorable human.

"Now it's your turn." Korvain offered his bloody palm to Mason, and the human bent down and drank from it without hesitation. When he finally righted himself, Mason looked like he was fucking high. But that was Korvain's blood. It was like being hooked up to an IV of the purest heroin in the world.

"All right, so what I need you to do is keep your ears open for any talk about an abduction. If you're right, and I think you are, and Bryn has been taken, we need to locate her ASAP. I'll keep trying to get into contact with her."

"How?" Mason asked, frowning.

Korvain's mood darkened. "That doesn't concern you."

32

Bryn was having the same dream over and over again. She was wandering around in a large open field filled with wild grasses and a thousand different wildflowers, and she was calling out to Korvain. For some reason, she felt as if he was near her, wanting to see her—needing to see her.

All of a sudden, a thick fog rolled in; it blanketed the landscape with puffy lines of smoke she couldn't break through. The temperature plummeted, goosebumps covering her skin. She kept searching, though, running through the field calling out Korvain's name. She could hear the desperation in her cries, but didn't care. He was close, so close to her now.

"Korvain!"

She strained her ears, listening, but only heard the soft caress of the wind over the tall grass and flowers.

Spinning around on the spot, she called again. "Korvain!"

Then she heard it. She heard her name being thrown back

at her, echoing her fear. She began moving toward the sound, running when he called for her again.

"I'm coming!"

She pumped her arms harder, her lungs burning. The mist seemed to be lifting each time he answered her.

"Korvain! Say something else! Anything!"

"Bryn," he called back.

The mist thinned even further. Up ahead she could see him— his tall, dark form taking shape in the field. Seeing him standing there sent a shiver of anticipation down her spine. She was only a few feet away now. He took a step toward her, reaching out his hands. She slipped into his arms and felt a jolt.

She blinked a few times, looking around, wondering where the field and the flowers had gone. The concrete floor beneath her feet was cold. She shivered as the temperature of her surroundings struck her. Where was she? A high-arched ceiling rose above her head, the dank, damp smells of earth pressing against her.

Pushing away from his chest, she looked into his dark eyes, questioning him. "Where am I?" she asked, her gaze dropping. She noticed she was wearing the same clothes she'd had on last night.

Korvain's finger under her chin drew her gaze back up. His eyes were gentle, his touch like silk. "I was hoping you'd be able to tell me."

She frowned, her head beginning to throb again. "I-I don't know where I am." She looked around again at the smooth concrete, the almost rounded walls, the cuffs around her ankles. Something cold was around her neck, and when she touched whatever it was, she discovered it to be a large metal collar covering her neck from the base of her skull to the tops of her collarbones.

That was when the panic began to set in. She attempted to yank the metal circle from around her throat, her fingernails breaking with each desperate pull. The feeling that she was being smothered was growing by the second. But the thing that bothered her the most was the fact that she was unarmed and vulnerable. Her sword—the only weapon she had—was unreachable.

"Bryn!" Korvain yelled, pulling her hands away. The look of anxiety on his face made her think he'd been calling her name for a long time.

"Korvain, get it off. Please," she whimpered.

He only shook his head. "I'm sorry, Bryn, but I can't."

She turned away from him, but he pulled her face back to his. The collar stung her skin and she winced. When Korvain saw the pain on her face, his eyes darkened. "I promise to get it off you soon, but right now I *need* to know where you are." He clutched her face in his hands, giving her no other option but to focus. "Bryn, think."

She frowned, her brain still feeling scrambled. "There were tunnels, and it was damp. Loki took me through a metal door. Wait . . ." Bryn squeezed her eyes shut and thought back. Had she seen . . .

"I think I saw a biscuit tin . . . like an old-fashioned biscuit tin."

"But you're underground? You're sure?"

"Yes," she replied in a whisper.

Korvain spat a nasty curse then quickly apologized. "You must still be in Boston. Loki wouldn't leave the city while Odin is still up for grabs. Bryn, are the other Valkyries with you?"

"I don't know. Loki faded with me to these . . . tunnels." She went to cradle her head in her hands. Why couldn't she remember whether Eir and Kristy were there or not?

He took her cold hands in his warm ones. "Don't worry about that. Just remember I'll come for you. I will come for you, Bryn. I will find you. Just hang on." And then he shocked the hell out of her. He leaned down and planted a very gentle, very subdued kiss on her lips. She took comfort in his words, in his warm welcome touch, then suddenly jerked away, her breath whooshing out of her. With a gasp she opened her eyes, blinking freezing water from her face. Loki stood before her, a cruel grin twisting the corners of his mouth.

"Wake up, sleepyhead."

Bryn was still sucking in deep breaths, trying to get her heart to calm. If she had thought she was cold before, she was freezing now. Her teeth began to chatter, the chill of the frigid air seeping into the metal collar around her neck and straight through to her bones. Loki placed the bucket down next to him and moved toward her. She stood up on shaky legs wishing she didn't feel so damn vulnerable.

The chains of her shackled ankles rattled against the metal pipe she was tied to, the sound of them sending a chill down her spine. She looked down at them, frowning. Why didn't she just fade out of there?

"I wouldn't try it," Loki said, unlocking the links around her ankles. He pulled up the chain and put them in her line of sight. She cursed. Each link was inscribed with the protection rune, which meant no fading. "It's the same on that collar of yours."

Why was she being shackled like this? Her brain was still too foggy to function properly. Then she remembered everything. It all came back to her with such ferocity that her knees buckled and she collapsed to the ground.

When she finally looked up at Loki, she demanded to know where Eir and Kristy were.

"They're safe as long as you tell me where your cloak is."

"I don't know where it is."

Loki shook his head slowly, chastising her like she was a child. "I suggest you start remembering where it is, otherwise the other two will die before your eyes, and I'll make sure I take my time with plucking their cloaks."

Bryn's throat was dry, but she licked her lips and said, "I told you, I don't know where my cloak is. Someone took it from me."

Loki's brows drew into a fierce scowl. With a guttural snarl, he took her upper arm and dragged her toward a large metal door in the corner of the room. As he opened it, she heard the whimpered pleas of the other two women, smelled death and rot.

It took a moment for her eyes to adjust, and when they did, she wished they hadn't. On one side of the room were the bodies of Svava, Sigrun and Astrid, carelessly stacked one on top of the other. A halo of their feathers surrounded them, all spattered in their blood.

On the opposite wall were Eir and Kristy. They were huddled together on the floor. Eir had a black eye, and Kristy had a split lip only just beginning to heal.

Anger surged through Bryn's veins. "Eir! Kristy! Are you okay?"

Eir managed to nod, but Kristy just buried her face in her sister's neck when Loki leered at them.

"He has our cloaks, Bryn," Eir said, her voice so soft Bryn hardly caught the words.

"I know."

"And I'm sorry," Eir added, breaking down into fresh sobs. The sound of her discomfort and regret tore the flesh from Bryn's bones. She hated to see her Valkyries hurting. She hated to hear it in their voices even more.

Loki pushed Bryn into a cold metal chair and chained her ankles to the legs so her thighs were forced open. Feeling exposed, she glared at Loki, her head still feeling a little fuzzy, the Valium Eir had given her no doubt compounded by the drug cocktail Loki had administered.

"Now Bryn," Loki moved to stand in front of her again, hand on his hips. "I know you're lying about your cloak. So why don't you tell me where it is and I'll be more than happy to let these two go." He waved a hand in the direction of her Valkyries. Bryn's gaze skated to them, too, but Eir was shaking her head, telling her not to tell him.

Fixing her eyes back on the trickster god, Bryn replied, "I don't know."

Loki glared at her for a long minute, as if she would cave under his stare. Clearly frustrated, he whirled around and pulled Kristy up by the hair. Eir screamed, still clutching her sister's hand. Kristy cried out for a second before tightly pressing her lips together. From the waistband at the small of his back, Loki pulled out a dagger.

With one final look over his shoulder at Bryn, he drew the tip of the dagger down Kristy's face. Starting at her temple, the smooth cut traversed her cheek and finally ended at the corner of her mouth.

Bryn didn't know how, but somehow Kristy stayed quiet throughout the whole thing even though tears trembled in her eyes, clinging to her pale lashes before tumbling down her face, causing clear streaks to run through her blood.

Eir pressed her lips together tighter even though she wanted to scream. Loki was holding her sister still, running his blade along the other side of her face. Eir felt it as if the god was actually doing it to her. Eir's fingers were wrapped around Kristy's hand.

She was taking her sister's pain for her, taking it into herself. It felt like acid. Searing. Burning. Agonizing. She would have taken the injury, too, but that was far beyond her power. Loki finally released Kristy, pushing her backward so she lost her footing and collapsed onto the ground in an undignified heap. Eir was forced to release her hold as she fell, Kristy feeling the sharp impact on her tailbone.

Bryn was watching on, horrified, but Eir could see she was confused. Why would Kristy cry out about falling over, but not about being sliced up? The truth was, Bryn didn't know about Eir's other ability. It worked best with the ones she loved, but at a push, she could shield anyone who needed it.

She glanced back at her sister. Blood was dripping off her chin now, raining down from her face and splattering the cold, grit-covered concrete beneath her. Kristy had started crying, the throb of her wounds finally crashing over her.

The hardest part about taking someone's pain away from them was that it didn't last. They would still feel it even after the worst of the trauma was over. That was another reason she didn't do it too often. Sometimes, she felt as if it was a cruelty to the person rather than a mercy.

"Tell me where your cloak is," Loki demanded of Bryn once more. The woman they all considered their leader just shook her head. Her face was stained with the tears she had shed for Kristy. That was why she made a good leader. She felt for all of them. In fact, she felt for all of them so much, it was the reason she had chosen to leave Odin's service . . .

Eir had been sitting in the drawing room of Odin's manse, attending to her needlework. Out of all the Valkyries, she was the most feminine. She was rethreading her needle when all the commotion outside caught her attention.

Putting down her work, she stood up, the sheer fabric of her shift dress moving easily with her gait as she went to open the sliding partition.

Out in the foyer were Kara, Bryn and Odin. Up above, looking over the balustrades were Mav, Mist and the other Valkyries who had made Odin's palace their home. Eir could see Kara had been crying. Bryn looked enraged, but her anger was nothing compared to the All-Father's. Eir shrank back into the room a little, but didn't close the doors.

"Odin, please," Bryn begged. "She made a mistake."

"A mistake she knew she could not make. She brought him into my house! She brought a human into my inner sanctum to fornicate with him!" Odin snarled, spittle flying from his lips. "I will not have it, Bryn. I will not have it!"

These words somehow made Bryn angrier. "Just remember you were the one to kill all our families. You took away the only people who loved us."

"Don't be ridiculous," he spat back indignantly.

"Kara was just looking for a little attention because she never received it from her father."

Odin paced, buttoning and unbuttoning his single-breasted coat. "Ridiculous!" he muttered again. "I am her father."

Bryn stepped in front of him, stopping him mid-stride. "Exactly. You drove her to this. You took away the only men who ever loved us and presumed to replace them yourself." Her antagonism toward him had finally reached its peak. For centuries she had held back the comments. Eir knew it was because she loved the All-Father. She probably always would.

Odin seemed to stumble back from her words as if she had truly wounded him with a physical weapon. "That's not true. I love all of you."

"Yes, but do you love us more than you love yourself?" She posed him the question, taking up her position beside Kara once more, showing him that she wouldn't be backing down. When Odin didn't respond, Bryn added, "I guess not. If Kara is to be expelled, I'm going with her."

Odin looked up, horrified. "You can't. Bryn, I forbid it."

Bryn shook her head, pity in her eyes. "I can and I will, Odin." Reaching around to the back of her neck, she took off the ash tree pendant she had worn for nearly one thousand years—the only personal gift she had been given by Odin. "You cannot push one of us out without another to follow. Just tell me if this is what you truly mean to do. If Kara leaves, I leave with her."

"Bryn, don't—" Kara started, but Bryn cut her off.

"Odin, what is it to be? Forgive Kara for her mistake, or lose her and me along with her?"

Eir held her breath. It was well known just how narcissistic Odin was. Would he sacrifice his ego to keep his Valkyries together, or would he wipe his hands of them forever?

He turned around, a hard glint in his eyes. The anger that had been so clearly directed at Kara before now turned on Bryn. "Go then!" he spat contemptuously, waving his hand as if to shoo them from his sight that very second. "Leave. You won't survive long in this new world without me."

The pendant slipped through Bryn's fingers and clattered to the floor. Softly, she said, "As you wish, All-Father."

Bryn had left, and no more than forty-eight hours later, all the Valkyries had left the All-Father's side. His ignorance had cost him his greatest creations. By slaughtering their families, Odin had hoped to erase them from their memories. But he hadn't taken love and devotion into account.

33

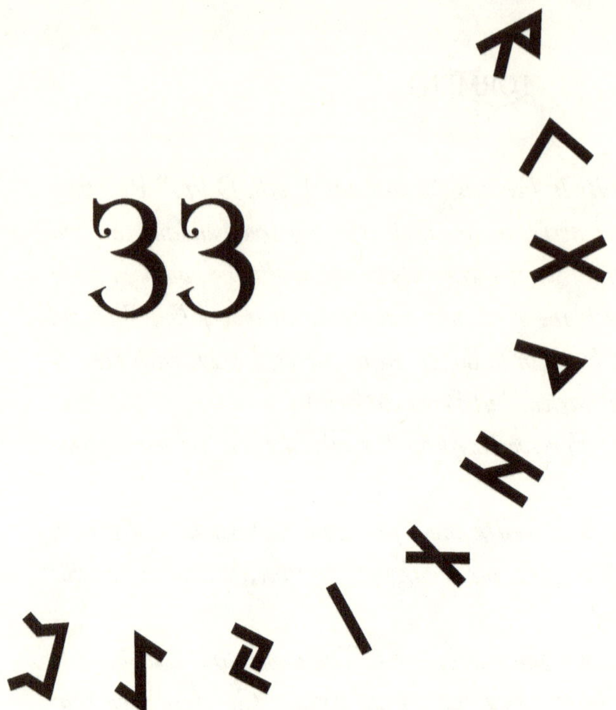

Darrion faded to Korvain's address, his anger a writhing beast deep in his gut. It had taken hold of him, shaken him violently until his dark thoughts consisted of blood and destruction. He had waited too long for Korvain to kill his target, and now that the fucker had been taken off the job, Adrian was taking too fucking long to kill Korvain and Bryn.

He pounded up the driveway, ignoring the front door altogether. By the cursing, Darrion could hear Adrian was inside the garage with his sister. No doubt Adrian thought if he trained her hard enough, she could survive Darrion's treatment of her. But he knew how to break women. He'd been doing it all his life.

He opened the side access door forcefully, letting his power and presence swirl into the room. Adrian had his back to him, but Taer had seen him. Her flushed face drained of color suddenly, and her inattention got her a punch to the jaw.

"Distractions will get you killed!" Adrian barked, roughly

hauling his sister up off the mat by the arm.

"Yes, they will," Darrion drawled. He enjoyed the way Adrian whirled around, placing his body firmly in between Darrion and his sister. If Adrian thought he could protect Taer from him, he was in for a big surprise.

He sneered at the other male. "You can't protect her from me."

"The hell I can't," Adrian said, letting his top lip peel back from the sharpened fangs at the front of his mouth. They were small in comparison to Darrion's, but the trait had been all but bred out of Mares.

"I'm not here for her," Darrion lied. "I'm here for you. We need to speak."

Adrian held his gaze for a long time before speaking to his sister over his shoulder, not taking his eyes off Darrion. "Taer, go inside the house."

The female didn't waste any time following her brother's order. She stepped around him, preparing to fade, when Darrion caught her around the wrist and pulled her toward him. With his hand still firmly attached to her wrist, she wouldn't be able to fade.

By the look in Adrian's eyes, he had realized it, too.

"I wouldn't be so quick to run away," Darrion whispered into her ear. He made sure to blow gently across her face as he spoke. Taer recoiled, trying to pull away, but he only clamped down harder.

Darrion laughed, which earned him a glare from Adrian. If it came down to a physical fight, Darrion would have him laid out flat before Adrian had a chance to draw breath.

Adrian's hands pumped into fists a number of times before the vibration of his anger quieted down.

"What do you want?" he spat out, his jaw tight.

"You really should relax. I hear stress is bad for you."

"I'd be more relaxed if you didn't have my baby sister pinned against your chest."

Darrion leaned down to Taer's head and drank in the scent of her shampoo and her fear. He rolled the scent around on the back of his tongue, biting it down and swallowing it whole. And he did all of that with a wide grin on his face.

Adrian took a step toward him. Darrion tightened his grip until bone ground beneath his fingers and Taer cried out in pain. That stopped Adrian where he was, glaring at Darrion like he was Odin himself.

"I didn't come here for a chat, so I'll just get right down to it, shall I?" Darrion asked, enjoying himself. Adrian may have survived the Final Test, but his control over his emotions wasn't nearly as good as Korvain's, or Darrion's own, for that matter.

In Darrion's opinion, emotions meant weakness.

Weakness meant death.

Darrion began stroking Taer's hair, but even as she squeaked in terror, all his attention was on her brother.

"You're resisting my compulsion."

"Yes," Adrian replied, his voice strained. Yes, he was resisting it, but not by much.

"I don't suggest you keep that up. It will break you. My will will break you." Just to prove it, Darrion broke past the barriers of Adrian's mind and pushed.

Just kill him, and all of this will be over. Taer will live a happy, fulfilled life with her big brother, and you will be able to protect her. Just give in.

He sent the message with a gentle push first, but when Adrian refused to listen, he shoved violently, kicking down the door to his mind.

Adrian screamed, clutching his head and doubling over. Taer began screaming at her brother, begging him to tell her what was going on. Darrion focused on the other male, pushing against his mind. It would have been a tidal wave, pounding against him and washing away his sanity.

Darrion truly loved being a guild master.

He eased back, enjoying seeing the beads of sweat that had formed on the other man's brow. When their eyes finally met, Darrion could see the glazed over look in Adrian's eyes, the desire to hunt down his prey like an animal.

"When are you going to do it?" Darrion drawled.

"Soon. I swear," Adrian replied, one hand still clutching at his head like there was some residual pain there.

"I don't believe you. I think you need more convincing."

"I don't." Adrian practically spat the words at him.

If there was one thing Darrion had learned in all his years as a guild master, it was this: Everybody could do with a little persuasion sometimes.

Darrion pulled one of his throwing knives from the small of his back, keeping it concealed until the timing was perfect.

"Now, let Taer go so we can get back to practicing," Adrian said.

Darrion laughed, startling the female in his arms. She even began to tremble a little. Such a delicate thing. No matter how hard Adrian dressed her to look like a warrior, she was just a beautiful butterfly destined to be crushed under Darrion's fist.

"Not when you have a job that needs to be completed. Finish this, Adrian, and finish this now, or I will have to do something I truly do not wish to do."

"What's that?" Adrian snapped back, his anger seething, thickening the air. No, that wasn't anger. Darrion drew in a deep breath through his nose and smiled a wide smile for the Mare.

Adrian was scared of what Darrion might do to Taer. His eyes kept bouncing everywhere around the room except to look at his sister. He didn't want Darrion to see how petrified he was.

"Adrian, look at me." It was a demand that Adrian could not even hope to disobey.

"What?"

Darrion smiled as Taer began screaming. She saw the blade glinting, coming towards her. He ran the length of the blade once across Taer's throat, opening it up, and her screams soon quieted, becoming gurgled bursts of anguish.

Adrian roared, throwing himself at them both. Darrion released the female and faded, rematerializing behind Adrian. The male was bent over Taer's twitching form. Bright red blood foamed from her mouth, while a much faster stream ran from the wound on her neck.

With his hands pressing against the wound, Adrian desperately tried to soothe his sister. "Just hang on, Tay. You're going to be all right."

Darrion stood directly behind Adrian, looking over his shoulder, looking down at the chaos he had created—delighting in it. Taer's pale eyes were fixed on him, but Adrian hadn't noticed.

"I'll kill him for this, Tay. I swear it," Adrian vowed, and that was what tipped Darrion over the edge.

Grabbing Adrian's hair from the crown, Darrion pulled up— lifting his head and exposing his throat. The blade in Darrion's hand was just an extension of his body, of his will. It arced down towards the base of Adrian's neck where it met his right shoulder—plunging into his skin. A sound more animal than man burst from Adrian's throat, pulling Darrion's lips up into a satisfied grin.

He pulled the knife free, blood spraying out onto his face, neck and chest. The heady scent of blood made Darrion's head swim, made his mouth water. Drawing back, he brought the knife down onto the base of Adrian's neck, determined to sever his head from his body. Adrian's spine gave way to the blade. As Darrion jerked the knife out, more blood ran from the wound, covering his hand in a warm scarlet blanket. He continued until Adrian stopped making any sound, stopped bucking uncontrollably. And even then that wasn't enough.

Darrion didn't stop until the Mare's head was hanging from his body by the barest shreds of bloody muscle, bone and sinew. When Adrian's body was dead weight in his hands, Darrion let him go, watching his blood mixing together with Taer's on the cold concrete floor.

Darrion could see the poetry in it.

They got to die together.

Taer's eyes had closed now, her face completely covered with Adrian's blood: He had slumped down onto his knees, his body covering hers.

Darrion stepped back and took in the carnage. He would just have to kill Korvain and Bryn himself now. It wouldn't be hard. Korvain was going to come home at some point and find the little present he'd prepared and come gunning for him.

The door to the garage suddenly slammed open. Darrion smiled sweetly and faded away, Korvain's savage roar following him into the darkness.

When Korvain finally calmed down enough to take in the room, his nose registered the tang of blood before his mind had caught up to the scene in front of him. Taer was on the ground. Blood covered her entire throat, and he knew there was no way she was still alive.

Adrian was crumpled on top of her, covering her chest completely. Korvain dropped to his knees and checked Adrian's pulse, but all he found were multiple stab wounds where his pulse should have been. Korvain roared wordlessly, rolling his brother over to get a look at his injuries, to see if there was any hope, but his carotid had been cut and left open—hemorrhaging. There was also very little left of Adrian's neck and throat. The bastard had tried to hack his best friend's head off. Korvain didn't even realize he was crying until his tears fell onto Adrian's hair, his head carefully cradled in Korvain's lap.

He placed his forehead against Adrian's and wept.

"I'm so sorry." The words wouldn't bring Adrian back, but in saying them, Korvain felt like maybe, just maybe, he could be forgiven for bringing Darrion's wrath down onto him and his sister.

A sudden noise nearby—a sharp intake of breath—caused Korvain's head to jerk up. Blinking the fresh tears from his eyes, he looked around the garage, but wasn't able to sense anyone else there.

He felt a new wave of grief crashing over him as he took in Taer's body. She was as close to a sister as he had ever had. He would feel her absence just as much as Adrian's.

Her eyes were closed lightly; blood covered her cheeks, forehead and lips. Reaching over a hand, he began to wipe away the still fresh specks. He ran his thumb down her temples, pushing the blood away. It ran in rivulets down her face and into her beautiful dark hair.

He brushed it away from her nose, pausing when he heard that same sharp intake of breath again. Frowning, he looked around and noticed Taer's chest pumping up and down in an irregular pattern.

Hope bloomed, but he didn't dare let it flourish. Running his fingers along the side of her neck, he felt for a pulse and found one. It was weak and thready, but it was a pulse.

Gently shifting Adrian from his lap, Korvain studied Taer's body, checking and rechecking to make sure he hadn't been mistaken. He hadn't. She was breathing. She was alive.

Carefully, he picked Taer up, cradling her to his chest as if she was the most fragile thing in the world. He knew he couldn't fade with her, even though she felt so light she could float away, but he decided he had to at least try.

To his surprise, when he closed his eyes and concentrated, he felt the familiar shift in the air before rematerializing a few blocks away from their house. Although it was mentally draining, he repeated the process again and again, moving a few hundred yards at time. Relief flooded him when he saw they were about a block away from the club, and he knew he'd made the right decision—the only safe option he had—in taking Taer to the Valkyries.

A minute later, he was pounding on the back door of the club. Mason answered it, a pinched expression on his face. His eyes dropped, and when he saw what was in Korvain's arms, his eyes bulged.

"What the fuck?"

Yeah, that pretty much summed it up.

"I can't explain right now." He pushed past the human and started toward the elevator. Over his shoulder, he called, "Get the Valkyries up there ASAP. I need help."

Mason didn't bother asking any more questions. Korvain was grateful for that. Punching the elevator button, he waited impatiently; it seemed to take forever to arrive. He was so focused on it that he snarled when a hand touched him gently on the shoulder.

Whirling around, he saw it was Mist, holding her arms out in front of her in the universal sign for surrender.

"Easy," she murmured, her eyes already fixed on Taer. Mist's hands touched her own throat as she looked at the injuries Taer had sustained.

"Gods, what happened?"

"She was attacked." The elevator chose that moment to ding open. He stepped inside, Mist squeezing in right beside him. "I need your help. I can't take her to a human hospital. They'll run tests and get more questions than answers, and . . ." He squeezed his eyes shut to stop the fresh tears, but it did nothing to stop the burn in the back of his throat. "I don't know of anyone else I can take her to that I trust." Yeah, it hurt to say those words.

Mist looked him square in the eye, showing she understood completely. "Don't worry. We'll take care of her in the best way we can."

Korvain let out a relieved breath. "Thank you. Thank you."

Mist nodded and the elevator came to a stop. When the doors opened, she led him in the opposite direction to Bryn's door. She opened up her apartment and ushered him in.

"Put her on the couch for now."

Korvain kneeled down and placed Taer on the couch, pushing some hair behind her ears. He could feel the heat radiating off her skin and took that to be a good sign.

The door of the apartment opened again. Kara and Mav came into the room. Mav seemed to glower at him. Kara smiled her saccharine smile, but when she saw Taer stretched out on the sofa, her expression went from playful minx to serious in a heartbeat.

"What the hell happened?"

"She was attacked. I found her like this."

"Who is she?" Mist asked, her voice far more level than Kara's had been. She passed Korvain some towels, motioning for him to hold them against the still bleeding wound. Korvain took them, carefully placing the soft cloth against Taer's throat.

"She's my best friend's baby sister."

"And where's your best friend?"

"Dead," he replied in a hollow voice, focusing all his energy on the one small task he could currently do for Taer.

Mist touched his shoulder, drawing his attention, and shook her head. "I'm so sorry."

"Not as sorry as I am," he replied in a dark voice. "But I need you to help her." He tilted his head in Taer's direction. "I need her to survive this."

"Of course. We'll see what we can do."

"Good." Korvain stood up, still holding the towel in place. "I have to go now."

"Where are you going?" Mist asked, taking his place by Taer's side. The towel was already soaked in blood and she changed it for a fresh one. "You just can't dump her and run."

"I can if you want me to get Bryn back."

Mist started. "What do you mean, get Bryn back?"

"Mason hasn't spoken to you?" Mist shook her head. "Fuck."

"Why? What happened to Bryn? Where is she?"

He glanced at the other women individually before finally looking back at Mist. His chest rose and fell as he prepared to voice the awful truth. "Loki has her."

Korvain felt the air shiver as Mav drew her sword. It was the deepest black, liquid steel.

"What?" Mav asked, her voice all gravel.

"Loki took Kristy then called to bargain for her life. In order to get Kristy back, he wanted Bryn and her cloak."

Kara moved to where Mist was crouched, taking the towel

from her.

"But why?" Mist asked, letting the other Valkyrie take over.

"I don't know," he said. "She didn't tell me. All I know is that I have to get her back."

"You know where Bryn is?" Kara asked, speaking up finally.

Korvain's gaze slid to hers. "I think so, but I need to get moving now if I'm to have any chance of getting her back."

"I want to help," Mist said, reaching for him before recoiling at the murderous glint in his dark eyes.

"No. I do this alone."

Korvain felt guilty for leaving Taer behind the way he did, but he didn't really have another choice. Bryn needed him, and he needed to get to her before Darrion could locate her, and before Loki—

He cursed, a stream of profanity pouring from his mouth in an uncontrollable wave.

He didn't want to think about what Loki could have done to her already. Ever since talking to Bryn, he had racked his brain trying to figure out exactly where she could be.

Boston was an old city with a lot of secrets. But he had discovered a lot of its mysteries in his years as a Shadow Walker. There were abandoned tunnels under the city streets. Lots of them. And Bryn had mentioned something that had struck him as odd.

That had narrowed down his search. She had to be in the old Tremont Street subway segment, somewhere between Boylston Street and Eliot Norton Park. That particular part of the tunnel had been deemed a suitable place for people to take shelter if there had been an attack during the Cold War.

At least that would have explained why she saw an old biscuit tin down there. Wrapping the shadows around him tightly, he faded to Boylston Station on the fringes of Boston Common. Descending the emerald-green tiled stairs, he kept his head down, his eyes sharp. He followed a group of humans down onto one of the platforms, his eyes scanning for a way below the tracks.

That's when he saw a security mesh covered doorway leading down to a disused section of track. This had to be the way. He faded onto the other side, the smell of damp growing stronger.

There were piles of dust and debris everywhere. Behind him was a dead end, which meant there was only one way to go. Pulling the shadows closer to muffle his footsteps, he started off in search of Bryn.

He was going in blind, but that wasn't what unsettled him. It was the fact that he had no fucking idea whether she was still alive or not. He hadn't been able to reach her in her dreams when he'd tried again. He hadn't even been able to find the door to her subconscious.

So this was either a rescue mission.

Or it was body recovery.

34

Loki clipped shut the last of Bryn's bonds and sat back on his heels to look the woman over. She had blood—congealed and tacky—on her forehead from the cut above her eye. The opposite eye was already beginning to discolor, her shattered cheekbone making a divot under her left eye.

He had beaten and tortured her until she had passed out, and even that hadn't stopped him. He needed her cloak. He needed it so he could finally kill Odin. What he couldn't understand was why she had turned up without it. She knew the stakes. She knew the other two Valkyries would be killed for her disobedience.

And yet she had turned up all the same.

Ensuring her metal collar was firmly in place, he stepped out of the small room he had chosen as her cell.

Bryn hadn't caved under his torture, but he had lost one of the Valkyries in his quest to make her talk. He wanted to keep her alive a little longer, but Bryn's denial drove him into a frenzy and he had ripped the feathers from the Valkyrie's cloak and driven his dagger through her heart.

Even though she had witnessed the death of her fellow Valkyrie, Bryn had withstood his torture, insisting till the very end that she did not know where her cloak was. He had done more damage than he had ever done to a body before, but she remained strong. He could understand why Odin had chosen her now.

He spat onto the floor, sneering over his blood brother's name in his head. Loki was so close—so incredibly close to killing him. The only thing standing between him and his goal was chained to a pipe just on the other side of a metal door.

As he stalked through to the main room, the other Valkyrie whimpered, but didn't move away from her sister's corpse. If anything, she drew it closer, protecting the body with her own.

Loki snapped his teeth at her, pacing in a tight line. He needed to get that cloak. He couldn't believe Bryn didn't know where it was. All Valkyries knew exactly where their cloaks were. It would have to be somewhere in the apartment she shared with the others, but how was he supposed to get in there to retrieve it?

The idea struck him. Loki laughed out loud, tipping his head back. His prisoner simply stared at him as if he had suddenly lost his mind. Tears trembled on her bottom lashes, small squeaks coming from her throat as she clutched her dead sister closer.

It was all too perfect.

They all knew Bryn was gone, which meant he could simply wear Bryn's face and go in there and retrieve the cloak without any questions being asked. Marching from the room, he opened up Bryn's makeshift cell door and stepped inside. She was still slumped over just as he'd left her.

Touching one shoulder, he began changing his form to mimic the fallen Valkyrie. Making himself shorter was always harder—it required a lot more concentration—but he managed to shrink his seven-foot frame into a semblance of her six-two body.

Her long braid fell over one of his shoulders, bouncing with a weight he didn't expect to feel. Touching it, he found the hair soft and thick and smelling of coconut. He transferred the same jeans and tee from her body onto his and looked down at his new body.

He abhorred being a female.

He let out a breath and faded to the club. Approaching the rear door, he knocked. A few moments passed before a human male opened the door.

"Bryn?" the man asked, eyeing him suspiciously.

Not bothering to acknowledge him, Loki pushed past the male and stepped inside. Ahead of him was a door and to his right a long hallway.

The human male was still buzzing around like an annoying insect. "Where have you been?" he asked, stopping Loki when he tried to pull open the door directly opposite him. Unable to speak in case his disguise slipped, Loki wheeled around, bared his teeth and shoved the human away.

Stalking off, Loki tried to find a way to get upstairs. The human remained where he was, staring at him from the other end of the hallway, which was a smart move—Loki would have been forced to kill him if he had come any closer.

At the very end of the long hall, there was a blind corner revealing the steel doors of an elevator.

He depressed the top button and waited, feeling more and more uncomfortable. He had to be careful. These were the women who knew Bryn best. If anyone was to see through his disguise now, it would be them. Stepping into the elevator, he waited for the doors to close and take him up.

The doors reopened with a soft snick and he stepped out into another long hallway. There were doors running the length of the hall—all closed. He had no idea which door he had to enter through.

He started walking down the hall, letting his nose lead him. At the end, he paused in front of one door, inhaling deeply. Bryn's scent was all over it. He tried the handle and found it unlocked.

He slid inside and closed the door behind him. He followed Bryn's scent until it became the strongest behind one door in particular. Opening it up, he started his search for her cloak, throwing things on the ground, tearing apart her bed and mattress, yanking all her clothes from the coathangers and dumping them with everything else.

And still he didn't find the box.

With a nasty curse on his lips, Loki turned around and stormed through the rest of the apartment. He tore it apart too, breaking glasses, plates, bowls. He pulled out all the drawers in the kitchen, dumping the contents on the ground and ripping the curtains from their windows. He even went so far as to tear apart the cushions on the couch. He stopped himself from screaming out in frustration at the last second, remembering who he was supposed to be and where he was.

Clamping his lips shut, he stalked out of there before the other Valkyries had a chance to investigate the source of all the noise. Coming back the way he had come, he pushed open the back door, shook off his disguise and faded back to the underground tunnel that had become his makeshift torture chamber.

Bryn was still unconscious, the swelling to her face looking worse than before. Seeing her again ignited his anger. Roughly, he undid the cuffs on her ankles, took her by one arm and dragged her from the room.

He needed that cloak.

And he needed it fucking ten minutes ago.

He picked her up and dumped her onto an old steel table he'd found in one of the other abandoned tunnels. He tied her arms and ankles with more links of chain inscribed with the protective rune and removed her collar.

"Please don't hurt her," the remaining Valkyrie whimpered. Loki turned his pale green gaze to her and she shrank back. She was still clutching the hand of her dead sister. He turned back to Bryn, his eyes roving all over her body.

His gaze was snagged by the tattoo on her neck. It seemed to glow in the low light. It was gold and incredibly beautiful. His finger skimmed over the ink, but he pulled away when her skin felt cold and hard over the blade itself. Loki's head suddenly turned around, scanning the rest of the room. He could have sworn he heard someone say motherfucker. He was losing his goddamn mind. He felt like he was in that cave again—hearing voices.

He glanced at the badly decomposing bodies of the other Valkyries, wondering whether they were the ones who had spoken to him.

Shaking himself of the thoughts, he retrieved a bucket of water and he threw it onto Bryn, stepping back to enjoy the show.

She came to with a loud gasp. Her spine bowed, coming off the metal table and rattling the chains that held her there. She was sucking in deep, rasping gulps of air, her eyes scrunching shut to clear the water away. When she was finally in control of herself, Bryn's head rolled in his direction.

Only one eye was functioning, the other swollen shut. When he'd thrown the water over her, some of the blood had melted away, leaving faint pink tracks down her cheeks. Blood plastered her hair to her head, matting it together. Her lips were cracked and bloody, weeping fresh tears as her mouth opened in surprise.

"Tell me where it is," he demanded before she was fully recovered. He took a step toward her supine form. She jerked against her bonds, moaning when the links cut into her already rubbed raw skin. "Tell me where your cloak is, Bryn, and I will set Eir free."

"Don't tell him!" Eir screamed, her eyes darting wildly between him and Bryn. Loki stalked toward the other woman, cuffing her. Bryn screamed out, but her voice was so quiet she could hardly be heard. Eir slumped forward, blood trickling from her newly split lip. Loki pulled the bottom of his jacket down, loosened his neck with a roll and turned back to Bryn.

He approached the table, finding one of the knife wounds he had earlier inflicted, and stabbed his thumb into her flesh. She pressed her lips together and writhed in silence. Loki got in nice and close to her, wanting her to feel his feathered breath on her face, wanting her heart to pound with fear. "Tell. Me." He penetrated further into her flesh until he forced the scream from her lips. She shrieked and there was no sweeter sound.

Loki removed his fingers and wiped her own blood on her cheek. She tried to pull away from his touch, but he took her chin in his hand and forced her eyes back to his.

"You have ten seconds to tell me where it is. Failure to do so will mean I kill Eir."

"Why are you doing this?" she asked.

"Why? Because you are Odin's only weakness. I eliminate you, and I eliminate him. It's simple."

Loki tipped his head back and laughed out loud when Bryn's frown deepened.

"He hasn't told you, has he? That arrogant bastard." Loki got in nice and close to her face, making sure he had her attention. "You are his first. When he gave you your immortality, he tipped too much of his soul into you. In doing this, he created an unbreakable bond between the two of you. Even being the All-Father didn't save him from his own arrogance.

"Your immortality and his are tangled together so tightly there was no way to undo it. You are bound together in life and in death. So, all I have to do is kill you and then I can kill him."

Loki watched her face, waiting for the anguish. Bryn's lips quirked . . . into a smile. Loki's anger flashed and he struck Bryn in the face. "What's so damn funny?" he demanded.

The Valkyrie laughed, coughing when blood got trapped in her throat. It stained her teeth. "You can't kill me."

Loki's rage boiled over. With a snarl on his lips, he drew his gun and pointed it at Eir's head. "Eir will die in ten seconds if you don't tell me where your cloak is."

The laughter died in Bryn's throat, the pulse beating against the side of her throat increasing in tempo as he flipped the safety off. "No!" Bryn screamed, bucking against the chains, pulling and twisting her body around.

"Ten."

"Fuck you!"

He smiled. "Nine."

She actually spat in his face this time. Wiping it away, he said with a growl, "Eight."

"You bastard! You fucking bastard!"

"Seven . . ."

Bryn listened to Loki count down, each number ringing like a tolling bell, signaling the end. Panic had taken root, making her pulse race. Desperately, her eyes found Eir. She found the

Valkyrie sobbing, clutching her sister as her whole body shook and shivered. This wasn't how Bryn had pictured she or any of her Valkyries would die, but there wasn't any hope left. There was no way Korvain could find her, and the realization of that fact sucked all the air from her lungs.

Loki leered at her, his weapon still aimed at Eir. Right before he could count down the next number, his eyes widened and he dropped the weapon. Both hands went to his neck, his fingers grappling for purchase on something that Bryn couldn't see. She watched in fascination as, just as suddenly, he dropped to his knees for no apparent reason. Gasping, choking noises filled the space where moments before nothing but fear and terror had reigned.

The god's legs scrambled on the concrete floor, flailing, kicking up bloody feathers with each spasmodic movement. His whole body bucked up off the floor, his breath forced out through his nose, his eyes bulging from their sockets. It looked as if he was being strangled.

"Bryn, what's happening?" Eir asked, her voice hoarse.

Bryn looked over at the other woman and shook her head. "I have no idea." Peering over the edge of the table, she found Loki's body had finally gone still, but knew he wasn't dead. She could still see his chest rising up and down. The shadows around the room shifted then, leaving Bryn blinking in disbelief.

"Korvain?" she asked.

"Hi, Cupcake," he drawled back with a lazy smile.

Bryn was so relieved that she couldn't stop the tears flowing from the corners of her eyes. He had come. He opened his mouth as if wanting to say something more to her, but clamped his jaws shut instead. She was glad—she didn't need to hear hollow statements like "Don't cry" or "It's okay" from him. Bryn knew they were far from being okay, far from being out of the woods.

Korvain moved to her shackled hands, breaking the bonds within a few moments and with very little effort. She sat up—wincing as she did—and tried to work one ankle while he did the other. She turned to look at him for a moment when he felt the air move behind him. Loki was up and moving again.

Korvain whirled around to face him, his tangible menace heavy in the air. Loki roared and charged toward Korvain. He readied himself, pulling his karambit free from a holster and holding it in a downward position.

"Duck," Bryn breathed in his ear. Thankfully, he didn't think or question her. He just reacted. Korvain hit the floor. Bryn's clumsy fingers swiped at her tattoo, and the air tingled with magic. Her fingers flexed around the hilt of her sword, determination flowing through her heavy limbs. All she had to do was nick Loki's skin.

Using the last reserves of her strength, Bryn raised her sword and took aim. Loki dropped to the ground in front of them.

Korvain stood up to continue the fight when Bryn's hand found his shoulder. "He's dead," she breathed, blinking rapidly. "He's dead," she repeated, feeling lightheaded and too hot all of a sudden. Was it even possible to pass out while lying down? Now that the threat was gone, Bryn could practically feel the relief washing through her entire body.

She slumped back against the table, willing her sword away before she surrendered to the cool darkness.

35

Bryn woke up feeling like her head was stuffed with wet newspaper. Everything hurt, even blinking. Through barely cracked eyelids, she looked around the room, terror filling her for a moment before she realized she wasn't in that tunnel anymore. Loki wasn't there to torture her. She was home.

Her whole body relaxed into the familiarity of it all.

She was home.

There was a gentle knocking on the door. Tilting her head toward the sound, she rasped, "Come in."

The door opened and Korvain slid inside. His broad shoulders held her attention first, as they always did. She looked away, sinking her teeth into her bottom lip. She still felt this burning attraction to him even when she'd been angry with him.

"How are you feeling?" he asked, his voice all gravel, doing something to the lower half of her body.

"Sore." Her voice didn't sound much better. She felt him sit on the side of her bed, not touching her even though her body cried out for it. She rolled her head to look at him.

"Would you mind telling me what happened?"

His dark eyebrows rose over his black-as-pitch eyes. "You don't remember?" Bryn tried to wiggle into a sitting position.

"Let me help you," Korvain murmured, his strong arm sliding behind her back. Her nose ended up in the space between his neck and shoulders. Bryn inhaled deeply, committing his scent to memory. He had saved her, but now he was going to bail on her as soon as he'd seen she was okay. She knew this because she had told him to get out of her life. What reason did he have to hang around now?

He chuckled. "Did you just sniff me?" he asked playfully. The gentle way he treated her seemed so at odds with his nature. His true nature. She could laugh. He was one of the most feared beings in her whole world. Yet when he was with her, she didn't feel threatened. She felt . . . safe. Protected. Even loved.

Bryn pulled away from him, shaking her head, looking into his eyes so suddenly filled with joy. "No . . . maybe . . ." She threw her hands into the air stiffly. "Okay. Yeah, I did." She looked at him from the corner of her eye, only to see him smiling at her, a smile that revealed all his teeth, including his incredibly sharp fangs.

That sobered her. "I'm still pissed off with you," she muttered. More like she was pissed off with herself.

"For what?"

"For lying to me about who and what you really are."

She expected him to blow her off, but he held her eyes, studying her face. "I'm sorry about that. Truly."

He had rescued her and Eir when she wasn't able. "I guess

you're forgiven then."

He shook his head. "No, Bryn. It's not that easy." He eased away from her, his expression serious. "There's more you need to know."

Bryn shifted away a little, too, taking a cue from his body language. There was something in the way his shoulders tightened that told her she wasn't going to like what he was about to say.

Letting out a deep breath that spoke of indecision and regret, Korvain said, "I've not been completely honest with you."

Bryn's whole body stiffened at his ominous words, her mouth suddenly dry. "What do you mean?"

"You're not out of danger yet. Loki wasn't . . . isn't . . . the only one after you. There's someone else."

Bryn's fingers tightened around the blanket at her waist. "Tell me."

"You already know I'm a Walker," he said and waited till she nodded in response, his gaze never wavering from her face. "My guild master also wants you dead, and he sent someone after you."

Bryn's heart leaped into her throat at his admission, her pulse galloping so hard and so fast she was sure he'd be able to hear it. "Who?"

Korvain's eyes told her everything she needed to know before he said the words. She held her hand up when he opened his mouth. She didn't want to hear him say it. Instead, she shifted away from him, picking up a pillow and hugging it to her chest protectively.

"You were the one to take my cloak, weren't you?" she asked, wanting to kick her own ass for not seeing it sooner.

When all Korvain did was stare, not denying it, she added, "And Winta's disappearance wasn't an accident either, was it?"

Her anger surged, fighting for dominance over her fear. "You killed him so you could get close to me." It was an accusation. It was a demand that he tell her the truth. Discarding the pillow, Bryn let her hands curl into tight fists, her nails cutting into her palms. Korvain's dark eyes dropped down, his nostrils flaring.

"You're bleeding," he murmured, waiting a beat then reaching for her.

Bryn pulled away sharply. "Are you here to kill me now?" She calculated she might just be fast enough to reach for her sword before he could attack. Warily watching him, she felt like a deer waiting for a circling wolf to strike.

When Korvain finally spoke, his voice was low. "Don't you think if I was going to kill you I would have done it already?"

Bryn sniffed. "I don't know what you're capable of."

His jaw flexed, betraying his exasperation. "Bryn, I'm not here to kill you," he said. "In case you've forgotten, I saved you. If I wanted you dead, I wouldn't have taken your cloak to protect you from yourself and I would have simply let Loki kill you." He sighed and shook his head. When he spoke again, his words were softer, more persuasive. "Bryn, think about it. I've had plenty of opportunities to kill you. But I haven't."

Bryn drew in a deep breath. She couldn't count the number of times she had been alone with him, yet not once had she felt threatened by him. She had felt everything else for him, though— attraction, need, desire. All those feelings had run through her blood, awakening her body.

Korvain added, "Even the thought of harming you was unbearable, so I refused to go through with the mission. My master—Darrion—forced the job of killing you and me over to Adrian. He couldn't do it either . . ." He paused, his throat working over a lump. "Darrion killed Adrian and nearly killed his sister as punishment."

Bryn sucked in a shocked breath. "Adrian is dead?"

Korvain only blinked at her, his grief obvious. "Taer is here now, though. Eir was able to save her life."

Bryn looked away, staring out the window across the other side of the room. "Why would your master want me dead?"

Korvain shook his head slowly. "Darrion never said. He just told me to get it done."

Bryn looked back at him and heaved a heavy sigh, rubbing at a tension headache behind her eyes. "This is all because of Odin, you know. All of it—Loki and Darrion included."

It suddenly made sense. Loki had explained it to her himself, and although he had every reason to lie, she knew what he'd said to be true—her immortality and Odin's were intertwined, and it had always been that way. That was why Odin wanted her back and why he cared so little about the fate of the other Valkyries.

Had Odin screwed over Korvain's guild master in some way, too—was that why Darrion wanted her dead?

"Odin and I are bound together in this life. If I die, he dies. That's why Loki was after me."

"Why would Loki go after all the other Valkyries first then, if you're the one he really wanted?" Korvain asked. "And where does Darrion fit into all this?"

Bryn thought uneasily of the role she herself had played in driving the dark elves to extinction. A thousand years ago, she had hunted Mares, and she had relished the hunt. Thinking about the innumerable kills she'd made left her feeling sick to the stomach. Now a Mare had saved her life. He had been sent to kill her, but instead he had saved her.

Bryn considered telling Korvain about her past, about the position she'd had in Odin's army—perhaps this was an opportunity to atone for her sins, the first step in her healing—but something told her not to reveal too much.

She shrugged. "I don't know about Darrion, but there's a lot of history between Loki and Odin. I'd say Loki wanted to hurt his blood brother in every possible way before he got to me." Bryn fixed her eyes on Korvain's face, letting him see her decision to absolve him of the part he'd played. "He'd have done it too if it weren't for you."

"Does this mean you forgive me?" he asked, his voice husky. Bryn blinked at him, unsure how to put what she was thinking into words.

"Bryn? I need this," he implored her. "Please. I've almost lost everything. Don't tell me I've lost you too."

Korvain leaned into her, his lips less than an inch from her mouth. Bryn stopped him, holding out her palm. She could practically taste her pulse on the back of her tongue as she planted her hand firmly against his broad chest, feeling the warmth of his skin through his shirt. He felt so real.

"In my other dreams, you came to me. Was what I felt then real, or did you make me think I wanted you?"

He pulled back from her, frowning.

"Korvain?"

He blinked at her. "Would you like to find out if the feelings were real?"

She nodded.

"Close your eyes."

Bryn did as she was told. A minute passed then maybe two. She kept her eyes shut, wondering what Korvain was doing. She couldn't smell his familiar spices anymore, but she hadn't felt him move, or heard him leave either.

Her door opened again, and she opened her eyes. Gods,

everything still hurt. She moaned as her palm hit her bruised cheekbone. That's right. One had been shattered. Hadn't she already gone through all of this?

"Bryn," Korvain said, stepping into the room and closing the door behind him. "Bryn, don't touch it. Eir healed you the best she could, but there was still some swelling left behind."

Korvain stilled her arm, sending a jolt of electricity down into the rest of her body. She hadn't felt that before. She blinked at him, silently asking him what was going on. Releasing her arm, he eased down onto the bed beside her.

He gave her a crooked smile. "You wanted to see if the feelings were real."

"That was a dream before? But you were just talking to me."

"Every time I've come to you has been in your dreams."

"They weren't real, were they?"

He touched the side of her face gently, stroking the skin along her undamaged cheekbone. "Everything you felt in them was real. It's true I can manipulate the dream, but everything you felt was real."

So he had actually rejected her before, after he'd made her come so spectacularly? She turned away from his feather caresses, ashamed with herself.

"Bryn? What is it?"

"Nothing."

His jaw tightened. "Tell me. You were thinking about something just then. I saw the look on your face. What was it?"

She turned back toward him. "So the rejection was real. That I felt." She wanted her words to wound him like a dagger through the heart.

"What are you talking about?"

"The last time you came to me, after Eir had been brought here unconscious, you . . ." She flushed even thinking about it. "You stopped before you . . ." Gods, why was it so hard to talk about this?

"I brought you and then did not take you?" he asked gently, once more stroking her skin. He had moved onto her neck. "You told me you were a virgin. I didn't want to your first time to happen like that. I wanted you to know that everything that happened between us was real."

He tucked strands of hair behind her ear now. The soft repetitive movements made her eyes droop.

"I'll let you sleep," Korvain announced. He was just getting off the bed when Bryn gripped his wrist. He looked down at her, a question in his dark eyes.

"Please don't go yet. Stay with me a while?"

She didn't understand why she needed him close. All she knew was she didn't want him to go. She realized just how precious life was, how much time she had wasted worrying about what Odin thought of her.

In the corner of her room was a chair that must have been brought in by whoever had kept vigil. Korvain reached for it.

"No." She moved over to one side with a wince. "Lie with me?"

He hesitated.

"Please?"

After a moment of uncertainty, he began lowering his body down onto the bed. His weight dipped the mattress, forcing her to either hike up the other side or simply roll into his warmth. She chose to let herself just be next to him.

His body was hard. He was all muscle, not an inch of fat on his frame. His familiar spicy, masculine scent saturated her, drawing her in. She was on her side, him on his back. She felt the long hot line of him against her, but craved more.

She wouldn't ask for it, though. He seemed almost afraid to touch her any more than a feather's caress. Putting the thought out of her head, she closed her eyes and began drifting off. Korvain woke her when he grunted, shifting his weight on the mattress.

"What are you doing?" she mumbled.

"Trying to get comfortable."

He had slipped out of bed, and when she peered around, she saw him stripping off a weapons harness she hadn't noticed. He pulled his snug tee up over his head too, and Bryn's eyes sank to drink him all in. Embarrassed at ogling him, she looked away to give him some privacy.

There were some more sounds: shoes coming off, and clothes being pulled away from his warm body. When he slid back into the bed, his heat was instant. She could feel his pecs and abdominal muscles against her spine.

He threw an arm over her waist and dragged her back into his chest, holding her there with his muscular arm. She was blanketed by him now, caged in by his warmth. With him there, she felt as if she could finally sleep safely.

Korvain finally had his woman where he wanted her: pressed against his chest, her hair in his face, her gardenia scent entangling in his nostrils and imprinting on his brain. When he'd first come into the room after stepping out of her dream, she'd looked so fragile, so broken.

Eir had done her best to heal the damage from the beatings Bryn had endured at Loki's hand, and she was healing. Just thinking about that bastard made Korvain's hands curl into fists.

But half of that anger was at himself. He had taken her cloak to protect her. He might have protected her, but he had made her suffer for it first.

His arm tightened around her waist, dragging her even closer into the line of his body. There wasn't a place on their bodies they weren't touching.

"Fuck," he muttered under his breath quietly. Bryn was trying to recuperate and he was as fucking hard as a rock. Korvain angled his hips away from her ass and thought about mundane things like the weather and football.

Fuck.

Bryn's breathing had finally eased off a few minutes ago, which was just where he wanted her to be. She needed her rest. He didn't know the reason she had asked him to stay with her, but he didn't care.

His cock throbbed between his legs, so he let his thoughts wander to distract himself. He couldn't sleep. He wouldn't sleep while Bryn was relying on him to keep her safe.

Taer was in the other room—the room where Eir was also set up. The Valkyrie had healed Tay's injuries, but she would forever have a scar across the front of her throat. Darrion was going to pay for killing his best friend and maiming his little sister.

Adrian had asked him once if Korvain would look out for Taer, if for whatever reason he wasn't there himself, to keep up with her training and protect her from Darrion. He'd sworn he would until he drew his last breath, and goddammit he was going to keep his promise. Adrian deserved that at least.

After bringing Bryn and Eir back to the other remaining Valkyries, Korvain had told them all he could about what had happened, and also about the bodies of the other Valkyries. They'd wanted to return straightaway, but Korvain had his own body to collect.

He'd returned to the house he had shared with his best friend only to find it going up in flames. The human authorities were crawling all over the place: police, ambulance and firefighters. Korvain had remained hidden, but managed to hear snippets of information. There had been a body found in the house, but there was a helluva large pool of blood in the garage. They assumed it had been the kill site and the body had been moved inside. The house had then been set alight by the perp to cover their tracks.

Darrion, that motherfucking bastard, had done it as one final fuck you to Korvain. He didn't even get to bury his brother after everything they'd been through together.

Korvain waited until all the flames were extinguished before moving in for a closer look. There was nothing but charred wood and a few barely recognizable pieces of furniture left behind. He picked through it all until he reached his own room.

Everything was gone, but as he shifted the rubble around, he discovered what he'd been hoping was still there. His gun safe was charred, but he got it open and took out the small arsenal, strapping it to his body. He'd returned to the club to check on Taer, and had fallen asleep in the chair beside her bed.

Bryn wiggled closer to his body, drawing him out of his dark thoughts. He pulled her even closer, despite the heat radiating from her body, despite how uncomfortable he was getting.

His body still raged for her. Goddammit, he was a perverted bastard for wanting her like this, but the connection between the logical part of his brain and the primitive part had shorted out and he could only see her, smell her. Fuck, he wanted to taste her again. When he'd taken her into his mouth, he'd drunk her down, savoring her gardenia flavor. Being here now, he wanted her again.

Leaning forward just a little, he placed his lips on the skin at the back of her neck. She sighed gently, but did not wake. Now that he had her taste on his lips, he needed more. He needed all of her.

36

B ryn woke up to the feel of Korvain's velvet lips on the nape of her neck. His warm breath brought a rush of goosebumps to her arms, making her nipples hard at the same time. She only had a thin cotton shirt on that wouldn't hide her reaction to him at all.

But, gods, did she care? She'd denied herself for too long. Now that she knew Odin had no real interest in her, or the other Valkyries, other than for his own selfish survival, she didn't feel as if she had to remain pure. Playing by Odin's rules for a minute longer was not an option. She wanted to play by her own now, and she was going to start by losing herself completely to Korvain and his satin touch.

The intoxicating scent that belonged to him and him alone rolled over her. The tip of his tongue skimmed the shell of her ear, drawing a soft shiver from her throat, her skin tingling in his wake.

She lay there for a few minutes, letting him kiss her softly, letting his fingers skim down her arms to trace over the goose bumps. He must have thought she was cold because he was suddenly pulling her closer into his hips, forcing her to mold into the line of his hard body. She gasped when she felt the long, hot length of his erection pressed into the top of her ass.

"Bryn? Are you awake?" he asked, kissing the nape of her neck again gently. She rolled over to face him. His hooded eyes let her know he had no interest in going to sleep anytime soon. She opened her mouth to answer him, but stopped when he placed two fingers against her mouth.

Unable to wait any longer, she sucked one of those fingers into her mouth. She pulled on the digit, swirling her tongue around it. She sucked it deep into her mouth, showing him with her eyes that she wished it was something else belonging to him.

Korvain groaned, his hips surging forward. He forced another finger past her lips and teeth, gaining access to the soft, warm, wet recesses of her mouth. Working on both digits now, she added her teeth to the suck and lick routine. Korvain's eyes actually rolled back, his mouth opening just a little, so Bryn could see the two sharp points of his fangs.

Moisture pooled between her thighs as she thought about him using them on her. Before Mares were routinely slaughtered, Kara had bedded a few and had shown no restraint in telling all of the other Valkyries what it had been like.

Korvain withdrew his fingers from her mouth slowly, his dark eyes locked onto her face. "Do you know what you've just done?" he asked, his voice husky.

She shook her head.

"You've given me an idea about what that luscious mouth of yours can do."

"Oh," she whispered. The truth was, just thinking about taking Korvain into her mouth made her squirm. He moved into her, raising his hand to her neck. His fingers moved toward her tattoo, but he stopped.

"Can I touch this?" he asked in a hushed voice. She nodded. His fingers brushed against the sword softly. "You know, when I saw Loki touching your tattoo, I wanted to kill him."

She shut her eyes. "I don't want to talk about him." Bryn opened them again when Korvain's fingers stilled. She smiled. "Tell me what you feel."

He stroked her neck again. "It's hard and cold like real steel."

Didn't she know it? It had taken her a long time to get used to it when the tattoo had first been done. Korvain's warm hand cupped her neck, his thumb making slow sweeps of her cheek and jaw.

"I'm sorry," he murmured.

"What for?"

"For taking your cloak. I didn't want you to rush into that situation without thinking it through properly. I could see that was what you were going to do, and you wouldn't let me help you in any other way. But if I hadn't taken it, Loki wouldn't have tortured you as brutally as he did and Kristy would still be alive. So for that, I'm so very sorry."

Bryn didn't want to think about all that. "Where is it now?"

"I put it in your office safe downstairs."

She frowned and Korvain straightened out the line between her eyes with his fingertips. "How did you get in there?"

He grinned at her, looking oddly sheepish. "It's a secret."

She should have been upset with him, but he'd been right to do it. Bryn placed her free hand on his chest. The warmth of his body felt so good beneath her fingertips. "If you hadn't taken it,

I would have given it up to save the other two, but Loki would have still killed them, then me, and then Odin." She brought his fingers to her lips and kissed each one. "You saved our lives."

When her lips touched his skin, a fire began to burn in his eyes. Her lips parted. Korvain brought his hand to her collarbone and swept the back of his bent finger down between her breasts. He slowly slid his hand over one of her breasts through her thin cotton shirt, forming a wide circle around her peaked flesh. Bryn bit down on her lower lip to hold back the groan.

His thumb flicked over her nipple, causing Bryn's head to roll back. Leaning in, Korvain's traced his tongue in a long wet line up the column of her throat. Bryn whimpered, pressing her breast into his hand.

He chuckled deeply and pulled away. The mattress moved beneath her. When Bryn finally opened her eyes again, she found him looking down at her. "Stand up for me," he told her. Bryn slid from the bed, pulling the bottom of her short cotton boxers down from her waist to cover more of her legs. Korvain approached her slowly, his hooded eyes never leaving her face. She felt his gaze like a shiver down her spine.

His palm found the nape of her neck as he slid his free hand down her neck, along her collarbone and onto her breast once more, dragging the top of her shirt down. Her nipples hardened under his touch. Her lips parted as he closed the distance between their mouths.

Korvain's tongue swept into her mouth, sliding and retreating, mimicking what she wanted him to do to another part of her body. He swallowed the moan escaping her lips. Bryn arched her back, her hands linking behind his neck.

He pulled back and dropped his mouth to the breast he'd been kneading. Korvain massaged her through the shirt, his tongue flicking back and forth along her hardened flesh. Bryn had to squeeze her thighs together to stop herself from rubbing directly up against his body.

He released the first breast and began working on the other. Bryn watched his mouth work her, watched his tongue lick and tease her, watched his teeth gently nibble at her. She saw his fangs, and gods help her, she wanted him to bite her right where his tongue was.

Her hips rolled forward, her head tipping back. Bryn's hands were in his short hair, moving him to where she needed him to be.

Korvain drew back from her and stood up to his full height. He caught her mouth again, biting down on her lower lip, nibbling it until he pulled long groans from her throat. He thumbed her already sensitive nipples, rubbing against them until Bryn felt her knees weaken. She'd heard the expression a million times before, but never truly understood what it had meant . . . until now.

He was breathing hard when he pulled back. Bryn hadn't realized she was leaning into him so much, so when she stumbled forward, it was only Korvain's arms that stopped her from going sprawling.

She laughed breathlessly, the soft sound stopping when she saw just how dark Korvain's eyes had become. She swallowed hard and stared up into his face.

His fingers inched down her torso, brushing the skin between the bottom of the tee and the top of her shorts. With one swift movement, he removed her shirt and dumped it onto the floor beside them with a cocky grin on his lips.

Her nipples puckered further. Korvain hadn't even touched her again yet. He was just staring at her with a hungry gleam in his eye, sending the muscles in her lower body into spasm.

She whimpered as he took one of her breasts into his hand, lowering his mouth to the other. Without the cotton tee separating them now, all the sensations were magnified. Digging her fingers into his shoulders, she held on as he suckled and plucked at her nipple with his lips.

When he was finished with one, he gave the other the same treatment. She knew she was making soft mewling noises in the back of her throat, but she was unable to stop herself from making them.

He released her nipple gently as he lowered himself to the ground at her feet. His mouth trailed down her torso, his tongue rimming her belly button before hitting the edge of her boxers. Bryn jerked uncontrollably when his fingers dipped below the elastic waist. She was suddenly nervous and Korvain paused, looking up into her eyes, asking her to trust him.

She let him see her answer reflected in her eyes before feeling the tug of Korvain's fingers on the fabric and the cool air kissing the tops of her thighs.

"Step," Korvain murmured. Bryn held onto his shoulder and stepped out of one leg hole. "Now the other." She obeyed and stepped out of the other, letting out a shaky breath.

Korvain was sitting back on his heels just staring at her. Her hands instinctively began to cover her breasts, and the juncture between her thighs, but she stopped when Korvain shook his head.

"Don't cover yourself up."

She frowned, his words dredging up another memory. "You've said that to me before."

He gave her a small smile, standing. "That's because you've tried to hide all your beauty from me before."

Bryn glanced down, a blush burning her cheeks. His hand

under her chin drew her face toward his. He kissed her gently, deepening it when she relaxed into his hold and slung her arms around his shoulders. She opened for him, letting him slide his tongue inside. But as the kiss deepened, as his tongue demanded more, she gave him back some of what he was demanding.

When her tongue dueled with his, he groaned and tightened his grip to the point of pain. Korvain slid his thigh between her legs and the sensation made her grind up against him. Gods, she was so wet already. She rubbed herself against the roughness of his pants, whimpering, panting, moaning for more.

Korvain maintained the contact at their mouths and drew his arms around her waist until her feet no longer touched the floor. He walked them backward, the softness of her sheets at her back once more.

He seemed to stumble back unsteadily a few steps, his fingers already working at the button on his pants. Bryn sat up on her elbows and watched the show, biting on her lower lip.

Korvain drew his pants down past his ass, over his thighs and calves before stepping out of them. He wasn't wearing anything underneath them, so what she saw was his long thick shaft standing proudly in front of him. She gulped and licked her lips.

"Show me how you like to be touched," she whispered. She didn't know where the words had come from—only that they had come.

Korvain's already heated eyes glowed, drifting down her body as he gripped himself near the base of his cock. Slowly, he started moving his hand up and down, up and down, running his thumb over the crown with each upward stroke. Bryn was transfixed, watching him, wanting him. She loved how his head kicked back and his breath quickened. She wanted to be the one to do that to him.

Sliding from the side of the bed, she fell to her knees in front of him, mirroring his previous position in front of her. Korvain looked down at her, a possessive heat in his dark eyes. Licking her lips, Bryn wrapped her hand around his shaft, gripping him like he had been gripping himself.

She started off slowly, matching the pace when his hands dropped away. "Gods," he gasped. She didn't break eye contact except to watch how his abdominals contracted and released with his erratic, heavy breathing. She smiled, enjoying how much control she had over him, but also at how much trust he was placing in her hands.

Leaning forward, she kissed him gently on the inside of his thigh, swiping her tongue against his skin. His hands swept through her hair, tugging it into a tight ponytail at the back of her head.

"I want your mouth on me." His voice came out as a long guttural sound that spoke to her mind and her body. With a smile on her lips, she leaned forward once more, her lips parted, her tongue ready.

Korvain groaned loudly when her lips passed over his head and slid down his thick shaft. He tasted of his particular brand of spice and of a man—a strong, virile man.

"I need to taste you again." The words were a rush against her eardrums. Bryn didn't want to stop. She loved what she was doing for him, loved the little groans and sighs she was drawing from him.

"*Sh'mai*, please," he begged. Bryn didn't know the meaning of the word, but did as she was asked. She rose from her knees, her eyes still fixed on his cock. He pulled her in the direction of the bed, laying her down gently, her hips hanging off the side.

Hooking her knees over his shoulders, he buried his head in

between her thighs. There was no warming up. It was just his long tongue sweeping apart her folds, sending little electric sparks shooting off in every direction. Her hips jerked forward with every lap at her weeping heart. Korvain laughed and planted his palm between her hipbones to keep her still.

Her heart was beating faster and faster in her chest. She felt the pressure beginning to bloom, and her hips lifted off the mattress again. Korvain stopped what he was doing to look at her.

"Don't stop, don't stop, don't stop," she pleaded. He smiled and resumed his oh-so-dedicated attention to bringing her. Her orgasm crested a wave so large it swept over her mind, body and soul. She was drowning in the sensation of his mouth on her, his tongue in her. Then he slid his finger into her, bringing her again.

She thrashed on the bed, still restrained by Korvain's hand on her stomach, until sweat beaded and her heart felt as if it would beat right out of her chest. When at last her body had quieted, she sat up on her elbows and looked at Korvain down the line of her body.

Korvain's eyes traversed all the soft and gentle slopes of Bryn's body as his gaze drifted languidly up to her face. He was between her legs—in his opinion there was no sweeter place to be—and he had brought her to orgasm.

The only thing bothering him right now was the fact he had called her *sh'mai*. It was an elfish word that translated to "beloved of my soul." He hadn't meant to let it slip out, but it had. He just thanked the gods Bryn wasn't familiar with the term. He was still trying to get his head around it.

Korvain climbed up her body until he lay alongside her on the bed. Her body was fluid and boneless; she was a woman well satisfied. She touched his face gently, stroking his bottom lip softly. He knew she was trying to see his fangs again. He had felt the thrill that had run through her body when she'd seen them before. They were practically vibrating again now. But he would not take her blood this time. They had plenty of time for that.

He captured her thumb in between his lips and bit down gently without breaking the skin. She gasped, her eyelids drifting to half-mast. His tongue swept over where he'd bitten, and she withdrew her finger.

"I want to feel you, Korvain. All of you."

"I don't want to hurt you," he murmured.

"You won't hurt me."

"You're sure?" he asked, his voice croaky. He had been fantasizing about this happening ever since he'd started invading her dreams. She blinked up at him, her blonde hair fanning out on the pillow beneath her, and making her look like the goddess she was.

Propping himself up on his arms, his hands beside her head, he lowered his body down until he was being cradled by her hips. He'd decided this was his favorite place to be. His erection was a bare whisper against her opening.

"Last chance to change your mind," he said.

"I'm not going to change my mind."

He kissed her gently and lifted his hips just a little. That first caress had him letting out a sharp breath. Gods, she felt so good, and he'd only just touched her. Bryn lifted her hips up, forcing the contact he had so badly craved.

Pushing gently, he began burying himself within her. He knew she was still a virgin, so he had to go slowly. He pushed a little further into the well of her body. Bryn gasped, her fingers latching onto his shoulders. Sweat broke out on his brow as he tried to maintain his gentle pace. When she inhaled sharply, he froze.

"I'll stop," he said, regretting the words instantly.

"No, don't," she replied with a grimace, sucking in a breath.

"I'm not going to hurt you, Bryn," he said darkly.

"You'll hurt me if you stop." Her back arched off the bed, forcing more of him into her body. He felt her stretch to accommodate his width and he swore under his breath, attempting to pull free of her body.

"More," Bryn whispered. "I need more of you."

She angled her hips to hold him within her. She was driving him crazy with her body. She was clearly in pain, and he was the one to cause it. He started to withdraw despite her little protests. They could try again later when she wasn't recovering from torture.

Bryn dug her fingers into his biceps, forcing him to look at her. "Make love to me, Korvain," she whispered.

He searched her eyes, hoping to find the answer to what he should do. "Fuck me," she commanded when he didn't react. "It'll be the same the next time we do this. And I plan on doing this with you again."

With a soft curse, Korvain penetrated her, stretching her wider and wider until he could go no further. Bryn called out his name when he started to rock into her, the gentle rhythm creating the friction he had been longing to feel.

"Gods!" Bryn gasped, getting a tighter grip on his shoulder.

He stopped. "Am I hurting you?" he asked in a panic. He had never asked anyone that question so many times, but Bryn was different. Hurting her was the last thing he ever wanted to do.

She looked into his face, smiling. "Yes, but it's temporary. It will pass. I knew it would be painful, but I know what I'm asking for here."

He accepted her answer reluctantly. "Okay."

Leaning down, he kissed her gently on the lips. Her tongue slid into his mouth, pushing against his. His hips arched against hers and she moved with him, absorbing the impact.

Korvain was so keyed up he knew he wouldn't last long. Bryn just felt too good. It just felt too good being buried to the hilt within her. As if those thoughts were the catalyst, he felt the familiar tightening down low in his body.

"I'm going to come," he managed to grit out. Before he had a chance to draw breath, Bryn flipped him over onto his back so she was riding him. Her face contorted at the deeper invasion.

He panicked, trying to flip her back over again. "Bryn, no."

"Shh," she soothed with a forced smile. "Trust me. Just relax."

She took his hands and placed them on the top of her thighs. He swallowed, his eyes drifting down to where their bodies were joined, then back up her lean stomach to her breasts, which were swaying with the steady rhythm of her rocking back and forth on his hips.

Sweat had beaded on Bryn's face, her eyes squeezed shut. Korvain could taste her pain, but Bryn wouldn't stop. Her mouth parted a little, her tongue darting out to sweep along her bottom lip. She was rocking and grinding against him. He could feel her inner walls clenching around his cock, squeezing. He clutched the top of her thighs suddenly, his knuckles turning white.

"I'm coming, *sh'mai*. I'm coming."

Bryn threw her head back and rode him harder. He came within the well of her body, jetting his seed deep inside her. Bryn cried out his name as she, too, came again.

He felt her inner muscles clenching down onto his cock, drawing yet another orgasm out of him. His hands went to her hips, fingers digging in. He threw his head back into the pillow, his back arching while Bryn held on.

His breath was beating out of him. Bryn's was matching his. He looked up at her and Bryn's dual-ringed eyes looked back into his. Leaning forward, with their bodies still connected so intimately, she placed a gentle kiss on his lips.

37

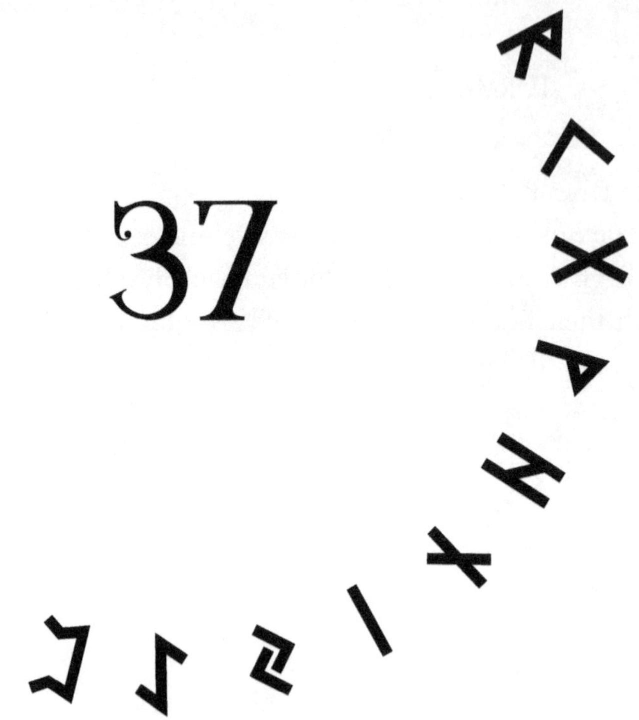

Taer stared at Korvain sitting in front of her and tried to make sense of the words he was saying.

"Tay? Adrian's de—"

"Yeah," she interrupted. "I heard you the first time."

Adrian's dead. Adrian's dead. Adrian's dead.

Yep, she got that message loud and clear. But why was she still here? She must have asked the question out loud because Korvain began speaking again.

"When I went home, I found you both in the garage. Adrian . . ."

She winced at the sound of his name.

Korvain sighed. "Your brother was dead. You had had your throat slashed, but you still had a weak pulse. I brought you here to be healed."

She eyed the room she'd woken up in again. It was plain, eggshell-white with plain and functional furniture. She was lying in one single bed while another identical bed was set against the opposite wall. Its sheets were still rumpled as if it had not long ago been slept in.

"Who healed me?"

"A Valkyrie named Eir."

"Where's Darrion?"

Korvain shook his head. "I don't know. I've searched his safe houses, even the ones he doesn't think I know about. He's nowhere to be found."

"Yeah? Well, I'm going to find him," she snapped, her anger starting to cloud her mind. She was going to find him and return the fucking favor he'd bestowed upon her and . . . her brother.

Taer felt the first tear begin to swell, but she blinked it away. She would not cry—not in front of Korvain or anyone. She had to be stronger than that. Ad . . . her brother had told her life was tough, and she had to be tougher. Well, guess what? She was going to be tougher. She would avenge her brother and she would make sure Darrion's death was a long and slow process. That bastard had just hurt the wrong Mare.

Revenge was coming.

Retribution was near.

Darrion watched the house burn, watched the humans swarm like flies to cow shit. He waited until the very end, until Korvain emerged, shrugging the shadows from his shoulders.

"Well, fuck me." He had no idea the bastard was capable of that. He knew he was powerful, but to be able to manipulate the shadows like that . . . well, he hadn't seen that happen since before he was an apprentice. The Mare moved silently through the burned remains of his house.

Adrian's body had been taken away in an ambulance, but there was no way they'd be able to ID the body without dentals. And Adrian didn't have any. Darrion shoved his hand into the front pocket of his pants and ran his fingers through the collection of teeth that were so fresh the blood was still drying on them.

They were his only trophy.

He should have had double the number, but he had discovered Taer's body was gone, which could have meant one of two things. Either she had somehow survived the attack, or Korvain had taken her body away first before coming back for Adrian.

Darrion faded back to his safe house in South Boston. He knew he had to get out of the city, if only for a little while. Korvain would be coming for him.

There was nothing more Darrion could do in any case. Bryn was still breathing, which meant Odin was still breathing. This particular attempt had failed, but the next one wouldn't.

He bit back a snarl. Over a thousand years had passed since his entire world had been ripped apart and left to hemorrhage. Odin had been responsible for severing the arteries of Darrion's life, and he'd be damned if he didn't make the All-Father pay for it.

He *would* strike again. Darrion would rid the world of Odin, but he needed to destroy Korvain for fucking around with him first; he refused to let his Walker's actions go unpunished.

Opening up his safe, he took out his collection of weapons and enough cash to see him through at least six months. He pulled a duffel bag from the hall closet, throwing some clothes into it, along with the cash. Leaving the apartment, he faded to a more secure location to bide his time—to plan his next move—swearing he wouldn't be defeated again.

EPILOGUE

MOMENTS AFTER
THE SWORD TOUCHED...

The concrete walls seemed to shudder with the motion of a subway train rolling past in a neighboring tunnel, shaking some of the dust and grit from its resting place. Loki watched from his dark, dank corner of the room, whiskers twitching as his beady eyes followed the body of the demigod he had used to carry out his plans falling to the cold, hard ground. The movement stirred some of the bloody feathers littered around the room, small eddies sending them skittering across the concrete floor. All around Loki was his destruction of their perfect world—the bodies of the Valkyries he had killed still stacked up in one corner.

Loki's timing had been perfect: he'd escaped the body at exactly the right moment. If he had left a microsecond later, his spirit would have been trapped, and he would have perished—just as the demigod had—fatally wounded by Bryn's sword.

He had brought down a reign of terror fit for any Edda, and he would have continued and had his revenge on the god Odin, had it not been for the Mare, Korvain, who was staring down at an unconscious Bryn as she clutched her golden blade to her chest, her knuckles stark white.

Korvain had been the one to discover Loki's hiding place, his place of torture. He had been the one to bring Loki's plot for revenge to an end. But Loki would not stop here. He had not suffered in that cave for longer than he could remember simply to walk away from his prize … and now he had two targets.

The clang of the metal brought Loki's attention back to where it should have always been. Loki watched as Korvain eyed the blade in Bryn's hand warily before whispering gently in her ear, trying to wake her. Loki could practically taste the metallic hum of blood on the back of his tongue. Bryn had lost a lot of that vital fluid, but she was still immortal. She would recover.

The Valkyrie's eyes peeled open sluggishly, and she sucked in a sharp breath. Blinking rapidly, she looked up into Korvain's eyes for a moment before glancing down. Her fingers tightened around the hilt of her sword.

"Korvain," she croaked. "I need you to get my Valkyries out of here." She raised a shaking hand to her neck, brushing her fingers against her tattoo. Loki looked on as the sword in her hand seemed to shiver and disappear. "Take Eir out first," Bryn added, cautiously sitting up.

The cuffs and collar Loki had placed on the Valkyrie to keep her from fading fell to the floor with a sharp clang that made him cringe, his hypersensitive rodent ears ringing with the sound.

"I won't leave you here," the Mare snarled in reply, his expression darkening, and if Loki weren't mistaken, there was also something else there, hiding behind his dark, shadow-filled eyes.

Bryn shook her head. "I'm not going anywhere. But Eir doesn't need to see her sister like that for any longer than she already has. Take her away from here." When the Mare hesitated, Bryn added, "Please."

Loki looked over at the only other surviving Valkyrie—Eir, the goddess of healing—and he would have smiled if his temporary rodent body had the lips to do it. Eir was still clutching the body of her dead sister to her chest, still rocking the corpse back and forth, back and forth, as if that would bring her back from Hel's frozen doorstep.

Korvain's growl drew Loki's wandering eyes. He was bending down to pick Bryn up, cradling her close to his chest.

"Put me down, please. I need to get to Eir," Bryn said, squirming weakly in the Mare's arms. After a seemingly long internal debate, Korvain begrudgingly did as she asked and placed her gently on the floor. Bryn collapsed at Eir's feet, crawling towards the woman. Loki scurried out of his hiding spot for a moment to get a better vantage point. Bryn looked up at Korvain, and without a word, he gently took Eir's sister from her hands. The Valkyrie didn't even fight him.

"Eir, we need to get out of here," Bryn murmured soothingly, rubbing the other woman's arms. When Eir nodded, Bryn stiffly got to her feet with Korvain's help. Hooking her hand under Eir's arm, Bryn said, "I need you to stand up for me, okay … That's it … Good, now lean on me for support."

"What about Kristy?" the woman asked with a cracked voice, slouching against Bryn.

"We'll come back for her. We'll come back for all of them. But right now, we have to get out of here. Come on," she urged, directing Eir towards the metal door. Korvain stalked behind them, his malice polluting the air.

When his rat senses couldn't pick up any other hints of their presence, Loki reverted to his true form. At seven feet, his heritage as a Jotunn could be seen by anyone bothering to look, but it was his pale hair and green eyes that had helped him to assimilate into Aesirean society so easily.

Popping the vertebrae in his neck, Loki took one final look at the scene of the first battle in the war against Odin.

"Soon, blood brother. Soon," he whispered into the cool air. Closing his eyes, Loki faded from the tunnel, his new plan already developing.

Need More?

Turn the page to read the first chapter of *Revenge*, book two in the Gods & Monsters Trilogy.

REVENGE

1

ONE MONTH LATER...

Taer didn't want to open her eyes.

She knew what she would find if she did, and she wasn't ready to experience it again. A deep, disembodied gasp finally forced open her eyes. All she could see was red. It was everywhere, pooling on the floor beside her head, splattered on the walls. Tacky, warm blood covered her face and neck.

The desperate sound of gasping made bile—hot and vitriolic—creep up the back of her throat, burning the delicate skin. Swallowing it back, Taer rolled her eyes around, trying to make sense of the scene she once again found herself in.

The gasping became louder then, and she recognized it for what it was … Hopelessness.

Suffering.

Death.

Focusing all her energy on her heavy limbs, Taer willed her fingers to move. She could feel a fine sheen of sweat on her forehead, but her hands remained motionless, and the gurgling breaths grew louder—

sharper. Taer let her eyes roll in their sockets, hoping to catch a glimpse of whoever was responsible for the desperate noise.

The sound ripped through her once more, tearing her heart to shreds with every beat that it took, because she now knew who was making those fraught sounds.

Adrian.

Taer wanted to scream out to her brother, but her body betrayed her and her tongue lay useless in her mouth.

Adrian.

He was in agony.

He was dying.

"Adrian." His name was barely a whispered croak from deep down in Taer's throat, but she cringed away from the sound.

She was to blame for his death. The crushing despair she felt overwhelmed her, threatening to suffocate her. How could she have let it happen? Tears leaked from the corners of her eyes and the back of her throat burned.

How could she have killed her brother?

"Taer, wake up."

Taer woke with a loud gasp. Blinking rapidly, she looked around the darkened room.

"Are you okay?" a woman asked. Still struggling to breathe, Taer managed to focus on the blonde-haired, blue-eyed Valkyrie sitting beside her on the bed. She knew this room—she had woken up in it for the first time more than a month ago, on the day her life had changed forever. She knew the Valkyrie, too—it was Eir, the healer.

Eir brought her hands to Taer's chest, her palms beginning to glow slightly. With a relieved groan, Taer slumped back into the pillows, feeling the tightness in her chest loosen.

After what felt like forever, Taer's breathing eased.

"You were having another nightmare," Eir said, repositioning her hands over Taer's throat. The near constant pain that lingered there eased just as the pain in Taer's chest had. Despite Eir doing her best to heal the muscular and arterial damage to her throat, Taer still suffered from pain. She didn't know how much longer her body would need to heal the slash to her throat that she'd received from her brother's former guild master, and in a way she never wanted it to go away.

"Do you want to talk about it?" the Valkyrie asked, flexing her hands into small fists a few times before placing them in her lap.

"No," Taer replied sharply. As she tried to sit up the sheet fell from her body, and looking down she noticed her tank top was soaked with sweat. Her nightmares were getting worse.

She knew what the Valkyrie was trying to get her to do, but she wasn't ready for that yet. If she spoke about Adrian, she would break down and there was no way in hell she was going to cry over the death of her brother.

"I'll be fine," she said defensively when Eir looked at her with concern.

Eir nodded and returned to the bed on the other side of the room. She was one of Bryn's Valkyries, and also the goddess of healing. Taer had been sharing her room since Korvain had brought her to the Valkyries to be healed. And with her house now nothing but a charred ruin thanks to the same guild master who had murdered her brother in cold blood, there was nowhere else she could go. She had no home. No brother. Nothing …

Taer had her tank top over her head when Eir spoke again. "I understand, you know." Her words were barely audible, and in the cocoon of cotton surrounding Taer's head, she couldn't be absolutely sure that she'd heard her right.

Taer bit her tongue. She had to remember that Eir had lost

someone too. Her twin, Kristy, had been killed in front of her by the god Loki. Although she must have been suffering just as much as Taer was, Taer couldn't find it in herself to give a fuck right now.

Pulling another tee over her head, Taer's eyes flickered over to the Valkyrie as she sat with her knees pulled up to her chest. Her loose blonde hair curtained the side of her face, making it difficult for Taer to see her expression and gauge her emotions.

Taer knew she should have said something comforting, but she had nothing but rage and sadness in her. She didn't even think it was possible to comfort someone else when she was still so messed up inside. Turning her back on the Valkyrie, Taer stripped the sweat-soaked bottom sheet from the bed and went to get another.

After making up her bed, Taer settled back on the mattress, letting the pillow cushion her head. She was afraid to close her eyes, afraid to dream of her brother again. Although she hadn't actually seen his death, Korvain had told her that he had died lying sprawled across her chest. Sometimes, she thought she could feel his blood soaking into her skin—and not always when she was dreaming.

"Taer!" Korvain barked. "Are you even listening to me?" Taer withdrew from her dark thoughts and tried to focus on her brother's best friend. The glowing ember of her anger flared at his provocative tone.

"Yeah, I'm listening," she replied defensively, keeping her eyes on his face. The Mare folded his arms over his muscular chest, stretching his shirt across his wide shoulders and firm pecs. She had no fucking idea what he'd been saying.

Her thoughts had been consumed with finding ways to get to Darrion. It had been a month since Adrian's death, and she still hadn't been able to find out where the bastard was holed up.

"All right, what did I just say?" Korvain asked. When all Taer did was stare impassively, his lips turned up into a smug smile, the tips of his enormous fangs peeking out. He moved towards her without warning, sweeping her legs out from beneath her.

She landed heavily on her tailbone, the thin blue mats covering the bare polished concrete floor of the Eye doing nothing to cushion the impact. Taer pressed her lips together to muffle the small grunt from escaping her throat. "Sonofa—," she started to growl under her breath as she moved to get up, but when the air shifted around her, she looked up and the words turned to ash on her tongue.

A shiver ran down her spine like a knife being wielded by an expert hunter skinning his latest kill. Korvain towered over her, and his violent eyes were all she could see. A vicious, raw sound came from his throat, setting the hairs at the back of her neck on end. Her instinct to get away from him was warring with her angry desire to stand and face him.

"Pay attention, Taer! I was teaching you how to avoid getting caught with a leg sweep. And if you'd been listening," he hissed, "you would have known how to evade that last attack."

She stood back up, maintaining eye contact with the male. She had to crane her head back a little for that, but she wasn't going to give him the satisfaction of winning this argument.

There was a time—not too long ago—when she would have been embarrassed to look at him, especially after she'd practically thrown herself at him and told him that she loved him … but things were different now. Adrian was dead, and she was going to kill the bastard that had put her brother in the ground.

Korvain must have seen the renewed determination in her eyes, because his thickly muscled arms wrapped around her back, dragging her against his hard chest. Taer could feel her eyes beginning to burn, could feel those traitorous tears threatening to spill over. Biting the inside of her cheek, she held them back. She would not cry. She would not cry in front of Korvain.

"We'll get him." He pulled away, forcing her to meet his eyes. "I swear on your brother's life that we will, Little—" Korvain shook his head. "Taer," he corrected. His eyes churned with pity. "You've been forced to grow up, Tay."

Taer felt his words hit her, rippling through her blood as their meaning struck home. She would never be his "Little Fox" again.

She had lost her innocence. She'd had her baptism in blood. She had crossed over to the other side and returned—bloodied and bruised—looking at the world in a whole new way.

He let her go and turned around. When he spoke again, his voice was painfully soft. "I lost my best friend when your brother died. He made me promise I'd look after you if anything happened to him, and dammit, Tay, I won't lose you to your anger and grief."

He turned towards her again, clutching her tightly by the upper arms, forcing her to look into his bottomless black eyes. "Your training is my top priority right now."

She wanted to scream that her top priority was killing Darrion, but she didn't need to say a word. Korvain could read the determination flowing off her body.

"The reason we're training is so that when the time comes, you'll be able to finish that motherfucker off by yourself."

Korvain released her arms, running both of his hands through his short hair. "We should stop for today," he muttered. "You're upset, and I've probably pushed you too far."

"No!" she replied, her voice hoarse. "I need to keep going," she explained when Korvain raised a dark eyebrow at her.

"We've been training for hours, Tay. You need to get some fuel into your body and you need to rest."

"I don't need food. Or sleep. What I need is to learn how to kill Darrion." He turned his stormy eyes to her. "I know you've been having nightmares, Taer, and believe me I see the fucking irony in that." Taer started at his words, but she chose not to acknowledge his assumption. The last thing she needed was to have him worrying about her even more than he already was. "If your body isn't working at one hundred percent, then neither is your brain. I need you sharp, so when I say we're done, guess what? We're fucking done."

"Fine," Taer conceded. "Give me an hour to get my head on straight. I'll eat. I'll rest, too, if that's what you want, but after that, we train until the club opens. Deal?"

Korvain's shadowed eyes narrowed on her face. "If I see you eat and rest in that hour, I'll continue to train you," he bargained.

Taer swallowed her irritation, but from between her clenched teeth, she said, "Deal." Like hell she was going to close her eyes, though. She followed him up in the lift to the apartment they now shared.

"Sit. I'll make you something to eat," Korvain commanded, pulling things from the fridge and setting them out on the bench. Taer bit her tongue and did as she was told. A minute later, a haphazardly slapped together turkey on rye was placed in front of her. Taer forced herself to eat it while Korvain watched on.

Seemingly satisfied, Korvain walked away, stripping the shirt over his head as he did. Taer caught the flash of black ink running the width of his shoulders. It was his contract with Darrion, inked with blood, and she wondered whether it was still active considering Darrion was currently off the grid.

"I'm going to take a shower," he called over his shoulder. "And Tay?" he added. She turned to look at him. "Get some sleep. You look like shit."

Eir's eyes opened, her body waking slowly from the small nap she'd taken before having to go work her shift at the hospital. Although she didn't feel like it, she knew she had to go. She had to maintain some sort of semblance of her life before her twin sister had been ripped from her by a deranged god.

The door to her room was slightly ajar, allowing Bryn and Korvain's faint whispers to filter through.

"How's Taer doing?" Bryn asked, her voice gentle. The leader of their dwindling little group had taken the young Mare into her care almost immediately when Korvain had brought her to be healed after Darrion's attack.

"She's doing all right," the Korvain replied, sighing. "I just wish she'd talk to me about it."

There was a long pause.

"Do you want me to talk to her? Or maybe Eir could? She lost her sister, so maybe they could help each other."

Eir squeezed her eyes shut, but a solitary tear slid free. Kristy. Gods, she felt so hollow inside with her twin gone. Watching the light fade from her sister's eyes had killed something inside of her.

They'd given Kristy and the other Valkyries the funerals they'd deserved the day after Korvain had rescued her and Bryn from Loki, but it would take a long time before Eir could forget. Grief didn't abide by time. She could only imagine the pain Taer must have been going through, too.

Korvain's coarse, rumbling voice drifted back into her bedroom. "I'll ask her."

Eir pushed the light blanket from her body and sat up. Picking up the small, silver fob watch from her bedside table, she noted the time. She had about an hour and a half before her shift at the hospital started.

Kicking her legs off the side of the bed, Eir sat on the edge of the mattress and finger-combed her blonde hair. Braiding it with practiced fingers, she secured the end and got up, stretching out her back until her muscles felt loose.

Eir crept to the door, listening carefully to hear where Korvain and Bryn were. Eir liked Korvain—now she'd got over the initial shock that he was actually a Shadow Walker. And Bryn seemed happy for the first time since she'd left Odin's service.

When the apartment door opened then closed, Eir padded out into the hallway. A touch to her shoulder from behind stopped her, spinning her around.

"Eir," Korvain said, taking back his hand and folding his arms across his chest. Eir took a small step back, that old fear rearing its ugly head. Korvain noticed the subtle shift in her behavior and loosened his arms, letting them drop to his side. He made a show of displaying empty hands.

"Sorry," she replied, taking a deep breath and shrugging. "Old habits."

His dark eyes were watchful. "You don't have to apologize. I get it."

She wondered whether he did get it. Eir guessed Bryn hadn't told him that Odin had personally ordered them to kill all Mares on sight while they were still in his service. The Valkyries had even gone on killing missions to known dark elf settlements to slaughter them all.

Bryn had been the most voracious in her drive to kill every single Mare in the Nine Worlds, all in her desire to please the All-Father.

How things had changed.

Eir lifted her eyes to his face once more. "Did you need me for something?"

Korvain reached up to scrub the back of his skull, and his bicep flexed and relaxed, reminding Eir that he was still dangerous. He was a tamed tiger right now, but he could unsheathe his claws at any time to protect what was his.

"Yeah. I was kind of hoping you'd speak to Taer about … about how she's feeling. She won't speak to me, and I know she's bottling things up." Eir nodded sympathetically. "She hasn't even cried about Adrian's death yet. Has she said anything to you about losing her brother?"

"No." Eir paused, wondering whether she should tell him what had happened that morning, and every morning since the death of Taer's brother.

"Do you know something, Eir?" Korvain pressed, reclaiming the small steps he'd taken away from her.

She blew out a breath, meeting his dark, intense gaze. "I had to wake her up this morning. She's been having nightmares, but today's one was unusually violent. She was in a cold sweat. Her vitals were all over the place, and I had to slow her heart rate down."

"Gods," Korvain muttered, his hand raking through his hair again. "I had a hunch about the dreams, and she didn't correct me earlier."

"After I stabilized her, I asked whether she wanted to talk about what she'd dreamed of. Her response was emphatic, and I didn't want to push her."

Korvain's concern for the young Mare radiated from his body, his harsh face etched with lines from the corners of his eyes and mouth. "Fuck, what am I supposed to do?"

Eir placed a tentative hand on his forearm, letting her natural healing ability take over, taking away some of his pain. "If you want my opinion, I'd leave her be for a little longer. Adrian's death is still a bleeding wound for her … she didn't have the opportunity to see his body and say goodbye." Eir paused to swallow past the sudden lump in her throat. "Give her a while longer to grieve."

Her voice cracked over the last word. Korvain moved towards her, wrapping his arms around her and pulling Eir against his chest. She stiffened in his embrace for just a moment—both terrified and unwilling to fall apart in front of him—but as soon as he uttered, "I'm so sorry, Eir. I didn't think," the tears began to roll unashamedly down her cheeks.

She wasn't sure how long he held her like that, but eventually, he gently pushed her from his body, thumbing away a stray tear from her cheek. Eir took a moment to realize what a contradiction Korvain truly was. He was a Shadow Walker—one of the most feared assassins in all the Nine Worlds. He was death, yet, here he was, holding her, cradling her and supporting her while she fell apart. Bryn was incredibly lucky to have him in her life.

The apartment door opened and closed at that moment, making Eir take another step back and hastily swipe at the tears still clinging to her cheeks. She looked at Bryn as she stepped into the kitchen. "I should get ready," she said. "I have to go to work soon."

TORMENT

1
GODS & MONSTERS